OR VANESSA MILLER

The American Queen

"Miller (*The Light on Halsey Street*) captivates with a propulsive historical based on the true story of a group of formerly enslaved people who founded a utopian society in the Appalachian mountains in the 1860s . . . readers will be won over by Louella's gumption, optimism, and tenacity. Miller brings to enthralling life a hidden gem in American history."

—*Publishers Weekly*

"*The American Queen* is beautifully told, a story rife with struggle, intrigue, and the indomitable spirit of a woman strong enough to carry the weight of a community, bold enough to dream the impossible, and determined enough to fashion dreams into reality. Louella Montgomery is a woman for the ages. I loved traveling alongside her and meeting the people of the Happy Land."

—Lisa Wingate, #1 *New York Times* bestselling author of *The Book of Lost Friends*

"*The American Queen* brings to light another hidden triumph in Black American history. Queen Louella is frankly a woman that everyone should know. Filled with bravery and cultural beauty, this marvel of a novel transported me while educating me on the sheer determination of an emancipated community to not only survive but to also thrive."

—Sadeqa Johnson, *New York Times* bestselling author of *The House of Eve*

"Some books just feel inspired. You feel blessed for having read them. They feel like a gift. This is one of those books. *The American*

Queen is definitely a story everyone should know, and a year from now, I have a feeling they will. Put it at the top of your Bookstagram reading list."

—Jamie Ford, *New York Times* bestselling author of
The Many Daughters of Afong Moy

"*The American Queen* by Vanessa Miller is a rich, multilayered saga of a little-known true story that completely captivated me with one of the strongest and most compelling protagonists I've ever read. The dreams of Louella Montgomery were strong enough to infuse an entire community and carry them on the wings of hope off the plantation. I had to blink several times to come back to the present after finishing the last page of this wonderful novel. Everyone should read this book!"

—Colleen Coble, *USA TODAY* bestselling author

"Regal, self-possessed with inner strength and dignity—that's the portrayal of Louella Bobo Montgomery in Vanessa Miller's *The American Queen*. Miller crafts a stellar image of resilience, giving life to a little-known story of American royalty. There's something special, soul-stirring to read of a woman, a wife, a queen building a space with her husband and found family that makes a community's hope of freedom come true. Everyone should read *The American Queen* and be inspired."

—Vanessa Riley, award-winning author of
Island Queen and *Queen of Exiles*

"Queen Louella, the American Queen, is a character so richly drawn, she writes the story of American history. Born into slavery, robbed of her mother and family, Louella has no reason to love or be loved. However, the superb Vanessa Miller has created a new world of possibility and the story takes flight. The impossible path to forgiveness is as arduous as the road to freedom is for the enslaved. When Louella decides it's her world, one that she will make her own in emancipation, the sky opens up and rains hope. This novel is a triumph."

—Adriana Trigiani, *New York Times* bestselling author of *The Good Left Undone*

The Light on Halsey Street

"*The Light on Halsey Street* is an emotional story that takes you on an up close and personal journey across the decades with two friends. The plot is woven with friendship, forgiveness, and faith. An unforgettable read from cover to cover by Vanessa Miller."

—Tia McCollors, bestselling author

"Vanessa Miller delivers a poignant story of friendship and betrayal, bringing Lisa and Dana full circle, with an uplifting ending that proves there is power in prayer."

—Lacey Baker, *USA TODAY* bestselling author

"Vanessa Miller set *The Light on Halsey Street* in Bedford-Stuyvesant, New York, but she takes readers on a decades-long exploration of the heart. In her coming-of-age story, two women learn about the impact of bitterness and resentment and the power of love to heal and restore what was lost. Readers will find it hard to put this novel down, and they'll hold on to these life lessons long after they turn the last page. Well done!"

—Robin W. Pearson, Christy Award–winning author

"Vanessa Miller's *The Light on Halsey Street* is women's fiction at its finest. Riveting and redemptive, *The Light on Halsey Street* vividly transports us back to 1980s Brooklyn with an unforgettable cast of characters and leaves you with the firm belief that light can truly never be extinguished by darkness."

—Joy Callaway, international bestselling
author of *All the Pretty Places*

"Vanessa Miller's latest, *The Light on Halsey Street*, reawakened memories of my own growing up in the neighborhood of Bedford-Stuyvesant in Brooklyn, which is a testament to her skill as a weaver of words. *The Light on Halsey Street* is not only a story of times gone by but the resiliency of friendship, family, and faith. This redemptive story of two friends, Lisa and Dana, poignantly demonstrates that we need not be a product of our circumstances and that the power to change is within all of us. Miller has created a timeless tale that will resonate long after the last word is read."

—Donna Hill, author of *Confessions in
B-Flat* and *I Am Ayah: The Way Home*

"Vanessa Miller serves a heartfelt and fulfilling Brooklyn, New York, literary buffet in this 1980s coming-of-age journey through friendships and hardships, all nourished by 'the light on Halsey Street.'"

—Pat G'Orge-Walker, *Essence* and national
bestselling author and creator of the
Sister Betty Christian comedy series

What We Found in Hallelujah

"Two sisters reunite with their mother in Hallelujah, S.C., in the satisfying latest from Miller (*Something Good*) . . . The result is a potent testament to the power of faith and family in the face of tragedy."

—*Publishers Weekly*

"Three strong women, family drama, secrets, and a setting that works masterfully with the plot—Vanessa Miller is at her best in this book! The complex, nuanced relationships between mothers and daughters captured my attention and drew me in from the very first chapters. This book is a heartwarming treat that will leave readers hopeful and singing their own hallelujah praise!"

—Michelle Stimpson, bestselling author

"In *What We Found in Hallelujah*, Vanessa Miller brilliantly tells a heartwarming, page-turning, beautiful story about family secrets, mother-daughter relationships, forgiveness, and restored faith, and I thoroughly enjoyed this saga from beginning to end! So well done, Vanessa!"

—Kimberla Lawson Roby,
New York Times bestselling author

"Vanessa Miller has created a soul-searching story in *What We Found in Hallelujah*. Her ability to weed through the hard topics with grace, humor, and family makes her stories like no other. I was invested in the characters and felt like praising with them in the end."

—Toni Shiloh, author of *In Search of a Prince*

"Vanessa lays a solid foundation for the fictional town of Hallelujah. Her characters are rich in diverse personalities. She layers the plot with an artistic flair that [has readers racing] to the finish line for the big 'reveal.' Redemption and reconciliation are sweet in Hallelujah."

—Pat Simmons, award-winning and national bestselling
Christian author of the Jamieson Legacy series

Something Good

"The enjoyable if familiar latest from Miller (*Once Upon a Dream*) follows three women who are connected by a car accident . . .

Prayer for 'something good' brings together the three women in an unlikely friendship, changing hearts and restoring marriages . . . Triumph of faith over tragedy will resonate with inspirational fans."

—*Publishers Weekly*

"*Something Good* by Vanessa Miller is a literary treat that captivated me from the first page. This story of three women drawn together by the unlikeliest of circumstances had me sitting back and realizing that no matter our backgrounds, no matter our struggles, when it's for God's purpose, we can come together. With characters that I could relate to and women who I wanted to win, I enjoyed *Something Good* from the beginning to the end."

—Victoria Christopher Murray, *New York Times* bestselling author of *The Personal Librarian*

"Vanessa Miller's thoughtful and anointed approach to crafting *Something Good* made for a beautiful page-turner full of depth and hope."

—Rhonda McKnight, award-winning author of *Unbreak My Heart*

"Vanessa Miller's latest novel is a relevant and heartwarming reminder that beauty for ashes is possible. This page-turning read inspires understanding, connection, and hope."

—Stacy Hawkins Adams, bestselling author

"This real-to-life story doesn't shy away from some hard issues of the modern world, but Miller is a master storyteller, who brings healing and redemption to her characters, and thus the reader, through the power of love and faith. I thoroughly enjoyed this book."

—Rachel Hauck, *New York Times* bestselling author

The American Queen

THE AMERICAN QUEEN

A Novel

VANESSA MILLER

THOMAS NELSON
Since 1798

The American Queen

Copyright © 2024 Vanessa Miller

Published in Nashville, Tennessee, by Thomas Nelson. Thomas Nelson is a registered trademark of HarperCollins Christian Publishing, Inc.

Thomas Nelson titles may be purchased in bulk for educational, business, fundraising, or sales promotional use. For information, please email SpecialMarkets@ThomasNelson.com.

Scripture quotations are taken from the King James Version. Public domain.

Publisher's Note: *The American Queen* is a work of fiction. All incidents, dialogue, letters, and all characters with the exception of some well-known historical figures, are products of the author's imagination and not to be construed as real. Where real-life historical persons appear, the situations, incidents, and dialogues concerning those personas are entirely fictional and are not intended to depict actual events or to change the entirely fictional nature of the work. In all other respects, any resemblance to persons living or dead is entirely coincidental.

Any internet addresses (websites, blogs, etc.) in this book are offered as a resource. They are not intended in any way to be or imply an endorsement by Thomas Nelson, nor does Thomas Nelson vouch for the content of these sites for the life of this book.

Library of Congress Cataloging-in-Publication Data
Names: Miller, Vanessa, author.
Title: The American queen / Vanessa Miller.
Description: Nashville, Tennessee : Thomas Nelson, 2024. |
Summary: "There is only one known queen who ruled a kingdom on American soil. This is her story"--Provided by publisher.
Identifiers: LCCN 2023029411 (print) | LCCN 2023029412 (ebook)
| ISBN 9780840708878 (paperback) | ISBN 9780840708908 (library binding) | ISBN 9780840708885 (epub) | ISBN 9780840708892
Subjects: LCSH: Enslaved persons--Fiction. | LCGFT: Christian fiction. | Novels.
Classification: LCC PS3613.I5623 A84 2024 (print) | LCC PS3613.
I5623 (ebook) | DDC 813/.6--dc23/eng/20230710
LC record available at https://lccn.loc.gov/2023029411
LC ebook record available at https://lccn.loc.gov/2023029412

Printed in the United States of America

23 24 25 26 27 LBC 5 4 3 2 1

This book is dedicated to my American Queen, my granddaughter, Amarrea Harris. Long may she reign in my heart. I love you dearly. My prayer is that you never forget to let the love of God reign supreme in your heart.

And to Louella Montgomery and the real-life people who built the Kingdom of the Happy Land. Researching this story was such a pleasure. It took grit and determination to do what they did. I pray I've done justice to their story.

This is a fictional account of actual events that
occurred between 1865 and 1889.

A Note from the Author

Dear Reader,

Thank you so much for picking up *The American Queen*. I hope it speaks to your heart in the way it spoke to mine. The hardest part of writing this historical novel was the hours, days, and weeks I spent researching information about the people in the Happy Land and the time period.

But one of the most difficult things to write in this novel was the N-word. I cringed when I had to reread the story during the editing process because African Americans have been subjected to that word and other hurtful words that degrade for far too long.

My editor and I debated about whether to use the hateful word at all. And believe me, if I were writing a contemporary novel, I wouldn't. Even though racism still runs rampant, we don't run into people who are willing to call Black people the N-word or other awful, debasing words to our face with no repercussions these days.

But I still vividly remember when I was a young girl in the seventies, walking to the bread store with my sister to get a cherry pie. (I can't even look at a cherry pie these days without gaining weight, but back then, I loved those little pies.)

We had just crossed the street and were happily making our way to the Wonder Bread Store when a pickup truck drove past us. A white guy in the back of the truck had a cup in his hand. He threw the contents of that cup on me and my sister and then called us the N-word. It was the first and only time a white person had ever disrespected me in such a manner, but I never forgot the tears I shed over that hateful act.

Now imagine how many times African Americans heard that word while they were enslaved or even right after emancipation. Imagine the hurt and the damage that being constantly called the N-word, and not being able to do anything about it, might do to a person. I use the word (and other words such as *mulatto*) sparingly in this novel. Hurtful as they are, they must be used in order to be true to the nineteenth-century time period. I believe it was necessary to viscerally show the treatment of African Americans during this ugly period in American history.

Some may think the word was used to shock or anger, but believe me, that was not my purpose. If I could have been true to the time period and the people who lived during those times without using those awful words, I would have. That might have been the easier route, but it wouldn't have been authentic.

In writing this novel, I also didn't want to insinuate that all white people treat African Americans in such a reckless and harmful manner. This is the reason I was only too happy to write about the relationship between Louella and Serepta Davis and her daughter Sarah.

I also developed characters like Dr. Morris and his mother in order to show that there is kindness in this world, and that color should not dictate kindness.

I hope you enjoy the journey. And I pray that *The American Queen* sticks with you long after you close the book. I hope the goodness of many of the people in this novel shines through and blesses you in some way.

Blessings,
Vanessa Miller

PART 1

THE HARD KNOCKS OF EMANCIPATION

Mississippi
October 1, 1864

CHAPTER 1

With hands planted in the dust of the earth, Louella Bobo's lungs filled with the smothering air of bondage while she listened to her daddy wax eloquent about freedom.

"Now listen to me and listen good." Samuel Bobo stood a few feet away from the cotton field addressing the enslaved men and women on the Montgomery Plantation in Mississippi. "Y'all heard what them Yankee soldiers said as well as I did." Samuel shook a fist. "Freedom is coming, but we got to be ready."

Louella's eyes lit up. She'd been on this plantation for all her twenty-four years, and the happiest day of her life was when those soldiers trotted onto Massa Montgomery's property like they wasn't a bit worried about being shot dead for trespassing. But the news they brung was the same thing Reverend William been telling them for months. Enslaved people just too full of fright to fathom the notion that freedom was in reach . . . as close as their feet were to the ground.

Louella wasn't shaking from fear but wonderment. Would the air of freedom be different, or would it be as stale and unrelenting as slavery air?

"I hear tell that Lincoln emancipated us back in 1863, but we still sitting here like we belong to these devils who stole us from our homeland. I say it's time to rise up and fight our way out of here."

"That sounds good, Samuel." Ruby, the housekeeper at the big house, wiped her hands on her apron. "But I'm not trying to be no runaway slave."

"Don't y'all see?" Samuel waved his arms around, then pointed toward his head. "You only enslaved in here. Once we free our minds, we can plan our way to freedom."

Later, after her father's speech, Louella found him. "Freedom has to come soon, Daddy. I'm nearly bursting with anticipation."

He patted her on the back as they walked home. "It's coming. We have to wait a little while longer." Rubbing his belly, Samuel said, "My stomach's grumbling. I hope your grandma cooked something good."

After the long workday ended, they were allowed to fill their bellies, then get some rest before heading back to that dreaded field and picking cotton with raw and bleeding fingers. The nighttime brought peace. It was usually so quiet in the slave quarters she could hear mice peeing on the cotton.

Louella wasn't thinking about peace or quiet tonight. She went to bed with revolution on her mind. Ready to fight for a new way of life. Ready to loose the chains that bound her to a place she wanted nothing to do with. But she woke to the *creak-creak* of the rickety old porch and the sad reality that she was still on the Montgomery Plantation. Still enslaved.

Most mornings, Louella woke with a sore back from picking cotton ten hours a day and then sleeping on a makeshift bed of straw and old rags.

The sun wasn't ready to brighten the new day yet. But no matter how early in the morning it was, Mama Sue had to do the washing. Louella's grandmother moved quiet like a house cat as she got out of bed. Louella normally didn't wake until she heard Mama Sue on the porch. Massa Montgomery's clothes had to be washed every other morning, rain or shine.

Only he wasn't their master no more. That's what them Yankee soldiers said last night.

Bang. Bang. Bang. "Gal, if you don't get out of bed and make your way to the field. That cotton ain't gon' pick itself."

Louella's makeshift bed was against the wall, next to the porch.

Her grandma's bangs against the wall not only shook the small cabin but sent waves of pain up her spine. She got out of bed, stretched, rolled her neck, then opened the door and stepped onto the porch.

Mama Sue sat on the stump between the rotted-out boards with the washboard in front of her and a soapy water tub beneath the washboard. The tub with clear water for rinsing was right next to the soapy one.

Mama Sue hummed the words to "Amazing Grace" as she worked. Louella had been blessed with a beautiful singing voice. Mama Sue said she got it from her. But Louella never sang or hummed while she worked . . . just seemed like Mama Sue was trying to find something enjoyable about scrubbing Massa Montgomery's britches.

Her grandmother had a rag tied around her head, with the same four braids she always wore. The hump in her back was pronounced as she slumped closer to the washboard. Mama Sue carried her grief in the slump of her back. With each endured loss, the slump became more pronounced and the hump grew.

Louella kept her hair in four braids as well. She had thick and wavy black hair. Silky and soft to the touch. But enslaved people didn't have much time for combing and brushing hair. It was easier to keep it braided.

Rubbing the sleep from her eyes, Louella said, "Mama, you heard what them soldiers said the other night. We free. I don't have to scar up my fingers in that ol' cotton field no more."

Mama Sue laid the shirt she'd been scrubbing on the washboard, leaned her head back, and cackled so hard her belly shook like jelly. "These white folks don't care nothing 'bout Lincoln's proclamation for some enslaved people. If we wanna keep this roof over our heads, then we gotta work and thank the good Lord for what we have."

Louella glanced up at the moldy, leaky thatched roof no one

had the time to clean or repair. She and her grandmother put pots on the floor when it rained. Louella had been coughing up phlegm for almost a year now. So she wasn't thanking the good Lord and nobody else for this shack. "We need to be making plans to get out of here. Daddy said a bunch of folks setting out on their own."

Mama Sue's head swiveled, eyes bucking as she looked over her shoulder. "Keep your voice down," she whispered. "And don't go talking behind your daddy. That man's the reason your mama got sold off, and we haven't seen hide nor hair of her since."

Louella's eyes rolled heavenward. "Why you keep blaming Daddy for what Massa Montgomery did of his own volition?"

"Fix your face. Don't roll them eyes at me. Get dressed and do as I tell ya."

"I said we free." Louella stomped her foot. "Don't want to stay here no more. I can't take being on this plantation. Wanna be free, like them Yankees said."

"What you know about freedom? You was born a slave. The Confederate army still out there fighting to keep us in chains. You think they gon' let us pack up and go on about our way?" Mama Sue kept scrubbing Massa Montgomery's shirt. "I done seen too many just-wanna-be-free Negroes drug back to this plantation in chains. You think I want you stuck on this plantation for the rest of your life?" Mama Sue shook her head. "But I don't want you dead neither."

Louella wanted to argue her point, but as a child, Mama Sue had watched as her father was beaten to death for refusing to lower his head as a white man passed him on the street. Mama Sue's husband, a free man who was half black, half Indian, had been run off the plantation for refusing to pick Massa Montgomery's cotton.

"And what Reverend William gon' say about you wanting to be free more than you want to be betrothed to him?"

"'Loving a Black man is like asking for a hole in your heart.'" Louella placed a hand on her hip. "Ain't that what you told me?"

"And now I'm telling you to marry the reverend. He a good man, and he can give you a better life."

Long, deep sigh. What was the use in talking to her grandmother about better days when she was stuck in what had always been? Louella went back into the house, poured some water in the basin, washed herself, and then threw on a dress that had been patched so many times it was more quilt than dress.

Louella then stood in the doorway, listening to Mama Sue humming again. Rolling her eyes, she opened her mouth to tell her it was too early in the morning for singing when her grandmother started rubbing her knuckles. Every time she got to the washing, without fail her knuckles would ache something terrible . . . terrible enough to bring tears to her eyes. "Have you been putting the liniment I made for you on your hands?"

"Mirabel got the rheumatism worse than me, so I let her have mine."

Louella walked over to her bed, got on the floor, and lifted up the hay and the rags to locate the last tin of liniment she'd been holding for Mama Sue. Once she found it, she got off her knees, went outside, and handed the liniment to her grandmother. "Don't give this one away. This is the only one I have left until I can rustle up more herbs."

"Thank you, dearest." Mama Sue put the shirt she was about to scrub against the washboard and rubbed some liniment on her hands. She flexed her fingers. "Girl, I'm so thankful you studied all them concoctions your mama was always putting together. Lord knows I could never figure any of it out. This liniment is a wonder."

Louella's granddaddy had taught her mother all about using herbs for healing. Louella learned as much as she could for as long as she could. Many on the plantation suffered from sickness and joint pains. The doctor only came around if one of the field hands was on his deathbed, so many relied on Louella's knowledge of herbs.

"We have to help ourselves 'round here. That no-count in the big house sure don't care how much pain we suffer. We still got to pick the cotton, wash the clothes, and whatever else need doing." Louella was tired of her lot in life. Needed God to show her that suffering don't last always. Then maybe she would hum like a bird too.

She left their small cabin. Headed up the dusty road on her way to go pick cotton, same as she'd done every day. Only she normally walked to the cotton field with her daddy.

She hadn't seen him since last night. Sometimes her daddy snuck over to the Bailey Plantation to keep company with some gal he had asked the master's permission to marry.

She had been standing next to her daddy when Massa Montgomery said, "You can find someone to belly up to right here on this plantation."

Daddy's eyes sparked with fire that day. He told Massa, "I had somebody, but you sold her away from me and my kids."

Louella had been seven years old when Massa Montgomery took over the plantation. Since he had brought twenty of his own enslaved people from South Carolina with him, he didn't need all the enslaved people the former master had. The journey from South Carolina to Mississippi had been long and costly, so he was in need of money.

He lined his pockets by selling off her mother, a cousin, and three others to a plantation back where Massa Montgomery come from. She hadn't heard from any of them since. Her daddy had said, *"Either the master gon' set us free, or we gon' fight our way out of this godforsaken place, where a Black man has to lower his head to white folk, thinking they better'n us."* That was when Louella had learned to hate . . . and her grandmother took up humming.

Louella's skin was dark like coffee with a little mix of cow's milk. But her skin color didn't make her any less than the lily-white women in the big house. That's why she lifted her voice and shouted, *"Hallelujah!"* after them soldiers left the plantation. Then she and a few of the other enslaved people danced in the red Mississippi dirt, praising the Lord for finally coming to see about them.

As she rounded the trail that led to the cotton field, the light of day pushed its way through the darkness, and the big oak tree stood tall with its canopy of leaves, which were supposed to provide shade. But that was white folks' shade. So Louella was surprised to see about a dozen or so colored folks standing around that big oak tree. Their eyes were lifted and focused.

Louella never stared at that tree. Whenever she was near it, the scar on her left wrist throbbed, causing her to stop picking cotton so she could rub the sting out of her wrist.

But this morning enslaved people was standing under that tree staring up . . . at a man who hung limp with a noose around his neck. The man was wearing the clothes her daddy had on when he gave his eloquent speech last night—dark brown slacks and a white shirt with tan suspenders. From the distance, she could see the dark skin . . . like her daddy's skin.

Louella covered her mouth and screamed inside her hand. Adrenaline-laced fury propelled her toward the oak tree.

Rocks from the dirt road made their way into her shoes from the holes in the bottoms. The rocks slowed her steps as they dug into her feet, causing her to limp, dread filling her belly with every step. Tears ran down her face like a river flowing into an ocean as she stood in front of her daddy's lifeless body. His neck lay crooked against the noose.

She shook like a winter breeze had swept by and chilled her from the inside out.

Her older brother, Ambrose, approached. He stayed in the small eight-by-eight shack with Daddy, while she'd moved in with Mama Sue after her mom had been sold off. Ambrose put an arm across her shoulder. "Turn around, sis. Don't look at him like this."

Her chest heaved back and forth, up and down. "I. Can't. Not. See. This." Louella shook her fist to the heavens. Glared up at the sky. "Why You hate us so much?"

Ambrose rubbed her back, then pulled her into his arms. "Woodrow ran off to get Reverend William. We'll get Daddy down from that tree."

Her heart beat fast like a locomotive as sweat beads gathered on her forehead. Mouth dry like cotton as it inched open with moans, groans, and then screams that escaped from the depths of her pain.

Someone said, "Cut him down, Overseer. His children don't need to see him like this."

But Overseer Brown snarled back, "He'll stay there as warning to the rest of you good-for-nothings. The South hasn't fallen yet, and y'all ain't going nowhere."

"Daddy was supposed to get us out of here." Eyes brimming with an ocean of anguish, Louella felt her heart break-break-breaking. "What we gon' do now?"

Then, as if she was tired of waiting on answers that never seemed to come, she kicked off her shoes and mustered the strength to plow between the field hands and was about to grab hold of a branch to begin her climb when Overseer Brown rushed over, snatched her away from the tree, and threw her to the ground.

"Leave me be, Overseer. This ain't right. My daddy don't deserve to hang on a tree like that."

Standing over her, he sneered. "There's more rope where that came from." He pointed toward the rope around her daddy's neck. Then the overseer pulled Louella off the ground by the back of her dress. He dug his dirty fingers into her neck as he turned her head so she was looking up at her daddy's lifeless body.

She had believed every word her daddy spoke about freedom

coming to them. About a day when enslaved people could hold their heads up and be somebody. Louella blinked several times. Tears glistened in her eyes. She couldn't turn away from what they had done to a man who only wanted to be free . . . wanted some dignity in this life. "No!" she screamed as the field hands stood like statues with a mix of fear and fury in their eyes.

"Why'd you do this to him? He only wanted the freedom that's been promised to us."

Louella reached toward her daddy. Took a step. Overseer Brown held on to her neck. She took another step, inching forward. She'd get to that tree and pull her daddy down. Dignity . . . Her daddy deserved dignity, even in death.

Overseer Brown yanked her back. But Louella didn't care about the repercussions. What good could come in living to see the next day when the next day still allowed a no-count like Overseer Brown to treat her as if her life and her heart and the things that brought her pain didn't matter?

"Let me go!" Louella struggled against him.

Somehow, she managed to get away. With determined strides, she approached the tree again, but Brown tripped her. Louella's head hit the ground hard and bounced back up.

The overseer sneered as he took off the belt from his pants. He snapped it, and Louella tensed as it crackled in the air. He looped his hand around the belt. The buckle whipped across the distance of decency and pain, striking Louella with a loud I-own-you *whack* against her back, legs, and head.

"Stop! Stop!" The buckle tore through her skin. Louella grabbed hold of the belt.

"I'll kill you!" he shouted, taking his heavy booted foot and stomping her until she rolled into a ball from the sheer pain of it all. Her eyes bulged with unshed tears.

"You're nothing. You hear me? Nothing but a nuisance."

Louella stretched her hand out toward the tree, longing to go with her daddy. Death would be better than living out the rest of her life as property that wasn't cared for or treated with any kindness.

His foot ground her face into the dirt. The blood and sweat of enslaved people filled her nostrils. Gagging, her throat muscles constricted, squeezing the breath of life out of her. She could hear others begging the overseer for mercy. But what mercy had they ever received on a plantation run by men who thought her kind was less than human? None.

Chapter 2

"Oh, Lord Jesus, don't let it be true!" Mama Sue wailed out her sorrow.

William and Ambrose carried Louella into the cabin and laid her on the makeshift bed.

Louella moaned, rolled onto her side. Eyes like slits as she glanced around the room.

William took off his hat. Pressed it against his white cotton shirt. "I'm sorry I didn't get to her sooner, Miss Sue."

"She's alive?" Mama Sue's eyes flashed with questions. Fear clung to her grandmother like black clings to the night.

Louella kept drifting in and out of consciousness. Every part of her hurt . . . hurt so bad she wanted to float out of her body and keep right on floating up yonder.

Through squinted eyes, Louella saw Mama Sue fussing over her. Grief rested on her grandmother's shoulders, like they were built for the heavy weight of loss. "Don't slump. We'll be free soon." Louella's words were jumbled and mumbled, like molasses had thickened her tongue and was slapping against the roof of her mouth. Her body was letting go . . . taking her far, far away. Far from misery and despair. Far from fields that needed pickin' . . . far from white folk that hated her without cause.

She drifted . . .

Louella was now walking down a dusty road. She had on a silk frock with a blue-and-black-striped petticoat and a bonnet to match. Everywhere she went, from the general store to the church house, she saw men and women who looked like her, dressed in their finery. They greeted one another with kindness and respect.

Where was she? She'd never seen colored folks act like this a day in her life. Heads were lifted, smiles wide, eyes bright. Bowed heads and frowns, with backs and fingers aching from the grind of the day, had become her norm. Not this.

A colored man trotted toward her, riding on a horse that wasn't pulling a buggy with a white man in the back seat being carted off for a day of leisure. Instead, it looked to her that the colored man was off for a day of leisure. Not a bit of hurry about his jaunt.

"Top of the day to you, Miss Louella," the man on the horse said as he came to a stop in front of her and then took off his hat and bowed his head to her before putting the hat back on.

Louella pointed at herself. "You know who I am?"

His head fell backward as he laughed. "Of course I know you. The entire province had better know, or they'll answer to me."

She didn't understand why he would say something like that. She was nothing . . . a nobody. Why did it matter if the people in these parts knew who she was? "What is this place?"

Eyes gleaming bright, he said, "Why, my lady, this is a happy place. A place where the formerly enslaved have come to find peace and restored dignity, but you already know that, don't you?"

❧

"Louella, my sweet girl, please wake up."

Wake up? Was she asleep? Was she only dreaming about this happy place? Eyelids fluttering, Louella wanted to keep them shut, but they defied her.

Mama Sue and William were standing over her. She wiped sweat from her forehead as her eyes adjusted. "Where am I?"

"You're here with us," William told her.

"Let me get you some soup." Mama Sue lifted from her slumped position in front of Louella. She straightened as she walked away.

A tear drifted down Louella's face. "But I don't want to be here."

April 1865

William's first order of business most days was to walk to the gate of the plantation to pick up the *Mississippian* and bring it to the big house so Massa Montgomery could read the newspaper with his morning coffee.

William normally waited until Massa Montgomery looked over the paper before he read any of it, but the headline this morning was "General Robert E. Lee Surrenders to General Ulysses S. Grant."

Surrendered? Was the war over? Although William had been enslaved since birth, the fact that Massa Montgomery was his father was the worst-kept secret on the plantation. He wasn't allowed to address the man who had set his mother free months before she gave birth to his younger brother, Robert, as "Father." But William had been allowed the run of the plantation. Had been taught to read, write, and to count and subtract money.

He understood the ins and outs of running the plantation, for all the good that did him. It wasn't like Massa Montgomery was going to leave the place to him in his will. But there wasn't much left of the Montgomery Plantation after the soldiers rode through, taking anything and everything that didn't bark or cry. There hadn't been any money for repairs around the plantation lately either.

William hadn't asked about it. He had eyes and could see that

Massa Montgomery wasn't bringing in the money he once had. The cotton was being planted, but piles of it were still stuffed into barns. No one had taken any of it to market in months.

His father read the paper, then snarled as he looked at William. "What do you tell your congregation in that church I had built for you?"

"I tell them that the Lord will make a way for us, sir."

"And you think the Lord wants me to lose everything so He can make a way for some ragamuffins?"

William stiffened. *Ragamuffins?* His lips twisted. "I think every man has a right to be free."

"That again." His father wiped his mouth with a napkin, then threw it on the table. "How long are you going to be jealous of your brother?"

"I'm not jealous of my brother. I'm thankful that he doesn't live a life of bondage. But I do believe that others would benefit from such benevolence."

Robert was a wanderer. He traveled whenever and wherever he pleased for two reasons: he was free, and his ivory skin tone helped him pass. William, on the other hand, had a caramel skin tone that could never be confused for a white man.

"Well, Lincoln has extended that kindness, as well you know, since you snoop and read my newspapers." Massa Montgomery pushed away from the table, stood, and stormed out of the room.

William picked up Massa Montgomery's plate, wiped the crumbs off the mahogany table. He folded the newspaper, placed it under his arm as he took the plate into the kitchen, and handed it to Mirabel.

Mirabel put the potato she'd been skinning on the table and looked at the plate. "He hardly ate anything at'tal. Is Massa Montgomery feeling poorly today?"

William patted Mirabel on the shoulder. "Just got a lot on his mind is all."

"Well, eggs have been scarce around here lately. No sense wasting them." Mirabel wrapped a towel around the plate and placed it on the table. "Waste not, want not. That's what I always say. When he gets hungry later, he can finish his breakfast." Mirabel went back to work on her potatoes.

William started to walk out of the kitchen but then turned back to Mirabel. "Oh, and I wanted to thank you for giving Louella a few things to do around here. Anytime she can get out of that field is a godsend to her."

"Happy to do it." Mirabel's voice got low. She shifted her eyes this way and that. "She's been teaching me to read when we have a spare minute."

"You couldn't have a better teacher." Louella was a quick learner and took to books like a fish to water. He'd started teaching her to read about a year ago. They'd also been keeping company. He was ready for marriage, but Louella's mind was on other things. Or maybe she didn't see him as a good fit since he was twenty years older. He'd pondered the matter and had finally decided to share his heart with her.

Mirabel nudged him. "When you gon' wed that girl?"

He grinned as he stepped away from the counter. "You never know, we might be jumping the broom and needing your famous peach cobbler one of these days."

"Don't you lie to me now. I'm telling Sue that we need to get ready for a wedding."

That evening William went to the church to meet Louella and a couple of the other members to do some much-needed cleaning. He hoped he would get a moment alone with her, but that was tricky. He didn't want wagging tongues claiming he was taking advantage of a young woman. And he certainly didn't want to tarnish Louella's good name.

He made his way past the bare cotton field. He wondered how long the cotton from the newly planted fields would sit in barns with no timeline for delivery to the cotton gins. The war had been bad for business, and William wondered if the plantation would ever recover.

The small church had been built on the back end of the cotton field so the preaching and singing wouldn't disturb anyone in the big house. Some Sundays, it seemed like the Lord Himself came down from glory to listen to the praises they sent up. William was blessed indeed to pastor such a congregation of men and women who put their trust in God.

"Steal away to Jesus. Steal away home."

William's ears perked up. Someone was singing. It wasn't a song they normally sang during worship service. "Steal Away" was sung in the cotton fields as a sign that the Underground Railroad was back in business. "Steal Away to Jesus" sounded like enslaved people were singing about going to heaven. The song actually symbolized escaping to freedom.

"I haven't got long to stay here. My Lord, my Lord, He calls me."

William opened the church door, eyes scanning the pews, looking for the songbird who had the voice of an angel. He'd heard her sing in the choir on numerous occasions, but never with the lilt of determination that was in her voice today.

Louella had a rag in her hand, wiping down the pew seats as she sang.

She was thinking about leaving again—always thinking about leaving this plantation rather than thinking on making a life with him.

He walked over to her and took the rag out of her hand. William sat down and patted the seat next to him.

"Ruth told me to wipe these seats down. I best keep working before she arrives and thinks I been slacking."

"It'll be fine." He patted the seat again. "Sit with me."

Sitting down, Louella placed her hands in her lap and glanced toward the window.

William put an index finger to the side of Louella's chin and turned her to face him. "I know you have misgivings about our marriage, but if you give me a chance, I'll show you how to love me."

"This place." Louella darted a finger in the direction of the big house. "These white folks have killed any love I ever had." Her cheeks puffed out hot air. "I'm sorry, Reverend." She lowered her head. "I hate so much, there's no room in my heart for love."

He handed Louella the newspaper. "God will remove the hate from your heart. Lean on Him."

Eyes glued to the newspaper, Louella read, "'General Robert E. Lee surrenders to General Ulysses S. Grant.'"

Louella's head swiveled in William's direction.

"The war is over. Things gon' be different now."

With a wide grin, Louella stood and put a hand to her heart. "We can leave now, can't we? No one can stop us."

He stood, took her hand in his. Squeezed it. "Stay. Marry me, and make my dreams come true."

She backed away from him. "What about my dreams?"

His heart cracked a bit at the thought that her dreams might mean more to her than all the love he had to give. William took hold of her hands again. They sat back down. "Tell me about your dreams, and I'll do everything in my power to make them come true."

Sighing, Louella turned to William. "Nobody understands me. Mama Sue thinks I should just marry and stay on this awful plantation, but I want so much more than this."

"Tell me."

The soft light of the setting sun shone through the small window as Louella expelled a long, deep sigh. She looked at him, and he winced as he caught a glimpse of eyes accustomed to pain filled with the dimming light of the sun.

Her voice was calm and contemplating. "After Overseer

Brown beat me, I dreamed about a place where people are happy . . . respected. That's what I want."

"I want those things for you as well."

"But you're content on the Montgomery Plantation . . . I'm not." She turned from him, shoulders slumping inward as sadness seemed to envelop her.

William placed a finger under her chin and turned her back toward him. "You are my sunshine, Louella. I promise you'll be happy with me. Can you make room in your heart for love?"

CHAPTER 3

May 1, 1865—Freedom

The air was hushed with quietness as Louella stood on the porch of the cloth house, breathing in fresh, free air. The war was over. The shackles had been loosed. And Mr. Lincoln had been shot dead.

Lots of people on both sides bled and died for the cause of freedom. Overseer Brown found out yesterday that his son, Anthony, wouldn't be coming home from the war. And although there wasn't a man more deserving of a broken heart than Overseer Brown, Anthony had been decent to her while they were growing up. He'd just chosen the wrong fight.

"Gal, will you get off that porch and come try this dress on?" Mama Sue said.

She was free, and she was jumping the broom with Reverend William, a forty-four-year-old man, twenty years older than she, and loads smarter. Louella didn't so much mind that since he'd taught her to read. "I'm coming."

"We got work to do before we present you to that fine reverend."

"Mama Sue, you shouldn't be talking like that. William is a man of God."

Miss Saddie harrumphed. "He still a man, and he's gon' be right proud to see you in this here dress." She lifted the cream-colored frock from her mending table.

Mama Sue's eyes lit up like Christmas morning when she saw

the lace on the arms and the waist of the dress. She waved Louella over. "I can't wait to see you in this."

Louella had only laid eyes on a dress this fine on white women entering the big house for fancy teas and other social gatherings. "That's not the Negro cloth you normally make our clothes with. Where'd you get such finery?"

Miss Saddie ran the cloth house, making all the clothes for the plantation workers on the loom or with needle and thread. The only fabric Miss Saddie had ever been permitted to use was something the white folks had branded "Negro cloth." It was cheap wool or low-grade cotton that itched something terrible.

"Never you mind where I got it from," Miss Saddie told her. "All you need to know is you'll be jumping the broom in this fine frock today."

She wouldn't be jumping the broom at all if Mama Sue hadn't refused to leave the plantation. Her grandmother was convinced that Louella needed a husband in order to be safe outside the plantation.

"Undress down to your shift," Miss Saddie told her.

"I don't have a shift."

Miss Saddie pinched her lips together. "I didn't think of that. Should've made one for you."

Since she didn't have a shift to wear under her gown, Louella slipped the dress on and prepared to feel the scratchiness of the fabric. When no itch came to her, she relaxed in the dress, which draped around her ankles. The silk of the fabric clung to her waist as the lace covered the cuffs of her sleeves. As she twirled around, Louella's eyes lit with delight. "I get to wear this dress, for sure and true?"

Mama Sue wrapped her arms around Louella. Tears rolled down her face. "It's yours, my sweet girl. You're going to be a beautiful bride—more beautiful than any other bride this plantation has ever seen."

Louella smiled at her grandmother, but she wondered how beautiful everyone would think she was if they knew she wasn't in love with William. She liked him . . . respected him. But too much hate was in her heart for love to grow for anyone else. She'd told William this, but he was determined to marry anyway. And her grandmother kept pushing her toward him, so Louella agreed to go through with the wedding.

❧

Reverend Wallace, Mr. Montgomery's pastor, stood in front of Louella and William and pronounced them man and wife. They were standing outside the big house. Mr. Montgomery and his new wife, Mary, were sitting on the front porch with Mary's three kids from her first husband, who died in the war. Overseer Brown and his wife, Constance, were also seated on the porch, sipping lemonade and scowling at them. On the opposite side of the porch, Louella's friends and family stood on the grass.

As the reverend pronounced them man and wife, ol' glassy-eyed Montgomery came down from the porch and placed a broom on the ground in front of them. William and Louella jumped over the broom and then shared a kiss.

The sun was like a bright light shining down on them. Louella lifted a hand above her eyebrows to dim the light as she came out of the embrace with William. Glancing around, she saw people were smiling, cheering for them. Shouldn't she be happy, full of smiles and bubbly with joy?

But then she heard Constance say, "Is that darky allowed to wear such finery while white women in Mississippi make do with the rags we have left?" Louella then remembered why she wasn't happy and could never be happy as long as she was tied to the Montgomery Plantation.

"Wouldn't have dared wear such a dress before that dang Lincoln ruined our way of life," Mary said.

Deflated, Louella lowered her head. She turned from the porch to the grass where friendly faces greeted her. But Mary swept down from the porch and demanded her attention anyway. "Gal, have you been stealing out of my closet?"

Louella shook her head. "I wouldn't take nothing from you."

Snarling at her, Mary pulled at the sleeve of her dress, tearing a piece of the lace. "This is my lace, and you stole it."

Louella shook with rage. Her fist clenched as she weighed the pleasure of knocking Mary on her coddled behind against the pain of being chained and imprisoned for the rest of her life.

William pulled Louella closer to him. "I'm sure all of your silk and lace are right where you left them."

"We'll see about that." Mary harrumphed, then swung back around and stalked up the porch steps. "If anything is missing, you'll pay for your thievery."

Louella unclenched her fists, but her cheeks puffed with fury. She nudged William away from her. "I knew we shouldn't've jumped the broom in front of the big house. Nothing good ever comes from mucking around with white folks."

"You've got it wrong, Louella. We're right proud to see you and William jump the broom." Mr. Montgomery touched his hand to his chest. "I gave that lace to Saddie for your dress."

A prickly sensation crept up Louella's back. She lifted a shoulder as she slipped her hand beneath the fabric and used her fingernails to scratch away the itch while Mr. Montgomery stared at her as if waiting on a thank-you.

Mary took her hand off the doorknob and swung back around. "You did what?"

"I gave Saddie the lace." He turned those glassy eyes that held no emotion in Mary's direction, then pointed toward the seat she had vacated. "Please sit back down and let William and Louella enjoy their day."

Mary's lips tightened, but she did as Montgomery bid her, then leaned close to Constance, and the two women whispered back and forth.

Louella ignored the hateful women on the porch because her hate was stronger. Mr. Montgomery could die waiting on a thank-you and that would suit her just fine.

Mr. Montgomery cleared his throat, patted William on the shoulder. "Thank you for letting us share in your day."

"Of course, sir."

Mr. Montgomery turned to the wedding attendees who were standing in the yard. He looked crestfallen as he said, "We thank you all for attending the festivities today. If times were better, we would have a nice meal out here in the yard for everybody." He stretched out his hands and let them drop to his sides. "The war hasn't been kind to us, so Mirabel and Sue have made a spread for y'all out by the cotton fields. Enjoy, and we'll figure a way forward from this debacle the North has gotten us in."

Louella didn't know what debacle Mr. Montgomery was referring to. The way she saw it, things were finally looking up. She needed to convince William and the rest of her family to get away from this plantation. Mama Sue was the only reason she stayed after the war ended. Her grandmother feared that something worse than what had already befallen them would come and crush their souls if they left this dreaded place.

So here she was, marrying the man of her grandmother's dreams. She prayed that William would love her enough to take away the pain that had lodged in her chest like a spreading sore.

William picked her up and carried her up the hill toward his church. A few of the men had gone hunting and come back with two rabbits and three coons. Mirabel pulled the collards she'd been growing in her vegetable garden. Mama Sue made corn muffins and grits.

The Montgomery Plantation had about forty workers—Louella refused to think of any of them as enslaved people any longer. All forty of the workers took part in the festivities. She even found herself smiling and enjoying the fact that she was a for sure and true married woman now. Then she turned to the left and caught sight of that oak tree. Rubbed her wrist as an itch tickled its way up her spine, reminding her that Mr. Montgomery was responsible for the fine dress she wore today.

Mama Sue pinched the back side of her arm. "Fix your face, girl. You a married woman now."

"Be right back." Louella went into the parsonage. The few clothes she owned had been brought to her new home this morning. She slipped out of the wedding dress and put on her brown skirt with a tan button-down shirt.

Louella then took the dress that she had been so thankful for earlier in the day back outside. She walked over to the fire Mirabel and Mama Sue were using to cook the food and dropped the dress. As the embers of lace floated up from the fire, tears of misery poured from her soul.

William pulled her into his arms. "Louella, what's this? Why'd you burn that dress?"

She wiped the tears from her face as flames danced in the air like they were in a hurry to get away from the ashes beneath. Her lips tightened, and her nostrils flared with the steam of hate. "I never asked him for that dress."

In all her life, she'd only asked Mr. Montgomery for one thing. Her pleas had fallen on a cold-hearted master with a need to line his pockets rather than give a little girl back the mother she desperately craved.

William shushed her. "I'm sorry. I didn't know he gave Miss Saddie the material for your dress. I think he wanted to do something nice for you."

Too late for that. "It's too much for me, William. I wish my mama and daddy were here to see that I done married myself a good man. Wish they knew that no massa can tear me away from you."

"What's wrong with Louella?" Ambrose asked as he came over to them.

William rubbed her back. "She's fine. Let's give her a minute. Help me move the food inside the church so we can eat our meal without all these flies buzzing around."

Mama Sue walked back over to the picnic table. She kept an eye on Louella. Once William asked that the food be moved into the church, she stood, lifted the bowl of grits off the table, and yelled out to the people, "You heard the reverend. Let's move this food inside."

"That's too much fuss," Louella told him.

William put his index finger under her chin, grinned at her. "Never too much fuss for my queen."

"So now you gon' call me a queen, huh? Queen of what, is what I want to know."

"Don't doubt it, Louella. My mother told me about our home-land. Our people came from kings and queens. We were never meant to be enslaved or to know the kind of pain you sorrow with."

His words were lyrical, soothing her soul. "I'd very much like to hear more about your mother's homeland."

"Then I'll tell you more later tonight when we're alone."

After they ate, their friends and family went back to their homes, and Louella stayed in her new home with William just to the left of the church. William's small house was supposed to make her happy—it wasn't as run-down as the shack she shared with her grandmother. But on her first night in the house, after she and William had consummated the marriage and her husband was asleep and snoring, she got up to get a drink of water.

She wrapped a shawl around her body to cover her nakedness, walked over to the keeping room, dipped the ladle in the bowl, and sipped the warm water. After quenching her thirst, she turned toward the window, staring out at the cotton field. That same rotten field that she'd worked in since her eighth birthday. The same day she'd asked her daddy why life was so hard for colored folk.

He sat her down on his lap and said, "I wish I could answer that for you. Plain and simple fact is, I don't know."

There was sadness in her daddy's eyes, so Louella put a hand on his cheek. "What's wrong?"

He took the handkerchief out of his back pocket and wiped the sweat from his forehead. "To tell you the truth, I been dreading this day."

"Huh?" Her face scrunched as her eyebrow lifted. How could her daddy dread the day she was born?

"Thing is, Massa say you old enough to work in the field with me. I gotta show you the ropes today."

She didn't get a cake on her birthday that year. Didn't get a doll. She did, however, get her first blister. From that day on, she dragged her feet every morning as she walked up the hill with her daddy to the cotton field. As years went by, she listened to her daddy tell stories about freedom and about the war and how soon Abe Lincoln would loose the shackles from their feet.

She no longer worked in the field. William had gotten her a job at the big house as a maid to that hateful Mary about a week after the war ended. She was trying her best to endure Mary's contempt.

Now she was living in a house that caused her to see the field and that oak tree every day. Why such gut-wrenching cruelness was heaped on her was something she planned to ask the good Lord about when she finally saw Him face-to-face.

She went back to bed, but the minute her eyelids shut tight, she saw her daddy hanging from that old oak tree. She wished she could tell her daddy that slavery days was over. Wished he knew that old Abe Lincoln had come through for them.

Tears seeped through her closed eyelids and rolled down her face. The horror show going on in her head wouldn't loose her. Whimpers set her soul on fire as her eyes popped open. Her hands reached out to grab hold of her daddy and bring him back.

William jumped up, looking around as if something or someone was about to do harm to them. He rubbed his eyes and then pulled Louella into his arms. "Beloved, stop crying. You're safe. You're with me."

"I saw him. My daddy's d-dead." She was shaking.

William squeezed her closer to his chest. She clung to his warmth, but it was only a momentary balm. Her eyes filled with buckets of pain, the overflow drenching both of them in a deluge of sorrow. "Why'd he have to kill my daddy? Why couldn't Daddy live to see this day?"

"I know this is hard, but I'm here. Let my love take away your sorrow."

Louella laid her head on William's chest. A dark cloud of misery was following her around, making prey of her. "Tell me more about your mother's homeland . . . about the people and how they cared for each other." She needed to be bathed in the warmth of other lands, to know there was a place she belonged.

William chuckled, wiped her face. "How many times do you need to hear the same old story?"

Sighing deeply, Louella told him, "If you can stand telling it, I need to hear it about a hundred more times."

CHAPTER 4

Louella's eyes popped open as William used his finger to trace the lines of the welts on her back.

"Don't do that. You know I don't like it." Getting out of bed exposed the curve of her belly. She and William had been married a little over five months and had a baby coming in the spring.

"I'm sorry," William said as she washed herself at the basin.

"Nothing for you to be sorry about. If that white devil hadn't scarred my back, I wouldn't have a problem with you touching me there." The tapestry of her body was a mix of joy and pain. She could share the joy of the swell of her belly with her husband and the other parts that gave him pleasure. But the patterns of the welts were her burden to bear alone.

Louella pulled on a black woolen dress, which was too heavy for the warm October day, but she could no longer fit into her brown cotton dress.

"Where you going?"

"Foraging. Mama Sue's rheumatism still bothering her something terrible, and since I have the day off, might as well make myself useful."

Louella took the basket she had weaved from straw and set out for a walk on the back side of the plantation where a lot of the foliage was. This area was thick with ginger plants. Louella had reseeded the ground with them as often as she could. She also reseeded another plant. Her mother had never told her the name of it, but it mixed well with the ginger. Louella named it the pain-free plant.

"Pay attention, Louella. Folks on my father's side are healers. I'm gon' teach you what I know so's you can help our people when they's feeling poorly."

"Okay, Mama. I'm listening."

"That's my girl."

Louella was four years old the first time Brenda took her to the back side of the plantation to teach her about plants and healing.

"God put everything we need in these here plants." Brenda clipped off a piece of the green leafy plant, then pulled up the root. Showed it to Louella. "When the old folks' fingers get to crimping and aching, make a paste out of the leaves and the root and rub it on their hands."

A grayish-green plant caught Louella's eye. She pointed to it. "What kind of plant is that?"

Brenda smiled. "That's catnip." She pulled a few of the leaves and let Louella touch them. "See the jagged, heart-shaped leaves?"

Louella nodded as she traced her fingers around it.

"Feel the fuzzy hairs on it."

Louella giggled. "Fuzzy."

"You 'member this plant. When somebody gets sick with a cold, come get some of this, then warm some water and give it to them in a cup of tea."

Louella scrunched her nose. "Nobody's gon' want leaves for tea."

"It tastes like mint. They'll drink it."

Her mother's words proved to be true. As folks took ill, Louella would always get the catnip plant. They drank it down without complaint. But she wasn't in search of catnip today.

She pulled the root of the ginger plant out of the ground and picked some leaves from the pain-free plant. Louella took her basket of plants and her supplies to her grandmother's house to begin making her mixture.

But along the way, she passed by the Bailey Plantation, which couldn't really be described as a plantation no more. They had rented out houses and sectioned off land for the Negroes who'd once been enslaved to do sharecropping. Louella wished that Mr. Montgomery had done the same thing with his plantation, rather than promising them monthly payments. They'd been working for the Montgomerys for five months now but had received only two of the promised payments.

As she passed by, she saw Gary out plowing the field. When they had spare change, William purchased potatoes and corn from Gary. She was getting ready to wave at him when she saw Lester Bailey ride up, angry as a bear disturbed from his winter's slumber. He held on to the horse's reins with one hand and a rifle with the other.

"Mr. Bailey." Gary tipped his hat to the man.

The frown on Bailey's face turned into a snarl. "Boy, didn't I tell you to get off my property?"

Gary let go of the plow, but he didn't raise his head. Didn't look Mr. Bailey in the eye. He stepped backward, keeping his head slightly lowered. "Now, now, Mr. Bailey, I'm working the land as we contracted. Not doing nothing wrong."

"You haven't turned over your crop, so you're in breach of that contract."

"I'm still waiting on payment. I farmed the land, deserve my fair share of them crops is all."

Louella was elated that Gary stood up for himself. Colored folks 'round here had been taking all the devilment thrown their way and then saying "Yes, sir" and "Thank you, sir" for everything that was dumped on 'em.

But then Lester Bailey lifted his rifle and trained it on Gary. "I said get."

Gary nearly fell as he turned and started running. Bailey cocked the rifle and then pushed back on the trigger. Louella screamed as the bullet narrowly missed Gary's head. Lester Bailey turned and narrowed his green eyes on her. "This is none of your concern. Get out of here before you get one of these bullets too."

Louella had a baby growing in her stomach, so she wasn't getting in the middle of no disputes. She prayed that Gary was able to run fast enough to get away from Bailey's rifle. Clara, Gary's wife, was her friend, so Louella sent up some prayers for her as well while she headed on up the road, hearing Bailey yell at Gary, "You bet not come back 'round here or I'm gon' grind you in the dust!"

It wasn't right . . . wasn't right. Heart racing, Louella ran the whole mile up the road to get back to the Montgomery Plantation.

She prayed that Bailey wouldn't turn his anger on her and come gallivanting down the road. But thankfully, he didn't bother with her.

When she was near the former quarters of the enslaved on the Montgomery Plantation, she stopped running. Sweat dripped down her face. Heart beat so fast, death would surely claim her if she didn't calm down. Panting, she heaved in and out, in and out, until her heart rate settled a bit.

"You all right, Mrs. Louella?" Woodrow, the cobbler, asked as he came upon her.

She nodded, still trying to catch her breath. "I'm fine. Saw Lester Bailey shooting at Gary."

"That Lester Bailey's been cheating him out of his earnings since he signed the contract," Woodrow told her.

"And now that Gary tilled the land, he put him off of it so he can get that crop for free." Louella shook her head.

She and Woodrow parted ways. She continued to Mama Sue's house.

Mirabel and Ruby were sitting on the porch with Mama Sue when Louella arrived. "Why y'all sitting out here looking like you got rocks in your jowls?"

As she rubbed her aching knuckles, Mama Sue said, "Miss Mary say she ain't paying us today."

Ruby harrumphed. "Said my housekeeping done got sloppy

since we been emancipated, but ain't a speck of dust to be found in that house."

Louella put a hand on Ruby's frail shoulder. The seventy-year-old woman had been cleaning the big house for fifty years without complaint. Miss Mary had been married to Mr. Montgomery for only a year, and suddenly, things weren't good enough for her. "I know you do your best to keep that house clean. I help you clean it four days a week, so I see it with my own eyes."

William normally brought her pay home when she had a day off, but if Ruby didn't get paid, Louella doubted there'd be any pay for her either. Two months ago, Mr. Montgomery had been short and asked them to hold on. Promised to pay what he could. But things wasn't getting no better.

Mirabel put her hands over her face and started crying. "I need my money. My Hank broke his hand plowing the field. He hasn't been able to work in over a month. I don't know what we gon' do for food if I don't get my pay."

"You work in the kitchen. Take your pay in food." Mama Sue laughed at her words.

Mirabel shook her head. "That hateful Mary would have me arrested if I took so much as a piece of bread from that house. She keeps count of the potatoes and the weight of the cornmeal bag."

Mama Sue waved her arm toward the front door. "We don't need to be worrying you about Miss Mary's penny-pinching. You go on in the house, sit down at the table, and rest your feet a spell."

Louella rolled her eyes heavenward. "I'm pregnant, Mama Sue. I'm not helpless." She did as she was told anyway and went into the house and started working on her herbal mixture.

But the more she pounded and crushed the leaves together, the more her mind kept running back what the ladies had said. Did Miss Mary really think she could work them like they were still enslaved? During slavery, the master at least fed and clothed them. The doing of that now fell on them, but how with no money?

How on God's green earth could they take care of themselves if they weren't getting paid? That was the exact question she asked William when she got back home and discovered that neither of them had been paid either.

"You've got to understand, Louella. The war put Mr. Montgomery in dire straits. He wants to keep all of us on the plantation, but he can't afford to pay right now."

"So is that Lester Bailey's problem too? He don't have no money, so he'd rather kill Gary than pay him for his sharecropping?"

William's eyebrow lifted and his head tilted slightly, like what she was saying was news to him.

"I saw it happen. I was passing by Gary's land when Bailey swooped down on him with that big rifle of his."

"Haven't I warned you about being on that side of the plantation?" William paced the floor, then stopped and wagged a finger at her. "There're people in Mississippi who're still spitting mad about the outcome of the war. No sense riling them up."

The look on his face clamped her mouth shut. No way was she telling him how mean old Lester Bailey scared her away. "I needed to pick from my plants on that side of the plantation."

"We have a child on the way. I can't protect you if you insist on going off, doing as you please."

Louella put a hand on her slightly swollen belly. "What are we supposed to do without any money? We do need to feed this child you speak of, and the Montgomerys aren't coming through with the pay."

"That might be true, but I have more to consider than our family alone."

Louella put her hands on her hips and stood flat-footed in front of William. "My child will not live the life of enslaved people just without the shackles."

Lifting his hand, he said, "I had nothing to do with nobody getting paid today. Mr. Montgomery is traveling this month, and I guess he didn't leave Miss Mary with the money to pay the staff, so she started going through the house making up reasons not to pay people. She didn't even pay me."

Arms across her chest, she blew out hot air. "Your loyalty has been trampled on for far too long."

He nodded, looked like he was beginning to see things her way. "Let's get ready for church. I'd love for you to sing something uplifting tonight. Think the congregation could use some encouragement."

"I'd rather sing 'Wade in the Water' 'cause we need to get out of here without leaving a trail for old Montgomery to sniff out."

Despite her anger, Louella went to the church house that night with William. But when she stood before the congregation of about forty people, nothing uplifting came to mind. Her soul pulled her toward another spiritual. So she opened her mouth and sang, *"Nobody knows the trouble I've seen . . . Nobody knows my sorrow."*

Those words touched deep down into her very soul. God had lifted their heads out of slavery, yet she was still in a land where she didn't belong. She might've been born in Mississippi, but this place would never be home to her.

She shouted, danced, and cried out to God and then sang, *"Sometimes I'm up, sometimes I'm down . . . oh yes, Lord, sometimes I'm almost to the groun'."*

She was overcome with sadness as two of the sisters helped her sit down and then used their hands to fan and cool her off.

She wiped the tears from her eyes and then looked over to her husband as he stood behind the pulpit. She hoped that her outburst and tears hadn't brought shame to him.

Woodrow stood. With a fist pumping the air, he shouted, "I'm tired of being low to the ground too! Anything has to be better than being here, dying of hunger."

Mirabel stood. "Miss Mary's cheating us out of our pay. We've got to do something, Reverend."

Before long, half the congregation was on their feet shouting and complaining about life after emancipation.

"We should've stayed enslaved if things wasn't gon' be no better," Ruby declared.

"Seems to me this land is being rebuilt on the backs of our free labor, and I'm tired of working for people who don't care if I live or die," Jerome, Mirabel's oldest son, said.

William lifted his hands, then did a downward motion. "Let's all calm down a bit. I understand where everyone is coming from, but we need to think things through before making any rash decisions."

"I haven't been paid in two months. My chillun going hungry," another complained.

Louella could see weariness settling on William's shoulders, and she was sorry that she'd brought this trouble to him when all she had to do was sing something uplifting without getting so over-wrought.

She lifted herself from the chair and stood next to William. Then she put her hand in his and whispered in his ear, "You're our leader. Speak to the people."

He closed his eyes. For a minute, he looked like he wanted to be anywhere but here. But then he sighed deeply and turned back to the congregation. "What we need to do now is pray. God made a way for us and loosed the shackles, so now we need to go to God and figure out our way forward."

CHAPTER 5

"I been praying like you asked us to do," Louella said to William after they woke the next morning.

William put his arm around her. "Good, good. The Lord will provide the answer for us."

"The Lord give me the answer last night." Louella rose up on one elbow. "This not the place for us. It's time to move on."

"But this is our home."

"I can't stay here no more, William. I can't."

Taking his arm from around Louella, William stood and rubbed his stubble-speckled chin as frustration knit the lines on his forehead. "We're married. We have a home here."

"This place never gon' be my home. Not as long as Overseer Brown and his kind still here."

"What you want from me, Louella?"

She stood in front of him, clenched his nightshirt with her hands, and pulled him so close her breath wafted into his nostrils as she said, "Take me away from my misery."

He pulled away. "You know I can't do that. Things are dire on the plantation. I can't leave Mr. Montgomery to deal with the fall-out of the war on his own."

"Listen to you. The man sired you, but you still have to call him Mister."

"That's the way things are. I can't ask for more."

Louella scoffed. "You deserve so much more. Never forget what your mother told you about the way things were where her daddy come from . . ." She touched a hand to her heart. "My daddy didn't have much to give, but I was his. He loved me, and I knew it."

"If you give it a chance, we can have a good life here. I promise you."

"No. Things ain't never gon' be good here."

"Louella!"

She turned her back to him and folded her arms across her chest. "Why am I talking to you about this? You'll never understand."

He bristled at the insult, picked his britches off the floor, and put them on. "I was enslaved same as you. Why wouldn't I understand?" He then opened the door and went outside without saying another word.

Louella hated that her words had caused him pain, but she couldn't be the person he wanted her to be. She would never be happy on this plantation. Her husband hadn't experienced the horrors she and others had. He could never understand.

❧

A few weeks later, William was sitting at the table eating a bowl of grits. There were no eggs or salt meat this morning. Just the grits. But he ate it like a man content with his lot in life. He was dressed and ready to go to the big house for another long day of uncompensated work. Not even so much as a three-cent copper nickel for his troubles.

He turned to her. "Shouldn't you be getting dressed? You have work this morning too."

"Decided to quit my job."

His eyes crossed as if two thoughts mixed in his head at once, but he didn't know which to dwell on first. Then he frowned. "Woman, what foolishness are you about this morning?"

"I was reading our Bible last night, then I starting praying, and—"

"I don't have time for this. Get dressed and let's go, please."

Louella narrowed her eyes at him. "Don't discount what I'm saying to you. You're not the only one who can get a word from the Lord, you know."

William wiped his mouth and then stood. He put on his coat, hat in hand. "I know I'm not the only one our God speaks to. That's why I asked the congregation to pray . . . and what do you mean, you quit?"

Hand on her left hip, lips slightly twisting, she said, "Ain't enslaved no more. I get to decide if I work for free, and I choose not."

"This is not the way to resolve the matter. I'm the house manager. You quitting is going to look bad on me."

"Why should it look bad on you when they the ones not paying nobody?"

"You're my wife, Louella. I beg of you to be reasonable." He held out a hand to her as if imploring her to come with him.

She wrapped her arms around her chest. Her arms rested on top of her swelling belly. Her foot *tap-tap-tapped* on the floor. "Are you gon' listen to what I heard while praying or not?"

William sat back down, put his hat on the table. "Go ahead, I'm listening. What has your prayer time yielded?"

Exhaling, Louella breathed a sigh of relief—hoping that her husband was finally ready to hear her. "I was so disturbed when we went to bed last night. My mind wouldn't stop thinking on our troubles. So I got on my knees."

Louella pointed toward their bed. "I stayed down there, praying for hours last night, and then I heard a voice say to me, 'Go. I have prepared a place.'"

"That's it? The voice didn't give you directions or tell you where this place is?"

Louella huffed. "Don't make light of me. What I tell you is the God's honest truth." She lifted a finger, indicating she had more to add. "After my prayers, I sat real quiet on our bed, and that's when my mind took me back to your mother's stories.

"You remember, don't you, William? Your mother used to tell you about the land she came from. How it was 'all for one and one for all'? That's where I want to be—in a place where colored folks are treated with respect. Not here where everything's for the white folks and the rest of us get the scraps, if there's anything left for the getting."

He looked away from her, then stood back up and put his hat on his head. "I'm going to work. I suggest you take off that nightgown, get dressed, and come to work with me."

She stomped her foot. "No! You should stay here with me and work on a plan to get us out of this place before we all starve to death."

"Don't be a nag, woman."

"Not being a nag, but we got a right to get paid for our work."

Her husband's nostrils flared. "I'm trying to figure a way to help all of us, but your constant nagging isn't helping." He then walked out the door without giving her so much as a kiss on the cheek.

Six months of marriage, and now that she was five months pregnant, she had become a nag to him. William was too focused on helping Mr. Montgomery rebuild this plantation to its former glory. The way Louella saw it, he needed to be more focused on bettering himself and his family.

❦

Two days later, Louella was tired of the constant arguments with William, so she got up early and fixed corn muffins so they could eat them with the last of the grits for breakfast. She then dressed and went to the big house with him.

When Louella stepped into the parlor, a floral scent with a hint of honey greeted her. She found Ruby down on hands and knees scrubbing the baseboards. Ruby glanced up as she put her rag back in her bucket of soapy water. "Well, look what the cat drug in," she said with a slight grin.

"More like what the house manager drug in," Louella whispered as she stepped closer to Ruby and helped the older woman stand. "You do the dusting. I'll wash these baseboards."

Ruby used the palm of her hand to rub her lower back. "Chile, I'm sho' glad you came back to work today. Miss Mary was fit to be tied after we complained about not being paid again. Barking orders all over the place."

"Well, while she's cross with us, we got to figure out how to feed ourselves." Louella got on the floor and wrung out the rag that Ruby had been using. The floral scent drifted in the air, then she noticed the purple lavender petals floating in the water.

"You right about that." Ruby rolled her eyes. "Let me go get the duster so we can keep this house spick-and-span."

Louella got busy wiping down all the baseboards. She kept breathing in the floral scent, hoping it would put her in a better mood, but then Mary entered the parlor and destroyed all her hopes.

"Look who decided to grace us with her presence." Mary folded her arms across her chest.

Louella lifted her head to greet the woman. "Good morning, Miss Mary. Is there anything you're in need of today?"

She smirked at Louella. "Don't you dare speak to me as if everything is fine and dandy." She shook a finger in Louella's face. "I have half a mind to throw you out of here—put you back in the field where you belong."

Putting her hands on her thighs, Louella took a deep breath, then another. She put the rag back in the water. "I don't wish to displease you, Miss Mary. I'll leave if you prefer, but I do not desire to work in the cotton field."

Mary put a hand to her chest and gasped. "Are you saying you won't go to the field if I send you there?"

Louella shook her head. "No, ma'am. I won't work in that cotton field ever again."

"Well, I never." Mary's hand flew to her hip. "You wait till Massa Montgomery gets back. I'll have him deal with your insolence." Mary left the room in a huff, heading toward the back of the house, yelling, "William!"

Truth be told, Louella would love to get up and walk out of this house, but she knew that Mary would bad-mouth her to other employers close by. Being with child, she doubted if William would take kindly to the idea of her walking into town each day to find work.

Louella also didn't want to leave all the housework to Ruby, so she finished in the parlor, then took her rag and bucket to the entryway and wiped down the front door, the wood trim around the windows, and the baseboards. When she was nearly done, Mary swept into the entryway with William following her.

Mary stopped in front of Louella and daggered a finger in her direction. "I want this girl punished for her insolence."

Louella looked from Mary to William as she put the rag back in the bucket and stood. "Punished? What did I do?"

Mary wagged that same finger in Louella's face. "You know what you did. No slave is going to put on airs with me and get away with it."

William stepped forward, moving Louella to his other side, farther away from Mary. "I don't think Louella meant to disrespect you, Miss Mary."

Mary put a hand on her hip. "Oh really? Then why hasn't she apologized?"

Louella was still waiting on apologies for all the wrong that had been done to her. She bit down on her lip as William turned peacemaking eyes to her.

Mary opened her mouth to say something else, but a team of horses rode up to the big house like they were trying to get away from the devil himself.

When the hooves stopped, someone stomped up the porch

steps and then banged on the front door. Louella would sooner dump that bucket of dirty water on Mary's head than apologize for anything, so she was thankful for the distraction.

William gave Mary a quizzical glance as if he was figuring on why someone was beating on the door and about to bust it wide open.

"Open it." Mary turned toward the door with her arms folded, lips pursed.

With his back ramrod straight, William walked to the door and inched it open. He held on to the doorknob with his right hand and the doorpost with his left. "Can I help you?"

"You tell Montgomery to keep his mulatto kids away from my store."

The man sounded angry enough to kill. Louella's stomach clenched in fear for her husband. William was one of Montgomery's mulatto kids. Was this man here to do him harm? She stepped closer to the door, needing to be near her husband, when she heard William shout, "My dear Lord, what did you do to him?"

William pushed past Stanley Johnson as he stood on the porch, looking like he was chewing on nails. Stanley's daddy owned the general store in town. He refused to give credit to coloreds, so many of them purchased produce from some of the sharecroppers in and around town.

Louella looked past Stanley toward his wagon. Two men in slopes stood in the back of the wagon. They were holding Robert. His white face was bluish purple in spots, and his jaw was swollen.

Robert was hog-tied. She heard her brother-in-law moan as if the death angel was coming to claim him, then the men threw him from the wagon to the dust on the ground.

William ran down the steps and got on his knees next to his brother. "Oh God, Robert. Can you hear me?" William shook him.

Louella's mouth hung open as she stepped out onto the porch.

Robert wasn't moving. William shouted, "Why'd you do this to him?"

Stanley stomped down the steps. "He's trying to take food out the mouths of good white men in our town. I don't care how white he looks"—Stanley spit on the ground next to Robert and William—"a drop of Black blood means he's a nigger. Make sure he knows it."

"What does he owe you?" William asked, trying to lift Robert off the ground.

"Two dollars, and if I don't get it, I'm going to kill that mutt the next time I see him."

"You'll get your money," William told him.

How? Louella wanted to know. They sure didn't have it. None of their church members had it either.

Stanley got in his wagon, snapped the reins. The horses kicked dust up as they galloped away from the big house.

Mary stepped onto the porch with her arms still folded across her chest. She had a smirk on her face as she glared in Robert's direction. "I knew all that passing for white would catch up with him one day or another."

"Louella, come help me. We need to get Robert inside."

Louella rushed down the steps and grabbed hold of Robert's arm.

Mary put her hands on either side of the front door, barring their entry. "You won't bring that nigger in here."

"But, Miss Mary, he's been hurt awful bad. I need to get a doctor for him," William pleaded.

"I don't care. You're not sullying my freshly cleaned house with the likes of him."

Louella's head twisted to the right, eyes squinted as she glanced over at Mary Montgomery. How had the woman perfected so much evil? Honestly, she didn't like Robert much herself, but she wouldn't let the man bleed to death without caring for him. With a deep sigh, Louella turned to William. "Let's take him to our place, and I'll put some liniment on his wounds. Hopefully he'll heal up some."

William nodded. "Can you lift his legs so we can carry him?"

Robert was going in and out of consciousness. There was no way he'd be able to walk. Louella lifted his legs while William entwined his arms under Robert's and situated himself so Robert's back was against his chest. They walked away from the big house toward their parsonage.

Mary stomped her foot and yanked her hands in a downward motion. "Louella, if you leave this house before your work is done, don't bother coming back tomorrow."

"Mr. Montgomery would want me to help Robert, and you know it. Why you hate us so much?" Louella yelled back, not caring if she angered the woman. She was tired as tired could be of dealing with the hatefulness she received from this woman for no good reason.

"Watch your tongue," William warned her.

"How dare you talk back to me in such a manner?" Mary shouted. "I want you off this plantation this instant. You can't live here anymore."

Louella's mouth hung open. She dropped Robert's feet at Mary's declaration. As she bent to pick her brother-in-law's feet back up, she caught William's glare of look-what-you-did.

Louella didn't care about losing her job, but she hadn't expected Mary to tell her to get off the plantation. The parsonage was on the plantation. Her grandmother's house was on the plantation. Where was she supposed to go? What would become of her and her baby if she had no place to lay her head?

CHAPTER 6

Once she and William laid Robert down on the floor in the parsonage, Louella took Robert's shirt off, revealing black and blue bruises on his chest. Louella scraped out the cream from the aloe vera plant and rubbed the liniment on Robert's face, chest, and back. She was about to remove his pants to see if he needed liniment on his legs as well, but William stopped her. "That's good enough for now. I need to get you out of here."

Even though Louella wanted nothing more than to get away from the Montgomery Plantation, her eyes clouded with fear. "Where am I to go? We haven't made plans yet. Will you come with me, or am I to go on my own?"

William's eyes were dark with sadness. "I can't leave Robert right now, but I can't have Miss Mary reporting you as a trespasser and then have you thrown in the penitentiary."

"B-but you can't think she'll really make me leave. What if I went back to work until we can plan things out? Maybe she'll forget about her cruel words and let me stay."

William shook his head. "Miss Mary is different since the war. I think she blames us for her first husband running off to the war and getting himself killed."

"How's that our fault?" Louella understood that she lived in a world full of injustices, but to hate a group of people for the folly of one man was beyond her.

"It's not, but we can't risk it. You will not deliver our baby in a penitentiary, so pack what you need and go to Robert's farm."

Robert turned to his side and moaned, "Elmira . . . I need Elmira."

Louella pointed to her brother-in-law. "Who's going to take care of him if I leave?"

William jabbed a finger toward his chest. "I will, but first I need to go down to the general store and collect Robert's wagon."

Louella's eyes grew big. "No! No! Don't you dare go to that general store. You see how they beat your brother? What you think they'll do to you?"

He didn't respond to that. "We don't have much time to waste. Grab your things and head to Robert's place while I go get the wagon."

Louella clamped her hands around William's wrists. "What if something goes wrong? What if you don't come back to me?"

William loosened Louella's hold on his wrists, put his hands on either side of her face, and let his lips touch hers for a fleeting moment. "You won't lose me, my sweet Louella. I promise you that."

His lips tasted of sweat and regret, like forbidden fruit hanging from a vine just out of reach. "I'm scared." William's safety mattered to her. She wanted him—no, needed him—with her.

"Be strong for me." He put his hands on her shoulders. "I have to do this for Robert."

Twisting away, she yelled, "Why? Why? Why do men always think they have to do things that don't need doing? Why can't Robert suffer a loss for being so foolish as to think those white folks cared anything about him?"

Robert rolled on the floor and moaned again as he pressed a hand to his ribs.

"I have to. Robert's horse, Elmira, is special to him."

Seeing that no sensible words would be able to talk her husband out of his folly, she grabbed her basket and walked around the parsonage, placing items of need in it. She then put her bonnet on her head and tied it under her chin.

William stepped onto the porch with her. He pulled her into his arms. The embrace was like heaven come down to earth.

"I love you. I'll come see you soon as I can," he whispered in her ear.

She wouldn't say those I-love-you words back. They were too dangerous. Loving put cracks in her heart. *Respect* and *admiration* . . . those were good words and all she could give.

But even as she refused to return his love, she couldn't stop the waterfall from coming at the thought of leaving him. Felt like they was still somebody else's property. Like slavery days was still here, and just like her mama, she wouldn't be able to have a family same as white folks had.

William went back into the parsonage. Louella started walking toward Robert's place. As she passed by the cotton field, her wrist throbbed, her heart sped up, and her world narrowed until all she could see was that dreaded oak tree.

Most days she turned from that tree and continued about her way. On this day, her heart wouldn't let it be. She couldn't turn away as her mind took her back to the day she got those scars on her back and her wrist . . .

"Louella, gal, didn't I say I needed two bushels of cotton from you today or I was going to tan your hide?"

"I tried real hard, sir. But it was powerful hot today. I almost fainted from the heat."

Overseer Brown had been sitting on a stump watching the enslaved people head to the gin house to get their cotton weighed. He stood and snatched Louella off her feet, carrying her all the way back to the oak tree in the cotton field.

Louella was only twelve years old, but she'd seen what happened to enslaved people when the overseer strapped them to the tree, and she wanted no part of it. "No, stop! I'll do better. I promise."

But Brown wasn't listening. Louella wiggled to escape his grasp. He threw her down on the ground and drug her the rest of the way to the tree. All the while, Louella was yelling, "I'll be good! I'll do better! Please . . . please don't hurt me."

The big oak tree's branches were thick and sturdy. On the left side of the tree was a long strap, a loop at the end of it. The same type of strap hung from the right side of the tree. Brown pulled Louella close to the tree and grabbed one of the straps. He put her left hand in the loop, tightened it.

"Please . . . please . . . please." Mama Sue was on the ground with her hands steepled as the enslaved people gathered 'round. "I'll do anything you ask. Please don't hurt my child."

Brown tightened the other loop on Louella's right hand. Her daddy ran over to him. "Whatever she done, I'll take the whipping for it. You don't have to do this to Louella."

Brown signaled for Oliver, his helper who spied on the enslaved people and toted a pistol on his hip. "Get them out of my way. This gal is getting three lashes, and I bet she'll get my bushels right tomorrow."

"You heard him!" Oliver shouted. "Get."

The enslaved people backed up as Louella's arms stretched out like Jesus' when He was crucified on the cross.

Brown tore off her shirt, exposing her to all eyes. He then pulled the whip from around his waist, reared back, and let it dance in the air.

When the first lash struck her back, Louella screamed, eyes rolling into the back of her head. By the second lash, the skin was ripping away from her body. She would have to use all the salve she had left to heal the fire that was raging on her back.

Trembling, Louella tried and tried to erase that memory, but it wouldn't go. Her arms shook as she cried for that twelve-year-old girl who learned the hard way that no one could protect her from the evil in this world. But tears weren't enough anymore, so she found herself running toward that tree with vengeance in her heart.

The straps that Overseer Brown used to tie enslaved people to the tree—the same straps that put the scar on her wrist—were still hanging from it. Even after slavery, the people on this plantation were too fearful to take those things down. "No more," she said through clenched teeth. "No more."

Louella placed her basket on the ground and searched for the pair of scissors she'd put in there. Once located, she took pleasure in cutting through the strap on the left and throwing the part that held the loop to the ground. She did the same for the one on the right. No one else would ever have their arms strapped to this tree while being beaten like an animal.

"Now I'll go!" Louella shouted those words to the wind as if declaring that she lived and moved by her own volition.

❦

It took Louella a minute to pull herself together. Walking the three miles down the road to Robert's place, she stopped several times to breathe in and breathe out, taking in the scent of the magnolias and wet grass.

Louella kept walking, not even once looking back. The farther she moved away from the Montgomery Plantation, the more her breathing settled. Relief at not having to look out her window and see that cotton field anymore overtook her.

Robert had a small farm down the road from the Montgomery Plantation. Before the war, he owned his kind and harvested corn that he sold at the market. The people he enslaved were now free but still living on his farm. There was no planting being done. The farm had been ravaged as the Union soldiers torched all his crops. Robert hadn't been able to put together the funds needed for his next crop, nor did he have anyone to sell it to.

She'd always hated the fact that Robert owned his own kind. Robert might look white, but his mother was colored, and she had been enslaved, forced to lie down with Massa Montgomery and have his babies. How Robert found no shame in building a farm on the backs of enslaved people, Louella didn't understand.

She found no joy in the fact that Robert had been beaten for needing credit on food so he could feed himself and the seven workers who were still on his farm. But sometimes what went around came right back around.

"What am I doing here?" Louella said as she entered Robert's home. She wiped down the table and chairs in his small dining area. She then got the wash bin out and washed the cotton sheets on Robert's bed. This, too, bothered Louella. She and William didn't own any sheets for their bed. They had an old blanket that Mr. Montgomery had given to William to wrap around their old mattress. Both the mattress and the blankets had been well used before they were given to William after being discarded from the big house.

But Mr. Montgomery's other son, who'd been born free and looked as white as his father, had been given a farm and was allowed to travel all around the country, pretending to be white, owning his own kind and having cotton sheets.

Louella wrung the sheet out and then took it outside and hung it on the clothesline. God only knew what Robert did in that bed, so she wasn't about to sleep in it without fresh sheets. As she headed back into the house, Abigail walked into the yard carrying a basket of folded clothes. She waved at Louella. "Hey, Mrs. Louella. What you doing over here?"

Abigail had long, wavy, brownish-blonde hair. Her skin was a sun-kissed tan, like the Black in her was fighting against the white that Lester Bailey left in her mama when he stole her innocence. After Abigail's mama died, Mr. Bailey sold Abigail to another owner. That owner then sold her to Robert when she was about fifteen. If Louella recollected right, Abigail was about twenty years old now.

Louella had once seen her on the Montgomery Plantation making eyes at Tommy. But as far as she knew, the two had never courted. "I'm staying at Robert's house for a spell."

Abigail's eyes lit with concern. She squinted. "Why you want to do a thing like that?"

Louella realized that Abigail thought she was staying at the farmhouse with Robert. She shook her head. "Robert's been hurt. He's at the parsonage with my husband, so William sent me here." She didn't bother to mention that hateful ol' Mary had thrown her off the plantation.

"Hurt?" Abigail put a hand to her chest. "My goodness. What happened to Massa Robert?"

Abigail's words rankled Louella, like teeth scraping together. "He's not your master no more. You're a worker, not enslaved."

Abigail lowered her head. "Well, let me get these clothes in the house before Mr. Robert gets back." She emphasized the word *mister* and walked inside the house.

Louella followed Abigail, not sure why the young woman seemed bothered about rinsing *massa* from her tongue. Louella decided to let it go. A lot of formerly enslaved people seemed stuck to her. They were all still in the same condition as they'd been before emancipation, so maybe they couldn't think past what they saw day in and day out.

Abigail put her wash basket at the foot of Robert's bed. She glanced around the house, then asked, "How long you think Mr. Robert'll be gone?"

Louella thought about how badly Robert had been beaten and how weak he looked when she left the house. "He'll probably be at the parsonage a few weeks."

Abigail let out a whoosh of air. Her shoulders seemed to relax. Glancing at the basket on the floor, Louella asked, "Is that all you needed to do?"

Clasping her hands together and then letting them swing by her sides, Abigail nodded. "That's it. I'll get out your way, but if you need anything, my house is directly across from the farmhouse on the other side of the cornfield."

"I'll let you know if I need anything." Louella closed the door behind Abigail and then began wringing her hands. Her mind hadn't been on the others at the farm. What if they told Mary that she was here? Would Mary get her thrown off Robert's farm too?

Placing a hand on her protruding belly, Louella looked up to heaven. "Lord, I done got myself in a pickle. I need You to direct William on what comes next for us. Need to be with my husband."

CHAPTER 7

While Louella was praying for the Lord to speak to her husband, William and Tommy were walking into town headed for the general store to see if Robert's horse and buggy were still outside the store.

"You think them boys gon' let us get Mr. Robert's horse? I brought my bag in case we run into any problems."

Tommy had been sixteen when the war began. He'd been forced to fight for the Confederate army alongside Overseer Brown's son. He'd learned a good bit about defending himself but still held resentment in his heart about being on the wrong side of the fight.

William patted Tommy on the shoulder. "Don't worry. We're not bringing them any problems, just collecting what's ours."

"They might think it's theirs now." Tommy's knuckles whitened as he tightened his grip around the strap of his bag.

William eyed Tommy. He was spoiling for a fight, itching to use the contents of that bag. Tommy was tall and bulky—could handle himself in a fight—but William wasn't worried about a fight. He was worried about the awful lies that might get folks stirred up . . . lies that could get them locked up—or killed.

Before the war, William didn't worry much on things like that. He'd been able to go and come as he pleased in this town. But even more hate than he'd seen during slavery seemed to fill the hearts and minds of these Mississippi white folks.

"The Lord will make a way for us."

Tommy's lips twisted to the left. "Pardon me for saying so, Reverend, but we sure been waiting on the Lord a mighty long time."

"He brought us out of slavery, didn't He?"

They were steps away from the general store. Tommy stopped walking, looked like he was stuck in thought, then said, "What good is not being enslaved if we're still treated like the dirt on the bottom of these white folks' shoes?"

"I been praying about the same thing. It'll all be made clear to us in due time."

Robert's buggy was not in front of the general store. At first, William thought Stanley might have taken it to his house. Making matters doubly hard for them. No way they'd win a court case against the white owner of the general store.

But then as he looked farther down the street, past the barber shop and the blacksmith, he saw Robert's horse and buggy in front of the tavern. Coloreds weren't allowed in the local tavern, but Robert normally wasn't thought of like the rest of the coloreds in these parts.

But this town wasn't welcoming to them no more, so they couldn't go about as they pleased. William pointed down the street. "There it is, in front of the tavern."

Tommy laughed. "Mr. Robert loves his whiskey."

"Yes, he does." William had been praying for his brother concerning this vice. Praying that Robert found another way to deal with the demons that beset him.

Peddlers had set up next to the tavern, calling out to people as they passed by. Money was scarce in town, so no one paid them much mind. "We've got the finest fabrics in town—silk, satin. The ladies will love how this fabric feels against their skin."

William walked over to the horse and rubbed her side. He wondered at the fine fabrics those peddlers were selling, when most people were struggling to pay for food. "Hey there, Elmira. I'm sure glad I found you. Robert will recover easier knowing that he still has you."

The horse lifted her head and neighed. Then lifted on her hind legs. William knew what this horse meant to his brother. That's why he was willing to risk life and limb to get her back.

"Happy to see you too." Rubbing the horse's mane, William turned to Tommy and whispered, "Get in the buggy. I'm going to untie her and then jump in alongside you."

Tommy did as he was told. William untied the horse's reins and hopped in the buggy. The peddler hollered, "Don't leave without some of these fine fabrics!"

William wished he had money for such things. He would love to dress his wife in fine fabrics, like the dress she wore on their wedding day. Sighing, he turned away from the peddler, planted his feet on the low front board of the carriage, and pulled on the reins. "Giddyap, girl."

The horse trotted down the red dirt road. Passing the general store, William breathed a sigh of relief. "I think we're okay."

"Think again," Tommy said as the door to the general store swung open and Stanley rushed out with a rifle aimed at them.

"Get back here, boy. I didn't say you could take that buggy." He aimed the rifle and fired.

The bullet grazed William's ear. "Oh my Lord Jesus!" The buggy swerved as William dropped one of the reins to touch his ear. He picked the rein back up and flapped it against the horse. "Let's go, girl!"

Tommy ducked in his seat. He pulled a bottle out of his bag, along with a piece of cloth that looked as if it was covered in a grayish-black substance. Tommy doused the cloth with the contents of the bottle and then flung it. It exploded and filled the air with smoke.

"*Woo-hoo!* That was amazing." William kept a tight hold on the reins as the wagon headed down the trail toward the Montgomery Plantation. "We just might make it out of here before that smoke clears."

"Wish I had a grenade. I'd blow them crackers all to pieces."

Tommy had been a quiet, not-looking-for-trouble kid before the war. But now he knew how to inflict the kind of pain that brought tears to a mother's eyes. And he wasn't a bit scared to use the skills the Confederates taught him. "Let's just get out of here in one piece," William told him.

Pow-pow.

"I'm gonna kill you, boy! Wait for it. It's coming," Stanley hollered after them.

More bullets flew past them. William was thankful that Elmira had taken off at high speed after the first bullets had been fired. They were out of gun range, but Tommy threw out another explosive.

The fact that the second explosive had been needed, along with hearing the threats and the foul names they were being called, shook something down deep in William's soul. Louella was right. This wasn't their home anymore.

❧

The next morning as Louella lay on Robert's bed, the wind whistled with a gentle rhythm as it blew against the house with a light *tap-tap-tap* to the glass and wooden door.

The tapping wasn't the only disturbance. She couldn't get comfortable. The baby was positioned awkwardly, causing pain to her left side. She got out of bed and paced the floor as swirling thoughts dropped her into the depths of despair. *Why is everything so hard? Why can't these white folks let us be?*

Louella stopped pacing as two images collided in her mind. That dream she had about people who looked like her going about their merry way, being happy . . . and the stories William told her about a land where Black people worked together and built something of their own. She needed to get to a place like that. Lifting her head, she prayed, *Please guide us, Lord. There has to be more for us than the lot we been given.*

A pain shot through her side as the baby kicked. Taking a deep breath, Louella was about to sit down when grumbling from outside startled her. Peeking out the window, she saw Stanley Johnson, Overseer Brown, and Lester Bailey jostling toward the farmhouse. A few other foaming-at-the-mouth white men rode behind them with lit torches.

"Come out here, Robert! I'm not leaving without my horse," Stanley yelled.

Louella clutched her nightshirt as she backed away from the window, looking around the room for any weapon she could use to protect herself. There was a poker next to the fireplace. Robert's rifle was under his bed. She was about to reach under the bed and grab it, but then the baby kicked again.

If she went outside with guns blazing, she might get shot herself—the baby might get shot. "I don't have no horse and don't want no trouble." Fear trembled her hands and her voice. She knew that no good would come from reclaiming Robert's horse.

"Where's the horse? Where's Robert?" Stanley said aloud.

Then another man said, "Let's burn the place down."

Abigail came running out of her house. She stood in front of Bailey's horse, hands steepled as if begging her father to do right by her. "Don't burn us down. This the only place we got to lay our heads."

"Get out of my way, gal. This here don't concern you," Lester Bailey told her, then averted his eyes.

Abigail could plead with that man from now till kingdom come for all the good it'd do her. Louella looked over her shoulder at Robert's bed again. She might take out one or two of 'em with his rifle before they got to her. But as she walked back toward the bed, she heard Abigail say, "Mr. Robert isn't here. He's at the parsonage."

"No!" *Thump-thump*. Louella's heart was about to beat out of her chest. She swung back around and opened the door, rushing onto the porch. "William lives at the parsonage. This is Robert's house."

"You wouldn't be here if Robert was in that house." Overseer Brown sneered at her. "Come on, boys. Let's go."

The gang of men flapped the reins on their horses and trotted away from the farm. Abigail ran toward her.

Louella's eyes darted this way and that. "Why'd you send them to the parsonage?"

"I'm sorry, Mrs. Louella, but I didn't want them to burn you and the baby up."

"But you done turned them demons on my husband."

"They won't hurt Reverend William. He's a man of God."

"When white men get a thing in their heads, they wouldn't care if God Himself said no."

Flashes of her husband being tied to that oak tree swirled around her mind. She couldn't let that happen. Wouldn't let that happen. Louella put her hands on Abigail's shoulders. "Run over to the big house and see if Montgomery returned from his trip. Tell him that William and Robert are in danger."

Abigail ran like a ghost was chasing her. Louella slipped into her shoes and tore out of the house, running as fast as she could while holding on to her swollen belly. She had to stop and catch her breath a few times, but she kept going.

Her husband hadn't listened to her, but she couldn't stand by and let him fall prey to a lynch mob. *Oh, God, please, let no harm come to William.*

By the time she made it back to the plantation and came up around the back side of the church, her foot got caught in her house-dress, and she fell to the ground, eyes popping with the sight of the blazing fire. "Oh, Lord Jesus, no!"

The church was on fire. She put a hand on her stomach and winced as she got off the ground. Limping, she made her way to the front of the building as a torch was thrown at the church and burst through the front window. Flames flickered in the very room where she first learned about God . . . and first learned to read.

"What are you doing? Why y'all destroying our church?" Louella screamed at them, her eyes wild with fury.

William opened the parsonage door and stepped out onto the porch.

Her eyes lit with delight. Relief caressed her body like a warm blanket on a wintry night at the sight of him.

"Get out of here, Louella. It's not safe!" William yelled at her.

"Look what they did." Louella ran over to William. A rolling fit of tears cascaded down her face. "The church is destroyed."

"It's either the horse or this noose."

Louella put a hand to her heart. Her chest tightened as she turned and saw Stanley holding a noose in his hand.

William pulled Louella close to him and whispered in her ear, "Go in the house."

As she stared at the noose, fear caused sweat to drip down her face like rain. She shook her head. "I'm not leaving you."

"Give us what we came for. Don't make this worse," Stanley said.

Worse? They were burning down the church and threatening her husband with a noose. She should have brought the rifle with her. The fire that blazed around the church was nothing compared to the fire of hate blazing inside her. She could kill all of them and sleep well tonight.

"What's going on here? Why you boys destroying property on my plantation?" Montgomery asked as he rode up to the parsonage in Robert's wagon.

"What's he doing with Elmira?" Louella asked William.

"I took her to him last night."

"Robert owes me money, sir." Stanley lowered the noose. "I was willing to take the horse for payment, but William stole it from me."

"Actually, this horse belongs to me, and I'm not partial to trading her for a two-dollar debt."

The flames from the church licked against the parsonage. Several men from the plantation ran through the cotton field carrying buckets of water. Larry, Ambrose, and Tommy threw water at the flames. As they ran back for more water, two other men also worked at dousing the fire with buckets of water.

"Are you siding with the likes of them over us?" Bailey demanded to know.

Montogomery waved a hand. "I'm doing no such thing, but I don't want my property burned to smithereens neither."

"I need to get what's owed to me," Stanley said. "That's only fair."

"I have a dollar." William pulled the bill out of his pants pocket and held it up.

Montgomery got down from the wagon, took the dollar from William, then walked over to Stanley. Pulling a dollar out of his pocket, he said, "I don't have much these days, but I do have a dollar. Take this and go. You boys have caused enough damage on my property."

"All I wanted was the debt paid," Stanley said.

Montgomery turned to Overseer Brown. He tipped his hat to him. "Did you have a hand in destroying my property?"

Overseer Brown shook his head. "No, sir, I only rode with these boys to make sure everything was on the up and up. We were headed to Robert's farm, so I didn't expect to be on your property."

William started helping the other men put out the church fire. Louella hated that William was giving up money they needed. But if it kept that noose from around his neck, then so be it. The troublemakers rode away like they hadn't left all sorts of mayhem for them to deal with.

Montgomery shook William's hand, said something to him,

then walked back to the big house on foot. Seven men were helping, but the fire continued to rage.

Smoke filled the air. It billowed and curled to the rhythm of the wind. There was no way they would put out the fire before it burned down the parsonage.

Louella hustled inside the parsonage. Robert was lying on the floor; his eyes sparked with fear as she entered the house. "Them boys still out there?"

"No, but you almost got your brother killed for that stupid horse you made such a fuss over."

"Looks like they were going to kill us both with this fire."

"Can you stand? I'm not sure how long the parsonage will hold." She took the blanket off the bed and threw as many items as she could carry in it.

"I need help."

She tied the blanket together, then scanned the room. Anything that wasn't nailed down was already in her blanket. But none of those items would help her get Robert out of here. The roof above their bed fell in, and flames tore through their lumpy mattress. Her eyes filled with the flames.

Hands to her face, she turned from the flames. Robert was still on the floor. She attempted to lift him; groans of pain escaped his lips.

A pain shot through the lower part of her belly. She grabbed her stomach. The heat of the flames inched closer to her back. She took a deep breath. "You have to help me."

"I'll try," Robert said.

She pulled him up. His legs were shaky. "Here, lean on me." She offered Robert her right shoulder to lean on while she drug the blanket on the ground next to her left foot as fire chased them out of the place she had called home.

The *crack, pop,* and sputter of the roaring flames around them ate at her heart. Black soot stained the front of the church and the parsonage. The windows darkened with smoke and Louella felt the familiar pang of loss.

Robert was heavy on her shoulder. The loss of the church and parsonage was heavy on her heart. She was about to succumb to the weight of it all when William ran over to her.

William took hold of Robert, then called to Tommy, "Come help me."

The smell of burning wood and smoke drifted from the house, causing her eyes to water. Louella wiped at her eyes as she took the blanket over to Robert's wagon. The smoke cleared in that area of the yard. In her peripheral vision, she saw someone standing under the oak tree. Her eyes focused on him: Overseer Brown. He was holding the loops from the straps she'd cut down.

Deep, heavy breaths, nostrils flaring with hot indignation. Her eyes scanned the yard. She picked up the biggest stick she could find, and then, like a tornado, she made her way toward her enemy. "You the devil. You don't belong on this earth!" Louella yelled, pointing her stick at the man who'd terrorized her for most of her life.

She would see him dead. She gripped the stick. He laughed, but she kept coming. "You and those other demons burned down our church. You killed my daddy and snatched my mother away from me when you knew I was too young to be without a mother."

She swung the stick in the air, making sure it was sturdy enough for the job. "If God don't make you pay, I'm gon' extract my payment from you this day."

"No! Louella, get back here!"

She heard William yell for her, but she wasn't listening for a voice of reason. Somebody had to rid them of this evil.

Overseer Brown leered at her. He threw the straps to the ground. "You cut these down, didn't you, gal?"

"Die, devil!" Louella lifted the thick stick and was about to swing it against his bald head when someone grabbed the stick from behind. Strong hands pulled her back.

Taunting her, Overseer Brown said, "I ought to tie you to this tree and beat you right now. Not a soul can stop me. You know that, don't ya?"

William shook a fist in the air. "You'll not touch my wife again."

Overseer Brown gave William a contemptuous snarl as his eyes bored into Louella's like he owned her every thought. "You remember how to beg, don't you, gal?"

The dam broke as Louella let out a guttural howl that expelled the hate that had been bottled in her heart. "Let. Me. Go!" She wrenched her arm away from Tommy. With William still holding on to her other arm, she inched closer and closer to Overseer Brown.

"He ain't worth it, Mrs. Louella," Tommy said. "Let's go."

"You want this beating, don't you?" Brown leaped forward, arm extended as he tried to pull Louella to him.

William released Louella, then stepped forward, fist balled tight. He punched the overseer so hard that he fell to the ground, holding his jaw and moving his lips about as if something had popped loose.

William then stood over him, fists at the ready. "My wife doesn't belong to you. I'll kill you before I let you touch her again."

The fire continued to rage, but the men put the buckets down and ran toward the cotton field. They stood with William, ready to do damage to the man who'd done so much to them. The overseer got off the ground, stumbling backward. He then turned and started running.

"Go after him!" Louella yelled. William pulled her into his arms. She beat on his chest. "You got to kill him. If you don't, he'll bring more tragedy upon us."

"That's not the way, my darling."

Eyes ablaze with fire and retribution, she said, "I hate him. Hate him with everything in me."

"You'll never see him again. I promise you that, so get this hate out of your heart."

"How can you know I won't see him again when he's everywhere all the time . . . even in my mind?"

"I'm taking you away from here. This place is no longer our home."

At William's words, even with all the devastation around them, Louella sighed in relief. She clamped her hands to his face and pulled him so close the tips of their noses touched. "For sure and true . . . Say you mean every word you said."

"I mean it," William told her and hugged her tight.

The rain came then. Drops beat down on Louella's head, mixing with the tears of bittersweet joy that tasted of loss and better days coming. She wiped away the rain and tears that drifted from her face into her mouth.

"Put her in the wagon with Robert," William told Louella's brother, Ambrose. "Take them to Robert's house. Tommy and I will round up the others. We'll meet at the farm."

She had emptied out a barrel of emotions on this plantation, but as they rode away, every sensation in her body was numb. This place would take nothing more from her. She would never turn this way again.

CHAPTER 8

William stood before his small congregation from the porch of his brother's farmhouse. The rain had subsided, but there was a chill in the air.

He looked out at the faces of men and women who had endured slavery until the very day they received news of their emancipation. They should be happy . . . should be jumping for joy. But instead, they looked more beat down than when the overseer was using the whip on them.

Overwrought from the ordeal they'd faced earlier that day, Louella sat in the rocking chair with a hand over her expanded belly. A consuming need to help her heal from the cruel hand slavery had dealt swept over him.

After those white boys left them to deal with the fire, Montgomery had put three dollars in William's hand, told him there was a rifle in the wagon. But he'd also said he could do no more for him and Robert. It was time for them to move on.

That was it . . . that was all the man who'd sired him and his brother said before turning his back and walking away. But even before Montgomery told him it was time to move on, William had gotten the message from Louella and people in his congregation.

"I want to say good afternoon," William said as he looked out at the people. "But from the looks on many of your faces, I doubt that you'd believe this is a good day."

Clenching his hand on the edge of the banister, William leaned into the reality they now faced. "I know things look bleak for us in this town that has been the only home some of us have known, but even though my dear mother has gone on to be with the Lord, it was my sweet and beautiful wife who reminded me of my mother's words."

Louella smiled, nodded her head as she waved in the air as if praising. "Tell the people, William."

With his wife's encouragement, he continued, "When I was a young boy, my mother used to tell me about the land her people came from. It's not like this land where people seem to only consider themselves and could care less about the welfare of other people . . . namely people like you and me.

"My mother told me that her people cared about each other, looked out for each other. They built a society based on an all-for-one-and-one-for-all mentality. I grew up as an enslaved child, but I always believed that there would come a day when our people would be treated as equals."

He lowered his head. "However, I have come to realize that we'll never be treated in that manner here."

He lifted a hand as a few grumbles sounded from the crowd. "I know I didn't always feel this way. I'll admit that Louella has been encouraging me to believe for something outside of this plantation, and I've been thinking more and more about my mother's words." With a clenched fist, he added, "I've been praying, brothers and sisters. The Lord showed me that this isn't our home anymore. My wife and I will be heading north.

"There's a land that God has prepared for us . . . . a land where we can be at peace and be happy. A land where we'll be treated as equals. We'd love to have y'all on the journey with us. Do you want to go to that land with us?"

One by one, the members of the congregation jumped to their feet and shouted, "Yes!"

"Then I need y'all to go and pack what belongings you can carry. We leave tonight."

Thirty-eight men and women from the Montgomery Plantation decided to make the trip north with William and Louella. But once Louella's nerves calmed down, her mind turned to another family who needed to get away from this rotten town.

That afternoon, she walked the path to where she normally went to get herbs. Gary hadn't been seen plowing his land since Lester Bailey shot at him. She knew it wouldn't be safe for his wife, Clara, or his teenage son, Jimmy, to stay in the house much longer, so Louella knocked on the door.

When Clara answered, her brown eyes narrowed in on Louella's belly. She touched the black scarf wrapped around her hair. "Girl, you swoll up quick, didn't you?"

Smiling, Louella patted her belly. "I'm five months."

"I'm sure Reverend William is right proud."

"He is. But I came here to tell you something." Louella leaned in closer to the door, looked around as if this secret was for Clara's ears only. "We're leaving the Montgomery Plantation. We'll be setting out tonight, and I was hoping you and Jimmy might go north with us."

Clara stepped onto the porch. She was a whole foot shorter than Louella, so she stretched forward a bit as she looked this way and that. "You and the reverend going north?"

"And the others on the Montgomery Plantation. This place is no good. We're going to find a place where we can be at peace."

"B-but Gary," Clara said as she looked off, eyes filling with sadness.

Louella put a hand on her shoulder. "I saw Gary run off after old Lester shot at him. I'm sorry y'all dealing with such things. But I had to let you know we're leaving in case you want something different than what's being dished out to us around these parts."

Clara chewed on her bottom lip, wrapped her arms around her chest. "I appreciate you thinking of us, but we best wait on Gary."

"I understand." Louella backed away from the door while whispering, "We gathering at Robert's farm tonight."

"May God watch over you on your journey." Clara hugged her, then went back in the house and closed the door.

While walking back to Robert's farmhouse, Louella prayed that God would watch over Clara and her son.

❧

When Louella got back to the farmhouse, Robert was rubbing salve on his legs and wincing with every movement. William paced the floor with worry lines etched across his forehead.

"Something happen while I been gone?"

William pointed in Robert's direction. "He wants to stay."

"Can't leave my people high and dry." Robert finished rubbing his legs and then lay back down as if he'd expended all his energy.

"You can't even stand up on your own. Who's going to look after you once we leave?" William rolled his eyes heavenward.

In all the times Louella dreamed of leaving this town, she never imagined that William's passing-for-white, slave-owning brother would be on the journey with them. Robert was thirty-nine years old. He owned a farm. He should stay here and deal with the trouble he caused.

There was a knock at the door. Louella peeked out the window. Abigail was standing on the porch. Four men and two other women who also worked on Robert's farm were standing in the yard. She opened the door.

"What's going on out here, Abigail?"

Abigail cleared her throat and spoke up for the group. "We don't want to stay here no more. Tommy told me that y'all heading up north."

Louella didn't know what Robert would say about all of his

workers leaving the farm, but something deep inside was telling her this, too, was a part of God's plan. Just as William's mother described, all for one and one for all. "Then y'all need to start packing. We leaving tonight."

The men and women in the yard erupted in cheers, then one of them yelled up to her, "Tell Mr. Robert I quit."

She smiled at that. Robert never should've enslaved people in the first place. It was no better for him that he'd now have to work this farm all by himself. "It will be my pleasure to let Robert know that y'all coming with us."

She went back in the house and told William. "Abigail and the rest of the workers on this farm say they leaving with us."

Robert's eyebrows lifted as his mouth flew open. "They what? Why would they do that?"

Louella's hand went to her hip, and with all the contempt she could muster, she told Robert, "Because they're free and able to live and move as they please, that's why."

William put a hand on Louella's shoulder, turned to Robert. "Your people are leaving. Will you listen to me now and let us pack your things so we can all go together?"

Robert's eyes held bewilderment, like he couldn't understand why free people wanted to be free. "I need to think on this."

"Don't think too long . . . or you'll be left here by yourself," William told him.

CHAPTER 9

As the sun went down and night filled the sky, almost fifty people beat a path to Robert's yard in the dark of night. They held hands as William prayed for their journey.

When the prayer was done, they packed the wagon Robert gave them. They took jugs of water, whatever food they had left. Miss Saddie, the weaver woman, put her cloth and supplies to make clothes in the wagon. Her son Woodrow, the cobbler, added the supplies he had left for making shoes.

They would need food, clothes, and shoes for the long and grueling journey to the Appalachian trail, the same trail William and Robert took when Montgomery left South Carolina seventeen years ago to get in on the cotton boon.

Standing on Robert's porch, looking out at the people, William said, "The mountain trail is not going to be easy. Our shoes will wear out, and there will be days when we won't be able to wash our faces, but this trail will keep us away from watchful eyes. So let's finish stocking the wagon and get moving."

Larry hollered up, "We can't put any more in the bed of this wagon. The oxen might not be able to pull the load."

The door opened behind William, and Robert leaned against the post. He pointed toward the smaller wagon that his horse, Elmira, was attached to. "Put the rest of the supplies in that wagon."

William turned to his brother and shook his head. "You're already giving us two oxen and a wagon. I can't ask you to give up Elmira too."

"I'm not giving up Elmira, nor am I staying here without my

brother. I'm coming with you." Robert held out a hand to William, and the brothers clasped hands. Then William helped his brother sit back down.

Louella had been standing at the bottom of the porch looking through packages, making sure the people were only bringing items that would be needed for the journey. When she heard Robert say that he was coming with them, she rubbed her belly as a sudden queasiness overtook her.

She climbed the steps of the porch and rushed over to William. Louella pulled her husband to the farthest side of the porch, away from his brother. "What you doing? We leaving these slave owners behind. We can't bring one with us."

"Louella!" He looked as if her words shamed him. "You know as well as I do that Robert isn't the only one passing as white and enslaving folks in the South. He did what the times called for, and not one of the people he enslaved ever so much as had a hair on their head plucked."

"You sure about that?" Louella challenged.

"The only thing I'm sure about is that we're in danger if we stay here much longer, so I don't have time for this." William turned away from her, walked back to his brother, and patted the man on his back as he told the people, "Hallelujah! We have another buggy. Put the rest of our supplies in Robert's buggy, but only use half of the space. Robert will need to ride in the wagon for the start of our journey."

Louella wanted to shout her objection. There had to be a reason that Robert's workers were packing up to leave, and she believed that Robert was the reason. But she swallowed hard and accepted their new passenger on this journey.

Ambrose walked over to her. "We packed up Mama Sue's things." He lifted the bag.

Louella pointed toward Robert's wagon, then glanced over at the porch. A smile lit up her face when she saw her grandmother sitting there. At that moment, she understood why William wanted Robert along for the journey—family was family, no matter what.

Louella waved her hands to get everyone's attention. A couple of kids were running around the wagons playing tag. Larry and Tommy held up lanterns so people could situate their belongings in the dark. "Okay, since we've got two wagons for this long journey, the fair thing for us to do would be to switch off who's riding and who's walking every so often. That way each of us gets to take a rest off our feet. Does that sound good?"

Cheers throughout the group went up, then one of them shouted, "All for one and one for all!"

William glanced over at his wife and smiled his approval, then clasped his hands together. "Okay, everybody, let's head out."

Flutters flittered in her stomach. She rubbed it as she whispered to her growing babe, "Don't be nervous. We're going to find a place where we can be happy. You'll see what I'm telling you is for sure and true."

Tommy held two bags up. "We still don't have enough room for all of our stuff."

William pressed his lips together. Louella put an arm around him. She recognized his expression. Lips pressed together meant that his next words were going to be displeasing but necessary.

"We may have to leave some of the items behind." William held up a hand as the grumbling started. "I know that each of us has so little that we can't bear to part with anything, but it is necessary."

Louella looked at the faces of the men and women gathered there. Even in the darkness of the night, a heavy cloud of despair descended on them. Leaving what little they had behind was too great an ask. She didn't want any of them to turn back for want of a skillet or toy for one of their children.

Walking down the steps of the porch, Louella shouted to the

group, "This journey we're undertaking is bigger than these small items that can be replaced once we find our land."

But Tommy shook his head. "I don't have nothing in this world." He held up the bag in his hand. "This is all my mama had, God rest her soul, and she left it in my keeping. I'll carry it on my back if I have to, but I'm not leaving it."

Louella had a keepsake of her mother's in her bag as well. Her hand went to her heart. "Tommy, we don't want you to lose any more of your precious mother than you already have."

Louella walked over to the bigger wagon. She was about to tell them to take everything off the wagon and go through their things one more time so they could see what could be left behind, but then Gary, Clara, and Jimmy rode onto the farm by way of Gary's ox wagon.

Gary loosed the reins and climbed down from his seat on the wagon. He walked over to the porch, looked up at William. "I hear tell y'all pulling out and going up north."

William nodded.

"Well, if you have need for a planter, then me and my family would be much obliged to join y'all."

William stepped down from the porch. He clasped hands with Gary. "Your skills will be most useful, and right now, we can use your wagon for a few more supplies."

"You're welcome to it, Reverend."

Clara smiled at Louella, then blew a kiss. Louella smiled back.

While several bags were thrown onto Gary's wagon, Louella glanced over at the porch, didn't see her grandmother, and called out, "Where's Mama Sue?"

A hand lifted from the group standing to the left side of the porch. "I'm here. You're not leaving without me."

"I wouldn't dream of it." Louella waved her over. "You and Miss Saddie need to ride on the wagon first. I'll walk."

William came over to Louella. "You need to be on that wagon. You're so far along, that baby has to be weighing down on you."

Putting a hand on William's shoulder, she told him, "I'm okay. Let me do this for my grandmother, please."

He turned from her, scanning the area. "Tommy!" William shouted. "You drive the wagon out of here. I'm walking with my love."

Love . . . Her mouth tightened and twisted. She turned away from him and studied the falling leaves. William coming so close to dying at the hand of those white devils was a reminder to guard her heart. Loving and losing was like a noose around her neck.

William shouted, "Onward!"

And so the journey began, with Louella and William walking arm in arm away from bondage toward a land they believed God would show them.

PART 2

THE JOURNEY

1865–1866

CHAPTER 10

It took three weeks to get from Jackson, Mississippi, to Mobile, Alabama. They mostly traveled by night and rested during the heat of the day, staying close to the Tombigbee and Mobile River so they could fill their water jugs and wash some of the road off them.

It would be a while before they reached the Appalachian trails. So when they passed by city areas, they spent some days selling what Louella touted as the cure for rheumatism in little tin cases they had purchased at a general store along the way.

The women cooked whatever the men were able to pull in with their fishing rods or raccoons and rabbits they caught. Most of the cooking was done in the early afternoon once the men came back to camp with their bounty.

The swelling of Louella's feet was troublesome. She tried drinking water during the day, but depending on which part of the river they camped at, sometimes the water was cloudy and made her sick to her stomach.

"I'm worried 'bout you," Mama Sue said as Louella sat on the ground next to the fire. Embers from the fire sparked as they floated away on air currents. Mama Sue was cooking the last of the rice they'd brought with them along with a pot of beans.

"I'll be fine. Just need more water."

"No, you need to be on that wagon more." Her grandmother stirred the beans, then shook her head. "All us appreciate you giving up your riding time to some of us older women, but we see how your feet swelling and how low that baby is hanging."

Placing her hands on the ground behind her, Louella leaned back to stretch out as the baby moved around. "This child laying on my bladder. Can't hardly rest my feet, I got to get up to relieve myself so often."

William and Larry helped her stand up. Louella held on to the bottom of her swollen belly as she wobbled up the hill and found a spot in front of one of the wagons to squat while trying not to wet her dress.

Breathing a sigh of relief, Louella righted herself and began the trek back down the hill. Her swollen feet ached something terrible.

She saw William standing next to Mama Sue. Louella almost yelled for him. She needed to lean on him to safely maneuver the rest of this hill. But his and Mama Sue's heads were huddled together, Mama Sue talking and pointing in Louella's direction. Louella stopped walking, took a deep breath. Hands on either side of her hips, she contemplated taking a seat in the very spot she stood.

But then William walked away from Mama Sue and lifted his arms, waving them in the air to get everyone's attention. "We've been on the road for several weeks now. Walking at night and selling our products during the day."

William took his handkerchief out of his pocket and wiped the sweat from his brow. "We need a rest. Let's stay close to the Mobile River for one more night before we make our way toward Georgia, where we will then find the trail for the Appalachian Mountains."

"William!" Louella yelled for him. She would've rushed over to him, but her feet felt heavy, like the chains of slavery were holding them in the spot she stood.

William trotted up the hill to Louella's side. "You okay, beloved? You need my help?"

"Why are we staying put another night? We're still far from our destination." Louella shook her head. "I don't think that's the right decision."

"Well." He kissed her on the forehead. "I reckon you've been overruled by your husband."

"I don't like that. You should listen to me."

"And you should listen to your body." William put an arm around Louella's waist and slowly walked with her down the hill. "You'd keep walking on those swollen feet until they bust wide open. You need rest, and from what Mama Sue tells me, you haven't been drinking enough water."

"The water's been turning my stomach. I can't drink it."

William helped her sit down. "I'll go foraging with the men in the morning. I'll find a creek with some fresh water and bring it back to you."

Louella lifted her hand and gently ran it down the side of William's face. "Thank you." Their eyes locked, but then Louella turned away.

They made camp that night, and Louella rested her feet. The next morning, William took Ambrose foraging. Mama Sue sat down next to Louella and rubbed her feet. "Why didn't you say anything? I could've given up my ride on the wagon the night before."

Louella shrugged. "We have so far to travel. I didn't want to be a burden by slowing us down."

"Stop talking foolish. If it wasn't for you, we'd still be on the Montgomery Plantation with empty bellies." Mama Sue stood back up and reheated the beans. A crisp, earthy smell wafted up from the bean pot with the steam of the salt meat.

Abigail was standing a little ways behind Mama Sue, helping Tommy chop wood. Abigail's eyelashes fluttered so many times as she laughed at whatever Tommy was saying, Louella felt like she was dipping into private matters, so she averted her eyes from the two of them.

"Abigail," Robert called out to her. "Get over here. Since we're just sitting around, you can keep me company."

Abigail's shoulders slumped, and her cheeks reddened with embarrassment. Louella was outraged for the girl. She swung around and glared at Robert. He had a grin on his face that she used to see on old Montgomery's face when he came sniffing around the women in the field. Grins like that stripped dignity from women who could do nothing but relent.

Louella wished he had stayed back in Mississippi. If she had anything to say about it, nobody was going to be "Massa" to her or anyone in this camp ever again.

Putting her hands to the ground, she tried to push herself up, but her belly was in the way and almost caused her to flop back onto the ground. It would have, if Clara hadn't run over and held on to her right arm while Mirabel grabbed her left.

"Girl, what you doing?" Mama Sue put her hands on her ample hips.

"I need to stand up, but this baby isn't making things easy on me." Louella grabbed hold of Clara and awkwardly stood on her swollen feet.

"Sit back down. You need to rest," Mama Sue told her.

"In a minute, Mama. Something needs fixing, and I can't be still." Louella then wobbled as she tried to walk gracefully over to Robert to give him a mouthful. She looked ridiculous, knew it, but didn't care. When she reached Robert, she got close and leaned into him as she said, "You need to leave Abigail alone. She don't belong to you no more."

Robert's head swiveled as if he'd been struck. Venom danced in his eyes. "How dare you speak to me with such insolence."

"Insolence?" She'd heard that word enough during slavery when white folks put her in her place for speaking her mind. But

Louella would never allow anyone to shut her mouth again. Not when she was right about a matter.

Robert stood. "I'm not going to put up with this from you."

"Just letting you know that the people on this journey no longer wish to be ruled by a massa, so Abigail won't be keeping you company tonight."

Sputtering, Robert turned toward the girl he'd once owned and yelled, "Abigail, get over here!"

Abigail put the log down and scurried over to Robert like a scared rat. Her head was lowered as she placed her feet next to his. "I was helping with the logs in case we get a chill tonight," she told him as if she needed to account for her time.

"You weren't doing anything wrong, Abigail. Raise your head," Louella told her.

Robert's hands tightened as he blew out a puff of air. "You don't tell her what to do."

Putting her hands on her hips, Louella harrumphed. "And neither do you. Abigail is a free woman. She don't answer to you no more."

Face red, Robert turned to Abigail. "Will you tell this meddling woman that I'm not forcing you to do anything?"

Inch by inch, Abigail lifted her head. She hesitated for a moment, stepped back, then told her former master, "You right as rain, Mr. Robert. You can't force me to do nothing."

"That's right," Robert agreed as he jutted a finger in Louella's direction. "Now tell her that you want to be with me."

Tommy stepped over to them. His eyes questioned Abigail. "Is it true, Abbey?"

Robert swung around, glaring at Tommy. "Why do you call her Abbey? Her name is Abigail." His voice rose with every word.

"I like when he calls me Abbey." Robert swung back in Abigail's direction. As her voice took on strength, she added, "And I don't want to keep company with you."

"Finally!" Louella hugged Abigail. "I knew you had it in you."

Smiling, Abigail said, "It's time for me to start acting like I'm free, right?"

Louella nodded. "For sure and true."

Tommy took Abigail's hand and walked away with her.

Robert turned his anger back to Louella. "Who do you think you are? I've looked out for my people all these years. Abigail and I have always been friendly. I haven't harmed her."

"And I'm sure your mama never complained about keeping company with Massa Montgomery either."

Robert raised his hand, getting ready to slap Louella, when William shouted, "What in the devil's going on?"

Robert's hand limped back down as William advanced on them. "Your wife is interfering in my business."

"You okay, sis?" Ambrose asked Louella while eyeing Robert.

"I'm fine." Louella lifted a hand, stopping Ambrose from advancing farther.

William pulled his wife close to him. "I don't care what she was doing. Don't you ever raise a hand to her again."

"William, now listen to me . . . ," Robert began.

But William shushed him and pointed toward a man, a woman, and two boys who were standing with Gary. "We have company."

"How we gon' have company, and we're basically sleeping outdoors?" Robert rolled his eyes.

William brought Louella back over to her seat. When she sat down, Mama Sue smiled at her but didn't say anything. William then handed her a ladle full of the water he'd brought back to the camp. She drank several ladles of water that tasted so fresh she wondered if God Himself had directed her husband to the stream.

William raised a hand to the group. "Gather around, everyone. I want to introduce you to some good people we met while hunting today."

The group pressed in. William had the newcomers stand next

to him. "This here is Marshal Johnson and his wife, Sooni Johnson." William extended a hand toward the children. "Their two boys are MJ and Mark. They come from the Johnson Plantation here in Mobile."

"Nice to meet y'all," Clara said as she shook Sooni's hand.

"The thing is," William began again, "the Johnsons have been hiding out from the Night Riders after they burned down their home."

All at once, the crowd seemed to groan at the mention of Night Riders. Since the war, they'd heard stories about ghosts chasing Negroes off their land. Many of the ghosts turned out to be the overseers or former slave owners, scaring colored folks into submission.

Gary stepped forward. "Marshal informed us that it's not safe to travel during the night while we're in Alabama. They've got night patrols looking to cause trouble and claim that our travels are unauthorized."

Louella was listening from her spot on the ground. Glancing down at her feet, she grinned. Dirty and swollen as they were, they might have kept them out of harm's way.

William lifted a hand to get everyone's attention again. "I suggest that we spend one more night at this camp and then head out in the morning."

Louella turned to the newcomers. "Thank you so much for delivering this important information to us."

"The Johnson family would like to take the journey north with us. I'd like a show of hands." William raised his first. "Can the Johnsons join us?"

Louella asked Marshal, "What was your trade on the Johnson Plantation?"

"I was a farmer, ma'am. You got crops need growing, I'm your man." He then pointed toward his wife. "Sooni be the best seamstress in all of Alabama."

"You all'll fit right in." Louella raised her hand. Mama Sue and Clara raised their hands. Then one hand after another went up.

William turned to the family. "Well, Marshal, looks like you're one of us now."

Marshal took his hat off as he looked upon the group. "From the bottom of my heart, I truly thank you."

"Now let's eat." Mama Sue opened her pot and let the smell of butter beans mingle with the air.

Once everyone had eaten, William sat down next to Louella and stretched out his legs.

"Are you full?" she asked.

He nodded, then leaned close and whispered in her ear, "Now, what was Robert so steaming mad about?"

Louella's eyes rolled heavenward. "Your brother thinks he's still massa around here."

William's head jolted backward. His face scrunched. "No, he doesn't. Robert is just as happy that slavery is over as we are."

"If that man could sell us right now and regain his wealth, he'd do it in a heartbeat."

"You're talking foolish, woman." William stood up and walked over to his brother.

Louella wished that William could see what she saw in Robert. She worried that Robert's behavior would disturb the happy union William wanted to build among the people.

Mama Sue took the empty spot William left. She rubbed Louella's shoulder. "You did the right thing, my girl. I'm proud of you."

"Oh, Mama." Louella laid her head on her grandmother's shoulder. "William's upset with me, but I couldn't let Robert treat Abigail like she still belonged to him."

Mama Sue patted Louella's shoulder. "It used to scare me the way you speak your mind, but lately I've been thinking that the good Lord must've put you on this earth to help those who can't help themselves."

Her grandmother then lay down on her pallet on the opposite side of the fire, as if she hadn't said anything out of the ordinary, but she'd said a mouthful. All her life Louella had been told to shut her mouth, mind her manners, and stop being so insolent. When all she ever wanted was to be heard. To be seen as more than some no-count enslaved girl. Her grandmother's words blessed her very soul.

CHAPTER 11

By morning, the swell in Louella's feet had slightly diminished, but not enough for William's liking. He piled lumber under her feet to elevate them while Mama Sue took some of the gel from an aloe vera plant and rubbed it on them.

They were preparing to leave, but then the rain came and muddied the trail they were following. If the wheels of those wagons got stuck in the mud, they'd have to rustle up the strength of Samson to get them out. William told the group, "Looks like we'll be holding camp one more night, but make sure all of your things are packed. We'll head out first light of day tomorrow."

Louella took respite under an oak tree that had enough leaves to hold off the rain from beating down on her head. Scratching the scar on her wrist, Louella turned her back to the oak but stayed put.

Sighing, she made peace with holding camp another day. God might be keeping them from danger on the road. After all, if they hadn't held camp yesterday, they wouldn't have met the Johnson family, nor would they have known about them Night Riders setting traps for formerly enslaved people who were traveling by night. Louella prayed that things would be different up north—prayed that they would find a place where they could have an ounce of dignity.

Abigail handed Louella a bowl of grits and a piece of the pheasant the men had brought back yesterday.

Louella took the offering. "Thank you."

"I'm the one who needs to be doing the thanking." Abigail sat down next to Louella.

Louella waved a hand in the air. "Don't even think on it."

"Can't help but to think on it." Abigail put her hands in her lap, then exhaled like she was trying to expel some demons from within. "Robert purchased me from a slave owner who did terrible things to children." Abigail's eyes clouded over with shame. "I kept expecting Robert to claim his due, as my former owner called it, but he never harmed me in any way. I think he's just jealous 'cause I'm keeping company with Tommy."

"Jealous or not, he had no business shaming you in front of everyone like that."

Tears glistened in Abigail's eyes as she gave Louella a weak smile. "When you told me to lift my head yesterday, something clicked inside my whole being."

The baby squirmed in Louella's stomach. It had been hours since the last time she ate, so she took a few spoonsful of the grits while listening to Abigail.

"I'm free . . . I'm not owned by nobody and no one can extract their due like my old massa ever again."

Louella shoved Abigail's shoulder. "Dry your weeping eyes, girl. You done stumbled on the truth, and you know what the truth will do for you, right?"

With furrowed brows, Abigail said, "I don't understand."

Patiently, like a teacher, Louella told her, "It's a phrase from the Bible. John 8:32 tells us, 'And ye shall know the truth, and the truth shall make you free.'"

"Oh," Abigail said quietly. Then she told Louella, "I wasn't taught to read or write. Don't know much about the Good Book or any other book."

Louella put her bowl down. "The world seems so small when we have only one way of seeing a thing. But reading takes your mind to places you've never been." She took Abigail's hand in hers and squeezed it. "I can teach you, if you want."

A tear rolled down Abigail's face. She wiped it away. "No fooling?"

Louella giggled. "No fooling. For sure and true."

Abigail jumped up and hugged her. She then ran over to Tommy and excitedly told him that she was going to learn to read.

Louella heard Tommy say, "I don't reckon that's a good idea. Don't want you getting ideas in that beautiful head of yours."

But Abigail put her hands on her hips, wagged a finger in his face. "Get used to it. I'm a free woman, and I'm gon' make something of myself in this world."

Louella screamed internally, *You tell him, Abigail!* These men weren't going to be the only ones getting opportunities when they made it to their promised land. Louella would see to it. And Abigail might help her with that mission.

Later that evening as they were sitting around the fire talking about the day's adventures, Marshal said, "A man from the Freedmen's Bureau come to my house right before them Night Riders burned it down."

"You don't say." William was stretched out next to Louella with an elbow on the ground holding him up. "I read something about that organization starting up a few months back."

"They say I don't have to keep my old enslaved name. Say I can change it to whatever I want, so when we get settled, I'm changing my last name."

Larry shrugged. "Don't see what all the fuss is about. People know me by Larry. What do I need a last name for?"

"My great-grandfather was stolen from the Ashante people," Marshal told them. "All my life, my family reminded me where I came from. If I can't go back, I'll at least take the Ashante name for my family. We shall be known as Marshal and Sooni Ashante." His chest puffed up as he said the name with pride.

Tommy stood and addressed the group. "My mama wanted to name me Femi, an African name that means 'love me,' because I was the only somebody who loved her." His face tightened, eyes took on sadness. "But Massa Montgomery wouldn't allow it, so if I get a chance, I'm changing my first name to Femi."

Abigail put her hand in his. "We don't have to wait. I'll call you Femi from this day forward." The two hugged and then, in front of God and everyone else in the camp, their eyes met, and they kissed.

Louella and several others clapped and shouted, "'Bout time!" But Robert scowled, got up, and stormed away from the group.

Gary stepped forward. He looked at Clara and their son, Jimmy. "We've carried the name Bailey since I was born, but I don't want that ol' enslaved name no more. I'd like to change our name to Freeman if that be all right with y'all."

Clara and Jimmy put their arms around Gary. When they parted again, Clara told him, "That sounds like a mighty fine name to me."

They continued talking through the night about the names they would prefer now that they were free to choose for themselves. Later that night as she and William lay side by side, she whispered in his ear, "What about you? Do you have a name picked out for us?"

Louella had been given the last name Bobo, same as her mother, grandmother, and brother, from their first owner before Montgomery came to Mississippi. She didn't mind getting rid of that name since it meant "fool." But William told her that Montgomery's ledger only listed the original enslaved people by their first name, so her husband didn't have a last name.

"Montgomery," William said without much contemplation. "I want our name to be Montgomery."

Louella clamped her mouth shut as bile from deep in her belly threatened to spring forth. They were finally away from their captors, and Louella wanted to fly all the way free. Why couldn't they have a last name like Freeman or Ashante?

He must've seen the look of horror on her face. He cleared his throat and said, "I know you don't like it, but that name is a part of my story. Can you be okay with it for me?"

She turned her back to him. Silence was her answer. She had great respect for William and for the good man that he was. But the Montgomery name was like dung flung in her face.

By morning, Louella's feet were back to normal. She rode on the wagon with William when they set out. William explained that they would have to go through Alabama, Georgia, and South Carolina on their way north. The journey was long, and traveling by the light of day scared Louella.

"What you fretting 'bout, girl?" William asked while flapping the reins on the oxen.

"Nothing much. Been praying for our safety."

William let go of one of the reins, put a hand over hers, then took the rein back. "I've been praying too. A lot of people are traveling to God only knows where with us. I'm responsible for each of them."

"We're all counting on you, William. You won't let us down."

"That's a lot of burden heaped on one man," he said as they made their way up a hill. The oxen were moving slow, so the walkers behind the wagon had to stop and wait for them to get up the hill.

"No more burden than these oxen feel trying to get us up this hill with the heavy load we have in the wagon."

Laughing, William said, "That makes me feel a lot better."

Louella put a hand on her belly as she shifted in her seat. "This baby wants to be out into this world. I just can't fathom what the hurry is all about."

Concern etched across William's face. "You okay? Do we need to stop and rest awhile?"

She shook her head. "I think I'll get out and walk at our next stop."

"We shouldn't have left before you had the baby. This trip has been too hard on you."

"We had no choice. Overseer Brown would've extracted retribution for how you waylaid him."

They made it up the grassy hill and started riding on level ground through a landscape of nothing but trees as far as the eye could see on either side of the trail. "Are you still cross with me?"

Biting down on her lip, Louella shifted in her seat again. Tagging her with that name, Montgomery, was like being reminded of the worst part of her life over and over. "I don't want to think on those people and their devilment ever again."

"This isn't about them. It's about me. And that's the name I choose for our family."

Louella turned back to him. She saw the longing in his eyes. Sighing deeply, she sat with her pain a moment longer, then relented. "Guess it won't kill me . . . long as I don't see hide nor hair of that plantation again."

They rode in silence for a little while, passing tree after tree . . . Why were trees everywhere? She could go her whole lifetime and be content never to see another tree again. Then suddenly, Louella screamed, "Stop the wagon! Oh Lordy, stop now."

William pulled on the reins. When the oxen came to a stop, he turned to Louella. "What's wrong? Is it the baby?"

She stared at the oak tree on the other side of the road. It was a thick tree with thick branches, ripe for lynching. "Help me down from this wagon."

"Do you need me to get Mama Sue?"

"Help get me down."

"What's going on up there?" Robert yelled from behind them. "We still have a few hours left of daylight."

William jumped down and ran around to Louella's side. He

held out a hand to her and helped her step down from the wagon. "Will you tell me what's got you upset?"

She pointed toward the oak tree. William turned to look. A noose was hanging from one of the thick limbs of the tree. "Louella, this is madness. Why'd you have me stop?"

"I can't leave that there." Her finger angrily jutted toward the oak tree as her eyes widened with indignation. "That noose is there, waiting for a body." Anger pushed her forward as she made her way to that dreaded tree. Her heart constricted with every step she took.

She wanted to climb that tree and loose that ungodly noose. But she couldn't get up the tree in her condition. She yanked and yanked and yanked. *"Argh!"* she yelled in frustration.

"Will you get your wife?" Robert demanded.

"Come on, Louella. We've got to clear more road before nightfall."

Louella folded her arms and let them rest on her belly. "I won't leave this spot until I have that noose in my hand."

"Girl, if you don't get back in that wagon and stop being a nuisance." Robert took his hat off and slapped it against his pants. He blew out air, his face showing his frustration. "If you take that noose down, what's that gon' do? Don't you think them boys will put another noose on that tree if they really want to lynch somebody?"

"They might," Louella said with a calmness she didn't possess. Her heart ached and bled for a soul she didn't know . . . a soul who would have to endure a lynch mob for no other reason than the color of his skin. "But I won't make it easy for them." She shook her head with conviction. "This noose is coming down." She turned back and yanked on it again.

Jimmy came forward. "I'll climb up there and get it for you, Mrs. Louella."

Louella nodded her gratitude, then he headed up the tree. Jimmy was young and spry, so he mounted that tree like a possum scurrying away from a hunter. He reached the limb where the rope was tied. Jimmy untied it, climbed down the tree, and handed it to Louella.

She turned to face the group and held up the rope so everyone could see the offending noose. "This, my friends, is a lie. They put the noose around our necks and kill us as if we're nothing and mean less than nothing to this world. But we're not what these Night Riders think in their cold, dark hearts about us."

Louella pumped the fisted hand that held the noose in the air several times as a river of tears cascaded down her face. She didn't want anyone else on God's green earth to endure the pain of finding a loved one hanging from a tree. "Repeat after me: This is a lie. Our lives matter."

The group stood tall and yelled back, "This is a lie! Our lives matter!"

She gripped the rope and began to sing, *"There is a happy land, far, far away, where saints in glory stand, bright, bright as day. Oh, how they sweetly sing, worthy is our Savior King."*

Louella lowered her head and wept as a pain so deep crept up and clawed into her heart. The white folks on the plantation used to sing that "Happy Land" song, but Louella never understood— could never imagine a happy land for her and for people who looked like her.

Clara stepped forward and continued the song. *"Oh, we shall happy be, when from sin and sorrow free."*

Wiping the tears from her eyes, Louella glanced over at her friend. They clasped hands and sang together.

When they were finished, William wiped his eyes and told the people, "I declare before you all this day, we will find this Happy Land, and we will all live in a place free from fear. We'll work together and build a nation that's built on mutual respect."

Cheers went up. Then Louella said, "Now let's get back on the road."

CHAPTER 12

I t took a month to go from Monroe County to Montgomery, Alabama. By the time they made it to Montgomery, Louella could go
no farther. Pain doubled her over as it shot through her belly again
and again. "It's not time yet."

Mama Sue told William, "It's time when the babe say it's time."

She was a little over seven months pregnant. She needed to
carry this baby at least another month. But no matter how much
she protested, Louella could do nothing but succumb to the nat-
ural course of things.

They found an abandoned barn that smelled of death and decay
and made camp. The men pulled a dead cow out of the barn, and
then Louella was brought in and laid on a pile of hay.

William paced outside the barn, and Louella yelled and screamed
bloody murder. "I'm dying! I swear 'fore God, I'm dying!" The
baby ripped her apart with each and every push.

Mama Sue fussed, "This child gotta come out. You been pushing too long."

"What's wrong? Why won't it come out?" Abigail asked.

Mama Sue and Abigail were tending to her. Abigail wiped the
sweat from Louella's forehead, but neither of them gave response to
her query.

"Push, Louella," was all Mama Sue said.

But there was something in her grandmother's eyes. A forebod-
ing that Louella had never seen before. Louella pushed, but the
baby had stopped kicking.

Mama Sue and Abigail grabbed hold of the child's head and shouted, "Push!" again.

Louella bore down with all her might and shouted, *"Argh!"* as she gave a push so strong that the baby gushed out from her body. Louella's head flapped back against the straw. It was done. She wanted to rejoice, but she hadn't heard the cry yet.

Exhaustion claimed Louella. She couldn't lift her head from the straw she was lying against. She rolled her head to the right. Mama Sue had the baby in her arm, pouring water on it and wiping fluids away. Drifting . . . eyelids heavy. "What did I have?"

Abigail gave her a woeful smile. "A little girl."

"A girl? Bring her to me." Louella lifted her arms, but Mama Sue backed away.

Her grandmother told Abigail, "Go get Reverend William."

"What's going on . . . What's the matter?" Louella squirmed against the hay, wanting to get up, but her body betrayed her.

When William stepped into the barn, Mama Sue whispered something to him, and then he came to sit with Louella. But Louella's eyes weren't on William. Mama Sue backed out of the barn with the baby close to her bosom.

"Bring her to me. I want to hold her."

As the barn door closed, William's shoulders rolled forward. "Thing is," he began. His voice cracked and he sniffed. "Th-the baby . . . didn't make it."

Her eyes squinted as she tried to make sense of what he'd said. "Huh?"

He repeated those foul words. "The baby didn't make it."

Her breath caught in her throat as if she'd been punched. She sobbed. Squirming, she tried to get up, but William held her down.

"Don't do too much moving. You lost a lot of blood and need to rest."

"Where's my baby?"

"I'm so sorry, beloved. Our precious little girl is with God. We can take heart that we'll see her again someday."

A guttural explosion of pain and why-me clawed its way up her throat and spilled out. She didn't want to wait to see her child in the sweet by-and-by. She wanted to wrap her in her bosom and love her like she deserved. God was always making mistakes when it came to the things that mattered to her. Through clenched teeth she moaned, "I. Want. My. Baby."

"It's best to let them bury her."

Louella's eyes went wild. "No! No! You can't do that. You can't put my baby in the ground without letting me hold her—like she doesn't matter." Tears blurred her sight. She touched her heart. "Like she meant nothing to us."

The barn door opened again. Louella wiped the tears from her face as Mama Sue brought her baby back in. Tears ran down her grandmother's face as she put the babe on Louella's chest. "I'm sorry, my sweet Louella."

"Take the baby back. It'll be better if she doesn't see her," William said.

But Mama Sue shook her head. "I know my granddaughter. Louella needs this."

Her little brown baby's eyes were closed, her lips turning purple, but she was still beautiful to Louella. This baby thoroughly possessed her heart . . . and broke it. A fresh tear dropped on the baby's face. Louella wiped it away, but there was plenty more to come.

William kissed the back of her neck as sorrow filled her soul. "I know it hurts. I'm hurting too. But we're going to get through this together."

"How?" The question eked out of her as clouds of sadness descended, drenching her in loss. Then rain beat down on the barn as if the sky was crying with her.

William took the baby from her.

"No! Give her back."

Taking a moment to look at his baby, William said, "I'm going to miss you, little one."

"She needs a name. You can't just dismiss her without a name."

"Of course she needs a name." He bit down on his lip. "It needs to be something beautiful. Something . . ."

"Lily. Her name is Lily," Louella told him.

He stood, handed the baby back to Mama Sue. "Thank you for letting us spend some time with our sweet Lily."

Mama Sue closed her eyes real tight for a moment, then backed out of the barn, breaking Louella's heart all over again.

❦

Louella hadn't eaten in the last three days. Mama Sue and William kept trying to feed her, but all she wanted to do was lie in the barn and sprinkle pity and sorrow on herself.

"Your food is getting cold," William told her.

Louella turned her face to the wall. Children were running around outside; she let the sound of their laughter linger in her ears while anguish streamed down her face, turning her cheeks into cascades of unbearable grief.

"Talk to me."

But she couldn't, wouldn't turn to him . . . couldn't share this pain.

"You won't talk to me, huh? Well, I know who you'll talk to." William left the barn, and within a few seconds, Mama Sue entered.

She put a hand on Louella's forehead. "Praise the good Lord . . . no fever."

"I'm not sick."

"I know, dearest. You're sad . . . and sometimes that's worse than sick. I been where you are, so I know."

Sighing deeply, she asked, "How did you go on?"

"Some days I wonder if I did go on, or if I'm still trapped in the horror of all that happened to us."

Louella turned to face her grandmother. Her eyebrow lifted. "But you're always so strong. I never even saw you cry when Mama was taken from us."

Mama Sue nodded. "I had to be strong for you and your brother. I couldn't fall apart when y'all needed me." She put a hand on Louella's shoulder. "I know you'd lay here forever if you could, but the people need you. You've made us believe that things will be better for us on the other side of this journey. But they're losing hope as this journey becomes more difficult."

"Let William talk to them. I want to lay here, Mama Sue. I need to be still. Can't you understand that?"

"I do, dearest. I do."

Wallowing in pity was her due. She wanted Lily—wanted to be a mother. But later that day as the people gathered outside the barn, she heard someone say, "We're running out of food."

Another said, "Louella losing that baby and us running out of food might be a bad omen."

"What you talking 'bout?"

"Talking 'bout going back to the Montgomery Plantation and seeing if they'll let me do some sharecropping."

As far as Louella was concerned, that was crazy. She would never turn back to her captors. How could they even think about going back to what God had brought them out of? The fact that she might be the cause of them thinking such foolery was beyond her.

Then she heard a voice that she recognized to be Robert's say, "I might be tempted to head back to my farm if a few men would come and help me with the land."

Later, when William came to sit with her, he brought a bowl of potato soup. Louella slowly raised herself up and leaned her back against the wall of the barn. She took the soup from her husband. "I heard someone say we're running low on food."

"We had a few complications. The hunting hasn't been good

in this location, but we did find some potatoes." He pointed to her bowl, encouraging her to eat.

Louella ate a spoonful.

"A new family joined our camp today. They said a lot of freed men and women are going hungry in these parts."

"They're coming with us?" Louella asked as she sipped her soup.

William nodded.

"Do they have a useful trade?"

William's lips tightened.

"What's wrong with my query?"

"I told you the family's going hungry. They don't *want* to join with us; they *need* to join with us."

Louella put her bowl down and placed a hand on William's thigh. "I'm not coming against your decision to allow them to travel with us, but I believe so much in this idea of a society where everyone pitches in and everyone is rewarded for their efforts."

"So do I," William retorted.

Louella lifted a hand. "If we're going to build the type of society your mother told you about, then we'll all need to be in accord. And everybody needs to have a skill that can benefit our community. That's all I'm saying."

"What makes you think we're not in accord?"

She pointed toward the interior barn walls. "These walls are thin."

William lowered his head, averted his eyes. "Some bandits broke into the camp last night. They stole some of our food and supplies."

"Why didn't you or Mama Sue tell me about that?"

"You have enough worries."

Louella held out her hands to him. "Help me up."

William stood. "You need to rest. I'll go and see about the grumbling."

"No, William. I need to go out there with you. The people are grumbling against me." She wanted to tell him that she heard his brother trying to get some of the people to go work on his farm, but the last time she said something about Robert, William had become cross with her.

When William didn't reach for her hands but stood there looking as if he was ready to put his foot down and command her to lie back down, Louella said, "Do you want the group to split up?"

William's forehead crinkled. "No, of course not."

"Well, someone out there"—she jutted her thumb backward—"is encouraging people to leave and go back where we came from."

"That doesn't make sense. What could I have done to make them want to go back to bondage?"

Still holding her hands out, she told him, "You've done no wrong, William. The people say I'm a jinx. I heard it with my own ears." She pointed at the walls again. "I've laid around too long. It's clear to me that it's time for us to move on."

"But you're not healed yet." His eyes held concern. "We can take grumbling bellies a few more days."

Her heart warmed all over, knowing the things William would endure for her. But she had never doubted his love. It was the Judas in the camp talking bad about her that got her blood to boiling. She reached out her hands again to William. "Help me up. We should talk to them together."

He took her hands and lifted her from the ground. A pull at the bottom of her stomach sent her mind on a journey of misery. Her hand touched the emptiness of what once possessed her baby girl, Lily. That was who she would always be to Louella. Her precious little Lily in the valley.

"Are you okay?"

Putting a hand on William's shoulder, she gave him a lopsided grin. "Right as rain." But the truth was, Louella doubted she'd ever be okay again. "Let me lean on your big, strong arm."

He smiled at that, then settled her close to him while putting a hand under her arm. They then walked out of the barn. Three days of lying on that straw, digesting the fact that she had lost her baby and finding the will to face each new day, was enough.

"He's a wood carver."

Louella's eyebrow jutted up. "Huh? Who's a wood carver?"

"The new guy. His wife does housekeeping."

A grin spread across Louella's face. How they could use a wood carver was beyond her, but the fact that William provided the information meant everything.

"Gather 'round, everyone," William said as they all came together around the wood-burning firepit.

The nights were colder now that winter had swept in. Blankets were being used at night and thrown back into the wagon during the warmth of daylight. Louella didn't know how many more seasons they would journey through or what else might be lost on their journey, but she wasn't ready to give up yet.

William squeezed her hand as he said, "These last few months have been more than a notion. But we ask for your patience as we allow God to lead us to the place He has prepared."

"How much longer?" one of the men yelled from the back. "My family can't take much more. At least we had a roof over our heads on the Montgomery Plantation."

"A roof that leaked." Louella wagged her finger as she said, "When y'all start reminiscing about the good old days of servitude, remember that I served with y'all, so I know it wasn't sweet."

"But we aren't making any money. How we gon' replace the food those bandits stole?"

Louella looked over at William. He shrugged as if he was fresh out of ideas. She then saw Robert. He was chewing on a piece of straw as he made his way toward them. She wasn't going to allow that man to act like the savior-come-down-from-the-cross, so she said, "We can sell my liniment. There has to be some cities nearby where we can peddle a few tins."

Eyes full of desperation looked back at her. She wouldn't let them down. "I need a few ladies to help me get the mixture together, then we'll be back in business in no time."

Abigail raised her hand and stepped forward. "I'll help."

Clara did the same, along with Mama Sue and Mirabel.

William clasped his hands together. "We'll let them work on the liniment, and . . ."

Larry lifted a basket full of fish. "I could use a few hands to clean the fish we caught today."

William said, "Okay, now we need a group on fish-cleaning duty, and I need another group to start loading up these wagons. We're heading out in the morning."

Shouts of "Hurray!" and "Hallelujah!" went up to the heavens.

Femi stepped forward. Standing next to Abigail, he took off his hat, cleared his throat, and puffed out his big broad chest. "Reverend William, Abigail and I love each other dearly, and we'd be right proud if you'd marry us."

Louella lifted her hands in praise. "Finally, some good news around here."

Robert took the straw stick out of his mouth. Threw it to the ground and then stalked off.

William said, "I'd be happy to marry the two of you."

"Thank you kindly, sir." Femi then pulled Abigail into his arms and gave her a kiss that showed he was ready to claim his husbandly benefits.

William grinned at the display of affection. "Hold on, young man. We need to take care of our chores before we can get to the ceremony, so save all of that for later."

The group laughed. Then everyone went about doing the work

that had been assigned. Abigail came into the barn with Louella, Mama Sue, Mirabel, and Clara. As they worked on the mixture for the rheumatoid liniment, Louella noticed that Abigail's hands were shaking.

"You ain't said nary a word since Femi told us y'all was getting wed." Louella kept an eye on the girl.

Abigail twisted her lips as she looked away from them. "Just nervous is all. After my first owner forced himself on me so many times, I don't know if I can join with another man without cringing inside."

Mirabel turned Abigail to face her. "Now you listen here. What your former owner did to you wasn't no kind of love. That's why you felt shame 'bout being with him. But the shame belongs to the man who done stole what wasn't his."

Mama Sue said, "If you truly love Tommy—"

"Femi. He wants to be called Femi," Louella corrected.

Mama Sue waved that off. "Whatever." She continued, "If you truly love what's-his-new-name, then you'll love being in his arms."

Tears were in Abigail's eyes. She wiped them away. "I do love Femi. I tried my hardest not to love him. Honestly, I never thought I could love a man because of all the hate I felt for my first owner, but Femi won my heart."

Louella knew firsthand how hate could fester and spread like wildfire. William promised to show her how to love, but that was too great a weight to put on his shoulders. No man could give what she must get from God.

Louella put a hand over Abigail's, her eyes filled with compassion. "If you love him, then let that guide you. But don't expect him to heal all your wounds. Give those to God."

Abigail wrapped her arms around Louella and hugged her tight. "Thank you for everything."

"Don't thank me. Live your life, and don't look back." Louella exhaled as she tried to take her own advice.

"I'm sorry about the baby," Abigail said.

"Me too." Louella closed her eyes, blocking out the pain that wanted to swallow her whole. She would be leaving a part of her heart in Montgomery, Alabama. A tear rolled down her face, but when she reopened her eyes, her mind was set on looking forward. "Let's go get you married."

After the wedding, William lay on the straw bed next to Louella and held her tight while she cried. His strong arms had always brought her comfort. These last few days had been filled with pain. His love and concern melted away some of the pain. The sadness would be with her, but on their last night in Montgomery, the smallest light broke through the darkness of her heart.

CHAPTER 13

Louella stood on a soapbox outside the general store in Macon, Georgia, with the heat causing sweat to trickle down her face on a powerful-hot August day, shouting, "Come get your liniment! Rheumatism will be a thing of the past after rubbing this"—she raised a tin of liniment in the air, waved it around—"on your hands."

Most of the passersby ignored her. Not even a wave of a hand as they marched up the dusty road. Louella didn't take it personally. There was a hollow, gutted-out feel in each town they passed through in Georgia. Maybe the whole South was like this, but she'd seen more abandoned plantations and dying-on-the-vine crops in Georgia than she remembered in the other states. But she might have been so happy to see the back side of Mississippi, and so focused on her pregnancy while in Alabama, that she didn't take in the devastation.

But the price of war was clearly seen in Georgia. Louella was getting ready to get down from her soapbox when an older, dark-skinned woman passing by said, "My hands ache all the time. What's that you got there?"

"Let me give you a sample." Louella got down from her soapbox, opened the tin, put some of the liniment on her index finger, and then rubbed it on the woman's knuckles. "My grandmother did the washing on the plantation we come from. Her knuckles got terribly sore. I'd make this liniment for her, and it would be healing to her hands."

The woman flexed her fingers after Louella finished rubbing

on the liniment. Her eyes brightened. "That stuff is wonderful." But then slumping shoulders told the story Louella'd been hearing since they arrived in Georgia. "Ain't got no money. What work there is around these parts, the old slave owners don't have funds to pay for it."

Louella gave the woman the tin of liniment. "I hope this helps you."

The old woman shook her head. "I don't have money, and I won't be the cause of your family going hungry."

"This is my gift to you. God will provide for my family." As the woman walked away with the tin in hand, Louella was about to get back on the soapbox when Sooni came up to her. "My turn."

A group of the women took turns selling the liniment. Louella handed Sooni the money bag and pointed toward the general store. "Don't forget to settle up with Mr. Watson before we leave."

"Sure thing," Sooni told her.

Sooni was five months pregnant. The slope of her belly had begun to show. Louella averted her eyes. A swell of jealousy filled her heart. Exhaling, she turned and walked to the wagon and sat down.

As they'd continued their journey from Alabama into Georgia, Louella's care for the people on the journey with them began to grow more and more in her heart. It was as if the Lord Himself was mending her heart with the kindness of others. Louella appreciated each person who refused their turn to ride in the wagon as she healed from the pregnancy and delivery. Her body was healed now, but she was still grateful for the kindness.

Femi rushed over to her with a cup of water. "Abigail told me to get this over to you."

"Thank you, Femi. I appreciate that."

She sipped the water. Louella's heart had expanded for her travel companions to the point that she was no longer challenging her husband about the skills each person needed to have in order to join with their group. As they traveled through Georgia, they gladly welcomed about thirty-five hungry and tired souls who'd been left with nothing and nowhere to turn after President Andrew Johnson took back the promise of forty acres General Sherman's Special Field Order granted them. They had plowed and grown crops despite the lack of rain until Johnson up and decided to give the land back to the former owners who'd abandoned their properties during the war.

"Hey, you can't loiter out here. If you don't have any place to be, we can find a place for you."

Louella's head swiveled to the right as the sheriff approached her wagon. He had on a wide-brimmed hat, a tan shirt, and brown pants. His sheriff's badge was pinned on his shirt close to his heart.

"I'm not loitering, sir. Just taking a break."

"We don't allow your kind to take breaks in these parts." He snarled at her. "Get down from that wagon."

"But why? What have I done?" Confusion etched across her face. Her heart rate sped up as she imagined a thousand different evils that could happen to her if she complied with the sheriff.

"Get down." The sheriff darted an angry finger at the ground.

Eyes wild with fear, Louella looked this way and that. William and Robert stepped out of the general store toting a bag of rice. Louella waved to them and bit back bile as she said, "Massa Montgomery, this kind sheriff thinks I'm loitering."

Robert glanced over at her, then at the sheriff. He and William put the bag of rice in the wagon, then Robert walked over to the sheriff. He tipped his tattered hat to the man. "Is there a problem?"

The sheriff pointed toward Louella. "We don't allow coloreds to loiter around here, not when there's work they could be doing."

"Believe me, my people work, day and night. Louella had been feeling poorly, so I allowed her to take a rest. But we'll be on our way and not trouble you further."

The sheriff lifted a brow. "Y'all not from 'round these parts, are ya?"

"We left Mississippi some months back. Them Yankees tore my farm all to pieces. I've got family in South Carolina. We're headed there to see if I can make a new start."

Sooni, Marshal, Abigail, and Femi walked over to the wagon. Louella turned to them and said, "We'll be taking off directly. Right now, Mr. Montgomery is speaking to this kind sheriff." Louella couldn't fix her mouth to call Robert "Massa" again.

Abigail eyed Louella, questions dancing in her eyes. Louella squinted, lips tight, as she stared back at Abigail.

The sheriff glanced around the wagon. He turned back to Robert. "Mississippi must have loyal darkies. The ones 'round here scattered. Can't hardly find enough of 'em to get a day's work done these days."

"I'm right thankful that my people aren't like the lot you're dealing with around here." Robert and the sheriff shook hands, and then Sooni and the rest of them got in the back of the wagon. Robert took hold of the reins and Louella exhaled as they drove away.

Later that night as they sat around the fire eating rice and pieces of the chickens they found at the abandoned plantation they'd rested at for the past two days, Robert told everyone how he saved Louella from winding up in the pokey.

Then one of the men who'd recently joined them told Louella, "You're lucky that Mr. Robert was there. The authorities in these parts been locking us up for little to no reason and then making us do involuntary labor on these plantations that don't have workers."

"*Involuntary labor* sounds like another word for slavery," William said.

Louella got up and walked away from the group. Emotions all over the place, she needed a minute. Inhaling the humid air, putting one foot in front of the other, she had to get away from the group—breathing and walking was all she could manage. Once she was far enough away, she stopped, put her hands on her hips, and looked to heaven.

"Want some company?"

Louella swung around. "I didn't hear you walk up."

"You looked deep in thought," William told her.

She turned away from him, then swung back around with hands beating at the air. "When will things change? When will these white folks look at us and see human beings? When will they stop looking at us as property, to do with as they please?"

"I have the same questions. The world's not fair, but we should at least be able to hold our heads up with some dignity."

Louella rubbed her temples and took a few steps, creating a bit of distance between them. "I had to call Robert 'Massa.'" She scrunched her nose to hold back tears that threatened to fall. As she wrapped her arms around herself, a trickle broke free and ran down her face. "Humiliating."

William crossed the distance between them. He pulled her into his arms. "You did what needed doing to survive. No shame in that."

Louella found shame in everything they experienced earlier in the day. "I can't take much more. I'm tired."

"Hold on a little while longer. We haven't come this far to turn back now."

Her head popped up and her eyes shot daggers at him as she pounded on his chest. "I'll never turn back. Get me out of the South."

CHAPTER 14

All minds were fixed on getting out of Georgia. It took two months before they were anywhere near South Carolina. Louella was starting to breathe a sigh of relief, but then she heard Robert yell from two wagons behind them, "No! No! No!"

"What in tarnation is he yelling about?" Louella asked William.

William pulled on the reins to stop his oxen. "Don't know, but I'm gon' find out." When the wagon stopped, he climbed down. The other wagons and walkers stopped as well.

Robert was hyperventilating when William reached his wagon. His horse, Elmira, lay on the ground moaning in pain. "What happened to her?" William asked.

"It's her leg," Robert said. "It's broken. She stumbled over a rock and then went down."

"No, not Elmira." William got on his knees next to the horse and rubbed her mane, soothing her. "I'm sorry, Robert. I know how much she means to you."

"The journey was too much for her." Tears drifted down Robert's eyes as he kicked at some of the rocks on the road. "I shouldn't have come . . . shouldn't have come."

Walking toward them, Louella could hear terrible moans from Elmira. The tears on Robert's face shocked her, gave her compassion she hadn't felt for him in a long time.

Louella put a hand on Robert's shoulder. "Is there anything we can do for her?"

Robert shook his head, wiped tears from his face. He then went to his wagon and pulled out his rifle. "I've got to put her out of her misery."

Louella's heart broke for Robert as she saw the pain in his eyes. His chest heaved up and down. Robert aimed the gun at the horse. Louella glanced at Elmira. The horse's moans had turned to whimpers as William kept rubbing her mane.

Robert lowered the rifle and wiped his eyes again. Louella lifted her hand. "Give me the gun, Robert. You go hold Elmira."

He looked at her a moment, then lowered his shoulders. "Thank you." Robert handed Louella the rifle and went to Elmira.

People were standing around, whispering to each other. A few men took their hats off, holding them to their chests. Some looked away, eyes downcast.

Sucking in air, Louella allowed Robert a moment to put Elmira's head in his hands. He kissed the horse. Louella raised the rifle. Elmira whimpered. Louella's heart clenched. She blew out the air that had gathered in her lungs, then positioned herself about six inches away from the horse. "I'm sorry," she told Robert, "but you and William have to move away from her head."

Robert looked up with questioning eyes.

"I need a shot to the skull so she won't suffer long."

Robert gulped. He and William moved to the body of the horse and held her tight.

Bang!

Louella put the gun down on the ground after firing the shot. Elmira convulsed a few seconds, then all movement ceased. Louella went back to the wagon as William put an arm around Robert to comfort him.

Robert wailed out his sorrow at losing his best friend, and Louella leaned against the wagon and cried like she, too, had lost something precious, something irreplaceable. And at that moment she realized that moving forward would never stop the pain that came to those who have loved and lost.

They made camp at the spot where Elmira died. The men dug a hole and buried the beloved animal. Somber faces sat around the campfire that night. Grumblings grew as some questioned whether they'd made the right decision to travel so far away from Mississippi.

Louella stood to say something to the weary travelers, but her mouth was dry, her tongue weighted down like it was filled with lead. She sat back down and silently prayed. *God, please help us. The journey is too much.*

As they were eating potato soup, a man rode up in his buggy. "Whoa." He pulled on the reins, bringing his horse to a complete stop. "I wondered why God directed me this way tonight. You folks look like you could use some Christian comfort."

William went over to the man. They clasped hands. "You're right about that, Mr. . . ."

"I'm Reverend Ezel."

William's eyes lit up. "I'm Reverend William. It is good to meet you."

Reverend Ezel sat down and partook in the soup with them. Louella asked, "You live around here?"

"I live where God sends me. But He mostly has me traveling and preaching to folks in South Carolina. I rarely cross the Georgia line, but like I said, I felt led to come this way."

William told him, "We come from Mississippi, picked up some of our travelers in Alabama and Georgia, but a few of us were originally from South Carolina."

Reverend Ezel stood. "Thank you for the delicious soup. I best be heading out. But before I leave, I'd like to pray for you all if that'd be all right."

Louella lifted her head to the sky and exhaled. When prayers went up, God was listening. She was thankful that Reverend Ezel stopped by to remind her of that. Standing with the rest of their group, she clasped hands with William and Reverend Ezel as he went before God on their behalf.

A refreshing wind blew in the camp that night as a heavy burden lifted from road-weary travelers. After Reverend Ezel's prayer, they had a mind to go on and see what the end would be like.

Louella and William walked Reverend Ezel to his wagon. As he was lifting himself back into his seat, Louella asked, "Did you live in South Carolina before becoming a traveling preacher?"

He nodded. "I was once enslaved there."

"My mother was sold to a plantation in South Carolina. I'm wondering if you ever ran into a woman by the name of Brenda Bobo."

He scratched his head, then lifted the reins. "Can't say that I have. But if our paths should cross, I'll let her know that her daughter grew up to be a beautiful woman inside and out."

"Thank you, Reverend."

Reverend Ezel then clicked his tongue at his horse, and the animal trotted off.

❧

The next morning, they got back on the road, again moving forward, leaving behind what they had lost but holding those things in their hearts forever.

"I was praying last night after Reverend Ezel left," William told Louella, "and I truly believe our journey is coming to an end. God is moving us in the direction we need to go."

Louella was thankful to hear that. It had been a little over eleven months since they left Mississippi, and they still had no place to call home. She put her hand over her belly. "That's good, 'cause I'm carrying life again."

William's hand slipped from one of the reins. He picked it back up. Turned to Louella. "You sure?"

"It's for sure and true, William. I wanted to tell you a few weeks ago, but I kept it to myself so you wouldn't refuse to let me help sell the liniment."

William laughed at that. "Louella Bobo Montgomery, I don't know what to do with you."

As they entered into South Carolina, Louella said, "Love me; that's enough."

"You've had my love since the first day I decided to tutor you."

"You mean to tell me that while you were giving me reading and writing lessons, I was unwittingly giving you love lessons?" Louella beamed as she set her eyes on William like he was the sun to her moon.

"I guess you were." William slapped the reins down on the oxen so they would pull up the hill faster. "I hope I've given you a few love lessons."

The fluttering in her heart wouldn't let her deny the truth of the matter. "That you have, darling. You've been the one to teach me most of the good lessons I've learned."

He laughed at her. "You can't even say it, can you?"

"I can say it."

"Then let me hear it. Three simple words: I. Love. You."

She grinned, put her arm around his, and leaned her head on his shoulder. "Are you excited about seeing the people you grew up with again?" They were headed to the low country in South Carolina. The town William and Robert had once lived in before Montgomery decided to set up his plantation in Mississippi.

"I am, Louella. I am," William replied.

❧

After about three more weeks of travel through South Carolina, they were close to the place Robert and William grew up. Robert took the lead, claiming he knew the way better than William. He now had a mule rather than his beloved Elmira pulling his wagon.

Louella wondered why they had gone off the trail, but she decided to sit back and see where Robert was taking them.

She received the answer a few hours later when they made it to Cross Anchor, South Carolina, and Robert's wagon came to a stop in front of a one-room log cabin. The rest of them pulled in behind him, making quite a spectacle with over a hundred of them lining the streets in these former quarters of enslaved people.

A young woman opened the door and came out to the yard. She wore a long tan skirt with a gray wool shirt. Her eyes were brown and searching. "Y'all not from 'round these parts."

William climbed down from the wagon and walked over to her. "We used to be." He pointed toward the shack that was right next to the one she'd walked out of. "Used to live right there eighteen years ago."

The girl glanced over her shoulder at the house William pointed to. "I was told my uncle used to live there."

The grin on William's face shone bright. He nodded. "I did."

The girl blinked, then blinked again. She looked a bit confused, then Robert came down from his wagon, opened his arms wide. "Elmira, girl, come give your daddy a hug."

Elmira swung around. Robert kept walking toward her. He then wrapped his arms around the girl and swung her in the air. "If you ain't a sight for sore eyes."

"Daddy?" She said the word like a question as they broke the embrace. She stepped back and squinted. "Granny said you looked like a white man."

Robert laughed. Took the hat from his head. "Maybe if I go hatless, I'll get a little more sun."

"Are you serious? Am I finally laying eyes on my daddy again?"

"I'm here. Wish I hadn't left you all those years ago, but things being what they were, I had no choice."

William put his arm around Elmira's shoulder and walked her over to where Louella still sat in the wagon. "Let me introduce you to your aunt." He pointed toward her. "This here is Louella, my bride."

Louella blushed and waved a hand in the air. "We've been married a year and a half. Can't exactly call me a bride no more."

"You'll always be my bride. What foolishness you talking?" William helped Louella down from the wagon and then made introductions. "This is my niece, Elmira."

Louella eyed William like he had some explaining to do. This was the first time she was hearing anything about Robert having a child . . . a grown child for that matter. Louella hugged the young woman and then asked, "How old are you?"

"Nineteen."

Louella glanced over at Robert as he made his way over to them. She didn't understand how Robert could have a nineteen-year-old daughter that no one knew anything about. She then glanced at the house and wondered how many more of Robert's kids might come running outside. Then Louella wondered how many of those tears Robert shed had to do with the loss of his horse and how many were for his daughter.

William whispered in her ear, "Remember, we lived in this town before moving to Mississippi."

"Uh-huh." She remembered about them moving from South Carolina to Mississippi. She would never forget. The week after Montgomery took over the plantation, he sold her mother and broke her heart.

Robert pointed toward the house that Elmira had come out of. "Is your grandma in there? She might not want to see me, but I want you to come with us, so I need to talk this out with her."

Sadness shadowed Elmira's eyes. "She passed on last year. Nobody but me left now."

Louella noticed that Robert didn't ask about the girl's mother. Had the mother been sold off as her mother had been, or had she died?

THE AMERICAN QUEEN 119

"You're not on your own no more." William hugged her.

Elmira told them that the owner of the plantation was in Georgia for a spell, so the group, which was now over a hundred, made camp on the former plantation for the night. As they sat around the fire waiting for Mama Sue, Louella, Abigail, and Clara to finish cooking the meal, Wiley Bennett and his wife, Rachel, sat with them.

Wiley had lived on a neighboring plantation when William and Robert lived in South Carolina. "Sho' didn't 'spect to see yo' faces around here again."

William nodded. "Things certainly have changed. It was time for us to strike out on our own."

Louella's eyes lit with a thought. She nudged her grandmother. "You think Mama might be in this town? This where Montgomery came from."

Mama Sue had been stirring the pot. She put the spoon down and exhaled. "To tell you the truth, I been wondering the same thing since we got here, but I didn't want to say nothing in case I was wrong."

Louella turned to the Bennetts and asked, "Do either of you know if a woman by the name of Brenda Bobo lives around here?"

Blank expressions turned to Louella. Rachel's forehead crinkled, then she said, "Never heard of nobody with the last name Bobo."

Lips pursed, Louella glanced over at Mama Sue. Her grandmother patted her shoulder, then went back to cooking and humming, back to pretending that her heart didn't bleed for the child she lost.

"Supper's ready," Louella called to the group. "Come get your bellies full." She then put the ladle in the pot and put some corn in a bowl along with a piece of rabbit and handed it to William. A short time ago they had come upon another abandoned farm. This one had stalks of corn. They'd loaded the wagon with the corn and had been eating it for the past three days.

"Corn again," one of them said as they lined up with bowls in hand.

"It's that or the swallow of your spit," Mama Sue told him.

Food had been scarce. Even with the money they earned from selling liniment, they didn't have enough to feed everyone, except for when they were able to catch enough fish or find food from abandoned farms or plantations. This was the last of the corn, so they wouldn't have to complain about this meal any longer. Louella prayed they'd be able to feed the people in the days to come.

Wiley and his wife, Rachel, ate the corn without complaint. As Wiley finished with his bowl, he looked to William. "Where are y'all headed after you leave these parts?"

"Wish I knew. Been praying for direction. The Lord has a place for us. But we haven't found it yet."

"And y'all traveled all the way from Mississippi?" Rachel asked.

Louella nodded. "Been traveling for a year now."

Robert plopped down next to William. "Something's got to give, or I might stay here with Elmira."

"The group of us that's still here go hungry most days. There's no work." Rachel shook her head. "You don't want to stay here."

"We're all tired and road weary, but we have to hold our patience a little while longer," William said.

Wiley rubbed his chin with his thumb and index finger, then he said, "Before the war, I 'member my white folks would travel from here to the mountains for vacation. There's land as far as the eye can see out there."

Rachel snapped her fingers. "Bessy Thompkins used to travel them mountains with her white folks years ago." Rachel stood. "Let me go get her."

Rachel walked down the street to one of the small houses on the block. Louella looked around. To her, South Carolina meant South. They were headed north, so she wasn't interested in anything this Bessy person had to say.

Bessy Thompkins and Percy Williams both came to their camp area. They made introductions, then Bessy told them about her travels. "Before the war, I was my missus' lady's maid. Whenever Mr. Thompkins would get it in his mind to take her to the mountains for a vacation, I would travel with 'em.

"What I saw up there is a heap better than what we're dealing with in the low country. Wagon trains were always on the go. Meat, molasses, and all sorts of produce were brought to them mountains. I'm telling you, they didn't lack for nothing."

"What about the land? Is there enough space for us?" Femi asked while wrapping an arm around Abigail.

Percy chimed in, "I know where there's land, if you can talk the owner into letting you have the former slave quarters on her land."

"We left Mississippi to get away from these kinds of shacks. Why would we want to trade that for the ones in South Carolina?" Gary rolled his eyes heavenward.

William lifted a hand. "Let's hear him out before we make any snap judgments."

Louella put a hand on William's back and tapped it a few times, slowing him down. They needed to think about this before making rash decisions.

Percy continued, "The enslaved people on that plantation left directly after the war. I hear tell that the old lady who runs the place been in dire straits and needs help. She's always been friendly to our kind . . . I'm thinking y'all might be able to work out something with her for a piece of that land."

"Exactly where is this place?" Robert asked.

"Over by the Enoree River, off that road House Representative Joel Roberts Poinsett had built right before he died of tuberculosis," Percy said.

"Who?" William's forehead wrinkled.

"I know you 'member the Buncombe Turnpike," Percy said. "It's over that way too."

Bessy said, "Stagecoaches travel them parts all the time. It crosses Old Indian Road. Over by Callahan Mountain and the Winding Stairs."

"Winding Stairs?" Louella was confused.

"Yeah," Bessy said. "Those stairs take you to the North Carolina state line, into Hendersonville. Then you run right into the Oakland Plantation. You won't miss it. Look for the big white house that's surrounded by oak trees."

Something foul dropped in the pit of Louella's stomach at the mention of oak trees.

"The whole place has gone to pot. Mrs. Serepta would probably be right pleased if'n y'all wanted to help with that place," Percy told them.

PART 3

A New Beginning— Building the Kingdom

1866–1869

CHAPTER 15

That night, as Louella prepared to sleep under the oak trees in the empty fields, trepidation iced over her heart. How could the Oakland Plantation be the place God was directing them to since she hated the sight of oak trees—hated lying under so many while they traveled? How could she make a home in a place that would continue to remind her of one of the most painful days of her life?

William went off to pray. He was gone until daybreak. When he returned, his eyes seemed bright and hopeful. Louella didn't know if she was prepared for what his prayer time had yielded, so she asked, "What's with Robert having a nineteen-year-old daughter that ain't nobody ever heard of before?"

"That's Robert's business to tell."

Louella put hands on her hips as she sat up. "You got any kids running 'round here? Am I about to be surprised by someone walking up to me saying that you they daddy?"

"Louella!"

"Don't *Louella* me, when you've held on to a secret like this for years."

Sighing deeply, William sat down next to his wife and rubbed her belly. "The only children I'll ever have will come from you."

She felt silly badgering her husband. William wasn't like Robert. She trusted him to be true.

He grinned at her a moment, then said, "We're almost home, Louella. We didn't just stop here so Robert could visit with his daughter. God directed us here."

Louella pulled her blanket against her chest. "What are you saying?"

"God has given us the Oakland Plantation. I don't know how, but I know it's meant to be ours."

Louella's eyes were explosive with disagreement. "But you said we were going north. We're still in the South."

Putting his hand in hers, William planted a kiss on her forehead. "Can you trust me on this? The people are weary. We've already lost Lily. I can't take the risk of losing anyone else. And with the baby coming . . ."

When she didn't respond, William added, "I heard you ask Rachel about your mother. She might not be in this town, but what if she's somewhere in South Carolina?"

She didn't want to be in a place with tons of oak trees, but she didn't want to give up on the chance of finding her mother either. And William was right about the weary state of the people. The journey had been long. They needed a place to call home.

With a deep, heavy sigh, she said, "Let's go and see if we can find a resting place for our people."

When they packed up to leave that morning, Percy, Bessy, Wiley, Rachel, Elmira, and several others from the low country gathered their few belongs and headed for the mountains with them. By the time they descended on the Oakland Plantation, the group of fifty that left Mississippi had ballooned into almost two hundred. Louella prayed they were headed to a land where they could once and for all find happiness.

❧

They traveled up the North Carolina mountains by way of the Winding Stairs and the cool winter breeze. It was now December, and the cold in the mountains bit harder than any cold Louella had experienced in Mississippi. They each donned scarfs and heavier clothes as they found their way to the Oakland Plantation. For miles and miles, wherever her eyes looked, Louella saw dry grass and leafless trees. More oak trees than she'd ever seen on one plantation.

Doubt set in again. But as they came upon dozens of empty cabins, Bessy said, "This where the enslaved people lived before freedom came."

"The cabins don't look like much," Robert said as they all walked the land, headed for the big house.

"Like the cabins we left behind," Femi said. "All in need of repair that we never had the time to do."

Louella saw a smile creep across William's face. He told the group, "God has given us an opportunity here. Did you notice the crumbling breastwork as we entered the city?"

Percy said, "The Yankees tore it down during the war."

"With all the disrepair I've seen since we entered this area, seems to me we've journeyed to the right place." William looked around at the group. "We have skills that can be put to good use in this area."

Louella was quiet, but she saw the logic in what William said. She also saw all the trees that surrounded them. Their group had the skills needed to repair these cabins. But they were supposed to be going north. To stop here almost seemed like giving up.

William turned to Robert. "We'll need your help on this one. I doubt it'll go over well if all of us descend on Mrs. Serepta's house at once. Maybe you should go ahead of us and tell her what we're about."

Gary slapped his knee as he laughed. "Robert is probably the only one of us that won't get shot walking up to the front door."

Other members of the group laughed and giggled about the comment, but Louella didn't find it so funny.

They camped out about a mile away from the quarters where enslaved people once lived, and they waited as Robert, William, and Louella took one of the wagons and rode to the Oakland Manor. While sitting in the wagon, Louella took in the expanse of the place.

It was a huge house with five arched pillars running the length of the front porch. Oak trees surrounded the sides and back of the house like a barrier. But that barrier hadn't stopped the treacherous mountain weather from putting a beating on the worn house, which had missing shutters and paint chipped away from what surely had once been a glorious white coating trimmed with black shutters.

"I hate these trees, William. Hate 'em with a passion."

He put his hand over Louella's. "Think on good things. Trees are used for more than lynchings and beatings."

Robert went to the manor and knocked on the door while William and Louella waited in the wagon. It took a few minutes, but a white man who looked to be in his forties or fifties opened the door. He stepped out on the porch and put his hands in the pockets of his overalls. He rocked back and forth on the heels of his shoes as he talked to Robert. Louella saw Robert point to the wagon. The man leaned forward and glanced over at them.

Robert shook the man's hand, then walked back to the wagon. "He's gonna see if his mother wants to talk with us."

William bit his lower lip, then said, "He didn't say no right off after you pointed toward the wagon. That's a good sign."

"The wood on the porch has rotted through in spots. And the shingles are falling off by the front door. I think they need our help," Robert told them.

"You really think this where God want us?" Louella asked William. "You really want to be all the way up in the mountains like this? It's cold."

"Let's see what the mistress of the manor has to say. You already know what I think," William told her.

Yes, she knew her husband believed that God had directed them to this location, but could God really be so cruel as to surround them with so many oak trees when He knew firsthand what white men used these trees for?

The front door opened, and a gray-haired woman stepped onto the porch. She waved to them. "Y'all get on in here."

The woman was smiling at them. Louella had to think hard to come up with a time a white woman had smiled as if she was pleased to be in her presence.

William got out of the wagon and then helped her down. As they walked closer to the house, the woman said, "My boy, Tommy, says you've been on your journey for over a year now."

"We have. It's been a long journey, but we believe that God has a place for us," William told her and then stuck out his hand. "I'm Reverend William Montgomery."

"Nice to meet you. I'm Serepta Davis."

And just like that they were invited inside the woman's house. No ifs, ands, or buts about it.

Serepta opened her front door and treated them like welcomed guests as they sat down in her living room. Louella squirmed in her seat. She couldn't get comfortable. The couch smelled old, not dirty. But the musty scent of age and family clung to the cushions.

Serepta came back into the living room carrying a teapot and a plate that had slices of bread and butter. "We don't have much to offer. My home used to be a showpiece for entertaining."

"You have a lovely home," Robert said.

Serepta glanced around the room. "That's kind of you to say, but the wear and tear is showing."

"That's the matter we bring before you today." William leaned forward. "As we traveled all the way from Mississippi, we gathered about two hundred other freed men and women. We're all looking for a place to call home, and we all have skills that are useful for restoring your home to its former glory."

"You don't say." A grin spread across Serepta's face as she looked heavenward. "God is always surprising me with His goodness."

William, Louella, and the rest of their group sat together around a campfire eating meat that had been caught earlier in the day. William wiped his hands on his pants and stood. "We talked to the owner of the Oakland Plantation, and she is truly a lovely woman."

Hundreds of weary eyes were on William as he spoke. "Mrs. Serepta has suffered greatly since the War Between the States began and hasn't recovered now that it's over. Her manor needs restoring."

Gary looked skeptical. "What's she offering?"

Louella understood Gary's skepticism. He had signed a contract to be a sharecropper but got chased off the land after all his hard work. Louella was skeptical herself. Should they put their trust in the kindness of white folks when their kindness was always fleeting?

"Good question." William nodded in Gary's direction. "Mrs. Serepta will let us use the empty cabins as long as we agree to work the land and do repairs around her home."

There was a look of apprehension on Abigail's face as she asked, "We don't have to sign some kind of contract and then be forced to stay here like we enslaved again, do we?"

William shook his head. "Absolutely not."

Then another stood. "I didn't come out of slavery to end up in quarters like this. I know we all need a rest from the road, but is this the best we can do?"

William looked dumbfounded by the responses of the people. Louella stood and took his hand. "I get what y'all saying. I don't want to live in these quarters neither, but maybe we should give this a chance. We can always leave and continue on to the North if it doesn't work out."

This wasn't Mississippi, and nobody was holding her prisoner, so she meant exactly what she said about leaving this place if things weren't as Serepta represented them to be.

CHAPTER 16

When they had set out on this journey, they all pitched in, all gave of what they had to ensure that each of them had the things needed to survive. Once they settled on the Oakland Plantation, Louella and William partnered with many of the businesses and homeowners nearby to secure jobs for their people.

Many of their group were hired out to work at Serepta's home or across the state line. A few miles away, some of the women worked at Ben Posey's grand house, which had once been the home of Joel Roberts Poinsett, who was a former secretary of war and had represented South Carolina in the House of Representatives.

Some of their people worked for a mere ten cents a day. Others sold Louella's rheumatoid liniment or the vegetables they grew to local markets.

No matter how the money was earned and no matter who earned it, all of the money was given to William. He and Louella then distributed the money as needed for food, clothing, and housing expenses. The money that was left over was being saved for repairs on the small shacks they'd been staying in for more than a year now.

In the time they'd been living in the former enslaved people's dwellings, Louella had given birth to a healthy baby boy. She and William named him Waties, because he would have no limitations to his independence. No one would ever take his freedom away.

He was eleven months old and still sleeping in the bed with them. She could barely turn around in this house, let alone find another space for Waties to lie. She wanted so much more for her child than what they currently had—wanted something more for herself as well. She'd read about the Freedmen's Bureau helping people find family members who had been lost to them. Maybe they could help find her mother.

While Waties slept, Louella sat at the table and wrote a letter to the Freedmen's Bureau.

Dear Sir,

I'm writing in hopes of receiving help. I was seven years old when my dear mother, Brenda Bobo, was sold away from me and my brother. I have ached for her ever since the overseer took her to the auction block. We once lived on the Montgomery Plantation in Mississippi. My family suffers every day from missing her. We don't know if she is still alive or what may have become of her.

We were told she had been sold to a plantation in South Carolina. If you have any information or can get this letter to my mother, I would be indebted to you forever.

Thank you,
Louella Bobo Montgomery

William came in when she finished writing her letter. "Good," she said. "You're here." She stood. "I need to get out of this house."

"I'll stay with Waties. Go take a walk or something," William suggested.

She'd been taking walks for a while now. Living in an eight-by-eight shack felt confining after traveling and camping in the great outdoors for so long. As she walked, her mind turned on the money they'd been saving. William wanted to use that money to fix the cabins, but Louella couldn't see throwing good money away like that.

Being in the mountains kept them away from the prying eyes of city folks. She was thankful for the peace of mind. But those cabins . . . She'd be willing to bet colored folks were living better than that up north. As she approached the top of the hill, Louella's lip twisted at the sight of all those oak trees. She could walk no farther. Those dreaded trees were in her way, covering the entire hillside like a forest.

In a huff, she turned to head back down the hill. Her eyes caught sight of the cabins she despised—cabins that were made of wood. She turned back to the trees as William's words floated around in her head: *"Trees are used for more than lynchings and beatings."*

A smile crept across her face and an overflow of joy bubbled within her. What they needed was land.

Land where they could build a place to call home. A society like William's mother had told him about. Her eyes scanned from one side to the other. Hundreds of trees would have to be knocked down before they could make use of the land.

It would be backbreaking work, but they'd be able to build homes with the wood from those trees. Her people had labored for others most of their lives. How much more for something they could call their own?

"What's that mind of yours fixing on today?"

Louella turned to her left and greeted Sarah Goodwin as she walked up the hill and stood next to her. Sarah was Serepta's oldest daughter. She and her husband, John Goodwin, lived over in Greenville, South Carolina, but she often visited her mother. "Pondering on a few things."

"Like what?"

A beat of time passed, then Louella stretched out her hand, pointing toward the overgrown area, past the run-down cabins she and the others occupied. Then she pointed at the trees. "All this land is just sitting here, profiting nothing for nobody."

Sarah raised an eyebrow. "How do you know we're not planning to do anything with it?"

"We've been here more than a year, and I haven't so much as

seen one tree come down in those woods." Louella looked Sarah in the eye. "There's money to be made with that lumber."

Sarah's head fell back as she gave a hearty laugh. "I've said the same thing, but none of my brothers are interested in cutting those trees down."

Sarah was straight to the point, like her elderly mother. Both women had been kind to Louella, but she still didn't know if she could trust what she saw. She kept wondering when they were going to change up on her.

She admonished herself to be bold, be courageous. Her people needed better living quarters. They needed a lot of things that their current situation didn't provide. "We could clear that land for you, then you could give us a share of the profits and let us buy the land."

❦

"You told them what?" William exploded as she discussed the matter of the land with him and Robert.

"If you think about it, this is the perfect solution." Louella held her breath, wanting to seem confident and knowledgeable so they would see things from her side. "We're nearly bursting at the seams in the small plot of land we're on right now."

"That might be true," Robert acknowledged, "but how in the world do you think we can clear that land with all those trees?"

"Where there's a will, there's a way," Louella told him.

William paced around their small cabin, a scowl of apprehension on his face. "I don't know. I honestly don't know."

Standing next to her husband, Louella put a hand on his arm. "Dear, when we left Mississippi, we promised the people that we were gon' build a land that belonged to us. What we got now belongs to Mrs. Serepta. And as nice as they are . . ."

Robert banged his cane against the floor. "Is there anybody on God's green earth that you trust?"

She swung around to face him with eyes blazing. "Has anybody on God's green earth ever given me reason to trust them?" Her chest heaved as anger clung to her like a close friend.

"Calm down, Louella. Let's be reasonable and discuss the matter," William told her.

Louella hated when anger took over and made her want to scream. But Robert was always getting in her way, opposing what she said simply because she said it. "Robert is the one who isn't seeing reason."

Turning back to her husband, she jutted a finger downward, indicating the cabin they stood in. "This ain't the place for us. Our promised land is out there."

William hoisted Waties into his arms and stepped outside. She glanced back at Robert. He was still sitting in their small cabin looking like he was sucking on lemons. She left the house and followed William as he walked up the hill she'd stood on earlier that day.

Bouncing Waties on his hip, he said, "Your mama is full of big ideas."

"Can't you see it?" Louella pointed toward the acres of trees that spanned as far as the eye could see. The branches waved at them as they approached. Leaves fell to the ground. The crackling of the twigs and leaves underfoot became a sweet melody to Louella.

"I see trees." William laughed. "Look, Waties, there's a squirrel." The squirrel scurried up one of the trees. "Your mama may have found some friends for you to play with."

Louella playfully punched William's shoulder. "Stop fooling around and open them eyes the good Lord gave you."

William looked from one side of the forest to the other. "I thought you hated trees."

"Didn't you tell me that trees could be used for more than lynchings and beatings?" She waved a hand. "Look at all this land, just waiting to be cleared out and claimed."

"And what would we do with so much land?"

Louella's eyes traveled for miles and miles down the way. This was what she had dreamed of for so long. Not the trees . . . never the trees. But a place to call her own. "We can build houses, a church, a store." Tickling her son's foot, she said, "*Ooh-ooh*, and a school for Waties and the other children. It would be something for our people."

William nodded as if he was beginning to see what she saw. "And will you finally be happy once I build this for you?"

Louella lifted her eyes heavenward as a smile eased across her face. She danced and twirled around on top of the hill, among the tall, tall trees, thick branches, and leaves. "The happiest, William. It would make me so happy."

Waties bounced on William's hip like he wanted to dance too.

"Then it's settled." William leaned forward and kissed Louella. "We'll call it the Happy Land."

Louella rolled the name around a few times in her head, and then she put an arm around William's waist and sang, "*There is a happy land . . .*"

As they began their trek back down the hill, Louella was still daydreaming about all the things she had imagined so many times in her head. "We can build us a fine home."

William lifted a hand, halting her dreams. "We still need to talk to Mrs. Serepta. Make sure we can get a fair price for the land."

"The good Lord will direct you what to say when you talk to her."

"And what of our people, Louella? What if they don't want to clear that land?"

"They want homes as bad as we do. They'll do it, seeing that it benefits all of us."

"I'll call a meeting. We'll talk to our people before we make an offer on the land," William told her.

CHAPTER 17

William, Robert, and Louella sat on one side of Serepta Davis's ten-seat dining room table. Sarah and her husband, John Goodwin, sat on the other side. Serepta entered the dining room carrying a tray of biscuits and butter.

"Mama," Sarah complained as she stood and took the tray out of Serepta's hands, "you know you shouldn't be doing this."

Serepta waved a hand in Sarah's direction. "I'm fine." She rubbed her hands. "My arthritis hasn't been acting up as much since Louella gave me that liniment of hers."

"There's more where that came from if you get to aching again," Louella said as Serepta sat down at the head of the table.

"Thank you, dear." Serepta turned to John and pointed toward the kitchen. "Since my daughter doesn't want me overexerting myself, can you get the coffee and bring some cups for our guests?"

"They're not guests." John scowled at them as if they didn't belong. Sarah put a hand on John's shoulder. He stood and shoved his chair back.

"Excuse my husband," Sarah told them. "He's used to the old ways."

Louella eyed him as he stalked off to the kitchen. She knew men like John Goodwin. Men who had no use for colored folks if they couldn't get free labor out of them. She wanted nothing to do with him. "Well, our business is with Mrs. Serepta anyway."

"Louella." William put a hand over hers.

She twisted her lips but kept quiet as John brought the coffee back to the table and slammed it down in front of Robert.

William smiled at Serepta as if John wasn't sizing them up for a noose. "We truly appreciate your hospitality, but we don't want to keep you longer than necessary."

"You're no bother at all," Serepta said.

Sarah agreed.

"Louella tells me that she and Sarah discussed the land on the other side of the cabins we now live in," William said.

Serepta laughed. She took one of the biscuits, put it on a plate and buttered it, then passed it down to Louella. "Try that."

Louella looked at the offering. She was stunned by the kindness of Serepta Davis and wondered whether she would've been as welcoming if Mrs. Serepta had showed up on her doorstep. "Thank you kindly." Louella bit into the biscuit. *"Mmm."*

Serepta turned back to William. "That so-called land is covered with trees. Can't do nothing with it."

Robert poured himself a cup of coffee. "It seems to me that a lot of your land has been sitting dormant and overgrown with trees and weeds."

"Daddy had planned to do more with the land, but he was always busy at the gristmill or at the store, and none of my brothers have any interest in clearing it," Sarah said.

Louella put the biscuit down. "What if we clear that land for you?"

"Your workers have already helped out so much around the house, and I'm grateful that I've been able to open my house to travelers again. But I don't have the money to pay for the clearing of that land."

William sat up straighter, cleared his throat. "That's where we come in. We have enough people to clear that land, and it won't cost you a dime. We want to be able to purchase the land we clear at a fair price."

"And what about all that lumber? I guess you want that too?" John narrowed his eyes on Robert as if he was the only one worth talking to.

Louella silently prayed that Robert wouldn't mess this up. He might not be happy with the fact that she was the one to come up with the idea, but he now realized that her plan made sense for their group.

Putting his coffee cup down, Robert put his elbows on the table and leaned in as he spoke to John. "We were thinking that you might want to handle the sale of the lumber. We'd need some of the lumber for our new homes, but after that, we're willing to take whatever you think is fair for our labor."

"But you don't get paid unless we sell the lumber, right?" John confirmed.

Robert nodded. "Yes, sir, that was our thinking on it."

Louella smiled. She glanced over at Robert. He wanted this as much as she did.

"And how much can you pay for the land once you clear it?" Serepta asked.

"We could do a dollar an acre, if that's all right with you," William told her.

"A dollar!" John popped out of his seat. "We could sell that land for three dollars an acre easy. Why would we give it to you people for less than we'd sell it to a white man?"

"Because you can't get any white men to clear that land," Louella told him. "We're willing to do that and put money in your pocket when you sell the lumber."

"She's got you there, John." Sarah grinned over at Louella.

Louella liked Sarah and wanted to grin back at her, but each time she was in her presence, Louella wondered if Sarah was one to extend her hand and then ball it into a fist the moment she didn't get her way.

John's lips tightened. "She's a mouthy one."

"Mouthy or not, she has a point." Serepta extended her hand. "You've got a deal. Let's get that land cleared."

The group gathered around the fire that had been set not far from where Louella and William lived. It was the end of a workday, and folks pulled up a chair or sat on the ground like they'd done while traveling from Mississippi to the mountains of North Carolina.

Mirabel, Mama Sue, and a few other ladies used the fire to fix a meal of yams, green beans, fish, and corn bread. When bellies were full and the plates empty, William stood.

"As always, it was so good to break bread with you all," he began, then clasped his hands together. "We had the meeting with Mrs. Serepta this morning, and she is willing to sell us some land that we can build houses on." He pointed toward the forest of trees. "But we've got to clear the land of those trees before we can buy or build on it."

Grumblings erupted as everyone turned toward those trees. "That will take forever," one man said.

"What we got to cut those trees down with?" another asked.

Then Gary stood. He rubbed his chin like he was trying to figure something out. "So we got to clear all of that land before they let you purchase it?"

William nodded. Then to Louella's surprise, Robert stood next to his brother and said, "It'll be a lot of work, but if we can pull this off, we'll have homes, which in my estimation is a whole heap better than what we've got now."

"That sounds good and all, but what if we clear that land and them white folks back out on the deal?" Gary shoved his hands in his pockets as he stood there waiting on an answer.

Louella understood Gary's concerns. She'd seen what had happened to him. She wished they could have brought a better deal to their people, but they weren't in a position to haggle any more than they already had.

William smiled as he looked up the hill toward those trees and glanced back at Gary. "Have you ever had faith in something that you couldn't rightly see?"

Gary shook his head. "Can't say as I have. Any faith I might've had been stripped from me."

Louella's heart bled for Gary. It also bled for herself and so many others who'd had the faith to believe in something good coming their way but had it beat out of 'em during slavery.

A couple of others in their group spoke up in agreement with Gary.

William lifted a hand. "Brothers and sisters, I do understand why there's so much misgiving about this, but where your faith is weak on this matter, mine is strong. Allow me to believe for something better for us."

By the time they put the fire out and headed back to their temporary homes, William had convinced the group to help him knock down those trees.

When Louella went to bed that night, her head should have been full of what was to come. She should've dreamed about trees tumbling down around them. Instead, her mother's face shone bright and clear. Louella reached out her hand as she had when her mother was carted off and sold like cattle.

Her mama's image faded into the distance. She couldn't see her clearly anymore, like her image was being smeared and wiped away. Louella's eyes popped open. She lay there in the darkness of the night, hand over her heart, protecting it from harm. She had a husband and a child now. Her grandmother and brother were with her, but she wanted her mama.

She ached for some of the faith that William had. The doubt within her and the not knowing if she'd ever see her mama again were tearing her apart.

CHAPTER 18

A year into the clearing and the men had chopped down a hundred trees. Once they had the trees down, Louella rounded up a dozen women to pull the leaves from the trees. They used the leaves and the grass in the overgrown areas for compost in the soil where they were growing vegetables to sell at the local markets. The vegetables they didn't sell were divided evenly among all the families.

"You shouldn't be here. This place is a mess." William gave Louella a hand as she stepped over a log that had been cut so it could be carried to John Goodwin's wagon.

Louella glanced around. Where William saw a mess, she saw progress. "It's beauty in motion."

He turned to Louella. "What are you seeing?"

Louella put a hand bellow her belly, which was now growing with their third child, and stepped forward. Bursting with joy and grinning like the sunshine beaming down from the sky was filling her soul, she waved an arm to the left. "We'll build the church over there so we can all gather on Sunday mornings and listen to you preach us happy."

He wagged a finger. "If we're naming the place the Happy Land, then the people must already be happy."

"We'll see about that." Louella then pointed to an area next to where the church would be. "A school should go right there." Her eyes glistened with excitement. "I can see it now. Our children and the other children in the Happy Land all getting an education so they can grow up and be whatever God says they can be."

Louella pointed to the right, a little farther up the hill. "And we'll have houses over there. Lots and lots of houses. Enough for all the families." Louella rubbed her hands together, giddy with excitement.

"If you can get all of that with the twenty-five acres we purchased from Serepta, then have at it."

Louella put her hands on William's chest and leaned into him. "I wish you could see what I see. What we're doing here is building a place we can call our own, where outside forces can't touch us. We're going to need many times over that twenty-five acres."

Taking her hands in his, William said, "I love that you're such a visionary. You remind me so much of my mother and how she was always dreaming of her homeland. But I don't want you getting your hopes too high. Let's be grateful for what we have, especially after the courts just instituted more of their so-called Black Codes against Black people owning property."

Shaking her head, Louella put a finger to his lips. "This is a good day. I don't even want to consider the things white folks do to keep us from dreaming."

"Have it your way, beloved."

"Thank you. I think I will." Louella turned back to look at the land. Even with all the trees the men had cut down, there were hundreds more. Acres and acres, waiting to be claimed. Land that they could put to good use. "Oh, William, I feel like singing. You need to hurry up and build that church."

"I love the sound of your voice. I hope I don't have to wait until we build the church before I hear that sweet voice of yours again."

Grinning at her husband, Louella leaned her head back and belted out, *"Happy Land, we're on our way. Even though it's cold and dreary some days."*

The men were working, chopping the lumber so John Goodwin's people could take it to the lumberyard. The moment Louella started singing, a few of them stopped to listen, even hum, as she continued.

"The dire effects of slavery we could no longer stand. We struck a blow for freedom or the grave, that's what we demand."

Tears rolled like diamonds down Louella's face as the men joined in, singing the chorus, *"This is the song . . . song of the free."*

William clapped as Louella sang the word *free* like she was trying to bury it deep, way-down deep, into all of their souls.

❦

Later that night, William called a meeting outside their cabins. There were now two hundred and fifty in their group. William brought two chairs from their cabin. Louella sat in one, and he sat in the other as they gathered in the empty lot next to the cornfield.

Louella looked out at the growing cornstalks and beyond them to the potato plants and cabbage on the other side of the cornfield. They were making a life for themselves in these mountains, surrounded by more oak trees than Louella ever wanted to see. She'd cheered as each tree came tumbling down.

William clasped his hands together and began. "Well, we've been mighty busy since we came here, and I wanted to take a moment to thank y'all for sticking with us and pooling our resources so we can build a place to call home.

"Mrs. Serepta has accepted payment, so we now own twenty-five acres of land, and Louella believes that God is going to give us many more acres. Enough for each of us to build a home of our own."

Cheers went up from the group. William raised a hand. "It's going to take a lot more work to have all the things my lovely wife has envisioned for us, so we wanted to discuss some of our plans with you before moving forward."

"We appreciate that," Gary said. "It's nice to be consulted about these things instead of being told the way it's gon' be."

Louella smiled at that. All she had ever wanted for herself and her people was a sense of dignity. And a place they could call home. She never imagined it would be in a place like this, but they'd found a place of belonging in these mountains. And soon they would have a place they could call home.

"After we finish clearing the acres we've already purchased, Louella thinks we should purchase more land for a church and a school," William told them.

Cheers went up among the group.

"Yes, sir! Our children need a school," one of them said.

"And I've sorely missed stepping into the church house on Sunday mornings," Mama Sue said.

Clara stepped forward. "It's nice and all that our children will learn to read and write." She lowered her head. "I've always wanted to read . . . but never been shown how."

Louella jumped out of her seat and clasped her hands together. "Why don't we begin night lessons for adults while the men are clearing and building on the land?"

William nodded. "Y'all see why I married this woman?" He stood and wrapped an arm around her shoulder. "Brains and beauty."

The flutter of butterflies shared space with the baby growing inside her. Putting her arm around William's waist, she tilted her head back as she looked up at him with adoring eyes. "My husband taught me everything I know, and I'm willing to provide lessons to anyone who wants them."

❧

Abigail was one of her first students. She worked as a lady's maid during the day over at Ben Posey's home. But each night, Abigail and a few others sat with Louella as she read from the Bible and taught them to do the same.

"'And God shall wipe away all tears from their eyes; and there shall be no more death, neither sorrow, nor crying, neither shall there be any more pain: for the former things are passed away.'"

Clara's eyes filled with wonder as Louella read the passage from the Bible. "I've never heard that before."

"And now you can read it for yourself." Louella handed Clara the Bible and pointed to the fourth verse in the twenty-first chapter of Revelation.

Clara took the book. She wiped the sweat beads from her upper lip, fanned away a bit of the heat, and began to read. "And God sh-sh . . . all."

"Shall," Louella corrected and then taught the group how to sound out words.

After Clara read the verse, Abigail was handed the Bible and she, too, read the verse. Rachel took her turn, then on it went. But when they passed the Bible to Elmira, she shook her head.

Rachel nudged her. "I took my turn. You need to do the same. You can't chicken out now."

Elmira lowered her head. "It's too late for me. Never had no book learning. Can't get it inside my brain."

Louella stood. Took her chair and moved it so she was sitting next to Elmira. "I know how you're feeling. When William first started teaching me this stuff, I struggled something terrible. Didn't think I'd ever learn the difference between a *B* and a *D*."

Elmira bit down on her bottom lip. "You're not like me, Auntie. All my life I've been told how dumb and stupid I am . . . I'm not good for nothing in this world."

If Louella had a nickel for every time Overseer Brown told her how useless she was . . . She took Elmira's hand in hers. "I'm more like you than you know."

Elmira put her hand over her face. "I can't read that in front of people. I just can't."

Louella nodded. "Me and you can carve out some one-on-one time, and that's the way it's going to be."

Elmira leaned over and hugged her so tight that Louella had to pull back. "Careful." She patted her belly. "Don't smush my child."

Louella found that she was more careful about overdoing it. She doubted she could live through the loss of another child. "Let's call it a day." Louella was getting ready to take her chair back to her cabin when Femi came up behind her.

"Oh no, you don't," he said. "I'll get that for you."

"Femi, you've been working all day cutting down those trees. You don't have to carry my chair."

"Allow my husband to be a gentleman, please," Abigail said. "He needs more practice."

The women in the group giggled.

Femi frowned as he carried Louella's chair. He turned to Abigail. "I treat you as good as I know how, Abbey. That wasn't called for."

Abigail's lips tightened.

Femi cherished Abigail and did anything she asked. How could they be having problems?

"Do you need anything else, Mrs. Louella?" Femi asked after depositing her chair back inside her cabin.

"Thank you, Femi. That will be all. Now go see about your wife."

His chest heaved as his shoulders rounded inward. "I try, ma'am, but I don't know what's gotten into her lately."

❦

Later that night as Louella and William lay next to each other, she found herself wondering if things were okay between her and William or if she was the only one happy with their marriage. Could she be fooling herself into believing that things were good and right between them?

Louella propped on her elbow and studied the fine lines beneath William's eyes and at the corners. Where did those come from? There had been no lines before they left Mississippi. Had the weight of the journey and of leading the people into this new land aged him?

Waties cried, then jumped up from the mattress that Louella had made of straw and cloth for him. "Mama." Waties lifted his hands.

Her son was almost two years old, and he was the joy of her life. She picked him up and then sniffed the air. Her joy had made a stinky. She got out of bed, dangling him a few inches away from her. "Let's get you changed."

William rolled over, putting a hand to his nose. "That boy has dropped a load."

Louella laughed at the disgusted look on William's face. But in truth, she wasn't so much concerned about the load in Waties's cloth. She laid Waties on his bed and cleaned him up. Then she turned back to her husband. "Tell me about your load. Is there anything I can help you carry?"

Wiping the sleep from his eyes, then yawning, William sat up in bed. "What do you mean?"

After tucking Waties in, she got back in bed and touched the lines at the corners of William's eyes. "You're tired. You can't be everything to everybody, and Robert has been running off to God knows where lately."

"Robert never worked this hard back in Mississippi. I think we wore him out. Let him have a little time to himself."

"While he's taking time for himself, you're stuck doing everything."

"Stop worrying, woman. I'm fine."

"You're not fine. You're tired, and I'm going to have Ambrose take over for you tomorrow."

William opened his mouth to protest. Louella lifted a hand. "Let me do this for you. A day of rest will do you good."

He pulled her into his arms. "Okay. I'll rest tomorrow, but tonight . . ." He leaned in for a kiss. She wrapped her arms around him and showered him with her unspoken love.

PART 4

A Kingdom Rises in the South

1870–1872

CHAPTER 19

The land they'd purchased sat on the border of South Carolina and North Carolina. Louella and William's house was on the South Carolina side.

The house had three bedrooms, a living room, a dining room, and a keeping room. The granite stone fireplace sat in the middle of their keeping room, which was just behind the dining room. The keeping room provided heat to the house. It was bigger than anything Louella had ever lived in. She couldn't really call the shacks she'd stayed in homes. They were merely structures with thatched roof coverings.

Louella's mouth hung open as she looked around the room. It wasn't the granite fireplace that left her in awe. It was the sofa, the matching chair, and the wooden dining table with six wooden chairs. Louella had never had a table that big. What would she do with all those chairs?

"I love it," Abigail said as she entered the house.

With a hand to the side of her face, Louella turned to her friend. "Where did all of this stuff come from?"

"Joe Freeman and his workers made it." Abigail gave a mischievous grin. "It was hard keeping the secret from you but well worth seeing the expression on your face."

Joe Freeman, the wood carver who joined them in Alabama, had been enslaved to a furniture builder and learned the skill well during his years on that plantation.

"Did he make furniture for yours and Femi's new home as well?"

Abigail shook her head. "Not yet. Your house was first on his list. Reverend William made sure of it."

"And I'll make sure there is enough money to have all of our homes furnished," Louella told her.

Abigail wrapped her arms around Louella and hugged her. "See, that's why we all love you so much. You're always thinking of others."

"What's our motto?"

Abigail grinned. "All for one and one for all." She then took Louella's arm and pulled her toward the front door. "Now come on. Let's get you ready for the celebration."

"Where we going? I have to check on Waties and Joshua." Waties would be turning three in a couple of months and her youngest child, Joshua, was nine months. Louella still thought of Lily and missed her terribly, but her two sons were the blessings she needed.

"Your grandmother said she'll keep them boys all day if that's what it takes." Abigail continued pulling her out of the house and back down the hill toward the small shacks they had lived in while their homes were being built.

This new land was a blessing. Never in all her days had she imagined that she would own land, let alone twenty-five acres. And even though the acreage they currently had wasn't enough for all of their residents, Louella trusted that they would soon have enough land to bring all of their community up from the lowly shacks some of them were still living in . . . all in good time.

For now, they were set to celebrate almost thirty homes that had been built on their land. Tonight, they were all going to march from the old cabins up the hill to their homes and have a great feast. But Louella didn't know why Abigail was in such a rush to get her ready. They were only marching up a hill.

When she stepped inside the one-room cabin, she first took notice of the wooden tub in the middle of the floor and the smell of lavender permeating the air. Elmira and Miss Saddie stood next to the tub with water pitchers in their hands. Clara stood behind a chair with a comb and brush in her hand. They were all looking at Louella as if she was the prize goose at the Thanksgiving table. "What kind of tomfoolery are you women about today?"

"None at all." A devilish grin swept across Clara's face as she pointed to the chair. "Have a seat."

Louella looked back at Abigail. "Where did you all get this tub from?" Louella washed by way of the basin in her cabin, and so did the rest of their group.

"Reverend William ordered it for you."

Confusion clouded Louella's face. "But why? I don't understand what's going on."

Abigail took her hand and moved her over to the chair. When Louella sat down, Abigail told her, "All will be revealed in due time. Please allow us to do something for you today, okay?"

Clara started undoing Louella's four big braids. While Clara worked on her hair, Miss Saddie and Elmira kept going outside, filling their pitchers with warm water and then pouring the water in the tub.

"Am I supposed to bathe like a lady in the big house? I already refreshed myself using my water basin this morning."

"You are a lady, and you will allow us to treat you in that manner," Elmira told her as she poured more water in the tub and then harrumphed.

"I guess she told me." Louella laughed and then eased back in the chair. Clara parted her hair down the middle and then stood on the left side while Abigail stood on the right. They both took pieces of her hair and braided it, then sectioned off another piece and braided it. This process continued all the way to the back of her head.

"Whew, Mrs. Louella, you have some long, fine hair. My fingers are cramping," Abigail complained.

"How many braids are you putting in my hair?"

"Ten," Clara told her.

"I've never had that many braids. I normally do the four big braids and then put my scarf over it."

"You look lovely in those braids," Clara assured her. "But we wanted to be able to put your hair in a bun on top of your head, and I think this will do nicely."

"How's Gary? I haven't seen him around much lately," Louella said.

While on her last braid, Clara told her, "He's fine. After helping to clear those trees, he and Jimmy have been using our wagon to drive over to Hendersonville and Greenville to sell crops."

"How very productive of them." Louella smiled at that. It seemed like someone in their group was always coming up with another way to bring money into their community. She was proud of each and every one of them.

"It was Jimmy's idea. Gary wouldn't let him help cut those trees down, so he spent his time growing the corn and the grain. He talked to a few people in Hendersonville and realized we could sell our crops over there."

"Jimmy loves Hendersonville." Elmira snickered.

"What's that supposed to mean?" Clara turned and stared at Elmira.

"I'm sure she didn't mean anything by it," Louella said. "Jimmy's a good boy."

"A good boy who has his eyes on the blacksmith's daughter down in Hendersonville," Elmira told them.

"Well, he'll be twenty in a few weeks. Guess my son is truly growing up," Clara said.

Miss Saddie poured water in the tub as she said, "We need to get that church built so Jimmy can find himself a good churchgoing woman."

Clara used a ribbon to tie Louella's hair into a bun on top of her head. "Okay. My work is done." She handed her a bar of soap and a rag. "Time for your bath."

"But we need to line up so we can all march up the hill. I don't want to hold everybody up."

Abigail took her hand and moved her over to the tub. "Relax. No one is going anywhere without you. We made a fire outside and warmed the water. Take as long as you need."

Lavender petals floated in the water. They were doing all of this for her? Why?

"Get undressed and take a dip. We'll wait outside. Let me know when you're ready. Got another surprise for you," Miss Saddie told her with a wink.

Another surprise? They'd done her hair and prepared her bath, all to march up a hill? What more could they have done? Louella had on a brown dress that had been worn so many times it was losing some of its stitching. Dust sprinkled the air as she dropped it to the floor.

She stepped into the tub and allowed the warm water to caress her skin as she sank down in it. *"Ahhh."*

She'd never imagined how good and relaxing it might be to lounge in a tub like this. Louella looked to heaven. Teardrops glided down her face like the flow of a river. "Thank You, Lord, for being a good God."

Those words made her cry even more. She still remembered days when she wondered why God wasn't being good to them—why He'd left them in the hands of people who misused them for so long. Days when she doubted God cared about them at all.

She lathered her hands, thoroughly soaping her body. When she touched her back, her hand traced the welts that were a forever reminder of what she had endured. The pain of that day lingered. She wanted to drown it out, cleanse her mind of the past. She put her face in the water and held her breath.

The swish of the water, the warmth surrounding her, the smell of lavender—all served to remind her that things were different.

She turned over and over in the water. As she turned, splashes of water wet her hair as her mind was being emptied of the pain . . . emptied of what once was . . . if only for a moment in time. A laugh bubbled inside her. Fun. She was having fun. Louella wanted to put Waties and Joshua in this tub so they could experience the complete abandon of such a luxury.

Twirling one more time, she put her hands on the tub and lifted herself up. "Okay. I'm ready!" she shouted.

Miss Saddie opened the door and came back in carrying a thin blanket. Louella wrapped it around herself and got out of the tub. "Ooh, the water is still warm. I hate to leave it, but we have a celebration to get to."

"Remember all the times we had to dip in those cold river streams to get the stink off us?" Miss Saddie said.

"Don't remind me." Louella shook her head. "The journey was hard, but we're home now."

Louella dried herself off and then reached for her old brown dress, but Miss Saddie snatched her dress off the floor and threw it against the back wall. "We've got something much better for you today."

Putting a hand over her mouth, Louella shivered with delight. "I should have known a dress was involved in all of this. Why else would you be in here?"

"Sooni and I have worked for months on your gown for the celebration, and I am honored to help you into it."

Miss Saddie handed her a shift. "I didn't forget this time. Put this on first."

Louella smiled. There had been no shift for the wedding dress Miss Saddie had made her when they were on the Montgomery Plantation.

Being careful not to disturb the bun on top, Louella pulled the shift over her head. Then Abigail entered the house again. She was carrying a pair of silk over-the-knee stockings. The kind that fine ladies wore.

"Your stockings, Lady Louella." Abigail curtsied in front of her as she held out the stockings.

"What's with this *lady* stuff?" Louella giggled, sat down, and put the stockings on.

Abigail used ribbons to tie the stockings below Louella's knees. "I would have tied them above your knees, but I have a feeling you're going to be dancing tonight."

The door opened, and Elmira entered carrying a dickey petticoat and a stay. The knee-length, white linen petticoat was worn underneath the outer petticoat for warmth and modesty. Louella stepped into it, and then it was tied around her waist.

The stay was a stiff piece of layered linen. It raised the bosom and narrowed the waist. Louella stretched her arms in front of her. Elmira slid the stay on and then began tying it in the back. Louella sucked her breath in at the jolt of the tightening. She had never had such a luxury in her whole life.

Abigail then put the stomacher on her and pinned it to the stay. The fabric of the stomacher was blue silk with gold lace.

Touching the fabric, Louella turned questioning eyes toward Miss Saddie. "You made this . . . for me?"

Miss Saddie *tsk*ed. "Of course we did. And stop looking as if someone's gon' bust open the door and tear these clothes off you. They're yours . . . bought and paid for."

Louella lowered her head. She hadn't forgotten Mary accusing her of thievery the last time she wore a dress that wasn't clothes for an enslaved person. She loved everything they were doing for her, but why did she need such finery? She wondered what Serepta and Sarah would say when they got a look at her in clothes that were fit for the lady of the manor—the big house.

"Stop it, Louella. You deserve everything that's coming your way," Clara told her as she stepped into the house carrying a beautiful blue and gold gown and petticoat.

Louella's hand went to her mouth. She looked to heaven. "Am I dreaming? Am I about to wake up and still be in my brown dress?"

"No!" Miss Saddie scrunched her nose. "I'm throwing that dress away. I've already made you a few other dresses to choose from after tonight's celebration."

This moment was too perfect—too beautiful—for her to allow Mary Montgomery any more space in her mind. She would not allow that woman to destroy another special moment in her life. She dismissed thoughts of Mary and leaned into everything that was taking place.

The smile on Louella's face couldn't be destroyed. She was walking on clouds . . . dancing with the angels. "Okay. Put this dress on me, and let's march up this hill."

CHAPTER 20

Everyone gathered to march up the hill to what would now become the Happy Land. Louella rejoiced at the two hundred fifty people who were with them. There were a hundred and ten women, eighty-six men, and fifty-four children.

Louella walked over to William. He looked quite gentlemanly in a black wool jacket, waistcoat, and trousers. He wore a white shirt with a black cravat about his neck. "Did they make you dip in the tub too?"

"I used the water basin."

"Well, you look real fine." Louella couldn't take her eyes off him. He was handsome and distinguished in her eyes whether he wore slopes while working in the field or a suit while handling business. But this fancy look was new for him, and she very much liked it.

Louella looped her arm around William's. His eyes walked the distance of her. "My, don't you clean up well. I'm a blessed man. I know that for sure."

Louella's cheeks reddened with the way William gazed at her. She swatted his arm. "Stop that. People are watching us."

"I can't help it. You're so beautiful." He lowered his head and kissed her, then turned to the group, waving a hand forward. "Let's go home!" he shouted.

The group began their trek up the hill. Dressed in her fine gown, holding on to her husband in his grand pantsuit, Louella felt a song bubble up in her heart, and she started singing.

"Go down, Moses, way down in Egypt land. Tell all pharaohs to . . ."

A chorus of people behind Louella sang, *"Let my people go!"*

As they continued up the hill, Louella bellowed out, *"When Israel was in Egypt land . . ."*

The chorus sang again, *"Let my people go!"*

William joined Louella on the next verse. *"Oppressed so hard they could not stand."*

"Let my people go!"

"So God said: go down, Moses, way down in Egypt land. Tell all pharaohs to . . ."

"Let my people go!"

Shouts went up from the front of the line all the way to the back as they made it up the hill and entered property that belonged to them. As they got close to the home that would be theirs, Louella shouted, "We're home!"

William lifted her hand in the air. "Never to roam again."

"Praise Jesus for that." Louella looked around. "Where's Waties and Joshua? I want to show them our new home."

"Allow them to stay in your grandmother's care awhile longer. There's something else we need to do."

"And what, pray tell, have you got up your sleeve now?" Louella glanced around again. A tall man with a gray beard stepped forward. He was holding a Bible.

"Do you remember Reverend Ezel?"

Louella nodded. They'd come across Reverend Ezel when they were in Georgia, just about to cross into South Carolina. He was a traveling preacher who had been enslaved.

William said, "He's going to handle our coronation service today."

Louella's eyes shifted in William's direction, then she spoke from the side of her mouth as they stood before the people. "What are you talking about?"

Reverend Ezel stood in front of them as the throng of people stood behind him. They leaned forward, eyes bright with great expectation. Louella scratched her forehead. Had she missed a meeting? Had she been taking care of the kids when a discussion took place about their entry into this new land? She didn't know what was going on or why people were acting so strange today.

William turned to her. Took her hands in his. "The day we married, I told you that you were my queen. Today, we make it official."

Leaning closer to him, she whispered, "What did you do?"

But Reverend Ezel held up his Bible and declared with a loud voice, "The people have spoken, and by God's will, I am here to-day to establish this new kingdom and to ordain William Montgomery as king and Louella Montgomery as queen."

Applause went up. She was sure that people traveling the Bun-combe Turnpike could hear their celebration. Louella's hands went to her face. Her eyes sparkled with wonder as she turned this way and that. Was everyone in on this? Mama Sue stood to the side. Waties was next to her while she toted Joshua on her hip. She blew a kiss to Louella and mouthed, *My queen.*

So overcome, so overwhelmed by the moment, Louella barely heard the words Reverend Ezel spoke over William . . . something about giving him charge over the people. Then she heard, "You must continue to build this kingdom and lead the people in the manner that God has shown you."

Robert stepped in front of William. He held a crown in his hand. It was made of some type of velvet fabric with a rounded dome top. Robert placed the crown on William's head.

Reverend Ezel said, "We crown you king of the Happy Land. May it flourish under your hand, and may you make your ancestors proud."

Louella's eyes filled with tears at this great honor being be-stowed on her husband. How could she ever have known when she said yes to marrying William, she was saying yes to a king—a man who would, like Moses, guide her and their people to their promised land?

As Robert stepped away, the smile on his face made him look as though he was happy for his brother, but then she noticed the smile didn't match the hard set of his eyes.

Reverend Ezel turned to Louella. Her hands were shaking. William was king. She was . . .

"The woman who stands next to the king is no less important to the kingdom they rule. She guides the head that leads the people, and therefore must be a woman worthy of the crown she wears."

Miss Saddie handed Mama Sue a circular item that looked like several thin tree branches had been woven together with green leaves and the most vibrant and beautiful yellow and white flowers cascading around it. Mama Sue came and stood in front of her.

Taking a deep breath, Louella touched her chest. Her heart was beating so fast she feared she might faint. Reverend Ezel continued, "Louella Bobo Montgomery, you are charged to always keep the people's best interests at heart, to seek to do good for the community you have been given charge over."

Mama Sue whispered to her, "Lower your head."

Oh yes, that's right. William lowered his head to receive his crown. She did the same, and her grandmother placed the crown on her head. Louella now understood why Clara braided her hair and then wrapped it in a bun on top of her head. The crown fit perfectly, and her long hair was completely out of the way.

She let out a whoosh of air as chants of "Long live the king! Long live the queen!" went up all around the land.

It was the most beautiful sound Louella had ever heard. William was king and she was queen of the Happy Land. What did it all mean? What would the people expect from her?

William guided her toward their home. Louella saw two chairs on their porch that hadn't been there this morning. They were made of wood. There was fabric on the arms of the chairs and each had a high back. There was a K carved on the back of the chair on the left and a Q on the chair on the right.

"Joe made these for us," William told her as he leaned close to her ear. "Have a seat on your throne, my queen."

Louella eased into the chair, at first not sure how she was supposed to sit on a throne. She scooted all the way back and let her legs dangle against the sturdiness of the wood. Her hands gripped the arms of the chair. The chair was too big for her. Could she ever measure up to what was required of her? Could she truly be a queen?

A fire was set in the open area in front of their home. Several of the men cleaned rabbits, fish, and pheasant. And Mirabel, Mama Sue, and a few other women were cooking corn on the cob from their harvest, collards from their garden, and corn bread.

"Everything smells so good," Louella said while holding Joshua in her lap. "I can't believe you planned all of this and no one told me anything."

"I swore them all to secrecy." William put a hand over Louella's free one as he added, "You deserve this, Louella. If it weren't for you, we might never have left Mississippi."

She put a finger to his lips. "Don't talk like that. You were born to be a leader, and like Moses, you brought us to our promised land. And I am humbled to be married to you."

William's eyes fluttered. "Now you're trying to make my face redden." Waties ran over to the porch, held up his arms, and William picked him up.

"Feels like I should be helping with something."

William wagged a finger. "Don't you dare. The Happy Landers want to do this for you."

"Happy Landers," Louella whispered. The words felt like butter on the tongue. Like a melody she had only just begun to sing. She looked out at everyone milling around. Many of them were busy with the task of making the first meal they would share together in their new land. Some were toting ears of corn, some were chopping the greens, while others were cleaning or cooking the meat.

Reverend Ezel stood before them with a dark-skinned man wearing a tattered straw hat. A thin woman stood next to him. Reverend Ezel said, "I brought John Markley and his wife, Sallie, to meet you fine folks. They might be of use to you here in the Happy Land."

Louella smiled her greeting, nodded to the woman, then asked the man, "What is your trade, Mr. Markley?"

"I'm a blacksmith, ma'am. I can tend to your horses, and I make pots, pans, and silverware out of metal."

William touched Louella's hand as he said, "You and your wife will be a fine addition to the Happy Land."

After sorting out where John Markley and his wife would sleep for the night, Gary came over to them with hat in hand. His head was lowered as he said, "I want to thank you and Queen Louella for keeping your word. My family is right proud of our new home and will work to clear more land so others can have a home of their own as well."

William stood and stepped down from the porch. He put a hand on Gary's shoulder. "We thank you for all that you and Jimmy have done. Especially with the selling of the crops."

"That was all Jimmy's idea," Gary said, looking like a proud papa.

"I'd like to talk to you and Jimmy tomorrow about an idea I've been mulling over."

"Sure thing, Will—uh, King William."

Louella smiled. All of Gary's complaints were now water under the bridge. He would work with them to ensure the kingdom flourished, and that was good news in Louella's opinion.

Gary put his hat back on and then tipped it to Louella. "You make a fine queen. Yes, sir, a mighty fine queen." Grinning, he added, "Reign forever, Queen Louella."

Louella nodded and thanked him. Then Joe came over to them.

"I hope those chairs are nice and comfortable."

"They are, Joe. Thank you so much. They're works of art. Must have taken a whole year to complete," Louella said as she admired his handiwork.

"I would have made them even if it took two or three years."

"You are a blessing to us," William told him.

But Joe shook his head. "It's you and Queen Louella who are the blessings. When freedom came, me and my family wandered around, not knowing which way to go, then y'all showed up." Joe wiped his eyes. "I'm grateful."

Ambrose walked over to her and bowed. "I can't believe my own eyes. My sister is a queen." He kissed her on the cheek and whispered in her ear, "I wish Mama could see you like this."

In the midst of her happiness, a piercing pain added more cracks to her heart. Louella patted Ambrose on the back. "Me too."

The rest of the night continued with members of the Happy Land expressing their joy at being in a land that belonged to each of them.

No matter the pain Louella carried in her heart, the people brought joy into her life. She stood, her heart full as she looked out at the people. "If this is to be a kingdom, it will be a place where people share with one another and treat each other with dignity. That's all I've ever wanted."

William stood and declared, "So shall it be."

But she should have known that the goodness of the night wouldn't roll on forever, not with so much hate in the world.

CHAPTER 21

Louella went to bed that night with so much joy in her heart. But she woke to a cross burning in her front yard.

"What in the world?" William jumped out of their bed, threw his housecoat on, and then rushed out the front door.

Louella went to the bedroom next door and checked on her children. They were sound asleep. She then stood at the front door as William hollered for the men to come out and help him.

The first to open his door was Femi, then Gary, then one by one, about fifteen men were standing out in the yard.

"Grab some buckets. We need to put this fire out!" William shouted.

"What kind of devil would do something like this?" one of the men yelled as they grabbed buckets of water and started dousing the fire.

"It was probably that John Goodwin. I see how he looks at us when he comes to get his share of the timber," Femi said.

Gary put fisted hands on his hips. "Same way ol' Bailey used to look at me. But ain't nobody running us off our land this time. I can promise you that."

"Did anybody see who came on our land?" William asked once the fire was out.

The men were shaking their heads when Abigail came running over to their yard. She ran so fast that she bent over, huffed a few times to catch her breath, then said, "I saw them." She pointed toward the road. "From where our house is, I can see the road that leads up here. It was two white men. One with blond hair and the other had coal-black hair."

Louella stepped out onto the porch. "Would you remember them if you saw them again?"

"I'm not sure. It was dark, and all I could make out was the color of their hair."

Glancing around, Louella wrapped her shawl around her body to stave off the cold night air. "Looks like they're gone. We all might as well get a little more sleep before the sun comes up."

She stayed on the porch, waiting as everyone dispersed, projecting an image of calm. She and William were the leaders of the group. They couldn't fall apart over some burning cross on the lawn. But Louella didn't plan to sit around and do nothing about it either.

When William came back into the house, she said, "We can't let that John Goodwin run us off."

"I don't think John has anything to do with this." William shrugged. "It doesn't make sense. Why would he sell us the land and then burn a cross in our yard?"

"He didn't sell us the land. Mrs. Serepta did that, with Sarah being in agreement. But didn't you notice how hostile John was to us when we sat at Mrs. Serepta's table?"

"I noticed." William lifted a hand and walked past Louella. "Let's get some sleep so we can think this through clearly in the morning."

She got back in bed with William, but Louella couldn't sleep.

❧

In the morning, Louella and Abigail took the wagon into town to sell some of the rheumatoid liniment.

They set up their table outside of the general store. As they were setting the product on the table, Abigail's eyes brightened. "You know what we should do?"

"Sell all of these tins of liniment so we can contribute to buying more seed for our crops?"

"Well, yes, of course that." Abigail picked up one of the tins. "But we should call this stuff Happy Land Liniment."

Louella crooked her head to the side. Nodded a few times. "I think you came up with something. I love it."

A gray-haired lady walked by. Abigail stopped her. "Excuse me, ma'am, but have you tried our Happy Land Liniment? It's the best thing for sore hands."

The woman shook her head and continued into the general store.

The next woman did the same thing. Then a gentleman passed by and heard them yelling, "Get your Happy Land Liniment here and cure your rheumatism in no time!"

The gentleman turned around and came back to their table. He picked up one of the tins. "Are you telling me that this liniment cures rheumatism?"

Abigail gleefully said, "It sure does. You should try it."

But Louella said, "I can't guarantee that it will go away forever, but I can tell you that my grandmother suffers from rheumatism, and every time she puts this liniment on her hands, she gets relief."

"Now that sounds like an honest answer." He grinned at her. "How much?"

"Five cents a tin."

He took two dollars out of his pocket. "How much will that cover?"

Abigail's eyes bulged. "My goodness. That'll be about forty tins."

Louella smiled. The lessons were paying off for her friend. They bagged up his order, and he was on his way. "We only have two tins left. We should be able to get back to the Happy Land in no time."

"Too soon for me." Abigail frowned as she leaned against the wall of the general store with arms folded.

Louella's eyebrows furrowed. "You don't like your new home?"

"Don't think that." Abigail came back to the table with Louella. "I love our new home. I'm what's wrong. I'm such a failure and a fraud in it."

Louella put a hand on Abigail's shoulder. "What's going on with you? Has Femi done something to upset you?"

"It's not Femi at all. That man has been better to me than I deserve. Wish I could give him what he wants most."

A woman came to the table. Louella sold her a tin of liniment, then turned to Abigail. "It's the baby issue, isn't it?"

Eyes widening, Abigail nodded. "How'd you know? Did Femi—"

Louella waved a hand. "Femi said nothing to us."

Dropping her head, Abigail said, "My womb is barren."

"Oh, Abigail, you don't know that for sure."

"Femi and I have been married almost four years, and I haven't given him a child." A tear trickled down her face. "I'm sure he regrets marrying me."

Louella grabbed hold of Abigail's shoulders. "You're talking foolish. If I know anything, I know that Femi loves you. If a baby comes, it comes, but don't lose sight of what you have."

Before she could say more, a woman came over to their table. Her hair was stringy and red. She had a scowl on her face as she approached them. Abigail lifted a tin. "Would you like to try some of the Happy Land Liniment?"

"What Happy Land? Where do you people come from?" The woman shot daggers at them as she put a hand on her hip and tapped her foot.

"We're up the road, ma'am. Over by the Oakland Plantation. Are you interested in our liniment? It soothes sore, aching hands."

"My hands aren't sore. I don't do colored women's work."

Louella's eyebrow arched, but she kept quiet. She would not let this woman's foul spirit disturb her.

"Why are you standing in front of the general store? Who gave you authority to loiter out here?"

Louella pointed toward the store. "Mr. Morris allows us to set up out here a few days each month."

"We'll see about that." The woman huffed and then stomped her way into the store. "Where is Freddie?" she shouted.

"We're not blocking the entrance into the store," Abigail said.

Louella clamped her mouth shut for fear that the ugly things she wanted to say about that woman would seep out.

Then she heard Freddie Morris, the owner of the general store, say, "Yes, Mrs. Anne, I do know those ladies are set up outside the store."

Louella sighed in relief, looked to heaven, and mouthed, *Thank You.*

But the woman wouldn't let it go. She kept screaming until Louella heard Freddie say, "Okay. You're right. I wasn't thinking."

Freddie Morris then ambled his way over to their table. "Good day to you, Louella . . . Abigail."

"Good day to you, Mr. Morris. How's business?" Louella asked. She kept her eyes directed toward him and didn't turn toward the foul-spirited woman even when she heard her say, "If this kind of thing is going to be allowed around here, I might start shopping in the next town over."

"Business has been good." Freddie looked back at the woman, who kept an eagle eye on him. "Have to ask you to pack up."

Abigail huffed. "I don't know what that lady said, but we didn't do anything to her."

Louella put a hand on Abigail's shoulder. She nodded to Freddie. "We'll leave now. Thank you for allowing us to use this space today."

Freddie walked away. Abigail whispered, "But we didn't do anything wrong."

"For some people, our very presence is wrong. If they can't enslave us, then they want nothing to do with us."

Louella and Abigail toted their table to the wagon and headed back to the Happy Land. Abigail asked, "Did you notice anything about Mr. Morris?"

"Nothing other than the fact that he'd rather please hateful people than keep his word."

"He has blond hair."

Louella laughed at that. "So did the man who bought forty tins from us. A lot of white men have blond hair."

Abigail tapped her forehead twice with her index finger. "I might be oversensitive to blond-haired men."

Louella held the reins tight as the horse trotted up the hill toward the Happy Land. "Something tells me that Mr. Morris isn't the cross-burning type, but I like that you're paying attention. We have to keep our eyes and ears open. Plenty people in this town are like Anne. We need to figure out which ones of them want to do us harm."

CHAPTER 22

Reverend Ezel came back to the Happy Land about a month after the Happy Landers had moved in. He brought with him a family that wanted to join with them. "This here is Harold Whitmore and his wife, Hannah. Harold fought in the war. Once it was over, his former owners turned them away."

"Nice to meet you." Louella shook their hands. "Where you good people from?"

"How you know we're good people?" Harold asked with a grin.

William shook Harold's hand. "Reverend Ezel would only bring good people to our land. So unless you've tricked the reverend . . ."

"Nobody's tricked Reverend Ezel." Hannah elbowed her husband. "My husband fancies himself a jokester. We're from Enoree, South Carolina, about fifty miles down the road."

"But we haven't been able to find work, and our two daughters have gone hungry more nights than I care to think about," Harold told them, the grin on his face washed away by the truth of their sorrow.

"Where are your daughters?" Louella asked.

Hannah pointed toward the wagon. "They fell asleep. We thought we'd wait until we found out if you'd allow us to stay before waking them."

All Louella needed to hear was that the children had gone hungry. "Get those children off that wagon and come into our home and have some supper."

The Whitmores, their daughters, and Reverend Ezel sat down

at Louella's dining table. She set fried chicken, golden yams, and collard greens in front of them.

William said grace, and they passed the plates. "*Mmm*," Harold said. "I haven't had fried chicken this good in years."

Hannah leaned close to her husband. "These yams melt in the mouth."

Smiling, Louella told them, "I can't take the credit. My grandmother lives in the house with us. She helps with the children and cooks our meals."

"Please give her our thanks. Our bellies have been grumbling for so long, we never imagined our next meal would be this delicious," Harold said.

"I should've prepared you for the hospitality you'd receive here in the Happy Land," Reverend Ezel said.

"I'm mighty thankful we've come to such a place," Hannah said.

Louella could see the woman's eyes filling with tears. Things had been hard for the Whitmores, that was evident. Hopefully, joining with them would ease some of their worries.

After they finished the meal, William explained how things worked in the kingdom. "All of our people share responsibilities in the Happy Land. We'll either find work for you outside of our community, or you'll work the land with us. Any money that's earned is brought back to me and—"

"Wait. Are you saying that I won't be able to keep the money I earn?" Harold scratched his head. "How am I supposed to feed my family . . . put a roof over their heads?"

"All good and valid questions, my friend." William patted Harold on the shoulder. "Our motto at the Happy Land is 'all for one and one for all,' so you'll eat, and your family will have a home."

Harold turned questioning eyes to Reverend Ezel. "I don't understand."

"Come with me," William said as he stood and walked toward the front door. The palm of one hand rested behind his back as he headed to the door, his posture ramrod straight. His walk appeared regal and of importance to Louella. She would follow him anywhere.

Harold walked out onto the porch. Louella then told Hannah, "You too."

Standing next to William, Louella put an arm around his waist while Hannah stood next to her husband. William extended a hand outward. "Do you see all of the houses and all of the land beyond those houses?"

Harold nodded. "Yes, sir. I see them."

With a puffed-out chest, William told him, "We built those homes, and as we continue to clear land and purchase more acreage, the people who lend a hand to the plow get homes for their families."

Louella's eyes beamed with pride as she looked at her husband. All of her dreams, everything she'd ever wanted, was coming to be. And her joy was being restored. She told Harold and Hannah, "Never fear, for we're good stewards over every dime that comes into our hands. After we hold what is needed for the building of this kingdom, William then evenly distributes the rest to all of our residents."

"We do not have any empty homes at this point, but we'll ask one of the families to take you in while we work to get your home built." William then stuck out his hand. "Does the Happy Land sound like a place you'd like to raise your family?"

An easy grin spread across Harold's face. He shook William's hand. "It does. It does indeed."

Louella walked Harold and Hannah over to the storehouse next to the barn. "This is where you'll come each week to gather food to feed your family."

Hannah's eyes widened as she looked from tables of potatoes, corn, and cabbage to tables of greens and so forth. "Never seen so much food in one place before."

"My prayer is that none of us go hungry ever again," Louella told her, then helped them get settled for the night.

Louella then walked Reverend Ezel over to the spot where they were building the church. There was only rubble, loose stones, and mud there for now.

"They're almost finished with the foundation," Louella said with joy ringing in her voice.

"My, my, my. Now this is something." Reverend Ezel glanced around. "Y'all truly setting up a society of your own. Our people need to be a part of what you and King William are building. That's why I bring as many as will listen."

Louella patted the kindly reverend on his shoulder. "You're doing God's work, Reverend, and we thank you."

"I hope I get a chance to preach at this church."

"Every time you come to visit us, the pulpit will be yours," Louella told him as they walked back to the house. When they reached her porch, before going back inside, she turned to him. "You still traveling all around South Carolina?"

He nodded.

"Have you run into anyone with the surname of Bobo yet?"

He put his hand on one of the posts that was holding up the porch. "I haven't forgotten about Brenda. I pray all the time that the good Lord would allow me to find your mother."

"Thank you, Reverend." She smiled at him but felt the pangs of sorrow in the tender part of her heart that still hadn't healed.

CHAPTER 23

"Good morning," Louella called out to the Happy Land Teamsters as she handed each of them a Mama Sue Apple Berry Muffin Special. They had the wagons loaded with corn, potatoes, and grain. Orders had been placed for their goods in neighboring South Carolina and North Carolina markets.

It was August 17, 1871. The sun was shining big and bright in the sky, and the Happy Land was flourishing. Jimmy's idea about selling goods to general stores and stagecoach depots proved to be a boon for their community.

"Don't forget to pick up the shipment from the Smiths down the road. They'll give you the delivery details when you get there," she told Larry.

The teamsters not only sold their own goods but picked up produce from other farmers who contracted with the Happy Landers to have their produce delivered near and far.

She handed Larry an envelope with several coins. "Take this for any expenses you have along the way."

Larry put the envelope in his pocket. "You're a blessing, Queen Louella. Thank you so much for the muffins."

Jimmy tipped his hat at her and took a bite of the muffin. He now had a mustache and was looking more the twenty-two-year-old man than the seventeen-year-old boy who first joined them.

"Be careful out there." Jimmy was headed to Hendersonville for a quick run, while the other teamsters would be gone at least a month. Louella waved goodbye to the team of men who were brave enough to fight off bandits and ensure that they didn't get cheated by unscrupulous store owners who still wanted free labor from Black workers.

Breathing in the humid morning air, Louella walked over to their new church building, unhooked the triangle bell, and clanged it a few times.

Front doors began opening all around the Happy Land, and children ran toward the church, which was also used as a school-house on weekdays. Louella had come to terms with not having two separate buildings since they needed all the space they could get to house the people who continued to find their way to the Happy Land.

"Good morning, my lovelies. Have a seat, and I'll be right in."

Louella rang the bell one more time, and then Abigail's door opened. Her friend waddled out, stomach leading the way as she labored with each step. A giggle bubbled up in Louella's belly as she remembered the years of doubt Abigail had about being able to bear a child.

"I'm sorry. Didn't mean to be late. It's so hard to get up now."

Abigail looked as if she was ready to burst any day. Louella said, "I'm sure Femi helped you."

Femi worked with the teamsters, but since Abigail had grown so big, he'd decided not to take the trip with them this week. In-stead, he would take the grain to the gristmill for grinding so he could stay close to home in case his wife needed him.

Holding the small of her back, Abigail smiled. "He did. God truly blessed me with a man like Femi."

"And don't you forget it," Louella scolded as they went inside the school. Abigail now served as Louella's teaching assistant.

They had twenty-three children between the ages of four and eight. The older children went to school outside of the Happy Land. That school was in Possum Hollow, and a Negro preacher by the name of Reverend Walter Allen was the instructor.

Clasping her hands as she entered the school building, Louella said, "Today, I'm going to read out of the book of Esther. This story is about a woman who became queen and saved her people from the hands of an enemy." She turned in her Bible and began reading: "'Now it came to pass in the days of Ahasuerus, (this is Ahasuerus which reigned, from India even unto Ethiopia, over an hundred and seven and twenty provinces:) that in those days, when the king Ahasuerus sat on the throne of his kingdom, which was in Shushan the palace, in the third year of his reign, he made a feast unto all his princes and his servants . . .'"

When she finished reading, she and Abigail then worked with the children on words that were in the first chapter of Esther.

"We don't have to sound out the king's name, do we? That looks hard," one of the kids said, causing the rest of them to burst out laughing.

"No," Louella assured the child. "We won't make you sound out King Ahasuerus."

"But we might make you spell *Esther,*" Abigail joked with them, "so pay attention."

Once the lesson was done, the children all gathered in a circle, and Louella taught them a song. She pulled her songs from Bible verses. In Louella's estimation, the Bible was poetic enough to sing.

Today's song came from Lamentations 3:22–23. "Okay, so I'll sing a few words, then you all will repeat after me."

"Okay," the children said in unison.

"It is of the Lord's mercies that we are not consumed," she sang.

The children repeated in song.

"Because his compassions fail not." Joy bubbled in Louella's heart at the sweet sound of children praising the Lord. Her childhood had been filled with so much grief and turmoil that she'd felt like a hypocrite singing praises to the Lord, but no more.

Louella lifted her eyes to heaven and sang the next verse of the Bible. *"They are new every morning: great is thy faithfulness."*

Those words made her heart glad. She took that joy with her throughout the day.

❦

On Saturday morning, as was custom, Louella and William sat in their royal chairs and listened to any thoughts the people had about making the kingdom work for all of them. Sometimes there were more grievances than thoughts. Louella's brother, Ambrose, served as the scribe, taking notes so that Louella and William could review the issues that needed further discussion and come back with an answer.

Some days only a few residents showed up when they held court. Other days, like today, there were many.

Jimmy Freeman, Gary and Clara's son, was the first in line. He stood there holding hands with a young girl with a yellowish-brown complexion and the prettiest light brown eyes. The girl didn't live in the Happy Land, so Louella was surprised to see her standing before them.

William said, "Good morning, Jimmy. What brings you before us today?"

Jimmy took off his hat and held it against his chest. "Good morning, King William." He then nodded in Louella's direction. "Queen Louella. I wanted to introduce you to Patricia Ann. She lives in Hendersonville with her parents."

"Good morning, Patricia Ann," William and Louella both said.

Clara was standing on the left side of Jimmy while Patricia Ann stood to his right. Clara nudged her son. "Tell 'em what you told me."

Jimmy took a few steps forward. "Well, you see, I don't want you thinking I don't love it here in the Happy Land, 'cause I do, but Patricia's parents won't let me marry her unless I agree to move to Hendersonville."

Patricia put a hand on Jimmy's back as he lowered his head and continued, "They don't understand our way of life here and refuse to let Patricia move into the Happy Land."

"Have your parents given you their blessing to marry Patricia Ann?" William asked.

Jimmy still wouldn't look up. He seemed tortured by the fact that he had to choose between his home in the Happy Land and the woman he had come to love. Louella put a hand on William's shoulder. "Give him our blessing."

William stood. He walked out to the yard and placed his hands on either side of Jimmy's head. He kissed the boy, who'd now grown into a man, on the forehead. "Go in peace, young man, and may the Lord grant you many happy years with your new family."

Louella stood and clapped for the young couple. Cheers went up all around them.

George Couch was next in line. He was new to the Happy Land. He and his wife, Maggie, had come by way of Reverend Ezel. They loved the good reverend so much that they even named one of their sons after him. George took his hat off as he stood before them. "Good day to you, King William." Then he nodded his head toward Louella. "Good day to you, Queen Louella."

"Nice to see you today, George. How's Maggie doing?" Louella asked.

"She's about ready to pop. That's the reason I'm here this morning."

Maggie and Abigail were both expecting in the next few days. Everyone in their community was aflutter about the babies that would soon be born.

"You see," George began again, "we've been staying with Hank and Mirabel. They're real nice people and all, but seeing as though we're having another baby, I was hoping we'd have our home by now."

William smiled generously at the man. "And you shall. The logs have been cut, and a space has been cleared for you."

George began backing up. "I'm sorry. I didn't know. I-I didn't mean to bother you good people."

"No bother at all. Things have been so busy around here, I forgot to tell you your plot of land is ready for building. Larry oversees all of the construction, so I'll make sure he gets with you next week so you can help build that house," William told him.

The next person to speak with them about a matter was Maurice, a resident for the past two years. "Before I say my piece, I want to let it be known that I truly love living in the Happy Land." Maurice looked around before adding, "But I'm having a hard time understanding why I receive the same dividends as the women when they aren't working as hard as the menfolk."

Mama Sue was inside the house with Waties and Joshua. Louella heard her grandmother harrumph. Her own eyebrow lifted at Maurice's statement.

William shifted in his chair, getting ready to respond, but Louella put a hand over his as she asked, "Are you saying that weaving, cooking, caring for the children, cleaning homes, and selling the Happy Land Liniment that brings money back to this kingdom aren't as important as the plowing you do?"

Maurice shook his head. "Not saying they ain't important. But women don't work as hard as men."

"I can assure you that's not the case, and we'll not take from the women in our land so the men can walk around with heavier pockets."

William cleared his throat. Louella turned to her husband. He hated when she took over their assembly meetings, but she would not allow any man in their community to downgrade the value of women's work. Maurice was young—had turned nineteen last month. Louella yielded the floor to William as she decided to give the boy some grace.

William rubbed his hands together. "We are a people who believe in the value of all and reward that value evenly."

"I appreciate being heard," Maurice said and then walked away.

Some of the women eyed him as if he'd received the last Sunday dinner at their table.

They listened to a few other concerns while Ambrose continued to write everything down in his notebook. Then Robert stepped to the front. He greeted his brother without so much as looking Louella's way.

"Brother, my prayer is that all is well with you," Robert said.

"All is well, but you would know that if you were with us in the Happy Land more often." William leaned forward with an easy grin as he looked at Robert.

"My heart is always with the Happy Land." Robert put a hand to his heart. "I stand before you today bringing concerns of many who live here with us."

At the word *concerns*, the grin disappeared from William's face. Louella put a hand on William's arm. Robert was up to something. She knew it like she knew her name. But her influence failed when it came to convincing William to be wary of his brother.

Louella asked Robert, "And what are those concerns? And why do they not come here themselves?"

Robert glanced her way, then turned back to William. "The people know you're a good man and don't want to overburden you. However, they've seen that we have delays on land clearing and homes being built. You need help."

William looked intrigued. "What do you suggest?"

"I know I've been traveling and away from the kingdom more than I've been here of late." Robert tapped his hand against his chest. "But I'm willing to sacrifice my time to help you build our kingdom."

William pressed his lips together. "I do need help, but I need someone who will focus on the needs of our kingdom. Are you sure you're ready to do that?"

Robert nodded. "You have my word."

William's hand gripped the arm of the chair. He turned jubilant eyes to Louella as if Robert's words were an answer to prayer.

Louella wasn't convinced. She asked Robert, "What exactly are you proposing?"

"Every good king needs a second-in-command." Robert beat at his chest. "I can be that for my king."

Louella's breath caught in her throat. When she recovered, she opened her mouth to tell Robert that William already had a second-in-command.

But William stood, stepped down from the throne, and hugged Robert. "Thank you. The kingdom welcomes your help."

Robert then took William's hand in his and lifted them as he turned to the group that remained in the yard. "So let it be said that the Montgomery brothers work together in the Happy Land. And as the second-in-command, I will help my king build this land."

The men standing around the yard broke out in cheers. They were gleeful at Robert's declaration, as if having another man to lead them was like the stars and the moon come down to greet them. Louella's lips tightened as her belly filled with fury. As queen, she was second-in-command, but William stood grinning like a dunderhead while Robert pushed her aside. Glancing around, Louella saw some of the women looking to her. They were waiting for her reaction.

She sat on her throne, not smiling, not frowning, just being still for as long as she could. If knowing that she and William would have help building the kingdom brought joy to some of their hearts, then so be it. But she wouldn't pretend that Robert taking a leadership role in the Happy Land was music to her ears.

Louella's hands were folded in her lap as William and Robert glad-handed the people who showered them with congratulations. Elmira rushed over to her. She leaned close to her ear. "Are you okay, Auntie?"

Nodding, Louella used her hand to fan her face. "It's a bit hot out here." She stood and went inside her home. The door almost slammed behind her, but she gripped it before it closed.

"Go on and let it slam," Mama Sue said as she stood in the kitchen scowling. "You been by that man's side all this time, and he lets that snake claim to be second-in-command."

With a gentle hand, she closed the door. "Stop that, Mama. The people look to William and me for leadership. I can't lower my character, even when my husband doesn't see what manner of man his brother is."

Grabbing hold of her wrist, Mama Sue pressed, "Make him see. That man don't mean you no good, and I'm not going to stand by and watch him destroy what would've never been built if not for you."

With eyes downcast, Louella shook her head. "I wish I could. This is one matter the king doesn't receive counsel from me on."

CHAPTER 24

The heat of summer had left them, and now the crisp, cool nights of fall were upon them. Louella and William were lying in bed; he had an arm around her as he slept. The nights had taken on a chill, so Louella snuggled closer to the heat of her husband. Lying in William's arms warmed her like the heat coming off the hearth. Even as he slept, she still saw strain on her husband's face. She wanted to trace the crow's-feet around his eyes but didn't want to wake him.

Turning over in bed, she felt her eyes droop. A mountain load of work would greet her in the morning. Not only was she teaching the children, but she also had her night class for adults learning to read and write. She would welcome a good night's sleep. But as her eyes were closing, she heard a noise outside, like hooves beating on the ground.

It was too dark for the crew to be getting the wagons loaded. She sniffed the air. Was that fire? She turned back to William and shoved his shoulder. "Wake up. I hear something outside."

"H-huh?" William wiped the corner of his mouth and sat up. He stretched. "What's going on?"

She whispered, "Someone's outside. I smell fire."

He sniffed the air, then jumped out of bed. It was dark in the room. He fumbled around until he found his pants. Louella lit the lantern next to her bed. "Blow that out," William whispered.

"I need to check on the boys."

"Not right now. Stay here." William put on his pants and slid into his slippers.

"Come on out, boy!"

Louella jumped. Her hands fisted the covers. "Oh, my Jesus!"

William headed for the door.

"No!" she screamed. "You can't go out there."

"Can't let them come in here."

Louella got out of bed. She rushed into the living room and peeked out the window. She blinked, refocused her eyes. A burning cross was in their yard. A ghostlike man sat on a horse. He held the burning ember that must've been used to light the cross.

A man directly behind the ghost wore the face of an animal with horns, another had a potato sack on his head, and another sat perched on his horse with his face painted black. She recognized the man wearing blackface. It was Mr. Morris from the general store. Louella didn't understand why he was in front of their home with the man who'd burned a cross in their yard. What devilment had gotten into him?

"Boy, if you don't get out here, I'm going to drag you out by your ears," the man holding the ember hollered.

William cracked open the door. Louella's eyes went wild. In the back of her mind, she was seeing William hanging from one of them oak trees on Mrs. Serepta's property. "Close that door, William. Those men mean you no good."

William's lips tightened. "I can't let them take you and the kids."

"If you're dead, you won't know any different. At least take the rifle out there with you."

But he shook his head, opened the door, and stepped onto the porch with his hands up as if he was surrendering to the sheriff. "It's late. You men should go on home. If there's a matter we need to discuss, we can do it tomorrow."

Mama Sue came into the living room. Pulling on her robe, she said, "What's going on out there?"

"The Klan, Mama. Go sit with the boys for me," Louella whispered.

"What you gon' do?"

Louella hunched her shoulders, then she heard one of the men say, "Your time is up here. You darkies won't steal another piece of land from poor old misguided Serepta."

"I can assure you we didn't steal any land. We've paid for every piece of land we own." William tried to reason with them.

But then the man in the white sheet took a rope with a noose off the back of his horse. "We brought this for you." Then two of the men dismounted and started walking toward William.

Louella's eyes flashed with the memory of her father hanging from that tree. She rushed back to their bedroom and pulled the rifle from under the bed. She wouldn't stand by and let them string her husband up, not without putting a bullet in one of them first.

"Louella, think of your children," Mama Sue called after her as she went out the door.

One of the men walking toward William had a rifle in his hand. Louella pointed hers in his face. "Don't come no closer, or I'll put a bullet in you."

"You're not going to shoot me," the man with the rifle said. He puffed out his chest, brash and cocky.

"Try me." Louella shot the rifle in the air and then pointed it toward the brash man's head.

"Go back in the house, Louella. I'll not allow you to tangle with these men."

Louella saw a few doors open as people in the Happy Land came out and stood on their porches. One of them called out, "We're watching, and we'll be sure to tell the sheriff everything we see."

The man with the white sheet over his head laughed. "The next time we have lunch, I'll tell him for you."

"You won't be telling the sheriff nothing if you don't get off our property." Louella's heart filled with rage as it had the night Overseer Brown burned down their church. She could pull the trigger over and over again, until all of them lay dead in her yard.

"Who do you think you are?" White Sheet asked.

"They call me Queen Louella."

A sudden explosion rattled the horses. A dust cloud formed, drifting into the air. Louella didn't know from whence the explosion came, but a couple of the horses took off running down the hill like they'd been spooked. Then Femi and Harold came and stood on the porch with her and William. Both Femi and Harold had rifles in their hands.

"Who wants to die tonight?" Femi asked, a crazed look in his eyes.

The men started backing up while a few residents came out with buckets of water and began putting out the fire.

"This ain't over," the man with the white sheet said as he swung his horse around.

"You come back here, and we'll bury you so deep no one'll ever find you," Harold told them.

William took the rifle out of Louella's hand. He glared at her as if her presence offended him. "You see, the menfolk have settled this matter."

She didn't see that at all. If she hadn't come out here with her rifle, those men would've hog-tied her husband and dragged him off to the nearest tree. But as her head swiveled from Femi to Harold, seeing them stand on her porch with their rifles at the ready, and then remembering the explosion, she wondered whether some plan had already been put in place that she was not privy to.

Louella went back inside the house and paced the floor, her cheeks puffing in and out as William talked with Harold and Femi.

When William came into the house, he placed the rifle against the door and then approached her. "Don't ever do that again. You could've been shot."

"Let me ask you something." She took a deep breath, calming her temper. "Do you think I could stand idly by and let you get hung as if your life meant nothing?"

He expelled a gust of air. "No. I don't suppose you could."

"Then why in God's name didn't you tell me you had already talked to Femi and Harold about protecting our land? If I had known that they'd come to your rescue, I wouldn't've put myself in jeopardy when we got children that need a mama to look after them."

"Robert talked to Femi and Harold. I didn't think to tell you. Hoped we wouldn't need to deploy them."

Folding her arms across her chest, Louella tapped her foot. Took a deep breath. "So am I no longer to be consulted about matters of concern for our kingdom? Do you and Robert now lead our people—without me?"

William shook his head. "Not trying to shut you out, Louella. Just didn't want to trouble your mind with such things."

She nodded and unfolded her arms. "Okay, then. I think we should call a meeting with the council in the morning."

"Council?" William's brow lifted.

"Of course," she told her husband. "We shall have a council to advise and protect our kingdom. I read all about it in one of the books Mrs. Serepta donated to our school."

"So we have a council now, do we?"

Louella nodded. "But I need y'all to understand that as queen of the Happy Land, I'm a part of this council, and I'll not stand for being kept in the dark about matters of import in this kingdom."

After saying her piece, she went back to their bedroom, but sleep still wasn't in her. Louella got on her knees and prayed for God to guide them. Scaring those evil men off tonight wouldn't stop them from coming back. How on earth would they protect their people?

She also prayed for God to open William's eyes to the truth of who was with him and who was not.

CHAPTER 25

"Thank y'all kindly for joining us for breakfast this morning," William said to Robert, Femi, and Harold as they broke bread together in the keeping room. Mama Sue had cooked eggs, ham, and grits. Louella brought the food to the table.

William said grace over the food and then they started passing plates. William sat at the head of the table. Louella sat opposite him, at the other head of the table. Her number one job today was making sure that the council understood she, along with William, made the final decisions for the benefit of the Happy Land.

"You men were spectacular against the Klan last night." William gave Femi a pat on the back. "I almost forgot about your gunpowder trick. That explosion was genius."

Femi grinned. "The army taught me well." But then Femi turned to Louella. "I'm sorry to say that I was sound asleep and didn't know anything was amiss until I heard the warning shot."

"Nothing at all to be sorry about," Louella told him. "You've been up 'round the clock helping Abigail as her time draws near."

Femi wiped a bead of sweat from his head. "I don't understand why she's so big. She can barely walk around our small house anymore."

Louella had wondered that a time or two herself. Abigail seemed unusually swollen, and she prayed nothing was going wrong with the baby. She couldn't bear the thought of Abigail enduring a loss like that.

"That baby's probably gon' have a big head like his daddy," Robert said with a chuckle.

Robert seemed in a good mood today. Louella's eyebrow lifted at Robert's joke about the baby Abigail was carrying since he had been vehemently against her marrying Femi. She also wondered why Robert had chosen Femi to be one of the sergeants at arms—that was the title she was giving them. But maybe Robert's disposition had improved over the years.

There was a knock at the door. Mama Sue opened it, and Ambrose and Elmira walked in. William turned to them. "We're in a meeting. Can y'all come back later?"

Ambrose's eyebrow rose as he glanced in Louella's direction.

She cleared her throat and addressed her husband. "I invited them for a morning meal today." Louella stood and hugged her brother and then hugged her sweet niece. "Sit down, y'all. Fill your plates."

Mama Sue handed Ambrose an extra chair so all seven of them could sit at the table.

William put his fork down. "Louella, what's the meaning of this?"

"All is well, William. Let Ambrose and Elmira fill their bellies, and then we can get into the whys and whatnot."

Robert harrumphed. "She's meddling in our business. That's why they're here."

Elmira frowned. "Don't be like that, Daddy."

Louella ignored Robert. She finished her breakfast while carrying on conversations with her guests around her table.

Once bellies were good and full, Louella looked from Femi to Harold and said, "I was so right proud to see the two of you come to our rescue. Can't thank y'all enough."

"No need to thank them. They did the job they were assigned," Robert said.

Harold agreed with Robert. "No need to thank us, Queen Louella. This what soldiers do. We protect."

"That may be true, but we're mighty grateful for your service to the Happy Land." William looked to Louella. "Isn't that right?"

"For sure and true," Louella agreed, then steepled her hands together. Her head tilted to the side. "But I'm wondering if the Happy Land might be more secure if some of our men took up posts at the bottom of the hill during the night."

"That's actually a great idea," Femi said. "But with Abigail being so close to delivering and not able to get around without help, I don't think I could spend many nights on duty right now."

"I know you and Harold been given the responsibility of protecting us, but I'm hoping we can enlist others to help as well." She pointed toward her brother. "Ambrose might not be a big and important former soldier, like the two of you. But he's willing to help."

"Anything for you, sis," Ambrose said.

"That's Queen Louella to you, boy," Mama Sue told him as she removed the dishes from the table.

"Mama, that's Ambrose. It's okay if he calls me sis."

But Mama Sue shook her head. "You gotta teach folks how to treat you or they'll walk all over you." She glanced in Robert's direction, then back at Louella before heading to the hearth to wash the dishes.

Louella got the message from her grandmother, but she had no intentions of letting Robert or any of the other men at this table walk over her or dismiss her worth to the Happy Land.

"We'll need more than the three of us if we're gon' set up a nightly patrol of the valley area," Harold said.

Louella nodded. "Since my husband and Robert selected you and Femi for this most urgent task, I'm hoping that the two of you can find other men who could be taught the things you both know that will keep us safe, as if we had our own little army."

"An army takes a lot of manpower," William said.

"And where would we get such manpower?" Robert interjected.

"We got three hundred people in the Happy Land. Should we take some of the men away from their farming duties? Should we disrupt the teamsters from delivering our produce to market?"

Trying to stop her eyes from rolling as Robert spoke proved to be an unmanageable task. "I'm not suggesting that we forgo our needed duties. Ten to twelve men should do." She waved a hand around the table. "And we already have three men for the job right here."

Louella then pointed toward Elmira. "And my lovely niece can keep record of who'll be on duty each night."

Robert barked at Elmira, "Why didn't you tell me about this?"

"Can't hardly tell you 'bout nothing when I can barely find you half the time," Elmira retorted.

Louella's heart went out to Elmira. She was in her early twenties, but still kept reaching out for the father she needed like water and air. At times it seemed as if Robert didn't notice or was too busy with whatever occupied his time outside of the Happy Land.

"Femi and Harold need only concern themselves with protecting this house and mine. Harm will not come to us if we keep our heads down and mind our own business," Robert said.

But Femi shook his head. "We could be doing absolutely nothing, and men like the ones who rode up here last night would still hate us. Queen Louella is right. We need to build our own army of men who can protect the land, even if it's only ten of us to start with."

Robert turned toward William. "You can't possibly agree with this nonsense. Our men already have enough to do around here. We're farmers and teamsters, not warriors."

William bowed his head as if in prayer. No one said a word. They waited for him to speak again. After a short while, he raised his head with a sigh. "The Happy Land is a place of peace, but if others should seek to harm us, we must prepare for such a battle."

With those words, William stood, indicating the meeting was

over. Louella looked at each man as they sat around her table. "You have your marching orders. Find out which men in the Happy Land would be willing to stand guard. Hopefully you'll get enough recruits so the men only have to spend one or two nights a month on duty." She stood. "Good day, gentlemen."

Turning to Elmira, Louella said, "We'll put you to work on this matter once we get some order to it."

"Okay, Auntie." Elmira came around the table and hugged her. "If you don't need anything else, I'll go with Daddy before he disappears again."

Louella patted her arm. "Go spend some time with your father."

Elmira ran out of the house. She called after Robert. He stopped, put an arm around his daughter, and then continued to his house with her.

Ambrose stayed after the other men left. William walked over to the church to work on his sermon for Sunday service.

"You really think we need our own army?" Ambrose asked her.

"There are men who seek to do us harm, and we must be ready. If we're not, you might find yourself hanging from a tree like Daddy."

"They can't treat us like that no more. We're free, and we're living on land that we worked for." Ambrose puffed out his chest.

"I pray you're right about that, but I need you on duty as a lookout. I trust Femi, and I trust you, but I don't know Harold that well yet."

"Your real problem is you don't trust Robert." Ambrose nudged his sister while laughing.

"Careful. That's a queen you're touching," Mama Sue said as she came back into the room.

"Mama Sue, that's not fair. I'm your grandchild too."

"Sho' are. That's why I'm making sure you show proper respect for your sister." Mama Sue then swung around to Louella. "And another thing . . . I'm getting real sick and tired of that man always having something to say whenever you open your mouth."

Without even asking, Louella knew her grandmother was complaining about Robert. That man worked her nerves too, but she was at a loss for what to do. "William is a smart man. He'll figure out that his brother only has his own interests at heart."

Ambrose then told Louella, "Jerry Casey's a good man to have on patrol. He loves the Happy Land and would be honored to protect it."

Louella patted Ambrose on the shoulder. "That's good, brother. I didn't think of Jerry, but he would be perfect for this assignment."

Before they could say more, Femi came running back to the house and banged on the door like he was getting ready to tear it down. Louella swung the door open. "What's wrong? What's happened?"

"It's Abigail. Her time has come."

CHAPTER 26

Femi was a warrior at heart. Wasn't scared of much, but fear crept into his eyes now.

"Let me get Sooni. She'll know what to do." Louella grabbed her coat and made her way up the hill. Besides being a seamstress, Sooni also served as the midwife for the Happy Land. She had delivered Joshua and a few other babies these last years.

Sooni didn't live far from Abigail, so Louella knocked on the woman's door while eyeing Femi running in and out of his house, looking this way and that . . . at a loss for what to do for his wife.

When Sooni answered the door, Louella told her, "It's time. Abigail needs you."

"Let me get my bag." Sooni went back into her house, grabbed her bag, and then rushed over to Abigail's.

As Louella and Sooni were about to enter the house, a god-awful scream from Abigail caused Louella's hands to tremble. They rushed into the room. Femi was pacing the floor, biting his lip while Abigail panted and screamed.

Louella wanted to help, honest to goodness she did, but watching Abigail struggle to bring her child into this world sent images of the day she lost Lily swirling around her head. Abigail was swollen. Her stomach was bigger than any Louella had ever seen. She wondered if her friend might have some kind of contamination that swelled her body. A trembling went down her spine and seemed to shake her whole body. As much as she wanted to stay, she couldn't. Louella turned to Sooni. "Can you help her?"

Sooni set her bag down and rolled up her sleeves. "This baby's ready to bless the world with its presence."

Sooni spread Abigail's legs apart. Femi looked as if he would soon be in need of some smelling salts. Abigail screamed again. Louella backed her way toward the door.

"I'm gon' let you get started. Gon' run over to the church . . . Be right back." Louella bolted out the door, needing to be anywhere but in the presence of travail.

When she arrived at the church, William was standing behind the pulpit, practicing his Sunday sermon. He looked regal to her as he stood behind that pulpit belting out the words of Psalm 91:

"'He that dwelleth in the secret place of the most High shall abide under the shadow of the Almighty. I will say of the Lord, He is my refuge and my fortress: my God; in him will I trust . . . Thou shalt not be afraid for the terror by night; nor for the arrow that flieth by day.'"

Louella leaned her head against the doorpost, mesmerized. What kind of God could protect them in such a manner? And why hadn't He protected them from all they suffered? Where was this secret place that a body needed to dwell in to receive such benefits from the Lord? A hundred questions ran through her mind all at once.

She loved God, truly she did, but she didn't know if she could trust Him with her life. Didn't know if she could leave matters of import to Him and trust that things would turn out for their good.

William looked up from the Good Book. "Hey, I didn't see you come in."

"I was listening." She walked toward him. "I've read Psalm 91 before, but after being attacked by the Klan, it takes on a new meaning to me, and I'm trying to gain understanding." Her eyes shadowed with doubt. "Or even the trust level that you have. It amazes me how you trust God no matter what."

William closed the Bible and then sat down in one of the pews. He patted the seat next to him and beckoned her to sit. "Talk to me. What's troubling your mind?"

Life, death . . . fear. So much was on her mind, the undercurrents of it all threatened to sweep her away. "Abigail's in labor."

Creases appeared on William's forehead. "Why'd you come to the church? Thought you were supposed to help Abigail through her labor."

"Sooni's helping her." Louella lowered her head, ran her hand over her hair. "To tell you the truth, I ran out of her house. I'm terrified for her. What if she loses the baby?"

"You think she might lose the baby?"

"I hope I'm being irrational, but the way she screamed reminded me of how I screamed when I delivered Lily. And her belly is so big. What if she has some kind of contamination?"

"But you've had two children since then. Surely you know that travail goes hand in hand with birth."

Louella put a hand on William's shoulder. "I don't need you being reasonable right now." She leaned her head against his shoulder.

William rubbed her arm. "Can you tell me why Abigail's labor made you think of Lily?"

She closed her eyes as her mind took her back to a place and time that stole a piece of her. Louella saw herself on that bed of hay pushing and pushing. Screaming and screaming. Her screams were like Abigail's screams. When she opened her eyes, she exhaled. "I didn't scream like that when I delivered Waties or Joshua."

William patted Louella's hand, then stood. "I'll walk you over there. I know you don't want to let Abigail down."

Louella stayed in her seat. She looked up at William, wanting to turn away from the hand he offered. She didn't understand why God always gave her the hard road. What if Abigail lost the baby?

But then resolve set in. "Abigail was there for me on my darkest day. I need to be there for her." She took William's hand and stood.

As they walked out the door and headed up the hill toward Abigail's house, he said, "I want you to do something for me."

She held on to his arm as they walked. "I'm listening."

"Start believing for good things, even before you see them. Can you do that?"

"See, that's where me and you are just different. My experiences cause me to plan for the worst."

A small laugh escaped William's lips. "And you think my experiences were superior to yours? I ask you, do you really think I enjoyed being enslaved while my brother was free and traveled where he pleased?"

Louella bit down on her lip. "I'm sure that wasn't pleasant for you, but you were given so much more than the rest of us."

He stopped walking, put his hands on her shoulders, and looked her in the eye. "Slavery ate at my soul each and every day I woke up and had to call my own daddy 'Massa.' It ate at my soul when Overseer Brown hanged your daddy, and I wasn't able to do a thing to stop it."

Sighing deeply, William continued, "I may not have the welts on my back to clearly show the brutality suffered by enslaved people, but they beat me down too."

As she looked into William's eyes, the pain she saw there shook her. Why had she been acting as if there were levels to slavery? They had all suffered and been dehumanized. Putting a hand on William's cheek, she said, "I owe you a thousand apologies."

"I'll accept every one of 'em, but right now we need to get up this hill to see about Abigail."

"Oh my goodness. Yes, let's get moving." As they ran up the hill, they could hear Abigail calling on Jesus for help.

"Her labor is terrible." Louella bit down on her bottom lip.

"All the more reason she might need to hold your hand to get through it." William urged her forward.

"Yes, yes, that's right." She called on her Lord Jesus and the angels sent to do God's bidding to give her strength, then entered the home again. Abigail's screams and the hugeness of her belly were signs of goodness about to come forth.

Sweat beaded on Abigail's forehead. She panted, then looked over at Louella. "Wh-where y-you been?"

"I stepped out for a minute, but I'm here now."

"The baby's coming, but I can't get it out," Abigail cried.

"Push!" Sooni told her.

"It hurts!" Abigail screamed.

Louella looked around the room. Femi was pulling at his hair as he continued to pace the floor. She pointed toward Femi, then told William, "Take him outside."

The man was absolutely no help at all. What had she been thinking, to leave Abigail the way she had? Louella took Abigail's hand in hers. "It's okay that it hurts. That's a part of labor. Now push like Sooni told you so we can get that baby out."

"Feels like I'm dying," Abigail told her while looking as if she was about to lose consciousness.

"Hey, we'll have none of that. You're not dying today. Today, you're bringing new life into this world, and I'm gon' be right here to see it." Louella squeezed her hand. "Push, please."

Abigail grunted as she bore down and pushed. "Sing something," Abigail said and then started panting.

Louella sat down in the chair next to Abigail's bed. Still holding her friend's hand, she started singing . . .

"There is a balm in Gilead
To make the wounded whole;
There is a balm in Gilead
To heal the sin-sick soul."

As she sang, Louella noticed that Abigail pushed without all of the panting.

"Sometimes I feel discouraged
And deep I feel the pain;
In prayers the Holy Spirit
Revives my soul again."

"I've got the head!" Sooni yelled. "Push again."

Femi rushed back into the house. He took hold of Abigail's other hand, and as Louella continued her singing, he joined in and sang with her. A look of joy spread across Abigail's face the likes of which Louella had never seen on any woman in travail.

She pushed one more time, and her baby boy flew out.

"Hallelujah!" Femi jumped for joy.

"You did it, Abigail. You have a son," Louella told her as she listened for the cry. Sooni cut the umbilical cord and then took the baby to the basin to wash him.

Sooni said, "I'll have him cleaned up in no time."

Abigail's eyes went wild. She screamed. "I'm still in pain. Oh God, what's happening to me?"

Sooni turned to Louella. "Queen Louella, I need your help. We need to get the placenta out of Abigail. Can you help her push one more time?"

Sooni washed out the baby's mouth, and Louella heard him cry out. Not realizing she was holding her breath, she exhaled.

Abigail faltered as she tried to lift herself on her elbows. Louella told Femi, "Take her arm, and help me lift her a bit so she can push one more time."

Femi did as he was instructed. Abigail bore down, grunted, and pushed while Louella started singing again. But the placenta didn't gush out of Abigail's body. Instead, Louella saw what looked like . . .

"Is that a head?" Louella's eyes bulged. Did the placenta look like a head? What was going on?

"Oh God! Oh God! Oh God!" Abigail kept repeating as she panted and pushed, pushed and panted.

"It's another baby!" Louella yelled as she turned to Sooni.

Sooni pointed to her bag. "Grab another towel out of my bag and stand between her legs so you can catch the baby."

Louella grabbed the towel, then followed Sooni's instructions. But her mind was turning every which way on this one. Two babies? She'd never seen such a thing. But after a push and another push, another boy inched his way into the world.

CHAPTER 27

As Louella and William walked back home talking about the beauty of life and what they had witnessed with Abigail giving birth to two babies on the same day, an idea struck.

Louella put her hand in William's. "Abigail was in great pain, but when Femi and I sang to her, she was comforted."

"Yes, ma'am." William nodded. "The spirituals have a way of calming the soul, that's for sure."

"Sooo . . . I was thinking about those hateful men who rode up to our house the other night. Been pondering on ways that we could calm our neighbors, help them to see we don't mean them harm."

William held tight to Louella's arm as they maneuvered down the hill. "People fear change is all. Can't rightly see how we can fix that."

"Maybe we need to see if we can calm the people with music."

❧

Christmas was upon them, so Louella filled the wagon with children and a few adults from their choir and rode into town. A lot of carolers went door to door, but Louella wasn't sure they'd be welcomed and didn't want to put the children in harm's way, so they found an empty spot on the street and started singing "Silent Night." When that song was finished, they rocked back and forth, clapping their hands while singing "Joy to the World."

When they started singing, many walked on by and averted their eyes, pretending to be too busy to take a moment to receive a bit of Christmas cheer from them. But when they began their last song, that's when the crowd gathered. Louella saw smiles on faces that looked different from hers as she and the others belted out . . .

"O holy night, the stars are brightly shining.
It is the night of the dear Savior's birth . . ."

After Louella sang the solo parts of the song, the onlookers were clapping. But when they got to the chorus and the choir brought it up a notch, Louella saw women weeping as they sang . . .

"Fall on your knees. O hear the angel voices!
O night divine! O night when Christ was born.
O night, O holy night, O night divine."

"That was a wonderful sight," Louella said as they rode back to the Happy Land.

"Leave it to 'O Holy Night' to make grown women cry," Elmira said as she rode next to Louella.

"I'd say the event was a success!" Clara yelled from the back of the wagon where she sat with the children.

When they arrived home, Louella ran into the house, giddy from the joy they had brought to their neighbors. She wanted to share the events of the day with William, but Robert was sitting at the table with her husband. They appeared to be in a heated discussion.

William lifted his head as Louella closed the door. He walked over to her and helped take her coat off. "How was the caroling?"

Pulling off her white gloves, Louella smiled bright. "It was lovely. The people clapped for us, and some of them even cried." She picked up Joshua as he ran into her arms. "We're going back on Saturday."

Robert pounded a fist to the table and turned in William's direction. "When will you stop encouraging your wife in all this tomfoolery that profits us nothing?"

Louella's hands went to her hips. "What we're doing isn't foolish."

"I say it is." Robert stood. "Those women and children could be busying themselves with work right here in the Happy Land instead of singing for people they don't know and may never see again." He said the word *singing* as if it was a dirty and disgusting thing.

Louella's nostrils flared as she handed Joshua to William and stormed over to Robert. "I'm not the one neglecting things that need doing around here. You're the one we can't find half the time."

Robert opened his mouth to say something, but Louella swung back around to William. Her thumb jutted back at Robert. "Your brother would rather put our children to work than allow them to gain a proper education and have field trips where they sow good cheer."

"What kind of education is singing Christmas carols?"

Louella swung back around to her brother-in-law. She wagged a finger in his face. "Slavery days is over, *Massa*. You don't get to throw our children in the fields before they even know how to count to ten or read. There's a whole new world opening up for our children, and I'm gon' make sure they're prepared to go out there and grab a piece of the pie for themselves."

"William, do you hear how your wife disrespects me? I'm not going to stand here and be talked to like this."

"Please don't continue to stand here. This is our home. You're free to go to yours," Louella told him as her neck rocked back and forth.

"Louella, that's enough. It isn't right to disrespect a guest in our home like this." William's chest heaved.

Louella had meant every word she said to her brother-in-law, but her words had grieved her husband. She stepped away from

Robert, took Joshua out of William's arms, and said, "I'll leave you gentlemen to your business."

Louella took Joshua to his room. She kissed him on the forehead and laid him down. "Time for a nap."

"Don't want no nap," Joshua told her.

She pointed to Waties's bed, where her older son lay sound asleep. "Your brother took his nap, so it's your turn."

Louella went to her room and settled in. The day had been tiring. All she wanted to do was lie down and rest before thinking about what came next. But no sooner had her eyelids closed as she began drifting than William came barreling into their bedroom demanding her attention.

"This thing between you and Robert has got to end."

Sighing, Louella sat up. "Did you tell your brother that, or am I the only one needing to bend?"

"Don't start with me. Robert objecting to your little project didn't give you cause to speak to him in that manner." William sat down on the bed and took his shoes off.

"It's not a *little* project. The Happy Land singers will help our neighbors see us as human beings. Then as they see our humanness, it is my prayer that they come to see we're entitled to the same benefits they enjoy."

William's demeanor softened. He walked over to Louella's side of the bed and sat down next to her. "You're trying to keep us safe. I know that, and I appreciate everything you're doing, but you got to learn how to disagree without being disagreeable."

William put his hand to the back of his neck and rubbed the spot that seemed to bother him every time he helped out with the plowing. Louella said, "Lay down on your stomach and let me take care of that kink in your neck."

He took off his shirt and stretched out on the bed. Louella kneaded his back with her fists from the top of his buttocks all the way up his spine until she reached his neck. She then used her fingers to massage his neck and shoulders until he moaned as if her touch was everything.

He rolled over, looking relaxed. "Queen of my heart, I thank you for ministering to your husband."

She leaned forward and touched her lips to his. Soft. She loved kissing him . . . loved being with him.

"You tired?" he asked with a cheeky grin.

"I'm whatever you need me to be," she told him and then snuggled in beside him.

❧

On Saturday, Louella and the Happy Land Choir went caroling again. This time they brought some of the Happy Land Liniment so they wouldn't be accused of not being productive. They sang and then sold the liniment, then sang another song. They continued the back-and-forth for about three hours.

When they were ready to pack up and go, the blond-haired man who'd purchased forty tins of liniment came to their table. "It's you," he said.

Louella couldn't tell if he was happy to see her or if he was there to complain about the product she'd sold him. They were trying to get the people in this town to trust them. It wouldn't do to have someone bad-mouthing her. They had made a little over two dollars today. If he complained, she would hand him the money and go.

"How are you doing, sir? It's been a while since I've seen you."

"I've been back and forth to the general store, but you never came back."

That's because the owner is a Ku Klux Klan member, Louella thought, but instead said, "We found a new location."

He reached in his pocket. "How many tins do you have?"

Louella counted the tins and then looked up at him. "We have ten left."

"I'll take them." He handed her a dollar and said, "Keep the change."

People 'round these parts rarely told them to keep the change. Money was always hard to come by, so people held on to what they had. Louella was thankful he wasn't complaining. "Thank you."

"No. Thank you." He smiled and then held out a hand to her. "My name is Dr. David Morris, and I'd love to introduce you to my mother."

Louella's eyebrow lifted. "Sir?" Did he ask her to meet his mother?

He pointed down the street. "We don't live far from here. My mom is the person I purchased your liniment for, and she's been asking about you since the first time she rubbed that cream on her hands."

It was strange to Louella's ears—a white man inviting her into his home. What if he was a member of the Ku Klux Klan and was plotting to do her harm?

"Your whole group can come if you'd be more comfortable. Maybe even sing a song with my mother."

Louella turned to Clara. "He wants us to go to his house to see his mother."

"His mother?" Clara questioned with a frown.

Dr. Morris put a hand over his mouth and laughed. "I promise I'm not some crazed killer. I heal people. I do not harm them."

Something in the doctor's eyes put Louella at ease. His mother used her liniment. Maybe the lady would continue to order if she met with her. "Okay. We were packing up to go. Let us put our table in the wagon, and we'll follow you."

❦

The house was white with a wraparound porch and three tall pillars on either side of the double-door entry. There were ten steps that led up to the porch. It was the stateliest home Louella had ever laid eyes on. And Dr. Morris marched all six of the Happy Land singers right through the front door like welcomed guests.

The high ceiling in the foyer and the spiral staircase took Louella's breath away. But it was the sweet sound of music coming from the grand piano beneath the staircase that enveloped her with warmth.

Dr. Morris urged them forward toward the piano, where a gray-haired lady sat playing it as if touching the keys and hearing the music breathed life into her.

"Mother, I brought someone for you to meet," Dr. Morris said as he stood to the side of the piano.

She stopped playing, gave her son a gracious smile, then turned toward Louella and her singers. Awe and wonder etched across her face. She had a kind face. She didn't have that superior tilt to her neck and those tight lips that Mary always had.

"Well, isn't this a nice surprise. Where do you all come from?"

Louella told her, "We live farther up the mountain over by Serepta Davis's place."

The woman slapped her hands to her skirt. "Serepta and I were once very good friends. But neither of us get around much these days. I haven't seen her in years. I hope she's doing well."

Louella nodded. "She is."

"Oh joy. So what brings you all here today?"

Dr. Morris told his mother, "Louella is the woman I purchased the liniment from."

At his words, the woman put one hand on the piano stool and held the other out to her son. He helped her stand up. She then went to Louella and hugged her. "God bless you. I'm so thankful my son ran into you."

Louella stiffened at the woman's touch. Had she ever been hugged by a white woman? No, not a single recollection came to mind. But as this woman blessed her and thanked her, Louella leaned into the embrace.

When the embrace ended, a warmth of acceptance spread through Louella. But could she trust what she was feeling? The Klan were certainly hateful men, but . . . Serepta hadn't been like the white folks she'd come up with. Maybe this woman wasn't either.

Dr. Morris held up the tins in his hand. "I purchased more."

His mother clapped. "I can share some with my friends."

Clara leaned close to Louella. "Are you okay?"

"I-I—" When words escaped her, Louella nodded. So many thoughts and emotions swirled inside her. She didn't know how to make sense of it all.

Dr. Morris then turned to Louella and said, "After my father died, my mother became so despondent, I thought we were going to lose her as well. Her hands hurt terribly. She could no longer play this piano. All my life, I've known how much joy playing the piano brought my mother. So when I saw you on the street, selling your liniment, claiming to cure rheumatism—"

Louella held up a finger. "I made no such claim."

Dr. Morris smiled. "I stand corrected. The lady who was with you made that claim. But anyway, I gave the ointment to my mother, and within a week, she was back to playing her beloved piano and finding joy in the world again. We wanted to thank you."

His words brought comfort to Louella's soul. "I'm thankful we played a part in your mama's healing."

His mother went back to the piano. "Would you all like to join me in a song?"

Louella turned to her group. Heads nodded; grins spread across their faces at the thought of singing alongside a piano. "We'd love to," she told the woman.

Joy filled the room as Mrs. Morris led them in song. Laughter bubbled up in Louella. Actual laughter . . . around white folks. But then the front door opened and wiped away all the merriment.

Freddie Morris walked in carrying a crate of apples. "The

bushels of red apples came in today. I know how you love them, so I brought you some."

Louella quickly grabbed two of the children and told Clara to grab the other two. "We best be heading back."

Mrs. Morris stopped playing. Her eyes were filled with confusion. "What happened? I thought we were having fun."

"We were." Louella eyed Freddie. "But the children need to get home for supper. I've kept them out too long as it is."

Louella rushed them to the door and was headed down the street when Freddie ran toward them. "Leave us be, Mr. Morris. We will not bother that nice lady again."

Louella and Clara helped the children get in the wagon. "You weren't bothering her. My mother has been asking to meet you for a while now. But I was too ashamed to tell my brother that I knew where you were."

Louella swung around, her back against the wagon, daggers shooting from her eyes. "You should be ashamed. I thought you were a decent man."

"I am a decent man," he declared.

"Oh yeah. Decent men always go around in blackface, scaring people away from their homes."

Clara climbed in the wagon and Louella did the same. She grabbed the reins, preparing to leave.

Freddie stuffed his hands in the pockets of his overalls. "Maybe I shouldn't have gone up the mountain with those fellows. But they said you and your people were stealing land while white men were going homeless in these parts."

"Did they also tell you my people spent years knocking trees down so we could have the space to build our homes? Which of your white men would have done that?"

The lowering of his head and the way his eyes no longer met hers was answer enough. She rode away, anger pricking her heart. Once again, the color of her skin meant she was doing wrong, even when she wasn't. Yesterday, that would have set her soul ablaze. But today, she had been in the company of someone who treated her as if color didn't matter.

Things would get better for her people. They would get the respect they deserved in this world. One day at a time, one person at a time. And frankly, it mattered less and less what others thought of her. Louella was a queen, and queens didn't bow to the foolishness of the world.

CHAPTER 28

Better to be on a rooftop than in the house with a brawling woman. Since William had given Robert the second-in-command position, things had been up and down with Louella. One moment she was smiling at him, the next moment she was snapping like a hungry alligator.

William rose early in the morning and went to his office at the church. They were knocking down more trees today, so he would make his way farther up the hill in a little while. Right now, he wanted to commune with his Lord. He opened his Bible and began reading from Psalm 23: *"The Lord is my shepherd . . ."*

After reading the Word, William left his office and went into the sanctuary. He kneeled in front of one of the pews to pray. He had no idea how long he'd been on his knees when Femi rushed in, needing his attention.

"I'm sorry to bother you, King, but we've got a problem at the gristmill."

William got up and dusted off his pants. "What's Robert saying about it?"

Femi shook his head. "Haven't seen him in a couple of days."

"I'll meet you over there." William got in his wagon and headed up the hill. Larry expected him this morning, so he needed to let his foreman know what was going on. He pulled up to the worksite and got down from his buggy.

"How's it going?" William asked Larry.

Larry said, "Well, I can give you the good news or the bad news, depending on which you want first."

"Hit me with the bad first." William braced himself, not wanting to deal with another problem before he could sort things out at the gristmill.

"A tree fell on Hank and the wagon we was using. Hank's got a broken leg, and one of the wheels broke off the wagon."

A worksite where trees were constantly falling was a dangerous place. Thankfully, they hadn't dealt with many accidents, but every now and again . . . "I hate to hear that about Hank. I'll check on him when I get back from the gristmill."

Larry's forehead crinkled. "Thought you was working with us today."

"I am. I'll be back after I check on an issue over there." As William got in his wagon and rode away, he saw Larry scratch his head, then roll his eyes.

Everyone in the Happy Land knew that Robert handled problems at the gristmill and managed the supplies needed for farming. Since Robert had once owned a farm, William thought those two assignments would work well for his brother, but Robert seemed more interested in being a man of leisure than doing the actual work it took to run the Happy Land.

When William arrived at the basement of the gristmill, the men were standing around with their hands in their pockets, looking up at the green chute that hung down through the ceiling from the floors above. The green chute carried the wheat to the two millstones that worked to grind the wheat into flour.

The millstones were flat and round with an opening at the top where the wheat fell from the green chute into them. The millstones sat one on top of the other. One of the millstones was called the runner. The workers turned the large wheel and the smaller wheel that was mounted close to the stones to grind the wheat.

The small wheel adjusted the distance between the two stones, fine-tuning it to create the best grade of flour, while the large wheel controlled the gate that delivered the flowing water needed to propel the turbines and allow the runner stone to work.

William looked up as the other men were doing. If there was a clog in the green chute, there might be too much wheat in the stones, which meant the turbine might not be pushing the water forward.

"I think we've got a problem," William told Femi and then walked the length of the gristmill scratching his head.

Where was Robert when he needed him? Having run a farm, his brother had used the services of the gristmill many times. He was more skilled to deal with this problem, but once again, he was missing in action.

William, Femi, and a couple of others spent hours going from the third floor to the basement trying to figure out how to fix the problem. When the problem couldn't be found, William sent one of the workers to get Tom Davis. He and his father had owned the gristmill before the Happy Landers took it over.

When Tom arrived, it took exactly twenty minutes for him to say, "I can tell you right now, you're not going to like what I'm about to say."

"How bad can it be?" Silently, William was praying that it wasn't as bad as the look on Tom's face.

"Looks like one of the turbines stopped working. It'll need to be replaced."

It was as bad as Tom looked. "How did this happen?"

Tom pointed toward the millstones. "You can't run those stones empty. Got to make sure there's always some grain in them. My bet is your boys been emptying out the grain from those stones every night. Then starting them back up without anything in them."

After Tom left, William went back to the worksite and helped chop some wood to take his mind off the money they would lose while waiting on the turbine to get replaced.

Supervision was needed at the gristmill. If Robert had been on his job rather than gallivanting off to God knew where, someone would've been able to instruct the workers on proper treatment of the equipment. Sighing deeply, he chopped the last log, then got in his wagon and rode over to Hank and Mirabel's house. He jumped down from his wagon and knocked on the door.

William stepped back, eyes registering surprise when Louella opened the door. "What you doing here?"

"Helping Mirabel get Hank settled. What took you so long to get here?"

Besides preaching, William also visited the sick. He thought it important to pray for healing and to let the sick or infirmed know that they would be cared for and still receive their normal monthly disbursement of funds while recovering.

Louella knew his routine, which was the reason she was standing in front of him with questioning eyes.

"There was a problem at the gristmill. It kept me away from the worksite for hours."

Her hand went to her hip. "Why should it have kept you? Robert takes care of problems at the gristmill, right?"

William's arm felt like a heavy weight as he lifted it to point toward the door, then used his other hand to rub at the back of his neck. "Can we discuss this later? I need to see Hank."

Louella's lips pursed but she stepped back and allowed him entry. William walked to the bedroom where Hank lay with his leg wrapped and elevated. Mirabel was standing to the side of the bed. William nodded in her direction. "Good evening, Mirabel. Sorry I'm late in getting here."

Mirabel came over to him, wrapped her arms around him, then placed a kiss on his cheek. "We're grateful for your visit. Let me get you a cup of tea."

When she left the room, William grinned at Hank. "I hear a tree got the best of you today."

Hank harrumphed. "Ain't no tree big enough to get the best of me. It was that wagon rolling on top of me that did it."

"Well, whichever way it occurred, I was sorry to hear of it." William sat with Hank for a little while, then prayed for him.

As he and Louella were leaving the house, he made sure to tell Mirabel, "When you pick up your disbursement later this week, Hank's disbursement will be waiting on you as well."

Mirabel patted William on the shoulder. "You're a blessing, King William. A true blessing."

He rode home with his queen by his side, wondering how much of a blessing she thought he was. She hadn't said a word to him during the ride, preferring to look at the scenery rather than face him. When he pulled the buggy in front of their home, she didn't wait for him to help her down as she normally would but got down and stomped her way into the house.

His wife was spoiling for a fight, but all he wanted to do was lie down and get some rest. Rubbing the arm he'd wielded the axe with, he went inside the lion's den.

Mama Sue greeted him with warmth as he walked in. "Sit down at that table and let me get a good meal in you before you go back to that room with the queen."

William grinned at Mama Sue and sat down as she instructed.

She put a bowl of beans and corn bread in front of him, then she leaned down and whispered, "That message you taught last week will probably help you some tonight."

Last Sunday, he'd preached about a soft answer turning away wrath. "How mad do you think she is?"

"From the way she stormed into that room and slammed the door, you'll be turning away a whole heap of wrath tonight." Mama Sue patted him on the back and then left him to eat.

All William wanted to do was sleep, but he took his time eating his beans while trying to figure a way out of the argument that was sure to come. When his belly was full, he pushed away from the table and left the house. He walked over to the church flower bed, where Louella had planted all sorts of beautiful flowers.

He picked some white irises and purple violets out of the flower bed, twined them together, and then headed home. Louella was standing on the porch, hands on hips as she tapped her foot on the floor.

Before she could say anything to him, he bowed to her and presented the flowers. "I thought you needed something pretty to put a smile on your beautiful face tonight."

Louella hesitated but then reached for the flowers. She brought them to her nose and inhaled as an easy grin spread across her face.

William stood on the steps watching her smell the flowers, praying he wouldn't end up on the rooftop this night.

"You got pain in your shoulders again?" she asked as she held on to the flowers.

He nodded. "Been troubling me since I left the worksite."

She waved him toward the front door. "Well, get on in here and let me fix you up with a massage."

❦

The next morning as William sat in his office at the church reading the newspaper, Robert came in with a peace offering of his own. He put the peach cobbler on William's desk and said, "You've got to try this. I brought it back from Spartanburg just for you."

William ignored the cobbler. He leaned against the back of his seat and folded his arms. "Is that where you've been?"

Robert held up a hand. "I know you're displeased, but I was only gone a few days—not long enough for anyone to miss me."

"The workers at the gristmill missed you. Their lack of training caused one of the turbines to break down."

Robert's shoulders rolled inward. The look on his face was crestfallen. "I'm sorry, William. I didn't mean to mess things up. I thought my men had everything under control. I'll head out there now."

Robert turned, getting ready to walk out of the church. William stopped him. "No need. Femi will take the lead at the gristmill from now on."

Robert swung back around. "You can't give Femi my job. Others will think I can't do the work."

William stood, pressed his lips together, then said, "Your irresponsible behavior has cost us enough. I can't afford to keep you at the gristmill."

"I'm not irresponsible," Robert objected.

"Prove it." William puffed out his chest as he blew out hot air. He then handed Robert the newspaper and pointed toward an article about the conviction of several Klansmen who'd been terrorizing South Carolina.

"Good," Robert responded after reading parts of the article. "President Grant is finally doing something about those terrorists."

"Real good for us, brother. With those Klansmen being arrested, we should be able to purchase more land, and I'll need you for the meeting since John Goodwin prefers discussing business with you."

"Just tell me when; I'll be there." Robert drew a cross above his heart with his index finger. "I won't let you down."

William sighed, then nodded. "You still have your position in the field, so go check on things over there."

CHAPTER 29

The dust of winter snow had lifted. Spring was shining through the mountains' peaks. Months after the Christmas caroling, Louella received friendly greetings from those who remembered the Happy Land Choir when she went into town.

Even John Goodwin came to the house, shook William's hand, and said, "Things have really improved around here since you Happy Landers showed up."

Sweet relief also came to them when President Grant finally got tired of the violence the Ku Klux Klan perpetrated against Black people and declared martial law. By December of 1871, about six hundred Klansmen had been arrested. Klan terrorism in their neck of the woods significantly decreased after a few of them were convicted.

William was pleased with the convictions. It felt like this was the perfect time to purchase more land, so he scheduled a meeting with Mrs. Serepta.

That meeting would take place in a few days, but today he told Louella to put on her best dress. He was taking her for a ride. Mama Sue, Mirabel, and Ruby were spending the day knitting and helping Miss Saddie boil cloth in indigo and madder root to add some color to it, so she asked Elmira to watch the children for her.

"Of course I will, Auntie." Elmira pointed toward Robert's house. "Let me go check on my dad while you get dressed."

Louella hugged her niece, then went to her bedroom and took out a yellow dress that had white frilly lace at the top. Miss Saddie told her this dress was for sunshiny days. Louella even had a yellow-and-white hat and gloves to match.

She got dressed and walked back into the keeping room. The kids were seated at the table, and Elmira was fixing them a snack. "I thought you were visiting with your daddy for a spell."

Elmira rolled her eyes. "He wasn't home."

"He was there yesterday. I saw him talking with Harold."

"I know. I told him I'd come see him today, but I guess he had more important things to do."

Louella frowned at that. Nothing was more important than a child, even one who was full-grown. "If you're frustrated, you should talk to your daddy."

Elmira huffed. She put bowls of berries in front of Waties and Joshua. "It doesn't make sense that I have to tell my own daddy he should spend more time with me."

Louella's daddy had been there for her. William was there for Waties and Joshua. She didn't understand why Robert preferred spending so much time outside of the Happy Land instead of being here with Elmira.

"I mean," Elmira continued, "he left me when I was a baby. You'd think he'd spend time getting to know me. But honestly, I have a better relationship with you and Uncle William than I do with my own father."

William walked in as Louella was searching her mind for something that would bring comfort to her niece. He took one look at Louella, then put two fingers in his mouth and whistled.

"I'm a lucky man. Yes, I am." He took her hand and twirled her around. "Boys, is your mother not the prettiest woman in all the South?"

Louella put her hands on her hips. "What about the North, East, and West?"

William bowed to her. "I stand corrected." He turned to their children. "Your mother is the prettiest woman in the whole world."

"I hope I'm at least second."

Grinning, William bowed to Elmira. "You most certainly are, princess."

Elmira nudged Louella. "See what I mean?"

"Stop fretting and speak your mind to your daddy." Louella kissed the boys on their cheeks and left the house arm in arm with her king.

Sitting next to him in the buggy, breathing in the fresh scent of spring, Louella set her mind on enjoying the day and appreciating all that was to come. "Where we riding off to?"

Holding on to the reins, William glanced over at Louella. "I was told about a lady selling fine fabrics outside of a general store in Spartanburg."

Louella touched the lace of her dress. "What kind of fabric do you think this dress was made of?"

"You're my queen, Louella. I want to give you more than the few pretty dresses you possess. You should have a month or two of fine Sunday dresses."

She put her hand on his arm and let it slide up and down. There weren't many easy days in the Happy Land. There was always land to be cleared, fields to be plowed, children to teach, and on and on.

Today, there was only time to enjoy with her husband. She leaned back in her seat, head resting on William's arm as the sun beat down on them. "It's been a long time since I've seen a day as beautiful as this."

"You deserve a thousand days like this."

"And you deserve all the love I have to give." After all these years, Louella was ashamed that this was as close of a declaration of love her mouth could give. But she prayed that he felt her love in every way she tried to show it. Why had she ever given a second thought to marrying this man? She was surely blessed by God when William Montgomery took a shine to her.

Louella found three bolts of fabric that she absolutely loved. William paid the woman and then put the fabric in the back of the wagon. As he did so, he remembered the day he saw those people outside of the saloon in Mississippi selling fine fabrics. He hadn't been able to afford luxuries back then but had desired to give such things to Louella ever since.

After shopping, William took Louella to a boardinghouse with a small restaurant on the lower level. "Robert told me this place serves some of the best smothered pork chops he's ever tasted."

"You better not let Maribel and Mama Sue hear y'all saying this. We'll be fending for ourselves, and I don't cook as well as they do."

"You cook just fine." William put a hand on her lower back as they walked into the boardinghouse.

"You folks looking for a room or a meal?"

William smiled at the woman in a brown skirt and white apron. "My brother told me y'all have the best smothered pork chops in the South, so I brought my lovely wife to sample them."

She showed them to a table. "You're in luck. I cooked pork chops, rice, and gravy today."

"You cook and serve the people?" Louella asked as William held out a seat for her.

"I do it all." The woman held out a hand to Louella and William. "I'm Lidia. I own the place."

William said, "I'm William, and this is Louella."

Lidia took a step back, gave them the once-over. "Who did you say your brother was?"

"Robert Montgomery. He raved about your food."

Her hand went to her mouth. "Oh my good Lord. Are you telling me I'm standing in front of a real live king and queen?" She started fussing around the room, wiping tables off, retucking her shirt in her long brown skirt.

Louella reached out and touched Lidia's arm. "Please don't fuss over us. We're just William and Louella, and we're so happy to meet you."

Lidia took a couple of deep breaths and fanned herself. "Ain't never been in the presence of royalty before."

William laughed. "Neither have we. Believe me when I tell you, we came out of slavery just as you did. We're not ones to put on airs."

Lidia bowed in front of them, then smiled as she left the room. She returned with two plates and a bowl of corn bread. "I wish I had cooked something fancier today. But here's your pork chop plates."

William said grace over the food and then they dug in. The smell of the gravy covering the rice and pork chops wafted upward into William's nostrils. He cut a piece of the chop, scooped some rice and gravy on his fork, and tasted it. "*Mmm.* Oh my goodness. Is this what I've been missing?"

Louella's eyes were closed like she was taking a moment to savor the experience. When she opened her eyes, she pointed her fork at him. "Don't be disrespectful. The food we're served in the Happy Land is very good."

"It really is," William agreed, "but we've never been served pork chops with gravy like this. This will have to go on the menu."

Louella was busy chewing. When she finished, she licked her lips and pointed toward her plate. "This thick gravy is so good." She reached for a piece of corn bread.

Lidia entered the keeping room with some lemon water. She put the glasses on the table.

William said, "Mrs. Lidia, can you give my wife the recipe for this delicious gravy?"

Putting a hand to her chest, Lidia asked, "You really like it?"

"We do. It would be a blessing to serve this in the Happy Land."

Lidia gave William a quizzical once-over. "If you don't mind my saying so, King, you and your brother are complete opposites."

William scratched by his hairline. "We're not so different."

William caught the twist of Louella's lips and the lift of her brow as Lidia said, "You and your wife are humble, but that brother of yours spends his time at the saloon down the street. By the time he comes here for a meal and his room, let's just say he's hard to deal with at times."

William's eyebrow lifted. He quickly brought it back down as he glanced over at Louella. Robert was selfish and entitled, but now William discovered that his brother was bringing shame to them with his drunken behavior. His emotions were all over the place as he tried to process this information.

After Lidia walked away, Louella put a hand over William's. "You okay?"

Measuring his words, William said, "Robert worries me at times." His brother was a poor second-in-command, but he couldn't admit that to his wife.

When Louella didn't respond, he added, "I need him for our meeting with Mrs. Serepta in a couple of days." He rubbed his forehead with three of his fingers. "I don't understand why he's down here running around as if he has no responsibilities."

"That's your brother." Louella waved a dismissive hand in the air. "He doesn't care about anyone but himself."

Mrs. Lidia handed Louella a piece of paper with the gravy recipe on it. "The secret is the onions and seasonings I use."

"I thank you for your kindness," Louella said as she held on to the recipe.

"Now, I don't go 'round handing out my recipes, but y'all special," Mrs. Lidia told them.

When they finished eating, William helped Louella back into

the wagon. While driving up the dusty road, Mrs. Lidia's words about Robert played over and over in his head. Robert's near whiteness provided a service to them from time to time, but with it came downright flakiness.

They were about to pass the saloon. Robert's horse and buggy were outside, as Lidia had stated. William pulled his buggy next to Robert's and hopped down.

"What are you doing?"

"I need to speak with Robert."

Louella leaned forward, trepidation on her face. "Wait until he comes back to the Happy Land. God only knows what's going on inside that saloon."

"Just stay here. I'll be right back." William stepped inside the saloon. There were at least ten tables with four chairs to each table. Men were drinking. Rowdy, boisterous laughs and cheers were heard from one side of the saloon to the other.

William scanned the room. He didn't see Robert at any of the tables. He walked over to the bar. A dark-skinned man with a long salt-and-pepper beard stood behind the bar pouring whiskey into a shot glass.

"What's your pleasure?" the bartender asked.

"I'm looking for my brother, Robert Montgomery." William pointed toward the outside, then raised his voice so he could be heard above the noise. "His horse and buggy are outside, but I don't see him."

"Robert Montgomery is your brother?" The bartender gave him a doubting-Thomas twist of the lip.

"He's been my brother all his life. I need to speak with him before I head home. Have you seen him?"

The bartender handed a man the whiskey glass, then jutted his thumb backward toward a door behind the bar. William figured that was the room where the gambling took place. He opened the door and found Robert seated at a round table with cards in his hand.

Three other men were at the table with him, smoking, drinking, and using language that burned William's ears. He stepped over to the table as Robert threw a card down. "What you doing here?" Robert slurred his words.

Holy indignation filled William. He took hold of Robert's arm. "Get up."

"Hey, let me go. I'm about to win this game."

William took the cards out of Robert's hand and threw them on the table.

One of the men at the table looked to Robert, then put a hand below the table. "You need me to handle this?"

Robert shook his hand. "Family business." He stood and walked over to the door with William. He whispered, "Get out of here. This is no place for you."

"It's no place for you either. Why do you come to this city making a spectacle of yourself?"

"Spectacle?" Robert's eyebrow shot up. "What am I doing wrong?" He stumbled and fell back against the door. "Enjoying a drink every now and then and a few games of chance makes me a bad guy?"

William reached out and caught Robert, steadied him, and then opened the door. He walked Robert out of the saloon. As they stood next to Robert's wagon, William told him, "You're embarrassing yourself. You're supposed to be a leader for the people in the Happy Land. Is this how you lead?"

"You're the king. I'm just your brother." Robert looked this way and that. "Who am I leading?"

"Is that what this is about? You're jealous that I'm leading our kingdom, so you fill yourself with strong drink and throw good money away?"

Robert laughed in his face and then started shouting. "Why would I be jealous of you? I was born free. I owned a farm. I never had to serve my father like a slave."

William's head jolted backward as if being punched. "It wasn't *like* a slave . . . I *was* enslaved. And every day I spent serving our father, I thanked God you never had to." William's eyes filled with sorrow. "Grow up, Robert. Our mother sacrificed everything so that you could be born free." Pointing at the saloon, William shook his head. "This is how you repay her?"

Robert flung his hands, lost his footing, then grabbed hold of the back of his wagon. "Our mother is dead, but I still hear her voice telling me how much I owe her. '*Go out in this world and make something of yourself, Robert. Don't let my sacrifice be in vain,*'" he mimicked.

"She sacrificed for both of us. Why do her words cut you so?" William's mother had told them that she wanted to run away but had stayed for her children. Took everything Montgomery dished out for her children.

"You weren't the one who reminded her so much of our father that she couldn't stand to look at you at times."

"That was a long time ago." William patted Robert on the shoulder. "Let it go."

Robert pointed toward the saloon. "I let it go in there."

William walked to his wagon. Louella was biting down on her lip as if she wanted to say something. He grabbed hold of the reins, then turned back to his brother. "If you'd rather drink your sorrows away, then stay here and I'll find someone else to do the job you keep running from."

CHAPTER 30

The meeting with Serepta was this afternoon. Robert hadn't returned home since William laid into him for shirking his responsibilities. The whole incident had left Louella without words. She'd been proud of William for finally seeing Robert for the irresponsible man he was, but the way Robert blamed his mother for his drinking had turned her stomach. She hoped he'd stay in Spartanburg and not attend the meeting today.

Whether Robert showed up or not, Louella needed to get out of bed and get organized. But as she woke, her five-year-old son, Waties, was jumping on the bed, shouting, "Breakfast, Mommy."

She rubbed her eyes as she lifted and rested on her elbow, glancing around the room. William wasn't in bed, but Joshua was sleeping next to her. He had snuggled into a ball. A smile crept across her face. She would love to stay home with them today, but there was too much to do in the kingdom.

"Didn't Mama Sue fix your breakfast?"

Waties jumped on the bed again. "She won't get up. I'm hungry."

Last night Mama Sue had complained of tiredness and then gone to bed. Louella decided to let her grandmother rest. Joshua was still asleep, but Waties was ready for breakfast. Waties was always hungry.

"What's for breakfast?" he asked.

"Grits and eggs this morning." She put a finger under Waties's chin, brought him close, and kissed his cheek. "And maybe a piece of salt meat if you're good."

"Yay!" Waties got off the bed and followed Louella into the keeping room while Joshua stayed rolled in a ball on her bed.

"Have a seat at the table, Waties. Let me check on Mama Sue, and then I'll get your breakfast."

It seemed a little too quiet in the house for Louella. Mama Sue was normally at the hearth working on her meals before Louella got out of bed. But the seasons were changing. It was warm during the day but cooler at night. She wondered if her grandmother had come down with a cold.

"Mama Sue," Louella called as she walked toward the left side of the house where her grandmother's bedroom was.

No answer.

Louella put her hand on the doorknob. "Mama Sue." She opened the door. Her grandmother was lying in the bed, but she hadn't stirred. Louella's heartbeat pounded in her ears; blood pumped faster and faster.

She inched over to the bed.

From the way Mama Sue was lying on her side facing the wall, Louella couldn't tell if she was breathing or not. Fear clenched her heart as she reached out and touched her grandmother's arm. She was hot—hot was a good sign. Too cold could mean death. But her grandmother was hot and clammy.

Louella shook her. "Mama Sue, wake up."

Mama Sue's eyes fluttered, but she could barely lift her head. "I'm feeling poorly this morning," she said.

"You're burning up, but don't worry. I'll take care of you." Louella backed out of the room. Concern etched her face. She went outside and picked some of the catnip plant that she grew on the side of the house. Started a fire to boil some water.

She poured some of the substance in a cup and took it to her grandmother. "I know you don't want to get up, but I need to raise your head a bit so you can drink this tea."

Mama Sue's eyes were slitted. She didn't respond.

Louella sat on the bed next to her grandmother. She adjusted her body so Mama Sue had her back against her chest and then she put the cup to her lips. "Sip on this for me."

Mama Sue's lips parted as Louella pressed the cup to her lips. She sipped a few drops but then fell back to sleep.

Louella stood. Sweat dripped off her grandmother like a waterfall. She would need to get that fever down before she could get as much catnip in her as she would need to break this sickness.

Rushing back into the keeping room, Louella saw Waties at the table. She touched his forehead to see if he had a fever. He wasn't hot.

Joshua! He didn't get up when she mentioned breakfast.

She went back to her bedroom. Joshua was still curled up in a ball. She touched him. He was hot. Why hadn't she noticed that earlier?

Waties yelled for her. "Breakfast, Mommy!"

"I'm coming. I need to get your daddy." Louella ran out of the house and into the church. She figured William had gone in there to get ready for his Sunday morning sermon, but he wasn't inside the church.

Louella ran back outside and was getting ready to find someone to go into town for a block of ice when Femi pulled his wagon up to their door. Ambrose was riding up front with him.

Ambrose jumped down the moment the wagon stopped moving, then Femi got down. They both went to the back of the wagon. Things moved in slow motion as they hopped into the bed of the wagon and lifted William up.

It felt like she was wearing cement boots with each step she took toward that wagon. "What happened to him?"

Femi looked befuddled. He hunched his shoulders. "King William came to the gristmill this morning to check on our progress. I turned toward the mill to show him how that thing has been locking up again. The next thing I knew, he was on the ground."

Louella touched William's arm. He was hot and clammy like her grandmother. "Take him to our room and lay him down, then I need you boys to ride into town and get me a block of ice."

"Yes, ma'am. Right away." Femi and Ambrose laid William on the bed.

As they were leaving, Louella yelled, "Tell Abigail that I need her to come get Waties! He's the only one not ill, and I need him to stay that way."

Ambrose said, "Hand him to me. We'll drop him at Abigail's as we head into town."

Louella brought Waties out of the house and sat him between Femi and Ambrose. "Tell Abigail that he hasn't eaten yet, so he might be a little cranky."

The oxen pulled the wagon up the hill. She went back in the house, poured catnip tea in two more cups. She woke Joshua and had him sip some tea.

Joshua didn't seem as out of it as her grandmother and husband, nor was his skin clammy. She took him to his room and put him back in his bed.

Joshua whined, "Mommy." He held out his hands to her.

Louella wrapped her son in her arms. She kissed his neck. "Mommy will be right back. Lay here like a good boy for me."

"My lips hurt."

"They're cracked." She had some beeswax, so she put that on Joshua's lips, then she went to her grandmother's room and put some on her cracked lips as well. She had her grandmother sit up and drink a little more tea. "I'll have an ice block here in a little while, and I'll be able to cool you off."

Her grandmother lay back down and moaned. Louella didn't know if Mama Sue understood what she was saying to her. But she had three sick ones to deal with, so she couldn't stay.

She went back to her bedroom, helped William sit up, and

pressed the cup of catnip tea against his lips. "Drink this, my darling. This will fix you up in no time."

But William couldn't open his mouth to receive the tea. She had never seen her husband so helpless . . . so weak. She needed to bring his fever down. She grabbed several rags and wet them, put one on Mama Sue's head, another on Joshua's head, and the third on William's head. As the cloth took on the heat from their bodies, she added cool water to the rags and placed them back on their foreheads.

On her third trip of replacing hot cloths with cool cloths, she looked to heaven. "Dear Lord, I need You. Nothing I'm doing is working."

When she finished praying, there was a knock at the door. Clara and Rachel were standing on her porch. She opened the door and the ladies came in.

"We heard you got a house full of sickness on your hands," Rachel said.

"We came to help," Clara added.

"Oh, praise God." Louella hugged the women and then set them to work taking care of Joshua and her grandmother. "Once the ice gets here, we'll be able to cool them off faster, but for now, we have to keep a cool, wet cloth to their heads."

"We might need more than one ice block," Rachel told her. "A few other families have come down with fevers."

This thing was spreading through the kingdom? "I'll have Femi and Ambrose check other homes when they get back." Louella went back into the room with William. His sweat had drenched the bed. She climbed in behind him and pressed another cool cloth to his head. He mumbled something that she couldn't understand.

"Are you coming around?" She picked the cup of tea off the table next to the bed, pressed it to his lips again. This time he took a few sips. "Oh, praise God."

Then she remembered how William encouraged her to believe for good things. She declared to him, "You're doing good, darling. I don't know what happened to y'all, but you'll survive. Do you hear me?"

William coughed and spit out some of the tea.

"There's more where that came from. Soon as I get this fever down, you'll be ready to sip on that tea."

She laid his head on her chest as she kept saying, "God will come see 'bout you. You believe so thoroughly in our Savior. He won't let you down."

After what seemed like hours, Femi and Ambrose returned with the block of ice. As they were bringing it into the house, Robert came in behind them. "What is this I'm hearing about William taking ill?"

Louella instructed Femi and Ambrose to break the ice so she could share it with all three of her patients, then she turned to Robert. "I don't have time to talk to you now. Please come back later."

"But we got a meeting with Serepta. William's sick, and you're stuck taking care of him. What we gon' do?"

Hands went to her hips. "I'm not stuck doing nothing. I want to be right here with my family."

Louella pointed to the remaining block of ice, then asked Ambrose and Femi, "Can you check with others to see how many families might need some ice to bring down a fever? You might need to get another block of ice as well."

"Will do," Femi said as he and Ambrose left the house.

Robert wouldn't let up. "You're a queen. You shouldn't be taking care of the sick. We have people in the Happy Land that can do this for you."

She folded her arms and leaned back as she challenged him. "Who are you to come in here telling me what I should and shouldn't be doing? Go back to Spartanburg."

Robert sputtered, "Y-you don't tell me what to do. I came back for this meeting, and you need to be there with me."

"Reschedule the meeting or take it yourself!" Louella shouted at Robert. "Leave us be."

Louella didn't care what Robert did at that point. She wasn't concerned about being the queen of the Happy Land today. She was a wife, a mother, a daughter, and a granddaughter, and that was all that mattered.

Her shirt was drenched as if she'd jumped in a tub with her clothes on. Her hair was braided on one side while the braid on the other side had unraveled.

"You're in no shape to take a meeting now anyway." Robert huffed and then stormed out of the house.

She took a few pieces of ice and wrapped a rag around them; Clara and Rachel did the same. Then each of them went back to ministering to the sick. Louella prayed hard that night. She was counting on God to come through for her.

CHAPTER 31

In the morning, William was still hot and clammy to the point of delirium. He called out to people who weren't there—his mother, his father. He talked about the cattle, the oxen, and the land, but his conversation didn't make much sense.

When he started talking to Lily, Louella wondered if her husband was transitioning and he was in some other realm, seeing things that only the spiritual eye could see.

Louella kept a cold compress to his head and put one on his back as well. "Come back to me. I don't want to do life without you, my love."

She didn't want to lead this kingdom without her husband. William had loved her for so long, but hate had filled her heart and love had been an afterthought. Now she needed him like she needed to breathe. Didn't know how she could go on without him. His mother and his daughter might love to have him walking 'round heaven with them, but she wanted him too. "Don't leave me. Stay here with the wife who loves you. Do you hear me, William? I said I love you." How many times had she wanted to say those words but bit them back?

She would not deny him those words today. Love was all she had to give, and she would pour out every ounce she had within her. "Love you so much."

Her chin quivered and thick tears flowed down her face, like the sap from a maple tree, congealing with the salty taste of her love and her regrets. "I don't want to love and lose. Stay with me."

She prayed that her love had comforted him through the years because it had been there; it grew slow but steady and had become unyielding. "I caused you too many headaches through the years. I'm sorry about that."

"Sue's fever broke," Rachel reported as she stood in front of Louella's bedroom door.

Then Clara came with news of Joshua. "Joshua's fever broke."

"Praise God," Louella said. Then she asked Clara, "Can you fix your famous chicken soup and give Joshua and Mama Sue each a bowl?"

"I'll get right on it." Clara left while Rachel stayed in front of the door.

Rachel asked, "How's King William doing?"

"He's gon' be fine. I expect his fever to pass soon." She gave Rachel a weak smile. "'Preciate the nursemaiding you done for Mama Sue."

"Happy to be of service," Rachel told her.

"You and Clara best drink some of that catnip tea. Don't want to take this sickness home to your family."

"Will do. And I'll bring you a cup of tea as well."

"Thank you. Oh, and get some of those horehound leaves and make some tea with that as well." She could always count on Rachel and Clara when she needed a helping hand around the kingdom. Their friendship was a blessing to her.

Louella pressed against her husband. The heat from his body and the moans of his delirium tore at the strings of her hope.

Rachel brought her a cup of tea. She drank it and then offered William a few sips of his tea, but he turned away from it. His lips were terribly chapped. She put more beeswax on them.

Through the day and into the night, William's body shook from either fighting or succumbing to the sickness. She heard him talking to Lily again. Louella whispered in his ear. "Tell her that Mommy loves her too, that I ain't never gon' forget her."

Her eyes drooped, but she refused to fall asleep. Needing to be with him every moment, every second. She stayed up, wiping sweat from his forehead and changing his clothes as his shirt and pants drenched through like a bucket of water had been poured on him.

William shivered as she replaced the wet clothes with dry ones. She climbed back in bed, rubbed his arms and legs, pouring warmth into him, even though he was hotter than a wood-burning fire. "You're a king. Long may you live." Louella repeated those words throughout the night as she fervently worked to get her husband's fever to break.

His breath came in rapid, shallow gasps. She clung to him like the sweet smell of a lover's sweat, daring him to leave after he had so thoroughly claimed her heart. "Stay here with me, my love. The kingdom needs you. I need you."

At one point, William's lips moved. He shivered again so she leaned in to rub his arms. As she did so, he said, "Bless God."

"What . . . what did you say?"

The words came again, this time like a whisper that floated in the air. "Bless God." Then his whole body shook as if the angels in heaven came down and trembled the earth. Then all at once, he went still.

"William . . . William." She hopped on her knees and shook him. "Sweetheart . . . dearest . . . my love, don't go. Not like this." An ocean of tears sprang forth and streamed down her face. It wasn't over . . . couldn't be over. Her heart was too full of love— love that needed to be shared.

Pressing her lips to his, tasting a mix of sweat, tears, and longing, she had one question for God. "Whhhhy?"

The patter of feet stormed toward her bedroom. Louella's glassy eyes barely made out the figures of Rachel and Clara as they stood in the entryway. Her tears puddled on the bed as a torrent of sorrow overflowed, encapsulating her in a tsunami of loss.

CHAPTER 32

Even while dying, William trusted in the Lord. Louella didn't understand her husband. How could he bless God when He didn't come through for them?

The king was dead. Her love was no more. Her children would have to grow up without a father, and the Happy Land had no king.

The plague swept through their land, taking four men, two women, and one precious child. Louella's heart ached for them all, but grief consumed her over the loss of William.

A grave had been dug for her beloved below the Davis Cemetery, where Serepta's husband, Colonel John Davis, and two of their children had been buried. Louella wore a black dress. Her children were in black as well as they walked behind the pallbearers who carried William's body down the hill toward the burial site.

William's body was wrapped in a gold linen shroud to represent his kingship. But his kingship didn't matter to Louella. All that mattered was that he was no more. She closed her eyes, shutting out the pain. Her heart ached so much that she doubled over and yelled out.

Abigail came up behind her. "I got you. Lean on me."

Then Clara took hold of her other arm, whispering to her, "We know it hurts a whole heap, but you gon' get through this."

Abigail and Clara had become so precious to her. More family than friends. She leaned on them today and would probably lean again in the coming days. They helped her continue the journey behind the pallbearers.

Her mind's eye took her back to the day when her mother was on the back of the wagon, riding away from the Montgomery Plantation, never to be seen again. *"Mama . . . I want Mama!"* she had screamed, running after that wagon. She would have jumped on it had Ambrose not stopped her.

Tears clouded her eyes as she once again saw her daddy hanging from that dreaded oak tree. So vivid was the vision that she reached out to grab him. If she could pull her daddy down from that tree, maybe she could make death go away—far, far away from them. So far that Lily would be here with them and Louella wouldn't right now be walking behind the men carrying William to his final resting place. But death wouldn't leave them alone.

They arrived at the burial site. The men placed King William in a wooden box that had been carved by Joe for the burial.

Reverend Ezel stood in front of the hole that had been dug for William with Bible in hand. As William's body was lowered into the ground, Reverend Ezel said, "Ashes to ashes, dust to dust. For we came from the dust and we must return."

But why did he have to return to the dust so soon? Why couldn't he stay with her and their children a little while longer? She wanted to ask Reverend Ezel those questions and many more as he waxed poetic about returning to the dust, but she clamped her mouth shut so as not to confound the many who gathered to mourn her husband.

"King William was a good man. He treasured the people in the Happy Land. And he loved his beautiful queen." Reverend Ezel nodded in Louella's direction. "He did everything in his power to ensure that you all had something to call your own."

"A good man with a good heart!" Robert shouted, standing next to Louella.

She glanced over at her brother-in-law and noted how sorrow clung to him like that shroud clung to her husband. She had been offended by Robert when he'd come into her home demanding that she take the meeting with Serepta while her husband was on his deathbed, but as she looked at him now, she knew William's death had disturbed his soul too.

She patted Robert on the shoulder, trying to bring comfort to someone who had loved her husband as best he could. But the gesture proved too much for her as tears cascaded down her cheeks. She turned back toward William's gravesite and shut her eyes tight, wiping the wetness from her face.

When she opened her eyes again, the men picked up the shovels and began tossing dirt on the coffin. Aching inside, she reached up and touched the beating organ that was so thoroughly disfigured and broken it couldn't possibly still be considered a heart. For she had loved and lost . . . again.

"I want Daddy," Joshua cried out.

Then Waties started crying. Louella wanted to comfort her boys. But she filled the void with her own tears. Her pain trickled out, leaking on everyone around her. It would have been better if she had never loved than to be standing in the place of loss.

When the pallbearers were finished throwing dirt on William's casket, Louella took Waties's and Joshua's hands and began walking back up the hill. But as she walked with her children, grandmother, and brother, she heard a sound that utterly froze her in the spot where she stood.

"The king is dead!" someone shouted. Then others shouted, "Long live the king . . . Long live the king!"

What were they talking about? How could they say, "The king is dead" in one breath and then "Long live the king" in the other? Didn't they realize that their king would never live again? But then she saw the same men who had served as pallbearers for her husband carrying Robert on their shoulders up the hill, moving past her as if they didn't see her standing there with the children that belonged to the king.

They carried Robert and continued to shout, "Long live the king!"

"Am I not their queen?" Louella pounded her fist on the table as she spoke to the women who gathered in her home after the funeral.

"Yes, of course you are," Mirabel told her as she patted Louella on the back. "I'm ashamed that my son was one of the men carrying Robert and being so disrespectful to you."

"They want a man, rather than to be ruled by a woman, their rightful queen." The disdain in Mama Sue's voice vibrated against the walls.

"If that's what they want, then they can have him." Louella shoved away from the table and stood.

"But you've done so much for us," Abigail declared. "How dare those men disrespect you like that?"

Abigail and Mama Sue were forever in her corner, and she loved them for it. But right now, she didn't have an ounce of fight in her. She wanted to lie down and shut out the whole treacherous world.

She went to her bedroom. The room she had shared with her king among kings. She needed to feel William's presence. She climbed in bed and brought his pillow to her face, breathing in his scent.

William loomed large in their room. They had spent many nights lying in bed after a long day of working with the children, helping the teamsters, or clearing more land. William would normally be exhausted and in need of a massage. Some days, Louella resented all the times he complained about back and shoulder aches.

But she'd give anything to be able to soothe his aching body today.

"Seems like those logs are getting heavier and heavier each day," William said as he stretched his arms and rolled his neck. *"Sure could use a massage."*

"*Come on over here and let me get you all fixed up.*" Louella put oil on her hands and then massaged it into William's back and arms.

"*Oh my goodness,*" he moaned. "*You've got the ministering hands of an angel.*"

"*I doubt that.*" She laughed. "*If they were angelic, you wouldn't be in need of a massage three nights a week.*"

"*I'm sorry to be so troublesome to you,*" William said.

"You were never any trouble," Louella moaned, praying her words drifted all the way to heaven and found their way to her beloved.

Fact of the matter was, they didn't rule a kingdom like the king and queen of England or France. They were hands-on in the Happy Land. All for one and one for all. So if there was a need and William could fill it, he'd jump in to help. Louella did the same. So aches and pains came with the territory.

Her hands itched to massage her husband's aching back. She looked at her fingers—fingers that had no one to caress, no one to soothe after a hard day's work. Rivers of pain cascaded down her face. Louella cried herself to sleep that night.

❦

The following days seemed to blend together, with Louella refusing to get out of bed for more than a few minutes at a time each day.

At night, when no one was bothering her, when no one was lying next to her, she opened the floodgates once more. Tears had become her companion, her ever-present friend. Normal was a wet pillow that she had to flip over so she could fall asleep.

"I know you're in pain, but you can't keep laying here feeling sorry for yourself," Mama Sue said to her about three weeks after William's funeral.

"Loving a Black man is like asking for a hole in your heart. You were so right."

Mama Sue lifted a hand. "I said that during slavery times. I knew firsthand the hurt that would come to a woman when some ol' massa decided to do away with the man she loved without a care to how it would break her.

"But there was never anything wrong with you loving William. That plague might have claimed his life, but it didn't claim his love. You had that." Mama Sue put a hand on Louella's shoulder. "Be comforted by that."

Louella turned to face the wall. "I know you want me to do the responsible thing." She closed her eyes and inhaled the bittersweetness of William's waning scent. "God was supposed to look out for my family, but my family keeps dwindling, and I'm too exhausted to go on."

The organ that was supposed to be a heart hurt so bad every time she got up, Louella expected it to explode. Then she would go to that sweet by and by, but maybe that was okay. She might even see Lily, as William did.

"What about Waties and Joshua? Don't you think they hurting too? They need you to hug them. Smile at them. Do something that lets them know they didn't lose you too."

Her babies needed her.

Then Mama Sue said, "What about the Happy Land? Don't you think the people here need you?"

"They have Robert." Louella was still angry about that "Long live the king" chant. It was all so disrespectful, and she honestly didn't know if she wanted to lead a group of people who so blatantly showed her their preference for a man. "They deserve what they'll get with Robert as their leader. Once he enslaves them again, maybe being ruled by a woman won't be such a hardship for some of these men."

Mama Sue *tsk*ed, but she left Louella alone with her anger. She also left the door open. And within minutes Waties and Joshua came to visit. Louella wanted to smile at her sons, but her lips couldn't pretend to be happy.

"When you gon' get up?" Waties asked.

"Why don't you play with us no more?" Joshua wanted to know.

And her heart broke all over again. This time, it didn't break due to all she had lost, but because she had allowed herself to forget what she had left. Her children were a gift from God. Mama Sue was right. She couldn't keep wallowing in self-pity when her sons needed her.

CHAPTER 33

Louella spent her days at the schoolhouse teaching the younger kids from a Bible she herself struggled to understand. At night, she lay in her bed and cried like tears were her refuge.

She was broken. Didn't know how much more she could take. She'd begun singing herself to sleep with the words from a sad song . . .

> "Sometimes I feel like a motherless child,
> Sometimes I feel like I'm almost done,
> A long way from home,
> A long way from home."

At night she let the pain of that song envelop her. When daylight came, she got out of bed, dressed, and tended to her children, then went back to the schoolhouse.

This morning Abigail stood in front of the class holding her Bible open. She read Psalm 27:13: "'I had fainted, unless I had believed to see the goodness of the Lord in the land of the living.'"

When Abigail finished reading those words, she closed the Bible as if she'd said enough and nothing more needed to be added. But Louella sat there as stiff as a statue, wrapping her mind around every word of that verse. If God wanted them to see goodness, then why so much pain?

Where was God in her darkest of hours? All these things were her inward thoughts, but she did not—would not—say any of it out loud. She lifted her face to the heavens, silently telling God, *I need answers . . . I am undone. My heart is heavy with grief.*

"You looked so sad after I read that scripture. I hope I didn't offend you with my choice," Abigail said as school ended for the day and she and Louella were leaving.

Louella shook her head. "You didn't offend me. The Word is what it is, whether I agree with it or not."

"I'm kind of shocked to hear you say that since you're the one who encouraged me to keep my head up all those years when I struggled with not being able to have children."

Louella's hand went to her mouth with a giggle. "Then you showed out and delivered two babies at once."

"I swear I thought Femi was going to faint when our second child pushed his way out." Abigail laughed with Louella, then she said, "It's good to see you smile, and I'm so sorry about King William."

"Me too," she said on an exhale. "Thanks for giving me something to smile about."

As Louella walked toward her home, Abigail stopped her with words that were meant to soothe. "Every day we're living can bring something to smile about, my queen."

Louella nodded and gave Abigail a half smile, then turned to go on her way, but Abigail wasn't finished.

"I still remember what you told me." A tear drifted down Abigail's right cheek. "And it guides everything I say and do."

Louella's eyebrow arched. Nothing important that she'd said to Abigail came to mind.

"Remember several years ago you told me that the truth would set me free?"

Louella nodded. They had left bondage and were headed for better days, then Lily died. "But what is the truth?" She didn't know anymore and truly needed God to open her eyes.

Putting a hand on Louella's shoulder, Abigail said, "The truth is, everything didn't go the way you planned it, but life can still be good, and we all still need your compassion and your guidance."

Louella hugged her friend. "Thank you, Abigail."

"Don't thank me. It's the truth. We love you, and Femi and I are here to help with whatever you need, so please call on us."

Tears cascaded down Louella's face as she made it to her front porch. She needed a moment before going inside. She sat down on her throne. But as she looked to the right where William's throne was, all she saw was an empty space. Rage overtook her. Robert could have the kingdom and all that was in it, but he could not have her husband's throne.

She wiped the tears from her face and marched next door to Robert's house. Even though they were next-door neighbors, Robert's house was on the North Carolina side while Louella's house was on the South Carolina side. She liked the fact that her brother-in-law was a whole state away from her. She wished he was on the farthest side of North Carolina so she wouldn't have to see him so often.

"Robert Montgomery, come out here and face me. I've got something to say to you!" she yelled as she stood in front of his house.

Robert opened his door, folded his arms across his chest, and stared at her as if she had gone mad. "Why you making all this noise in front of my home?"

"I see what you done." Using her index and middle fingers, she pointed from her eyes to Robert's. "But I'm not gon' let you get away with it."

"Get away with what? What you talking 'bout?" Robert stepped onto the porch.

He was standing next to the throne. The throne that had been hand carved for William—the throne that had been on her porch. She pointed a finger at it. "How dare you take that chair off my porch. It doesn't belong to you! It doesn't belong to you!" she kept screaming.

She was yelling so loud that doors opened and residents of the Happy Land peeked out. Louella didn't care. It was high time she let this so-called king know what she thought of him.

"Calm down, Louella. I didn't steal William's throne. I only brought the chair over here so I could serve the people while you're in mourning."

"'Serve the people.'" She scoffed, turning this way and that, looking at the land she and William labored over. "You never served anyone but yourself. You'll never have the heart your brother had for these people. They never should have made you king."

Robert looked past her, waved a hand. "Come over here and help me."

Louella turned to see who he was talking to. Harold and Ambrose were standing behind her. "Help you with what? If you think they gon' move me away from your door, think again. I'm not leaving until I get what I came for."

Robert didn't reply to her. He told Harold and Ambrose, "Can you move this chair back to Louella's porch?"

Her mouth went slack. Was he giving the chair back without a fight? Ambrose and Harold picked up the chair and carried it back to her house. As they moved the chair, she was still standing in front of Robert's house, mouth itching to let everything spill out.

But Robert turned back to her and said, "I apologize. I never meant to upset you. You're my brother's widow, and I'll do whatever needs doing to help the Happy Land. You have nothing to fear from me."

There was so much more she wanted to scream and shout at him, but his apology softened her. Made her take a few steps back. She nodded and walked back to her house.

"You okay, sis?" Ambrose asked when she sat back down on the porch.

She reached out and held on to William's throne as she turned to Ambrose. "I'm trying to get to okay. Think I need a little more time, though."

"Good . . . good," Ambrose said and then went inside the house, scurrying away from her grief.

Breathe in . . . breathe out.

When Ambrose opened the door, Waties and Joshua ran out. Waties sat in his father's chair and Joshua jumped in her lap. "Mommy, I've been waiting on you to read me a story."

Breathe in . . . breathe out. "Oh my goodness, I almost forgot about story time." She was about to get up and go in the house when Clara came running over to her.

"Got me some good news today!" Clara shouted.

While Joshua bounced in her arms, Louella smiled at Clara. "What's got you so excited?"

"Patricia Ann gave birth to my first grandchild. I'm so thrilled, I had to share my good news with somebody."

"I'm glad you shared it with me. What did she have?"

"A little boy. They're naming him Jimmy Freeman Jr." Clara grinned and then held out her hands to Joshua.

He left Louella's lap and climbed into Clara's arms. "He doesn't leave me for nobody but you or Mama Sue."

Looking at Joshua with adoring eyes, Clara said, "We became fast friends the day I took care of him."

The day William died, Louella thought.

"Honestly, though, I was terrified that he wasn't going to make it, but once his fever broke, I knew he'd stay here with us." She kissed Joshua's cheek, then added, "He's a gift from God."

Louella was still coming to terms with the gift God had allowed to slip away, so she didn't know how to respond to that. "Are you going to Hendersonville to see your grandson?"

Joshua started fidgeting in Clara's arms. Louella set him back on her lap. "Yes, ma'am. That's the other reason I ran over here. I'm gon' need someone to fill in for me at the Poseys'."

"How long you going for?"

"I'm thinking two weeks. Jimmy wants me to help Patricia Ann with the baby while she's recovering from the delivery."

"Don't worry about a thing. Enjoy your new grandbaby. I'll find someone to take your place."

"Thank you so much. I better head back home so I can pack. Jimmy's waiting on me."

"Tell Jimmy I said congratulations." Clara's joy was overflowing. Louella was happy for her friend. As Clara walked away, Louella looked over at Waties sitting in his father's chair like a big boy and then at Joshua as he bounced in her lap.

Maybe her children and Clara's grandchild were a part of the goodness of the Lord. Maybe they were on this earth for as long as God allowed to impart goodness into their children and their children's children.

❧

A few days later, Louella was in her room with Waties and Joshua playing a game of tickle and enjoying the sound of her sons' laughter when a knock came on her front door.

Mama Sue hollered to Louella, "I got it."

"Who is it?" Louella asked while getting off the floor and wiping her hands on her skirt. Joshua was still rolling around on the floor giggling.

A smile crept across her face like a cobweb across a window, one strand at a time. Then Mama Sue hollered back, "It's the king." And the strands broke.

Louella's eyes shifted heavenward. She expelled a do-I-have-to-do-this-today sigh, then headed for the front of the house. Freshly burning wood from the fireplace filled the air. Mama Sue put a pot on the fire as Louella stepped onto the porch. Her hands were folded across her chest. Lips tight. "Robert."

"I'm sorry if I disturbed you, but I came to discuss a few matters of importance concerning the kingdom."

Her lip curled as she leaned against the post. "I thought you men did whatever you please around here. Can't imagine what you need to discuss with me."

"For one," Robert began, "the teamsters are headed out. They need money for the supplies they bring back."

Louella walked back into the house. She went over to the fireplace, moved a piece of the granite, then took out several coins. Walking back outside and down the steps to where Robert stood holding on to the banister, she put the money in his hand and then headed back up the steps without so much as a goodbye.

"When you're ready, we need to talk. We can't rule the Happy Land together if you and I can't communicate."

The wind whistled through the trees and the tall grass. The grass turned with each gust, moving like the sway of her emotions. If they were blades, they would cut. "What communication do you speak of? I don't remember no communication when you claimed the mantle of king before the dust had dried over my dear William's grave."

"That wasn't my doing. The people wanted a king."

The elongation of her neck was profound, with the lifting of her head and the thunder in her voice. "They had a queen."

Robert stood there a moment, staring up at Louella as if seeing something that froze him in his steps. Sighing, he said, "I didn't come over here to fight with you. I'm sorry for the misunderstandings we've had through the years."

Her eyes filled with fire, but she said not a word.

"You are the rightful queen of the Happy Land. The people need you. But they need me as well." When she still didn't say anything, his voice rose. "We can help each other, if you allow it."

She lifted her hand and pointed out toward the houses, the fields, and all the things that she had envisioned for the place they would call home. "My husband and I built all of this. Brick by brick, timber by timber. We put together a system that prospers us all, so I will not dishonor him by standing aside while you tear it all down."

Robert rubbed the front of his forehead with three of his fingers. "William was my brother, Louella. I want to honor him too. But you can't keep fighting against me."

His words penetrated the space between them. William loved his brother, flaws and all. She could hear her husband somewhere in the whip of the wind urging her to be forgiving and to do the right thing for the kingdom.

She stuck her hand out to him. "All right, then. We rule together."

Robert smiled, climbed the steps, and shook her hand. "You won't be sorry. We'll do this for William."

She hoped and prayed that Robert wouldn't do anything to make her regret this truce. As he walked back down the stairs, she told him, "Don't think you can play me for a fool. We're equal partners in this, and I'll make sure of it."

PART 5

CRACKS IN THE KINGDOM

1882–1889

CHAPTER 34

"What a fine, glorious morning it is," Robert said while holding the reins of his horse and guiding it down the long winding hill.

Louella was seated next to Robert. After years of struggling, the two had finally come to terms with each other. The Happy Land had grown to over four hundred people. Louella couldn't meet the needs of all those people by herself, and neither could Robert. Working together had been good for the kingdom.

They were headed to the Henderson Courthouse to file papers for the hundred and eighty acres of land they'd purchased from John Goodwin, by way of Serepta Davis, a few years back.

Sarah's husband, John, handled all property matters for Serepta. The day they approached him to purchase more land, he'd said, *"I was skeptical about you people when you first arrived here, but except for that king and queen business, you've been no trouble at'tal."* He signed over the land without further complaint.

"It's a right fine day, I must agree." Louella wore a bonnet and white gloves. The crisp March air was ripe for the shawl the women had gifted her at Christmas.

"Thankfully, we've already cleared the land we purchased."

Louella nodded. "We've got the lumber and the bricks. We'll start building again shortly."

The last few years had been good for the Happy Land. The waggoners carried dried fruit, meat, lard, potatoes, and other vegetables tilled and produced in the Happy Land to the farther parts of North and South Carolina. They sold all the produce, lard, and meat to stores and stagecoach stops. They even set up their own farmers' market from time to time, purchased needed supplies, and then brought the remainder of the profits back to the kingdom. Robert held the money in their treasury, and he and Louella doled it out to the residents as needed.

Times were good, and Louella had to admit that having Robert help her lead their people hadn't been so bad. He had settled into life in the Happy Land and wasn't gone for months on end anymore—more like a week every month. While he was gone, she didn't have to discuss any decisions that needed to be made with him, and that was fine with Louella.

Toot-toot.

"Oh my Lord, here we go again. I get caught by this train at least once a week." Robert pulled on the reins and stopped the progression of the horse as the train went by.

"Serepta said they're losing business at her depot. The stagecoach isn't coming through as much anymore."

"They're talking about stopping the stagecoach altogether since they laid down the tracks for this railroad from Spartanburg to Hendersonville," Robert told her as the caboose rolled by. Then he shook the reins to get the horse moving again.

Louella looked back at the railroad tracks. "There's still places where the railroad hasn't been built yet, like Asheville. Those places can still use a stagecoach."

"Face it, Louella, the old way of doing things is gone. This railroad is the way of the future."

If the railroad was the way of the future, Louella wondered what that meant for their way of life. Most of the money earned in the Happy Land came by way of the waggoners. Would their customers abandon them as the railroad was built throughout Asheville and beyond?

As they continued to travel down the sandy clay road headed

for the court building, Louella wondered about the changes coming to the Appalachian town she had lived in for almost fifteen years.

She was so deep in thought, she didn't notice that Robert had pulled the wagon in front of the courthouse until Reverend Walter Allen approached her. "Good day to you, Queen Louella." He tipped his hat.

Louella smiled. The reverend was a good man and lived near Hendersonville. He served the surrounding Negro communities by opening a school so Negro children could receive their lessons like children of white folks. Several of the older kids in the Happy Land attended his school in Possum Hollow. It was a distance from the Happy Land but well worth it since the kids received a good education.

A wagon packed full of kids left the Happy Land each morning and returned with them in the evening. Her Waties and Joshua were now on that wagon also. Her boys were growing up, fifteen and thirteen now. Louella was thankful for the education they were receiving.

"Good day to you as well, Reverend. I'm surprised to see you by the courthouse this early in the day."

He helped Louella down from the wagon and then turned to Robert. "Good day to you, King Robert."

Robert came over to Louella's side and shook Reverend Allen's hand. "I hope the Happy Land children haven't run you away from the schoolhouse today."

"No, no, not at all. I'm picking up a few supplies before I head back. But rest assured, I left the children in capable hands."

"Isn't Abigail helping you today?" Louella asked.

"She sure is. And I thank you for allowing her to assist me from time to time."

"Abigail loves teaching the older kids, so I'm thankful you've been able to use her skills."

Reverend Allen tipped his hat again. "Well, I best be getting those supplies." He then headed down the street.

"Such a nice man," Louella said as he walked away.

"I'm sure you wish I was as nice and refined as the good reverend, but I am who I am."

Louella nodded and then let Robert lead the way into the courthouse. He was who he was, but she had come to appreciate the things that he had been able to do for the Happy Land through the years. Like what he was about to do right now.

When she and William had purchased the first twenty-five acres of land, they didn't bring the signed documents to the courthouse for fear of what might happen to a Black man owning property in these parts.

However, the Klan had found out about their purchase and the building of their community anyway, so they had held off on buying more land. Once she and Robert did purchase more land, they held on to the deeds until Louella was comfortable with the filing. Today was the day.

Robert handed the signed agreement they'd received from John Goodwin to the clerk of courts. "I'd like to file these documents with the court."

"Yes, sir. I'm here to help with that." The clerk put on his glasses and reviewed the document, then glanced back up. "I presume you are Robert Montgomery?"

"That's correct."

The man's forehead crinkled as he glanced back at the document. He looked back up at Robert. "There's also a Louella Montgomery?"

"I'm Louella." She raised a hand as if indicating her presence.

The man sputtered as he turned back to Robert. "But she's a . . . a . . . You can't be owning property with these people. They're not like us."

Louella wanted to give this man a good dose of what she was thinking at the moment, but she and Robert had already rehearsed what he would say if they had any trouble with the good white folks at the Henderson Courthouse. So she clamped her mouth shut and waited on Robert to speak.

"My people were good and loyal to me before and after the war. It's only fitting that I share my land with them. So, yes, Louella Montgomery's name will be on the deed as well."

The man's lip twitched upward as he glared at Louella. "It's your funeral. If they kill you in your sleep to get their hands on your property, don't say I didn't warn you."

Louella recoiled at the words that came out of this stranger's mouth. She was queen to the people in the Happy Land but still a nothing to those outside her kingdom. She would be fine with shutting herself inside her place of peace and never coming back to Hendersonville to deal with those who thought of people who looked like her as less than.

When the papers were processed, Louella smiled sweetly. "Thank you very kindly." She then turned and walked out of the courthouse without so much as a backward glance.

"You handled yourself well in there," Robert said as they got back on the road, heading home.

Louella tossed her shawl over her shoulders, leaned back in her seat, and got comfortable. "I'm getting older." She would be forty this year. "I don't have time to deal with the stupidity of others anymore. Let the rest of the world think what they may. All that matters is what our people think of us in the Happy Land."

It stung to have that man treat her as if she didn't deserve anything good in this life. And if she got something good, then she would be stealing it from Robert, which was a hoot. Although he looked as white as that man in the courthouse, Robert wouldn't have anything if it hadn't been for her and William.

"What are you laughing about?" Robert asked.

Louella put her hand to her mouth. She hadn't realized her laugh had seeped out. "Oh, just thinking about the injustices outside of the Happy Land."

"And there are no injustices inside our land? Is that the way you see it?" Robert arched an eyebrow.

"That's exactly the way I see it. We treat our people as equals." Louella nodded as if approving her own words. "We aren't called the Happy Land for no reason, Robert. Our people have joy that they didn't have when so-called masters took advantage of us."

"And you don't think we take advantage of our people . . . I mean, all the money they earn comes right back to us. How different than a master are we?"

Rolling her eyes, Louella glared at Robert. Of course he would see it that way. He was probably happy to receive the money and play the role of Mr. Big and Grand, but he had it all wrong. "You will never understand, will you?"

Robert shrugged and whipped the reins to have the horse move faster as they made their climb up the hill toward the Happy Land. "What is it that I don't understand? Please enlighten me. Better yet, tell me again how I'm a poor substitute for your beloved William."

She wasn't going to feel bad for saying that or thinking it. It was true. Sighing deeply, she turned to her brother-in-law. "When William and I decided to set out on our own and then others decided to follow us, we knew then that we had to set up a system that would help all of us succeed.

"You see, William had a heart for people, even those who couldn't do for themselves, so we told the people they all had to give into one pot. But it was never for the enrichment of ourselves. It was so we could also lift the heads of the elderly and sickly in our community."

"'All for one and one for all,'" Robert quoted.

"That's exactly it. One day I pray you understand all that entails and the responsibility we have to our people."

He pulled the wagon in front of her door, then got out and walked to the other side. He helped Louella down. "And one day I hope you come to see that I am not your enemy."

CHAPTER 35

Fall 1886

The railroad had come in like a thief in the night, snatching away resources needed for the growth of the Happy Land. Louella now had to concern herself with new ways to bring money into the kingdom since the waggoners had lost most of their contracts. The land was no longer yielding enough corn, and they were now rationing out the food to the Happy Landers.

They could survive this season of lack with a little tightening of the belt. The waggoners still had some business, but not enough for the purchases they made while on the road. The last purchase list she saw contained loads of sugar and yeast, but Louella couldn't figure out what they needed those supplies for.

"What's going on with these supplies the waggoners are bringing back here? I don't see them on the list of items being rationed to our people," Louella had said to Robert a few months back.

"I'll check into it," he'd told her, "but I'm sure it's nothing. Maybe Mirabel and some of the other cooks are making cakes and pies to sell."

But as the days lingered on, Louella busied herself with other matters in the kingdom and forgot about the extra supplies. She was at the church placing the hymnals on chairs for Sunday service. Reverend Ezel was coming to town and would preach the Word at tomorrow's service.

Clara and Gary came into the church. Gary took the hymnals out of her hand and finished placing them on the chairs.

Clara asked, "Anything I can help you with?"

"Finishing up," Louella told her. "What brings you and Gary out today?"

"Clara needs to tell you something." Gary came back to stand by his wife.

Clara looked away as she said, "Ben and Julia Posey are leaving Basin Springs. They have a new house in Hendersonville."

"I'm sorry to hear that," Louella said. Several residents of the Happy Land worked for the Poseys at Basin Springs. They would have to find new employment for their people, and right now, jobs were hard to come by.

"The thing is," Clara began, wringing her hands and biting her bottom lip.

Gary nudged her. "Tell her. Queen Louella will understand."

Clara looked as if she was struggling with something within her. Louella didn't like to see her friend so distressed, so she said, "Don't worry about losing your job with the Poseys. Something else will come up. It always does."

"The thing is," Clara began again, "the Poseys have asked us to come with them. They have a job for Gary, and we'll be closer to my grandchildren if we live in Hendersonville."

Clara wasn't the first to decide to leave. There were more jobs in Hendersonville and Greenville, and in the last few years, they had lost about fifty of their residents to those areas. But no one was trapped or enslaved in the Happy Land. They were free to choose whether they wanted to stay or go.

"I'm sad to see you go, but happy for you. I know you've been missing those grandbabies." Louella smiled as she hugged Clara.

When they let each other go, Clara had tears in her eyes. "It's just . . . I don't want you to think we're ungrateful for all you done for us."

Louella shook her head. "I don't think that way. We all built the Happy Land. I'm grateful for everything you, Gary, and Jimmy did to help, but you aren't tied to this land forever if your heart is leading you elsewhere."

"See." Gary nudged Clara again. "Told you she'd wish us well."

"I do, Gary, and please don't be strangers. Come back and see us sometime."

"You can count on it." Clara wiped the tears from her face.

Things were changing in the Happy Land. The railroad had made sure of it. But Louella hadn't changed. Even after nineteen years, she still wanted the best for herself and the people she loved.

Louella went home and opened her front door. Waties rushed over to her. He was now nineteen years old and a whole foot taller than her. "Mama, make Joshua help me clean up. Granny isn't feeling well, and he won't help."

"Aren't you and your brother supposed to be tending to the cows?"

"Yes, ma'am, but we got to clean the house if we want supper."

She should have known that Waties's stomach was leading again. "Let me check on Mama Sue, and then I'll see about supper."

"What about Joshua?" Waties asked.

Louella hollered to the back of the house, "Joshua, get out here and help your brother with the cleaning!"

Louella knocked on Mama Sue's door and then entered. Her grandmother was lying in bed. "Hey. Waties said you weren't feeling well."

Mama Sue giggled. "That's what I told him. If that boy wants supper so bad, let him help me clean this house."

"But you're not sick?"

Mama Sue waved that notion off. "Child, please. I'm fine. I'll be up as soon as them boys clean behind themselves."

Louella exhaled. Mama Sue was getting older, but she was still active and got around better than others half her age. The only issue she had was rheumatism, which Louella's Happy Land Liniment took care of when she had aches and pains.

"All right. Tell you what. This is your day off. I'm cooking for them hungry men, and I'll bring your supper to you."

As Louella turned to leave, Mama Sue grabbed hold of her arm. The look in her eyes revealed her tiredness. "You always been a joy to me. The good Lord sure blessed me when I birthed your mama."

Walking away, Louella found herself once again wondering about the goodness of the Lord. If her mother was a blessing to her grandmother, then why had God allowed her to be sold away from them? Why had they not seen her again, even all these years after freedom came?

Sighing deeply, Louella threw up her hands and got to the business of cooking supper for her family. The only way she had been able to get back up after William's death and to take over William's preaching on Sunday mornings was by understanding one simple thing: she loved God, and that was that.

She didn't understand the God she sang about, nor did she think she ever would. But as her grandmother was grateful for her mother, Louella was grateful for William being in her life. Her husband had showed her his love for God, even when he couldn't trace Him, so she had learned to say hallelujah anyhow.

❧

Reverend Ezel arrived later that night. He brought four others with him. Each time he arrived, Louella found herself glancing at his wagon in hopes that she would see her mother, but Brenda Bobo was never there. She'd stopped asking Reverend Ezel about her mother a few years back, but that longing in her heart hadn't gone away.

"This is Queen Louella," Reverend Ezel told his passengers. "I'm going to leave you all in her capable hands while I get ready for Sunday service."

There were two women and two men. They got out of the wagon and bowed to her. Louella laughed. "There will be no bowing around here. I'm not royalty that cannot be touched. I'm the queen of the Happy Land. And you'll soon discover that we all pitch in and work together around here."

CHAPTER 36

The choir sang "Rock of Ages." Louella hadn't thought much of this song when she first heard it. But through the years, she'd come to think of it as her call to God.

"Rock of Ages, cleft for me,
let me hide myself in Thee . . .
Not the labors of my hands
can fulfill Thy law's commands;
could my zeal no respite know,
could my tears forever flow . . ."

When the song was finished, Reverend Ezel stood behind the podium and preached a fire-and-brimstone message that set the church on fire. The parishioners raised their hands in praise. They even came to the altar and cried out to God for forgiveness. Louella hadn't seen God move so thoroughly in a service like this in a long while.

After the service, she went to the reverend. "You got some extra fire from the Lord to deliver that message today."

He nodded, his face shadowed with sadness. "I truly did, Queen." He then took her hand in his. "The Lord brought me here this time to warn your people to get right or this whole thing that y'all built is gon' come tumbling down."

Louella pulled her hand out of Reverend Ezel's grasp. Stepped back as if pricked by his words. "But, Reverend, why would you continue to bring people here if you think the Lord is no longer with us?"

"Can we take a walk?" he asked while tying a string around his well-used Bible. The string kept the loose pages from falling out.

"Yes, yes, of course." Louella left the church with Reverend Ezel. He placed his Bible back in his wagon and then they took a walk around the valley side of the Happy Land, waving at folks who were standing outside talking or gardening in their front yards.

"We missed you at church today," Louella said to one of them.

Another said to Reverend Ezel, "That was a mighty fine message you delivered today."

And on and on it went, until they reached the lower part of the land where there was quietness. That's when Louella turned to the reverend. "What has the Lord shown you about the Happy Land?"

"Can't say it was the Lord so much showing, or if it was word leaking out about the goings-on around here lately."

Louella hadn't the faintest idea what the good reverend could be talking about. Not much had been going on. The economy was bad in the Appalachian Mountains. Travelers and sellers of goods had taken to using that new railroad system, but things would pick up. She was sure of it.

"Hasn't been much going on around here of late."

Reverend Ezel stopped walking as they came upon the brook that separated one part of their land from the other. He turned to Louella. "I hate bringing this news to you. You and your husband built this land to do something positive for our people after emancipation."

Louella raised a hand. "William might be gone, but we still have concern for our people. Look at all the homes that have been built. Our people have security here."

"And that's why it tears at my heart to tell you what's been going on behind your back."

Louella scrunched her nose. She squinted as she looked at Reverend Ezel, wondering if age was taking his mind. Not much went on in the Happy Land that she didn't know about.

Louella checked on the residents as time permitted. She and Robert still held monthly meetings where anyone could come and make a request or spark a fire with a grievance. No one had need to fear her, so why would they keep anything from her?

"Now, Reverend, you know I work hard to keep abreast of all the needs and goings-on of our people. So I can't rightly say that anything has been kept from me, but you go ahead and speak your mind."

"The Happy Land waggoners have taken to selling corn liquor. They're contaminating the parts of South Carolina where I travel with strong drink."

A gasp escaped Louella's lips. She'd thought that Reverend Ezel was about to say something about the waggoners being inappropriate as they traveled from town to town. She would have given them a stern talking-to and then the matter would have been resolved.

But if what Reverend Ezel was saying was true, Louella didn't think a stern talking-to was going to take care of the situation. "The Happy Landers are good and productive people." She blinked, looked around as if something in the grass or the stream would provide guidance. "Are you sure about this?"

"I wouldn't bring this to you if I wasn't."

Corn . . . corn. The reverend said it was corn liquor being sold. But from what she knew, most of their corn had been destroyed in the last storm they had a few months back. At least, that's what Robert had told her.

"Reverend, what would be needed to make this corn liquor?"

"What the waggoners are selling is more like whiskey. I saw it produced in my younger days while I lived on a whiskey-producing plantation."

"I don't believe you ever told me that before."

"It's not something I'm proud of. I saw from an early age how whiskey could destroy a man. It's more like demon liquor to me, causing men to act in ways they never would if they had their wits about them."

"I've seen men act outside of themselves once they got into a bottle of liquor too, Reverend." Her brother-in-law had been one of the men she'd seen as a falling-down drunk.

"Does this whiskey need a lot of corn?" Louella asked.

Reverend Ezel nodded. "Fermented corn, sugar, and yeast. Once you have those elements, you'll be on your way to some strong whiskey."

Sugar . . . yeast . . . Louella thought back to the sugar and yeast she'd seen on the supply log. All the corn the men loaded onto their wagons that she'd been told wasn't fit to sell or eat. Had Robert let the people in the Happy Land go without in order to line his pockets with ill-gotten gain?

❧

The next day, Louella asked Abigail to teach the class while she got in her wagon and rode over to the farthest side of their property—the side where Robert had built his new barn.

Robert wanted her to believe that he wasn't an enemy, but at the same time, he had taken money from the kingdom to build a barn they didn't need. He put that barn on the farthest part of their North Carolina land, far from her inspection. Louella had ignored this new barn for over a year. She didn't have time for Robert's new toy project.

But today, she made time. Several men were standing outside the barn when she pulled her wagon to a stop. A few of them scurried inside. But Harold, their sergeant at arms, one of the protectors of the land, placed himself in front of the barn door as she stepped down from the wagon.

"Harold," she said by way of greeting.

"It's good to see you, Queen. My wife and I don't see you much since we built our home on this side of the Happy Land."

"No, I guess we don't see much of each other. I hope your family's doing well."

He nodded. "The kids are growing like weeds."

"And your wife?"

"Doing good. You should visit with her sometime. She misses being on the South Carolina side."

"I'll do that." Louella folded her hands in front of her long woolen skirt, then pointed toward the door. "I need to go inside."

Harold didn't move. "I'm sorry, Queen, but King Robert has instructed me to open these doors for no one without his permission."

"I see." Louella stepped back, cleared her throat. "Robert doesn't lead this land alone. I'm the queen of the Happy Land, and I have come to inspect this barn." Her eyes bored into his as she added, "I will not be denied."

Harold didn't respond.

Louella silently counted *One, two, three*, as she'd done when her boys were young and she'd made a request of them. If it wasn't done by the count of three, her boys had learned there would be consequences.

"Harold." She said his name with a bit of bass in her voice.

The door opened behind Harold. He turned and stepped out of the way as Robert joined them outside. He had a piece of straw in his mouth.

"Louella, what brings you out here?" His eyes jumped from her to the yard, to Harold, and to the side of the barn.

"I had some free time today and thought I'd see why you were so excited about building this new barn."

"Sure you want to get your fine clothes sullied in a dirty barn?"

She held out an arm and moved Robert aside, then walked into the barn. Each heated step she took sparked images of the fool she was for trusting Robert Montgomery to ever do anything for anyone but himself.

"What in tarnation is going on in here?" There was a burner on the floor. The fire was lit beneath a huge metal contraption that had a copper pipe connected to it. The copper pipe went down into a barrel, and then another part of the pipe came out of the barrel and connected with another barrel.

"Calm down, Louella. This really isn't as bad as it seems."

Louella swung around to face Robert. "If it isn't so bad, then why'd you hide it from me all this time? Why are you stealing the corn our people could be feeding their families with to do your devilment?"

He coughed and then coughed again as if something had gone down the wrong pipe and was choking him.

"You all right?" Louella stepped toward him.

"I'm fine." He held up a hand while clearing his throat. "I found a way for us to earn money after that railroad took most of our business. You should be happy."

"Happy?" Louella's head bobbed backward as she contemplated being happy over the king of the Happy Land causing others to stumble and become possessed by this demon liquor.

"Why would I ever be happy about this abomination you've brought on us?" Louella turned around, pointing at one contraption after the next. The burner, the pot still, the boiler, and the condenser. "I want this whole operation shut down."

Robert laughed in her face. "I can't shut this down. We're doing good business. I'm bringing money back to the Happy Land."

"If you're bringing so much money to us, why we been tightening our belts?" Louella turned to the men who were all standing around, looking as if they'd rather be anywhere else but here. "Is he splitting the profits with y'all, or are y'all going home and watching your wives scrounge up enough food to feed the family each day?"

Louella pointed at the pot still and told the men, "No one has had corn muffins in the Happy Land in six months. We been rationing out the corn to each family. I'm sure you men done heard complaints from your wives about that."

No one responded.

Louella turned back to Robert and shouted at him, "You're a thief, and you're no good for this kingdom! I knew it from the beginning, but these men wanted you to lead them . . .

"They stand by you now, even though you're taking food out of their families' mouths. But I won't stand by you."

Robert took the straw out of his mouth and threw it to the ground. "What you gon' do?"

He looked as if he wanted to challenge her authority to tell him what he could and couldn't do, but Louella wasn't scared of Robert or any of his cohorts. She told him, "The first thing I'm going to do is appoint watchers over our crops. You won't take another ear of corn out of the mouths of our children. The next thing I'm going to do is report you to the authorities."

He laughed again. "There's no law against selling liquor."

"There's a crime in not paying the taxes on your liquor sales, and since I keep the books and no liquor sales have ever been turned in to me, I know you're not paying taxes."

Robert huffed. "You wouldn't dare."

"Try me." Louella started walking toward the door. She pointed back toward the moonshine equipment. "I want it all torn down." She stopped and glared at him. "I promise you this: I will see you in jail before I let you pervert God's people with your wicked ways one day longer."

CHAPTER 37

The night took its sweet time . . . seemed like it went on for hours longer than it used to when William lay beside her. Most things took more effort now that William had gone home to glory.

But when the night released its hold, Louella jumped out of bed ready to tackle the new day. To see if it would bring sweetness or sorrow. But no matter what, her boys brought her joy every day.

Joshua took the wagon over to Possum Hollow so he could attend his last year of school. Waties went to the field to harvest the potatoes. If nothing else, they would all have some potato soup and mashed potatoes with their meals. They would have to wait another six months to harvest the corn. But Louella would make sure that everyone in the Happy Land received their fair share of that harvest.

"Good morning, Mama Sue. How are you doing?" The sun had cracked the sky. Her grandmother could have slept in if she pleased. But she'd gotten up early for so many mornings that her internal clock wouldn't let her sleep too late.

"I'm doing much better this morning. These old bones get tired sometimes is all."

"That's why I want you to rest more."

Mama Sue waved that off. "I'll have plenty time for resting when they bury me. But as long as I'm able, I'm gon' keep getting out of that bed and taking care of you and these chillun."

"Okay, but don't talk about being buried. I don't want to hear that."

"I'm sorry, chile, but I'm getting older. The good Lord is going to call me home sooner rather than later, and I don't want you crying over me when you've got this whole kingdom to run."

Her grandmother was eighty-seven years old. She'd lived a good, long life. But Louella wanted more and couldn't bear to think about losing another person. Yet she understood the cycle of life, so she said, "I pray that you've known peace these last few years."

Mama Sue put scrambled eggs on a plate and handed it to Louella. "Don't you ever doubt it. You have lifted my head, sweet girl. There's only one thing left for me to see in this world and then I can die a happy woman."

Louella knew the one thing her grandmother desired. It was also her desire. She didn't know if it would ever come to pass, so she didn't entertain it with further conversation. She ate her eggs, then washed off her plate. "I'm heading over to the school. I'll see you for lunch."

Louella worked on vowel sounds with the children on the right side of the room while Abigail worked on handwriting drills on the left side of the room. When their session was over, Louella sent the children home. Then she turned to Abigail. "What's going on with you? You've been kind of quiet today."

"Thinking over some things."

While taking papers off the kids' desks, Louella asked, "Like what?"

"For one thing," Abigail said with a grin, "Femi told me how you shut down King Robert's moonshine operation."

"You knew about that?"

Abigail shook her head. "They kept everything they were doing in that barn hush-hush. Femi didn't even know. But last night while on patrol, Larry told Femi what had been going on and how you put a stop to it."

"I told him to stop. I'm not sure if he actually stopped, but he won't be stealing any more corn from us for his moonshine. I can promise you that."

"Oh no, he stopped. Larry told Femi that you put the fear of God in King Robert. He had the whole contraption taken down. Said something about not wanting to spend his last days in prison."

Louella sat down in her chair at the front of the classroom and took her pencil out to review the paperwork. "He made the right decision."

"I wish I could've been there to see his face when you threatened him." Abigail laughed.

"It's not funny. I didn't want to do that in front of his men, but he left me no choice. But I'm glad I could put a smile on your face."

Abigail sighed. She walked over to Louella and leaned against one of the kid's desks. "I do have something to tell you."

Louella put the papers down. "Nothing's wrong with the kids, is there?"

Abigail shook her head. "The boys are fine, but I have an interview for a teaching position in Greenville."

Louella let out a whoosh of air, like she'd been punched in the gut. Others had left the Happy Land, and she was okay with that. Her people were free to do whatever was best for them. Losing Abigail was different.

But no matter how much it hurt, she wouldn't take this moment from Abigail with her own selfish desires. Forcing herself to smile, Louella said, "This the moment you've been dreaming about. You've helped me and Reverend Allen teach for years."

"Thanks to you, I was able to receive my teaching certificate. So when I heard about the position in Greenville . . ."

Silence mingled with missing-you-already sighs. Louella got out of her seat and came around to Abigail. She pulled the woman into her arms. "I'm so proud of you."

"I don't have the job yet," Abigail told her as they ended their embrace.

"They would be fools not to hire you. I'll give you a reference, and I'm sure Reverend Allen will do the same."

Abigail sniffed as a tear rolled down her face. "If I get the job, we'll have to move to Greenville."

Louella started crying as well. She wiped the tears from her face. "I know."

"I'll miss you terribly."

"Me too," Louella told her. But then a glimmer of a smile crept across her face. "But you know what . . . Clara moved to Hendersonville. She and I have promised to visit each other, so now I'll also have a friend in Greenville to visit."

"I'm not only a friend, Queen Louella. We're sisters. No bit of distance will ever change that."

"No, it won't change that." But that didn't stop Louella's heart from hurting. She was losing her sister . . . her best friend. Even as her heart hurt, she thought back to the day she first offered to teach Abigail how to read.

Abigail was about to make something of herself, and Louella couldn't wait to see her sister shine. They parted ways. Louella was headed home with a heavy heart when Larry ran over to her with frantic and fear-struck eyes.

"Queen Louella, we need you. Come quick."

"Who needs me? What's got you out of sorts?"

"It's King Robert. Something's wrong with him." Larry took off running toward Robert's house. Louella followed him, walking as fast as she could. Then when Larry stood on Robert's porch, waving her on, she ran the rest of the way.

"We got him to his bed, but he don't look good," Larry told her.

Louella opened the door and walked into Robert's house. She took note of the Elizabethan sofa and chair and found herself wondering if he'd had that furniture shipped in or if Joe had made them.

Louella held her breath as she stepped inside Robert's room.

She didn't know what she would do if she saw him unconscious in the same way William had been brought home to her the day before he died.

His eyes were open and he was alert, but he reached out to her. "Help me, Louella. Death is upon me."

CHAPTER 38

Robert didn't die that day. He had the kind of sickness that lingered on. Louella brewed every herb they had in the kingdom and gave them to him, but nothing raised him up again.

Dr. Morris came to the Happy Land to check on him. When he finished looking Robert over, Dr. Morris told Louella, "I've seen this before. It doesn't end well."

"But you know medicine, Dr. Morris. There has to be something you can do."

"I wish there was, especially after what you did for my mother." The look on his face didn't bring her comfort. He reached in his bag and handed Louella a pill bottle. "Give him this for the pain."

Louella took the bottle, but she questioned Dr. Morris again. "You went to medical school, right?"

He nodded. "I did."

"And there's nothing in any of them books you studied that can help Robert?"

Dr. Morris patted her on the shoulder. "Make him as comfortable as you can." With that, he left her standing there with pills in her hand and no good news to share with her brother-in-law.

She set up around-the-clock nursemaids to give Robert the best care they could. She had to oversee the kingdom during the day, but she sat with her brother-in-law several nights a week.

"Those nephews of mine are growing up to be fine men."

Louella was seated next to Robert's bed. She smiled. Waties brought Robert breakfast every morning before he went off to the fields, and Joshua made sure his uncle had his nightly meal when he arrived home from school.

She'd told them that the nursemaids could take care of Robert's meals, but they assured her they wanted to help in this way. *"Our father would want us to help his brother during his time of need,"* Waties had said.

The little imp that crept up Louella's spine from time to time when dealing with Robert wanted her to tell her sons how shameful Robert had acted during their father's time of need and even after his death—by claiming the mantle of king before she and others in the Happy Land had time to mourn their deceased leader.

Each time those thoughts rose up in her, she reminded herself about the blessing of forgiveness.

"William would have been very proud of the men his sons have grown up to be," Louella responded.

"Elmira thinks I wish she had been a boy, but that's not true at all."

Elmira sat with Louella on many nights. One night, as they talked, Elmira confessed that she and her daddy weren't getting along. She didn't understand why he left her behind after her mother died, and she held that against him.

"I think she wants answers," Louella told him.

"She thinks I was wrong for leaving South Carolina and heading to Mississippi when my father suddenly got a mind to grow cotton." Robert coughed, making his body jerk.

When he settled, Louella said, "You and your mother were free. You didn't have to go if you didn't want to."

"It may have seemed that way, but my father was taking William with him, and he kept threatening to revoke my mother's papers if she didn't travel to Mississippi with him. I was a young man back then, and I was terrified at the thought of never seeing my family again."

Letting out a deep sigh, Robert continued, "Elmira's mother

had died, and Elmira wasn't free. I didn't know how to take care of a child on my own—didn't know what would become of me if I stayed—so I left her with her grandmother. But I thought about my child every day."

Louella remembered the horse Robert had named Elmira. It had been so precious to him that he cried when she had to be put down. She patted his hand. "I believe you."

He fell asleep.

Robert slept a lot. He needed his nurse to get out of bed. His legs weren't steady enough to hold him. After relieving himself and being helped back into bed, he would often fall right back to sleep, drained by those few minutes of being on his feet. But most nights Robert would lie in bed, ready to converse with Louella when she arrived at his bedside.

Tonight he said, "I need to confess something to you, but I'm afraid you'll hate me even more than you already do."

"I don't hate you, Robert. I've never understood you, but *hate* is too strong a word to use against family."

Robert tried to sit up, but the struggle was too much for him. Louella helped him lift his body into an upright position. He coughed and then said, "You're a good-hearted woman. I gave you a hard time for years, but you've served the Happy Land well."

"I appreciate you saying that. I've done the best I could for everyone."

"I know you have. That's why it breaks my heart to tell you what I've done."

Holding on to her chair, Louella took a deep breath to prepare herself for whatever Robert had to say. The man had done so many terrible things without batting an eye down through the years, so Louella couldn't fathom what sin he was holding on to now.

Robert put a hand to his chest as he winced in pain. Louella had rubbed her ointment on his chest more times than she could count, but it only momentarily relieved the pain. She gave him one of the pills Dr. Morris had left for him. "Maybe we should get you to the hospital."

But Robert said, "No. If the good Lord has decided that this is my time, then I'll go to the sweet by and by right here—in the land that we built."

"Okay." Louella nodded her agreement. "You are the king of the Happy Land, so I won't force the issue of the hospital with you again."

The truth of the matter was that Robert didn't look as if he had many days left in him. If being in the Happy Land brought him comfort in his last days, then she wouldn't take that away from him.

"I finally get you to acknowledge me as king, but what I have to tell you isn't very kingly." Robert adjusted himself. "I can't get comfortable."

"Take your time. If this thing is too much for you, we can talk about it tomorrow."

He lifted a hand. "I don't know how many more tomorrows I got. You have to know what I've done. It might affect the kingdom once I'm gone."

"I'm listening." She projected calmness and light, but she was sitting on pins and needles while waiting for Robert to say more.

"I used to love going over to Spartanburg, so much so that there were times when I wouldn't come back home for months."

"I remember those days."

"I've been a drinker and a gambler since I was young. Found a saloon out by Spartanburg where I was able to take care of both my vices."

She knew about the saloon but was still confused by his statement. "What do your vices have to do with us?"

"I wish I could say nothing, but I lost more than I won. When I built the barn and bought the equipment to make the moonshine, I had to borrow from someone I thought was a friend."

"William and I never borrowed from anyone. We didn't want to be in debt, and you knew that. Why would you put our land in jeopardy like that?"

"William was perfect, and I'm the rotten seed. I get that, but I tried to make the money back with the moonshine runs. Equipment and supplies were costly, and then I got sick . . ."

"What exactly are you telling me?"

"Carter Wilson came to see me the other day. He says if I don't pay what I owe, he's gon' take the land from us."

"No!" Louella shouted. Then lowered her tone. "This isn't only your land. It belongs to all of us. We shouldn't have to pay for your sins."

"In the Happy Land, you're a queen and held in honor, but"— he pointed behind him—"the real world don't care what a Black woman wants."

"Ten cents a day." Cheap labor . . . ten-cents-a-day labor built the Happy Land. They all worked hard, long hours and brought the money back to her and William with the promise that they would forever have a home to call their own.

"He's been pressuring me to sign over the deed to him since I got in debt. Thought I'd be able to pay what I owed, but . . . I ran out of time."

Sweat dripped from Robert's forehead. Louella grabbed a rag and wiped his head. "If you've owed this man for a couple of years, why am I just now hearing anything about this?"

"You always said I wasn't fit to be king. I couldn't bear proving you right."

Her brother-in-law had been sick for so long that it took the bite out of Louella's anger. "I'll admit that I needed your help after

William died. He did so much in the field with the men, and I was always so busy with the women and children . . . I doubt I would've been able to handle everything on my own."

"Not to mention that you were a total wreck back then."

"Well, I had lost my husband."

"I've only envied my brother two times in my life: when he became king and when I saw the look in your eyes after you lost him. It made me wish that I'd settled down with someone who loved me as much as you loved William."

"He made me love him, and I'm better for having had him in my life."

"And he was better for having you." Robert grinned a bit. "It's strange how an illness can make you put things in perspective." He looked at Louella. His eyes were glassy, looking as if they were about to spill over with tears. "I'm sorry."

Louella stood. She put a hand on Robert's arm. His misdeeds would surely bring harm to the Happy Land. But all the unforgiveness she had harbored in her heart against the men who enslaved her and controlled her had almost kept her from loving William.

If she had not released the hate, she never would have been able to let love grow in her heart. And what kind of life would that have been? "I forgive you, Robert, and I'm going to pray that the Lord raises you up so we can take care of this situation together."

CHAPTER 39

That night, when Louella left Robert's house, her legs wobbled. Her vision was spinning . . . spinning. The church was a few feet away—her house was even closer—but her eyes blurred the distance as she turned this way and that, grabbing hold of her racing heart.

A mountain of dust and trouble swirled around her. A trap had been set. She was falling into a hole. Her mouth opened, sucking in air and then blowing it out. Sucking in and blowing out again and again.

"Mama, what's wrong? Is he gone?"

Waties grabbed her shoulders and shook her. The spinning stopped, and her eyes focused on her son. "What?"

"Is he gone?"

Robert . . . He wanted to know about Robert. "No, chile, he ain't gone." Louella patted Waties on the shoulder and then let him help her to the house.

She needed some sleep but kept falling into a pit of leeches. Pulling them away from her mouth, she hollered each time her eyes popped open.

She had to figure a way out of the mess Robert had gotten them in. Louella had not allowed him to throw all of their money away on the gambling tables or strong drink and his barn. She had squirreled away gold coins here and there. She kept them hidden in her home. After lying awake most of the night thinking and thinking, she'd come up with something.

❦

In the morning, Louella took twenty-five dollars' worth of coins from her stash along with the deed to the first plot of land she and William had purchased not long after they moved into the mountains. She rushed up the hill to her beloved niece's home.

Louella knocked on the door and waited. Elmira opened the door. Her eyes sparked with the is-he-gone question families dealt with while waiting for a loved one to pass on.

"Your father's still with us, but you might want to go see him soon. He's getting weaker by the day."

"I want to, Auntie, but I don't like seeing him like that."

Louella walked into the house with Elmira. She sat down with her in the living room. "I know you and your daddy have your differences, but don't stay away too long and then live with regrets."

Elmira nodded, then lowered her head.

"I didn't come here to get on you about your daddy." She used her index finger to lift Elmira's chin. "Go see him soon. There may not be a later."

"I will, Auntie. I promise."

"I need you to do me a favor. That's why I'm here today."

"You"—Elmira pointed toward Louella—"need a favor from me?" Then she pointed toward herself as if she couldn't believe the queen of the Happy Land was requesting favors.

"I do." Louella took Elmira's hand in hers. "You're the only one I can trust to do this for me, so I must ask, but I can't tell you why at this moment."

"What you need?"

Louella opened the envelope. She poured the coins out into Elmira's lap, then she took the deed for twenty-five acres of land out of the envelope. "I need you to buy this land from me. I'm willing to sell it to you for twenty-five dollars."

Elmira slapped a hand to her cheek. "You're giving me twenty-five acres? I can have all this land?"

Louella shook her head. "It's more like I'm loaning it to you. I'll tell you everything I need you to do, but no matter what, you'll be able to keep the purchase price all to yourself."

Elmira stuck her hand out. "Fine with me."

After handing over the first twenty-five acres, Louella could breathe again. She had a plan, and only time would tell if it would work or not. At least she wasn't sitting on her do-nothing waiting for what would come next.

Abigail came out of her house as Louella was headed back down the hill. She waved to Louella and then caught up with her.

"Hey," Louella said. "I've been meaning to come see you."

"I know you're busy," Abigail said.

"How'd the interview go?"

"Really good. I think I'm going to get the job. But of course, I'll let you know before anything is final."

"I appreciate that," Louella said.

Then Abigail pointed toward Robert's house. "How's he doing?"

Louella looked away, then shook her head. "Not good."

"Can I see him?"

Louella's eyebrow went up. "But you don't like Robert, right?"

Abigail sighed. "I'm conflicted. A long time ago, he did something for me, but I never thanked him."

Louella put an arm around Abigail. "Well, this I've got to hear. Come on, let's see if the king is up for visitors."

Robert was feverish when Louella and Abigail entered his house. The nursemaid had just given him some catnip tea and a pill, and a cold rag was placed on his head as Louella had instructed. "I don't know if he's up for visitors," the nurse told them.

Robert turned toward them. His eyes seemed to light up as he glanced in Abigail's direction. "Come over here," he said.

"I don't want to tire you, King Robert. I came to check on you." Abigail walked over to his bed and took the chair Louella sat in most nights when she visited.

"Well, you're a sight to see. How are your children?"

"Getting bigger every day," Abigail told him. Then Louella saw sadness shadow her face. Abigail fidgeted in her seat. Sighed. "I never thanked you for what you did for me back in Mississippi."

"Don't even speak of it. You don't owe me anything, then or now," Robert told her.

"Yet and still, I should have said thank you. But even though I didn't appreciate your kindness back then, I see it as plain as day now and . . . thank you."

Abigail stood and rushed out of the room. She looked as if she was about to cry, so Louella followed her. They stood on the porch. Louella asked her friend, "You okay?"

"I will be."

"Want to talk about it?"

Looking off into the distance, Abigail knocked her fist against one of the pillars, then turned to Louella. "I still wake up screaming some nights when my dreams take me back to those slavery days. I was used in terrible ways by my first owner."

Tears flowed down Abigail's cheeks as pain etched across her face. "He liked young girls, so when I got older, he put me on the auction block. Robert was there with his daddy. Old Montgomery started bidding on me, but before it was over, Robert had outbid him.

"I thought he wanted the same thing from me as my former master, but Robert never touched me. I still don't understand why he bought me, but I'm grateful that I didn't have to go home with his daddy."

Abigail's words left Louella questioning things about Robert enslaving his own kind before emancipation. She'd thought he'd treated Abigail the way her first owner had, but knowing that he hadn't left Louella in a quandary.

Louella said goodbye to Abigail and went back to Robert's room. She considered him for a moment, scratched her head, then sat down. "Why'd you enslave those people? I've always hated that about you, but now I'm wondering if I misjudged some things."

"Somebody had to protect them. I didn't have enough money to purchase as many as my daddy had, but with what money I had, I made sure at least some of our enslaved brothers and sisters wouldn't be whipped or controlled by a master who could do whatever he wanted with 'em."

"You bought Abigail even though you knew your daddy wanted her." Louella was looking at her brother-in-law in a new light. "Was that to keep her from living the life your mother endured?"

Robert's eyes shadowed over, like ugly memories flooded his soul. "Mama used to say, '*Master* is just another word for the devil himself.' I tried to honor her by being a different kind of master. I never wanted to harm my people. But I guess the mere fact that they were considered someone's property was harm enough."

Louella had read many newspaper articles through the years with white folks claiming they had happy throngs of slaves and that the war had ruined their wonderful way of life. She could tell them different.

Robert had never been anyone's property, so she understood why he didn't get it. But then she thought of something that might help him with the matter. "You see how kind and good Serepta has been to us since we arrived over twenty years ago?"

Robert nodded. "Kindest woman in these mountains."

"But when we arrived, she was in need of help. All of the enslaved people had left the moment slavery ended."

Robert winced and put a hand to his chest.

Louella waited for the pain to subside, then said, "We suffered many hardships under your daddy, his wife, and that awful overseer, but I doubt Serepta was anything like Mary, and yet her people still left. Something about being owned, being somebody's property, makes a person yearn to throw off them shackles."

Robert's eyes fluttered as he said, "Freedom." Then he went to sleep.

Louella went home. But her heart was heavy with the things she had discovered about the king. He had not done right by the kingdom in some of the decisions he'd made, but he wasn't her enemy either. She'd made him out to be the devil on many occasions, but that wasn't the man she had come to know.

"How's the king doing?" Mama Sue asked when she came into the house.

"It's not looking good." Louella sighed. "Now that I'm finally getting to know him, it's almost over." She went to her room and lay down. The house smelled of butter beans and fried chicken, but Louella wasn't hungry. She was drained.

The next morning, Louella's body ached all over. She wanted to lie in bed and act as if nothing that was happening in the Happy Land concerned her, but she threw off the covers and got out of bed even though everything in her wanted to stay put.

She was the queen. She had responsibilities to her people, and that wouldn't change until she went to glory and was able to see her husband, daughter, and father again. But in truth, Louella sometimes wondered if her mother was also in glory. No one had been able to provide information on her whereabouts. Maybe she needed to stop hoping and dreaming for something that wasn't to be.

"Good morning, children," Louella said as she stood before her class later that morning. "Today, I am going to teach you how to spell three-letter words, so it's gonna be a fun day."

One of the children in the back of the room raised a hand.

Louella acknowledged the hand, then her student said, "But I don't know how to spell two-letter words yet."

Other kids laughed at him.

Louella shushed them. "Stop. It's not nice to laugh at your friends. He joined our class a few weeks ago and wasn't here when we went over two-letter words."

One of the students got up from his seat and walked toward the back, where the student who asked the question was seated. "I'm sorry for laughing. I can help you with those two-letter words."

Joy bubbled up in Louella's heart. She preached kindness to her students, but to see it in action on a day when she was so tired that she hadn't even wanted to show up for class was simply wondrous to her.

She clapped her hands a few times, then said, "I love you all. Now let's get started."

Louella began writing three-letter words like *dog*, *cat*, and so forth on the chalkboard. When she turned to face the class again, she saw a wagon coming down the hill. It was Reverend Ezel. She asked the class, "Can y'all practice these words for a minute? I need to speak with Reverend Ezel."

Louella rushed outside and stood in front of the school, waving the reverend forward. She was thankful he had arrived. Reverend Ezel's prayers were always welcomed in the Happy Land, and Robert could use some of that fire in Reverend Ezel's belly.

Reverend Ezel pulled his wagon up to the school. He smiled at her as he jumped down. Bowing as he was wont to do, he said, "Good morning, Queen. I'm so sorry to disturb your lessons, but I had to rush over here first thing this morning."

"I'm thankful you came. I'm hopeful you'll be able to sit with Robert and pray with him."

"Yes, yes, of course. It would be a great honor to pray with King Robert. But before I go over to his house, I brought someone that has been dying to see you."

Louella was too drained to get excited about a new resident for the Happy Land. She hoped the person wouldn't take her demeanor the wrong way. She moved her neck from side to side, needing to release the tightness around her shoulders, then walked to the back of the wagon with Reverend Ezel.

He held out his hand to a woman and helped her step down. A young man stepped down behind her. Louella wiped her hands on her skirt and lifted her head as she prepared to welcome a new resident, but the tears on the woman's face took her by surprise. In all the years Reverend Ezel had been bringing folks to the Happy Land, none of them had ever cried at the sight of her.

Then the woman pulled Louella into her arms and hugged her so tight that Louella instantly closed her eyes as her nose brushed against the nape of the woman's neck. The scent of her was familiar, like the neck she had nuzzled up to many nights as a child.

Louella pulled back and looked at the woman. Gray hairs lined the front of her head. Crow's-feet danced around her eyes, but other than that, Louella was looking at the same woman who had sat in the back of that wagon tied like a hog as she was driven away from the Montgomery Plantation.

"Mama?"

"Yes, child. It's me."

"B-but how can this be? Am I for sure and true looking at you?" Louella touched Brenda's face. Was she dreaming? "Mama!" Louella hugged her all over again.

Brenda raised her hands in the air. "The good Lord done answered my prayers." Then she put her hands on either side of Louella's face. "I can't believe that I lived to see this day."

Holding up a finger, Louella said, "Wait . . . wait." Then she ran from the school to her house. She swung the door open wide. Mama Sue was at the hearth. Tears of I-can't-believe-this-joy streamed down Louella's face.

"Oh, chile, I'm so sorry." Mama Sue wiped her hands on her housecoat and walked toward Louella.

Shaking like a cold wind had blown through and chilled her bones, Louella held up a hand. "It's not the king."

Mama Sue's eyebrow jutted upward. "Then what's got you all riled?"

"Come outside! Come now!" Louella ran back outside and grabbed her mother's hand, moving her closer and closer to the house.

Mama Sue stepped out onto the porch. She had a hand on her hip, eyes flashing with questions as she turned to where Louella was pulling a woman toward her.

Entering the front yard, Brenda stopped and put her hands to her face. As her eyes got big, she cried out, "Mama!"

Mama Sue put her hand on the banister and made her way down the steps. Brenda went to her mother and pulled her into a tender embrace. Her voice was an earthquake of emotion as she said, "I dreamed about this moment, Mama!"

"Are my eyes deceiving me?" Mama Sue pulled back, staring at Brenda, and then went right back into her arms. Tears flowed down Mama Sue's face. She lifted a hand in praise. "The Lord done blessed me real good in my old age."

Brenda then called the young man over to her. "This here is Henry. He's my son, Mama."

Mama Sue walked over to Henry, who looked to be about thirty or so. She put her hands on his face and kissed him. "All these years, I kept dreaming about a little boy. I thought I was dreaming about Ambrose, but it must have been you all along. And now the missing part of my heart has been restored."

Tears wouldn't stop rolling. She had another brother. Louella hugged Henry. "I'm so glad to finally meet you." She then closed school for the day and sent someone to get Ambrose.

When Ambrose came to the house, Brenda started crying all over again as she looked from him to Louella. "Look at my children. Y'all's grown now." She sighed deeply, like a pain way down deep was dislodging from one spot and resituating itself. "Thought I'd never see you two again, but God done kept us. And we're all together, like family's supposed to be."

There was a pang in Louella's heart at her mother's words. Her father was family, and he was no longer with them. He had sacrificed his life to get to freedom, but it was still a blessing to see her mother in the land of the living.

She went outside and stood on her porch. Her heart filled with joy as she sang the words to a new song. *"I'm no longer a motherless child . . . It took a long while, but the good Lord, He done threaded my heart . . . Me and my mama, we no longer apart."*

CHAPTER 40

Robert got weaker by the day. He could no longer tolerate food and only took sips of water. On Sunday, as Louella and the other congregants left the church, she saw Elmira standing on Robert's porch, leaning against one of the posts that held up the roof.

The look on Elmira's face wasn't sadness; it was anger. "What's troubling you?" Louella stepped onto the porch.

"Ask my father," Elmira said and then stormed away from the house.

Louella had no idea what Robert had done this time, but whatever it was, it didn't sit well with his daughter.

The nurse opened the door as Louella was pondering on Elmira's anger. "Queen Louella, come quickly."

Louella rushed into the house. As she entered Robert's room, she could hear the death rattle with each labored breath he took. Standing beside his bed, she took Robert's hand in hers. "Look to God now, King Robert. Ask Him to forgive you and receive you."

Robert's eyes fluttered, then lifted, but he wasn't looking at her. He had his eyes on something that Louella couldn't see.

"Be with my king on this day, dear Lord. Forgive his trespasses." One thing was certain: earthly kings and kingdoms would all pass away, but God's kingdom would reign forever. After all these years, after all their disagreements, in the end the only thing that mattered was that Robert got things right with God. She kept praying.

Robert's body heaved. She heard that rattle one last time, and then he was gone. Another king was gone, and Louella had watched them both transition. She was calmer with Robert, but there was still an ache in her heart.

His hand went limp. Louella placed it back on the bed. She closed her eyes and took in a deep, long-suffering breath, then exhaled. She couldn't sit here and fall apart. The people would need her now more than ever.

Louella walked outside. She went to the school and rang the triangle bell. As a tear dropped from her eye, she shouted, "The king is dead!"

Reverend Ezel stayed on at the Happy Land to perform the funeral for King Robert. Louella was pleased that so many had turned out for the burial. She laid him to rest next to his brother below the Davis Cemetery.

As they left the burial site, Louella looped her arm around her grandmother's and started singing "Amazing Grace." Robert had left a mess that she would have to clean up, but for now, she only wanted to celebrate the king that once was.

Her prayer for Robert was that he had received grace from God for his sins on this side of heaven. She had forgiven him and had let the past reckon with itself. Now she needed to get Elmira to do the same.

After the meal was served and everyone had eaten, Louella took Elmira to the side. She hugged her niece. "You look like you need a hug today."

"I do, Auntie. I'm so torn." Mountains of sadness filled Elmira's eyes. "I love my daddy, but some of the things he's done . . ." She shook her head. "I can't get behind them."

Louella put a hand on Elmira's shoulder. "Do you want to talk about it? I saw how upset you were before your daddy passed."

Elmira leaned against the post as Louella sat in her chair on the porch. Looking out toward the hill where more houses were, she said, "He apologized to me."

Louella figured the apology had nothing to do with the anger she'd seen on Elmira's face that day, so she kept quiet and waited.

Elmira wiped tears from her face as she turned to Louella. "Then he told me that I wouldn't be alone in this world when his time came."

"Of course you're not. You've got me, your cousins, and the rest of the Bobo clan."

"I know that, Auntie, but he wasn't talking about y'all." Elmira looked around, then she walked closer to Louella and whispered, "He told me that I have other sisters and a brother over in Spartanburg."

A hand went to her face. Louella figured there had to be something that kept pulling Robert away from the Happy Land. He told her about the gambling and drinking in Spartanburg, but he hadn't said a peep about children . . . children!

"I didn't know anything about this. Did your daddy marry some woman in Spartanburg?"

Elmira shrugged. "He didn't say anything about a marriage."

Louella's eyes grew wide, but she was silent . . . couldn't speak on it.

"Wasn't that nice of him to tell me something like that but provide no other information? I don't know their names . . . where they live . . . nothing."

Louella wondered how old Robert's other kids were. She wondered if William knew what his brother had been up to. Children . . . in Spartanburg? She couldn't blame Elmira for being upset. Why Robert waited until he was on his deathbed to tell his daughter something like that was beyond her.

But she desperately wanted her niece to forgive her father. She didn't want anyone to harbor unforgiveness in their heart the way she had. But Louella knew all too well that forgiveness wasn't easy, so she would pray for Elmira and wait until God healed her niece's heart.

Elmira didn't want to move into the home that had belonged to her daddy, so Louella gave it to her mother. The same day that her mother moved next door, Mama Sue said, "I hope you don't mind, but Brenda wants me to stay with her a spell."

Louella's heart tightened. "You're leaving me?"

"I'll just be next door, my sweet girl." Mama Sue put a gentle hand to Louella's face. "Not but a stone's throw away."

Louella sighed. "At least you'll be close so I'll be able to check on you."

Mama Sue gave a big belly laugh. "You mean you'll be able to come right on over for supper."

"Me too," Waties said.

Mama Sue patted him on the head. "Don't worry, I'll still cook for y'all."

Things were changing in the Happy Land. The children they had started with were now grown. George and Maggie Couch's children, Ezel, Anderson, and Mary, were all grown up now as well. Louella's children were grown, and so many others had grown up and left the Happy Land.

Louella's mother was now with them, but Louella hadn't imagined that finding her mother would take a bit of her grandmother from her. Things were not the same in the house without Mama Sue.

A few days later, Louella glanced over at her mother's home. Mama Sue and Brenda were sitting on the porch sipping on tea as they chatted. Mama Sue said something, then her mother's head fell backward as laughter spilled out of her.

Sniffing the air, Louella walked to the edge of her porch. "I smell those greens cooking. I'm coming for supper. I hope you made enough."

Brenda waved to her. "You better get over here and eat this food with us. I want to see each of my children every day of my life from here on out."

She had her mother back. She still had her grandmother. God was good.

❦

The next day Louella sat on the porch with her mother, enjoying the light springtime breeze. "Your grandmother told me everything you've done for her and your brother, and I want to thank you for keeping the family together."

"We had lost enough . . . didn't want to lose each other too. I stayed on that rotten plantation after slavery because Mama Sue didn't want to leave." Louella reached over, took her mother's hand in hers, and squeezed it. "I think she was waiting on you to find your way back to us."

"Wish I had run into Reverend Ezel sooner. I missed all of you dearly. It got so bad, I had to tell myself that I wouldn't see any of you again until we met on the other side. That was the only way I could get up and keep going every morning. I had to stop hoping for what I didn't believe would ever happen."

"It's a terrible thing to lose hope." Louella wiped the sweat from her forehead. The days were getting longer and hotter. "I have to admit that I stopped believing this day would ever come."

"And yet here we are." Brenda pointed heavenward with tears rolling down her face. "It's been forty years since I was sold away from my family, but God heard my cry, and He brought me back to y'all."

There were so many days that Louella had wondered if God was listening or if she was praying in vain. She had no way of knowing how or why God answered some prayers and left others hanging out in the wind. Even so, she had learned to bless God through it all and wait on the miracles He sent her way.

CHAPTER 41

As Louella was making peace with the God she couldn't trace, two things happened that almost took the fight she had left. One day as she was in the field overseeing the corn harvest, a wagon rode into the Happy Land. She glanced over her shoulder and saw that the Henderson County sheriff was guiding his horse and buggy toward the field.

Louella put a hand on Larry's shoulder. "Let me see what the sheriff wants, and I'll be right back."

But Larry said, "Queen, you don't have to watch over us. I promise, we're out of the moonshine business. The corn will be delivered to our remaining customers, and anything left over will be kept right here for everyone in the Happy Land. You have my word."

Louella nodded and patted him on the shoulder. "Tell the men I said thanks for all the hard work. I'll leave you to it." She couldn't be everywhere and do everything on her own. She had to leave certain things in the capable hands of others and trust that they would do what was right for the kingdom.

When she walked over to greet the man who'd rode onto their property, her trust suffered a blow.

"Louella Montgomery?" he asked.

She put her hand over her eyes as the sun blocked her view. "That's me." She'd never had any dealings with the sheriff in these parts, but she'd seen him from time to time as they passed through Hendersonville. "What can I help you with?"

He climbed down from his buggy and handed Louella an envelope. "Your appearance is requested in court."

"My appearance?" Louella put a hand to her chest as her eyebrows furrowed. "But why?"

"It's in the letter, ma'am." He tipped his hat to her. "Good day." And then he was back in his buggy, riding down the hill toward the valley.

Louella stood next to the cornfield, staring at the envelope for the longest time. What on earth could she have done that required her appearance in court? She opened the envelope and read:

R. I. Barnwell, Administrator, seeks authority to sell property of Robert Montgomery to provide funds in order to pay debts in the amount of $500.

The letter also indicated that the property they had purchased for a dollar an acre was now worth two dollars an acre.

"You look like somebody struck you. What's wrong?" Concern was in Brenda's voice as she approached Louella.

Louella glanced up. She let the mountain air fill her lungs as she leaned on her mother's shoulder. Sighing deeply, she lifted the letter. "Robert owes money to someone and now they want to take the land in order to pay his debts."

Brenda put a hand to her cheek as her breath caught in her throat. "Oh, sweetheart, I'm so sorry to hear that."

"Me too." Louella was befuddled by this. Even though Robert had confessed about his debts, no one had bothered them for months. She had hoped they were in the clear.

"What you gon' do?"

"Got to figure out what comes next, I guess." She walked home with her mother, then an idea struck. "I'll be back." She got in her wagon and rode over to Serepta's house.

But when Sarah opened the door with tears in her eyes, Louella experienced her second shock of the day.

"You heard?" Sarah bellowed while using a tissue to wipe her face.

Louella's nose scrunched. She looked around, not sure what Sarah was referring to. "Did something happen?"

"It's Mama. She's been ill, and the doctor thinks her time is near."

"Oh no!" Louella closed her eyes as the familiar pang of heartache snatched at her again. Serepta was eighty-seven years old, but there were some people God should let live forever, and Serepta was one of them. She was the first white person to ever show Louella a crumb of kindness.

Sarah hugged Louella as she continued to cry. "It's terrible. I'm not ready to lose her."

"We never are," Louella told her. "But what I want you to consider is all the good your mama done. Think on that grand smile of hers and let that fill your heart."

They ended the embrace, then Sarah blew her nose. "Thank you for that, Louella. Mama always said you and the others in the Happy Land were sent by God."

"Do you mind if I sit with her? I'd like to thank her for everything."

Nodding as a smile broke through the sadness on her face, Sarah said, "I think she would like that."

Louella took the stairs with Sarah leading the way. She had become acquainted with love, loss, and grief. Serepta had been good to the Happy Landers, so she would not let her pass this earth without knowing how special she had been to them.

They entered Serepta's room. It was hot outside and hotter in Serepta's room. The fireplace was stacked high with wood, and the fire was blazing.

Louella stepped closer to Serepta's bed.

"She keeps complaining about being cold," Sarah told her.

Sweat beads formed on Louella's forehead. "It's fine." Sitting down next to Serepta, she could see that the vibrant woman she once knew was no more. She'd lost weight, and her face was both thin and pale. Green veins ran through her frail hands as if they were mapping their way to glory.

"Came to see the old lady, huh?" Serepta said, glancing over at Louella.

Louella looked from right to left as if she was trying to find someone. "What old lady? I don't see no old ladies 'round here."

Serepta looked too tired to laugh, but she grinned. "I knew there was a reason I liked you on sight. You're smart."

No white person had ever told her that she was smart. "And you're one of the kindest women I've ever met." Louella chuckled. "Never thought I'd say that to a white woman."

A small snicker rose up in Serepta. "You didn't trust me one bit when y'all first arrived. Always looking at me like you thought I was saying one thing but going to do another."

Nodding, Louella admitted the truth of that statement. "After all that had been done to me during slavery days, it was hard to trust a white person to do anything but wrong. But you're different."

The fire crackled, and sweat dripped down the side of her face. The world didn't seem so black and white as Louella leaned back in her seat and held on to Serepta's frail hand. Her chest heaved forward as she enjoyed a moment in time with . . . her friend.

"You and I had to fend for ourselves when our men left this earth. But we did it. We held on to what was ours. Yes, we did," Serepta said as she started drifting.

Louella leaned forward. She didn't know if she would see this kind woman again. So she had to get the words out now. "Thank you, Serepta, for everything you done for us. And you're right, I'm gon' find a way to hold on to what belongs to me and my people."

Louella had planned to ask the Davises for help in fighting this court case, but she wouldn't put her burdens on their shoulders at a time like this. She went back home and stewed around the house, racking her brain to figure a way out of the mess Robert got them into.

The Kingdom of the Happy Land was a place of peace for so many who had been wounded and scarred by slavery and the injustices in this world. She couldn't do nothing and let them take everything they had scrimped and scraped to pull together.

The hours, days, months, and years the men spent sawing down trees and clearing the way so they could build homes for the people in their land had been too much of a sacrifice. All the aching fingers and sore arms and bad backs that resulted from the building of this kingdom weren't for nothing.

As she entered her bedroom, the first thing she saw was William's Bible on the table next to the bed. It was a well-used Bible with pages falling out, like Reverend Ezel's. She picked it up and looked to heaven. "Is it all over? Did we come all this way to be left with nothing?"

Lifting the Bible up, with tears streaming down her face, she asked, "Are the words in this Bible true? Can we trust You, or are we all on our own?"

She closed her eyes as she got on her knees, wiping tears from her face. "I need answers, Lord. I don't know what to do anymore. I've given this place everything I have, but it wasn't enough. We're about to lose everything, and I don't know what to do."

She stayed on floor long into the night, waiting for answers that didn't come. After a while, her eyes began to droop. She stretched out on the floor with the Bible still in her hands. Louella didn't know how long she had been asleep, but when she woke, the Bible was open to the book of Ezekiel, chapter 37.

Louella was mesmerized by the words she read. Was the Lord telling her that her situation was not dead, and He was going to make sure she kept the land?

Then she heard William's voice as clear as day telling her, *"Start believing for good things, even before you see them."*

She got off the floor and picked up the court papers again. The trial would begin next month. Louella didn't know much about the judicial system, but in these last few years, she had learned to trust God to the very end. William had showed her how.

CHAPTER 42

Louella took her place in front of her throne as was custom. They had now lost a little over a hundred people to surrounding areas like Hendersonville, Greenville, and Spartanburg. A deep sense of responsibility clung to her shoulders for the three hundred residents left in the Happy Land. She would not let them down—could not let them down.

"Greetings to all of you. As we gather here this morning, I am duty bound to share with you some unfortunate news." Louella squared her shoulders and clasped her hands in front of her. This would be a hard pill to swallow. Many in the kingdom believed their king and queen were flawless people. Although she had come to realize that Robert wasn't the terrible human being she'd always made him out to be, he wasn't perfect . . . He'd made costly mistakes.

"It appears that the king had debts outside of the kingdom." She lifted the court papers that were in her hand. "I received court papers earlier this week, and I'm sorry to inform you that they're seeking to sell our land in order to cover those debts."

Grumblings rose up as about fifty or so of the residents stood in the yard in front of her home. She raised a hand. "I've been praying about this, and I don't know how, but we're not going to lose our land."

Harold was the first in line to question her. "Queen, if you don't mind me asking, how much did King Robert owe?"

Louella had no problem sharing that information. These were her people. She would not shrink or hide the truth from them. "Five hundred dollars."

Gasps went up.

Harold then said, "I don't understand why this has gone to trial, putting homes that we built with our own two hands in jeopardy."

A man in the back shouted, "Where has all the money that we pay to the kingdom gone? Why didn't you pay his debts?"

It was always the men who questioned her. Being ruled by a woman was an abomination to some men, but that was the problem of small minds.

Her voice boomed. "For one thing, money hasn't been plentiful in the Happy Land of late. But even so, the administrator of this case never gave me that option. They processed the court papers and then informed me of the proceedings."

Her mind went back to when Robert told her, *"In the Happy Land, you're a queen and held in honor, but the real world don't care what a Black woman wants."* If it was the last thing she did, she'd show them all who she was.

Elmira stepped forward. "How can we help, Auntie? I don't want you bearing all this on your shoulders. Let me know when you need my help."

The piercing look Elmira gave her told Louella that she now understood why she had been temporarily gifted those twenty-five acres. But twenty-five acres was not enough. Louella wanted to keep all of what they had built. Sitting down at her throne, Louella nodded to Elmira. "I will. Just hold on a little while longer."

Wiley Bennett was holding his wife's hand as he said, "We love the Happy Land, so if there's anything we can do to help, we want to be a part of that."

Jerry Casey stepped forward. Anger flashed in his eyes. "I'm here to help as well, Queen. I'll defend this land until the very end, and I promise you, I'm not going nowhere."

Louella believed him. Jerry had proven to be a man with leadership qualities and someone who loved this land. With Femi and

Abigail now living in Greenville, they were going to need Jerry more than ever. "I need you to take over Femi's role as sergeant at arms."

"Thank you, Queen. I would be honored," Jerry said as he stepped aside.

She was about to stand back up and dismiss the crowd when Harold stepped back to the front. "Excuse me, Queen Louella, but with all due respect, I should be the one to pick the next sergeant at arms since he will be working with me."

She hadn't forgotten Harold's allegiance to Robert. He probably wanted the Happy Land to have another king and was vying for the job, but that would never happen. She stood, breathed in deeply, then pierced her eyes in Harold's direction. "You defied me once, and I forgave that transgression, but we'll not have a repeat. Jerry will be the new sergeant at arms, and I'm positive he will be an asset to you."

A man yelled from the back, "It's time to pick a new king! You can't handle this on your own."

Louella stretched forth empty hands. "I have no more kings to give you. But let this be known: I will fight for what is ours with everything in me."

❀

Fires on every side had to be put out. But all the fires, great and small, were put on hold when Serepta died. The day was October 13, 1889. Louella took a day to sit on her porch and breathe in the cool fall air.

Louella would miss the woman she now thought of as a friend, even though she'd fought hard not to attach herself in any way to the white lady who'd treated her like a human.

She'd been fighting all her life for others to recognize her somethingthingness. Serepta had seen her for who she was. Louella would forever be thankful for that.

But most importantly, Louella had opened her heart as she learned to forgive. She credited William with giving her the ability to sort out the bad and see some good in others. His goodness helped her release the hate that had grown in her heart for those who sought to harm her and her family.

Forgiveness was a beautiful thing. It allowed her to see Robert as a flawed man but still have respect for the man who loved this kingdom as much as she did.

❧

Forces outside of the kingdom now sought to destroy everything they had built. God help her, but Louella doubted she could ever forgive something like that. She looked to heaven, where she prayed certain members of her family and Serepta now resided. Maybe they were speaking to God on her behalf, reminding Him to breathe life into her dead situation. Then an idea struck.

She wrote a letter to the judge:

Greetings,

My name is Louella Montgomery, and I am writing to make sure you are aware that the land R. I. Barnwell wants to sell in order to pay debts incurred by Robert Montgomery is not solely owned by Mr. Montgomery. My name is on the deed as well, and I don't owe anyone but God.

Furthermore, this land was never owned by Robert Montgomery and Louella Montgomery alone. Hundreds of residents in the Happy Land worked their fingers to the bone as we all pooled our resources together to buy and build this land.

Times have been hard for us and others in this area, but I currently have $350. I am willing to give it all to Mr. Barnwell and make payments on the rest of the debt if you

would be so kind as to cancel this lawsuit and allow us to
settle this matter with Mr. Barnwell ourselves.

Thank you,
Louella Montgomery

Louella's request was denied. With a heavy heart, she turned to God. "I want to put all my trust in You as William did, but I need You to show me something. Fix this dead situation."

A week after her prayer, Louella was sitting at her dining table with Clara and Abigail. "You don't know how happy I am to see both of you."

Mama Sue brought tea and warm biscuits to the table.

"Thank you, Miss Sue. And I wanted to tell you how happy I was to hear that your daughter found her way back to you," Abigail said.

Mama Sue smiled and backed away from the table as she said, "God is good!"

Louella wanted to believe in the goodness of God that she'd heard spoken of. Bringing her mother back to them was certainly something to be thankful for, but now Louella needed God to help them keep their homes.

"We know you're busy, but Abigail and I heard about the troubles you've had since King Robert passed."

Louella pointed toward the biscuits on the table. "I don't want to trouble you with my problems. Eat up. The biscuits are the best that's offered in the Happy Land."

Abigail grabbed one. "I'm not turning down one of Miss Sue's biscuits."

"I'll take a biscuit too." Clara bit into the biscuit and savored it. "We took up a collection from some of the people in Hendersonville who used to live in the Happy Land."

Louella rubbed her forehead with the palm of her hand, too shocked to speak.

Then Abigail said, "I did the same thing in Greenville. We raised twenty dollars." Abigail handed Louella the money.

"Here's mine." Clara took an envelope and handed it over. "Twenty-five dollars came from Hendersonville. I know it's not enough to cover the debt, but we gave what we had."

Holding both envelopes in her hand, Louella felt her eyes fill with tears. "You didn't have to do this. You both have your own lives and your own bills."

Abigail *tsked*. "Don't talk like that, Louella. Whether we live here or not, it will always be all for one and one for all."

Crying now herself, Clara said, "That's what you taught us. So how dare you think we wouldn't help in your time of need."

❧

The next day, Larry and some of the other men began cutting down trees in the area they hadn't tilled yet. More homes were being built in Greenville, and lumber was needed.

Louella stood in front of all those oak trees remembering how much she hated the sight of them when they first arrived on the Oakland Plantation. But through the years, each one of the trees that had been on this land had aided in providing homes for her people, either by the money earned from the sale of them or by the wood used to build the homes.

Oak trees had been her nemesis, but if they could sell enough trees to gather the remaining funds needed to pay Robert's debt, they just might become her saving grace.

❧

Louella was granted a meeting with R. I. Barnwell the day before the trial. She sat across the desk from him in his small office in Hendersonville. She had the deed to the Happy Land in her hands. "Thank you so much for meeting with me today."

He nodded. "It's a part of my job as administrator to meet with all interested parties."

Louella got right to business. She handed him the deed. "How can you sue for the Happy Land when my name is on this deed, as well as Robert Montgomery's, and I don't owe anyone any money?"

"Yes, we're aware that your name is on the deed as well, but that doesn't stop us from collecting on his debts."

"What if I pay the amount owed?"

"That would have been fine a week ago, but now we have other complications." Barnwell handed her back the deed.

She didn't have the money a week ago. She and the other members of the Happy Land had spent the last two weeks coming up with the hundred she was short. They'd sold the Happy Land Liniment, and she'd even kissed the last oak tree that left the Happy Land for the lumber yard. "What complications could stop you from taking my money?"

"We've received notice that Robert Montgomery has three children in Spartanburg." He shuffled some papers, then said, "A Robert S. Montgomery Jr., age fifteen; Cornelia Montgomery, age seventeen; and one Julia Ann Montgomery, age nineteen."

The hairs on the back of her neck rose at the name of each child Barnwell mentioned. Robert had three children but had not brought them to the kingdom to meet his family . . . their sister. "Robert also has another daughter. Her name is Elmira Montgomery, and she is forty-one this year."

"And where does Elmira Montgomery live?" he asked.

"She lives in the Happy Land."

He was jotting information down on a notepad. He looked up. "What's the Happy Land?"

"The property you seek to sell is called the Happy Land. This is the place where our people have built their own homes and built a community of people who work together and treat each other with respect."

"Makes no difference to me what you call it. I've got a hundred and eighty acres of land that needs to be sold to cover these debts, and Mr. P. J. Hart is interested in about eighty or so acres. We'll auction the remainder of the land to cover the rest of what Montgomery owes."

"Selling the land at two dollars an acre will still leave you short of the five hundred you seek. I am offering you the amount owed. Why won't you take it rather than sell the land in pieces?"

Barnwell had been writing something on his notepad. He turned a questioning glance to her. "What do you people need with so much land anyway?"

Remain calm. Deep breath. Remain calm. His "you people" comment would not distract her. "You said I couldn't pay for the debt, said the children presented a complication, so how do you already have a buyer and we haven't gone to court yet?"

Barnwell sputtered, "I-I won't have you speculating about my business practices." He stood and adjusted his jacket. "It's amazing that anyone even wants the land after you people lived on the property for so long."

Barnwell was so sure he could do anything he wanted with their land. Men like him thought white was right and Black was always wrong, even when it wasn't. The problem was, other men were only too willing to help them with their dirty deeds.

Louella stood. She stared him down. With a determined set to her jaw, she told him, "What's amazing is that you think you can take our land—land that nobody wanted when it was nothing but trees as far as the eye could see. Now suddenly, the property is worth more than we bought it for, and you can't take my money to cover Robert's debts."

"I assure you that these proceedings are all very legal."

Louella wasn't stupid by a long mile. She saw what was happening. They were being treated as Gary had been back in Missis-sippi. After he'd tilled the land and grown the crops, he was run off so someone else could profit. "Legal or not, my people have been dealt blows like this from your kind since y'all first stole us from Africa, but God don't like ugly or shameful, so watch out."

"Are you threatening me?"

Louella shook her head. "I don't threaten people, Mr. Barnwell. Just know that the grave you dig for me needs to be big enough for the both of us." With that, Louella walked out of his office.

But as she was heading out the door, she noticed a woman seated with teenagers. One boy and two girls. The boy looked like his father.

CHAPTER 43

Louella brought Robert's children to the Happy Land and spent the rest of her day showing them around. "I'm so thankful that I was able to meet each of you," Louella said and meant it.

Tears welled in her eyes as she hugged Robert Jr. and then Cornelia and Julia. "I'm so sorry that you weren't able to see your daddy before he died. If I had known . . ."

But Julia shook her head. "It's not your fault, Auntie. We knew that our father had another life outside of us. We didn't understand why he never let us be a part of it, though."

Louella didn't understand that either, so she couldn't speak on it. She took Robert's children around the Happy Land, letting them see everything from the crops they grew to the schoolhouse-church to the hundred homes that had been built on the property.

"This is amazing. Our dad owned all of this?" Robert Jr. asked.

"My name and your daddy's name may be on the deed, but this land doesn't belong to us," Louella told them. "It belongs to the people. They're the ones who broke their backs knocking down trees and helped us build everything on this land."

Louella pointed toward the homes all around them as she continued, "The people in those homes went out to work each day for little to no money until it all added up and allowed us to purchase and build what you see here today."

"Wow. So you're like the queen around here," Cornelia said.

Louella humbly said, "They call me Queen, but I consider myself more of a servant to the people."

"How can a queen also be a servant?" Julia's brow furrowed.

"If I'm to serve anyone, let it be the people of the Happy Land." For Louella would gladly fill her days in service to those who'd known the evils men and women could heap upon them, and still they rose . . . kept fighting . . . kept believing. Those were her kind of people.

She continued, "Come on, let's go to the house. I want to introduce y'all to your sister."

"Daddy told us we had a sister," Julia said, "but since I never met her, I've always felt like the oldest."

"And the bossiest," Robert Jr. said.

Julia shoved Robert Jr.

Louella guided the buggy up the hill. When they arrived at the house and saw Elmira, each one commented about the age difference, but they hugged their sister and enjoyed her company.

"So you actually lived here with Daddy?" Cornelia asked her older sister.

Elmira pointed to the house next door. "Daddy lived in that house. I have my own place farther up the hill. You're welcome to visit me anytime you like."

"Are you the reason he couldn't stay with us for more than a few days each month?" Julia asked.

Robert Jr. nudged his sister. "Don't be cantankerous. These are nice people."

"It's all right." Elmira put a hand on Robert Jr.'s shoulder. "I know how Julia feels. Daddy left when I was a toddler, and I didn't see him again until I was nineteen." She sighed. "I hoped we would spend more time together once I moved here with him. But we didn't spend as much time together as I wanted."

Robert Jr.'s eyebrow jutted upward. "How's that possible? You were right here with him."

"Wish I could answer that for you." Sorrow clung to Elmira's voice.

Louella's heart went out to them. She cleared her throat. "What you need to understand is that the evil of slavery separated men from their wives and children. Black men had no control, no say in what happened to their family. Even if a man was free, he couldn't tell the master what to do with his family if they weren't free.

"Robert suffered that atrocity with Elmira." Louella used to think that the enslaved people working in the big house and the ones who'd been set free didn't suffer as she had. But William had opened her eyes. They all suffered. "Your dad may not have known how to handle his responsibilities, but I do believe he loved each of you."

Tears flowed from each of Robert's children. Louella prayed that her words had given them a bit of compassion for their father. Elmira wiped the tears from her face, then hugged Louella. "Thank you, Auntie. I think I can forgive him now."

Elmira then turned to her siblings. "He loved us the best he could. We have to take comfort in that." Then the four of them hugged.

They enjoyed each other's company long into the night. Julia and Cornelia spent the night at Elmira's house. Robert Jr. stayed at Louella's house with Waties and Joshua.

The next morning Mama Sue came over and fixed a big breakfast for all of them. She nudged Louella while stirring the grits. "I always knew that man was hiding something. But a whole family?" She leaned her head back and cackled like a hyena.

Louella gave her an exasperated stare. Then she whispered, "Don't be like that. His children went next door to see Robert's old house. But they'll be right back. You don't want to offend them."

Mama Sue stopped laughing. "Okay. I'll be good."

The door opened. Joshua walked in with Robert Jr., Cornelia, and Julia behind him.

"Breakfast will be ready in a minute. Y'all go into the keeping room." Louella glanced out the door, then asked, "Where's Elmira?"

"She'll be here for breakfast, but she didn't want to go inside Daddy's house," Julia told her.

Louella looked toward Elmira's house. Her niece opened the door and started walking down the hill. Hands in her pockets, she looked to be deep in thought. Baby steps. Her niece needed more time to sit with her grief.

When Elmira came inside the house, Louella spotted tear stains on her face. "You okay?"

"I will be. I get sad sometimes since Daddy left. That must mean something, right?"

"It means you loved him." Louella hugged her niece. "And he loved you."

They had breakfast together as a family. Louella truly enjoyed getting to know Robert's children. She prayed they would not be strangers. "If we're able to keep this land, you're welcome to live here with us," Louella told them.

"That's very nice of you, Auntie," Robert Jr. said.

After breakfast, Ambrose drove Robert's children back to Spartanburg.

When they left, Elmira said, "Thank you, Auntie. Don't know if I ever would've met them if not for you."

"I'm thankful I ran into them and could bring them out here. Those kids need to know they have family who cares about what becomes of them."

"Speaking of that . . ." Elmira took an envelope out of her purse and handed it to Louella. "I care about what becomes of you, so I'm giving you the deed back. I've already signed my twenty-five acres over to you."

Louella took the envelope. "Now we have to convince that judge to release the rest of our land." Louella looked to heaven. "I'm still waiting, Lord." The twenty-five acres would not be enough for her people, but she'd given it to Elmira for safekeeping because she hadn't known what else to do at the time.

On the first day of court, Louella's mood was dark like the black mourning dress she wore. She sat on her throne, thinking over the years that had come and gone. Hard years. Fruitful years.

This thing that Robert had done wouldn't beat them. They'd survived worse.

Harold and Jerry rode up to the front of her house. The horses they rode on were black with the most beautiful black manes. She remained on her throne and received them.

They dismounted, and Harold took his hat off and lowered his head. "Good morning, Queen."

She nodded to Harold and Jerry. "Morning, fellows." She left the "good" out. She wasn't sure how good it was to have to go to court to fend off the vultures who wanted their land.

Jerry took his hat off and lowered his head before saying, "We bring news from our patrol last night."

Harold stood ramrod straight. He cleared his throat. "A man passed by last night, said he wanted to come up the hill to see the land."

A prickly feeling crawled up her spine. "And what y'all tell him?"

Jerry's lips stretched into a grin. "We told him this is private property, and no one comes on or off at night without our queen's say-so."

Louella stood and walked down the steps. "They spying out our land. That Barnwell is piecing it out even before the judge says yay or nay." She patted them on the shoulders.

"Tell them bigwigs what's what. Everything's gon' be all right." Harold lifted a fist in the air as if rooting her on.

Jerry helped her into the wagon. Louella picked up the reins, waved to them, then headed down the hill to the place where no one cared what a Black woman wanted. Determination built in her. She would find a way to make them care.

The court would not recognize her as a defendant in the very same case that sought to take her land. She was a Black woman with no rights as far as they could see. "My name is on that deed. I am Louella Montgomery. How can you take land that rightfully belongs to me and my people?"

The judge yawned, then put a fisted hand under his white-bearded chin. "Money is owed on that land, so it's not all that clear whether the land is yours anymore."

Fix your face, Louella.

There had been many occasions when Mama Sue told her to fix her face. Frowns had been her weapon against the people who would do her harm. But she had much more than frowns now. She had God on her side, and she was determined to win this fight.

"My people worked that land. We built the Happy Land by knocking down one tree at a time. The menfolk have the bad backs to show for it." She shook her head. "The swipe of a fountain pen can't take away all that we built." Louella glanced around the courtroom, which was full of white men with hands itching to snatch what didn't belong to them.

"My people survived trespasses from men like you." Her pointer finger stretched the length of the court. "And we'll survive this injustice as well."

The judge banged the gavel. "That's enough. We have allowed you your say. Now sit down and let us get on with these court proceedings."

Louella took her seat, but all day long the frown of her lips displayed her displeasure. She couldn't fix her face . . . not today.

Barnwell stood before the judge. A grin of self-importance spread across his face. "Your Honor, this case is as simple as the ABCs or one plus one equals two."

The judge barked at him, "No need to be cute, Barnwell. Just give us the facts."

His self-important grin dissipated. "Why, yes, Your Honor. The facts of the matter are that Robert Montgomery left this earth owing a great sum of money. The aggrieved party wishes to receive the funds owed, and therefore we are petitioning the court to sell all land in the possession of Mr. Robert Montgomery and Louella Montgomery."

"Do you have documentation you can present to the court so I can verify this debt?"

Barnwell handed over the documents. The judge took a moment to look over them, then said, "All appears to be in order. Robert Montgomery signed this contract and has defaulted."

"Those are the facts, sir," Barnwell said.

The judge asked, "Will the sale of the land cover the debt?"

"It will cover approximately three hundred and sixty dollars of the debt."

"And will Mr. Wilson be satisfied with that amount?"

Barnwell lifted his hands and let them fall back to his sides. "He would prefer to receive all of the funds owed, but we have to work with what's available to us."

Louella stood. She shouted for all to hear. "I can pay the entire five hundred of the debt! I've told you this. Why won't you take my money?"

The judge banged the gavel again, then pointed an angry finger at Louella. "You've overstayed your welcome in this courtroom."

She was escorted out, all the while yelling, "Let me pay the debt! Don't take our land. We'll pay the debt."

Standing outside the courthouse, Louella looked to heaven. "I need help." She had to find another way to save the land. She had failed with the court—or more accurately, the court system had failed her and so many others who looked like her.

CHAPTER 44

In the end, no amount of kicking and screaming from Louella stopped the judge from siding with Barnwell. The date of November 4, 1889, was set to auction off the land.

The autumn winds blew. Louella wrapped her wool shawl around herself as she stood before her people on the cold and cloudy last day of October. The leaves from the surrounding trees had dried, turning yellow and brown. The color contrasted with the green of the grass as each leaf tumbled slowly, catching in the wind and drifting until it came to rest on the ground like the last notes of a sad song.

There were no joyful notes left in the Happy Land, but Louella found joy in her memories. She told them, "Many years ago, before freedom came, I was beaten unconscious right under the same tree they hanged my daddy on. While I was out, I had this vision of people going about their daily lives, smiling and being kind to one another. Lending a helping hand to lift one another up."

She stretched forth her hand as she pointed at the crowd in front of her home. "You all became the manifestation of my vision. I pray that you've known some form of comfort in the Happy Land after the misery most of us endured during slavery."

Cheers went up among the crowd.

Louella took no pleasure in the cheers. Her next words would not bring comfort. Sighing deeply, she told them, "I'm standing before you today to inform everyone that the judge has sided with Barnwell concerning King Robert's debts. About ninety acres of the Happy Land has already been sold to a Mr. P. J. Hart."

She pointed north of where they were standing. "Over by the barn that Robert built, they are auctioning off most of our land in five days. All we have left is the twenty-five acres William and I purchased when we first began building the Happy Land."

Grief stood before Louella like a boxer, ready to strike a blow. Face blank, eyes hollow as if she'd witnessed an unspeakable horror, she said, "I'm sorry." Her head lowered with each word. "I have failed you."

"You didn't fail us. I know for a fact you did everything in your power," Jerry declared. "Now it's time for us to take up arms and fight fire with fire."

"Yeah!" someone else yelled. "We'll die before we let them take our land."

Another shouted, "I helped build my house, and I'm not leaving!"

"No more death!" Louella shouted. "I won't lose this land and the people on it as well."

"We got to do something. Why haven't you paid them?" someone shouted from the back.

"I tried and tried to pay them." Her hand went up and fell back down. Despair weighed her shoulders down as tears flooded her face. "They won't accept the money from me, so what more can I do?"

Mama Sue and Louella's mother slowly walked to the front of the crowd. They were singing. Louella lifted a hand, too heartsick for music, but Mama Sue ignored her and kept right on singing . . .

"Don't be weary, traveller,
Come along home to Jesus;
Where to go I did not know,
Come along home to Jesus;
Ever since He freed my soul,
Come along home to Jesus."

The words to "Don't Be Weary, Traveller" pierced the distance between slavery and the road they'd traveled to get here. They weren't the same people who journeyed from Mississippi in search of a place to call home. They'd found their land. They'd endured sorrow, pain, and joy. And they'd known true happiness . . . even if it had been fleeting.

The song moved Louella. She opened her mouth and belted out the last verse . . .

"I look at de world and de world look new,
Come along home to Jesus."

By the time they finished singing, Louella had found some semblance of peace. She prayed it was enough to get her through the days to come. The crowd dispersed. Louella stayed on her porch. She sat on her throne looking out at all they had built. The church, the homes, the barns, the crops . . . Everything she had envisioned was here. But how long would it remain?

Mama Sue sat on William's throne and held her hand. Her mama stood beside her chair and rubbed her back. Ambrose and Henry walked over to the porch. Family. At the lowest moments of her life, family had always been there. They would ride this storm together and see which way the wind and waves blew them this time.

"Sis, Henry and I—"

Mama Sue loudly cleared her throat and glared at her grandson.

"Uh, Queen," Ambrose began again, "Henry and I were talking about the fix we're in."

Henry chimed in. "I know a fellow who purchased a home from the sheriff's auction last year, so I been thinking about going down to that auction myself."

Louella shook her head. "Your last name is Bobo. They would probably deny you since we're related."

Ambrose's nostrils flared. "We worked too hard for what we got. The days of us just laying down and letting them destroy us is over." Wringing his hands, Ambrose looked to his sister, eyes pleading with her. "Has to be something we can do."

Leaning back in her chair, Louella's fingers thumped against her chin. She stared out at their land as a smile replaced the frown. "We may have one more card to play."

❧

The auction was to take place at the sheriff's office. Louella pulled her wagon as close as possible. Her mother was seated next to her. She took Louella's hand. "Dearest, relax. You've done everything you can, so now we must put the rest in the Lord's hands."

Louella let out a whoosh of air. She leaned back against her seat, thankful that her mama was with her so she had a shoulder to lean on.

She looked to Brenda now and confessed, "It's been hard to put my trust in God through the years, but I've come to accept that God's will is not always my will. His ways are not my ways." Squeezing her mother's hand, she nodded. "I got peace with that."

The auction began with a crowd of men standing outside the county jailhouse. The sheriff announced that they were going to be auctioning ninety-five acres of property just up the hill from the Oakland Plantation.

Louella wished those bidders understood that the place the sheriff referred to had been dubbed the Happy Land. It was the place where their crops grew, where homes were built, and where families enjoyed peaceful lives. Their land was priceless. God Himself had brought them to this land, and only God could determine when their time was up.

The bidding started at twenty-five cents an acre. Several hands went up. The hands stayed up at thirty-five cents. Then fifty cents.

When the bidding went up to a dollar, several of the men walked away.

Brenda put a hand on Louella's shoulder. "You see what's happening, don't you?"

Louella wasn't sure how any of this was going to turn out. She wished she could stand in front of the sheriff's office and bid on the property herself, but even though women were allowed to own property that had been left to them by their husbands, they weren't allowed to buy property without a male cosigner.

Six white men and one Black man remained as the bidding went up to a dollar twenty per acre. When it went up to a dollar fifty, three more white men dropped off.

Brenda started kicking her feet. The wagon moved forward. Louella steadied the horse. "Calm down, Mama. We don't want to draw too much attention to ourselves."

"Sorry." Brenda put her hands in her lap. "I'm excited. God is working this thing out for us."

The bidding went up to a dollar seventy-five, and two more white men stepped away. Now it was Wiley Bennett and the last white man. "Can I get a dollar eighty?" the auctioneer rattled off.

The white man raised his hand. Wiley Bennett raised his hand.

"Can I get a dollar eighty-five?" Wiley Bennett raised his hand and the white man raised his hand. The two men battled it out all the way up to a dollar ninety-five. Then, as the auctioneer went to the two-dollar mark, the white man shook his head and stepped away.

Wiley raised his hand and accepted the two-dollar-an-acre asking price for ninety-five acres of the Happy Land.

As Wiley and the sheriff shook on it, Louella snapped the reins and rode back to the land that God had promised to give them. She pulled the buggy up to the house. Brenda hugged Louella, then got out of the buggy and walked to her house.

Louella sat on the porch with her memories. In her mind's eye, William was perched on the throne next to hers, taking care of kingdom business. His chin was lifted, eyes bright with devotion to the land they built . . . to the people who came before him.

He stood and stretched out his arms. Arms that were muscular and strong from swinging that axe day in and day out until all those trees came tumbling down. He'd made promises to her and left nary a one unfulfilled. He'd made her a queen and she had loved a king. Would love him for the rest of her life.

Wiley rode up to the house on his horse. He climbed down and walked over to Louella. He grinned as he bowed, then handed her the deed to the Happy Land and a hundred and seventy dollars. "Looks like we got a discount on King Robert's debt."

Louella nodded. "Indeed we did." She handed Wiley twenty-five dollars. "Do something nice for Rachel with some of that."

He nodded, put the money in his pocket, and then got back on his horse and rode to the home he shared with Rachel. The home he would continue to live in.

Louella wrapped her shawl around her shoulders. She left her porch and took a walk up the hill. Many years ago when she'd stood in this very spot, there had been nothing but trees as far as the eye could see. The hillside was covered in trees and the valley contained cabins for enslaved people. But she'd imagined what this land could become.

Breathing in the mountain air she'd come to love, Louella lifted her hands to the heavens, and she exhaled. All that they had built was before her eyes. Louella's heart rejoiced.

Thanks to Wiley representing her at the auction, they now had a hundred and twenty acres. No, they hadn't been able to keep all of their land, but as she walked back down the hill, her eyes were set on the homes, the building they used as both a school and a church, the barns, and the crops. She looked at the people milling about, happy to be in a place of their own where they could hold their heads up and be respected.

Waties and Joshua stepped out onto the porch and waved at her. A smile crept across her face. Louella's mind rolled over good things as she waved back to them. Slavery hadn't beaten her. She'd survived . . . Her people had survived. And they had built a kingdom to be proud of.

She'd lost a lot along the way, but she'd gained a lot as well. Her heart had expanded as William taught her to love, laugh, and forgive. Louella didn't know what the future held for them, but one thing was for sure and true: this was good . . . very good.

THE END

A Closing Note from the Author

It has been my greatest honor to write this story about a moment in our history that most people know nothing about. Yes, there once were a king and queen in America, and they had been enslaved before the Civil War. They built an all-for-one-and-one-for-all society—something that we might consider a socialist society. But it was their way of making sure that *all* would be cared for and treated with respect after enduring the dehumanization and demoralization that came with slavery.

It may have been smaller than what we typically consider a kingdom, but William and Louella ruled it with grace and honor. As I researched for this book, I fell in love with this story and Queen Louella's compassion for the people she served, for their kingdom was not about what the people could do for them but more about how they could benefit each other.

I live right here in North Carolina but knew nothing of the story of the Kingdom of the Happy Land until #1 *New York Times* bestselling author Lisa Wingate (a very kind and beautiful spirit) mentioned it to me. It happened on a normal morning when I had sat down in front of my computer to begin writing. But first I decided to send Lisa an email and thank her for taking the time to read my novel *Something Good* and for giving me an endorsement. I also told her that I enjoyed her book *The Book of Lost Friends*.

When Lisa emailed back, she dropped a bomb by telling me about the Happy Land people. She said that a Facebook friend had told her about the story. Since I lived in North Carolina, she thought I might be interested. Was I ever!

I googled everything I could find on the subject. Turns out, this kingdom wasn't such a secret in the North Carolina Appalachian Mountains, where article after article had been written about King William and Queen Louella. I was intrigued. I knew I had something, but what? Was this a story that anyone would believe? I certainly believed it, but I kept digging to make sure I had enough information to write this story.

That's when I met Ronnie Pepper. He works at the library in Hendersonville, North Carolina, which houses a book (more like a pamphlet at only sixteen pages) about the Kingdom of the Happy Land by Sadie Smathers Patton. In the 1950s, Ms. Patton had interviewed people who once lived in the Happy Land. Some of them had moved there after the first king died, so they knew nothing of William and had recollections only of King Robert and Queen Louella. Once I read Ms. Patton's information along with many other books on that particular time period, I was ready to write my story.

When taking on the challenge to write women's historical fiction about people who once lived but weren't included in history books—so not much was written about them—a lot of research is needed. For example, not much is known about the Happy Land people before they arrived in the mountains of North Carolina. They told people that they came from Mississippi. And others knew that the two brothers, William and Robert, were sons of the owner of the plantation they came from. It was also noted that Robert was born free and was so light-complected that he passed as white during slavery times.

William was enslaved from birth and based on his complexion could not pass for white. However, both brothers were well educated. William had been the house manager during slavery, a position that would have equipped him well for running the elaborate kingdom that he and Louella set up.

Since I couldn't locate the exact records of when and where the Montgomerys lived in Mississippi, I researched the circumstances of enslaved people during that time period in order to deliver the story of their decision to leave Mississippi for a land they knew nothing of. It is a fact that formerly enslaved people entered into sharecropping contracts with their former owners. The book *They Left Great Marks on Me* by Kidada E. Williams includes an account of a formerly enslaved man testifying to Congress concerning being run off the land because the owner refused to pay for the crops as had been agreed.

There is further evidence to support that many of the formerly enslaved people, who stayed on their plantations after the war and worked the land, were not paid because their former owners didn't have the funds to pay for the labor they had once received for free.

Once William, Louella, and the other members of their group left Mississippi, it is noted in the numerous articles I read on the Happy Landers that they traveled from Mississippi through Alabama, Georgia, and South Carolina to reach the Oakland Plantation in the Appalachian Mountains of North Carolina.

Based on the research, it is also highly possible that William and Robert Montgomery lived in South Carolina with their enslaver/ father before they moved to Mississippi. This likelihood is based on the daughter of Robert Montgomery, who was the oldest of his children and was about nineteen years old by the time the Happy Landers traveled from Mississippi to North Carolina. Elmira Montgomery lived in Cross Anchor, South Carolina, until she moved to the Happy Land with her father.

It is also a fact that a woman named Serepta Davis sold the Happy Landers about two hundred acres of land that spanned from North Carolina to South Carolina, as noted in Serepta's grave announcement. (I have provided the website in the references.)

Serepta Davis had received several hundred acres of land after her husband, Colonel John Davis, died in 1859. After the war, she was left penniless and unsure of what to do with so much land. She no longer had enslaved people to help her care for the land, and she was getting older. Then along came about two hundred formerly enslaved men and women, offering to help her repair her property. She would eventually sell this group the land that would become known as the Kingdom of the Happy Land. Can you imagine the symbolism in that—formerly enslaved people wanting to be happy?

Land purchased from Serepta by the Happy Landers is also recorded in Henderson County Courthouse's Book 15, page 37. The deed recorded indicates that Robert Montgomery and Louella Montgomery purchased land that spanned from Henderson County, North Carolina, through Greenville County, South Carolina. The deed further states the land was purchased from John H. Goodwin, whose wife was Sarah, the daughter of Colonel John and Serepta Davis.

Book 22, page 306 further indicates that Elmira Montgomery sold twenty-five acres to Louella Montgomery for the sum of twenty-five dollars. But there is no mention of how Elmira acquired the land. Therefore, I give you my best possible explanation within the story.

Names and Events Mentioned in the Book

I did extensive research around the area, time period, and even many of the people mentioned in the book. The sad incidents that happened to formerly enslaved people during the period of Reconstruction, some of which appear in the storyline, occurred all too often in those days. The forty-acre plots that had been given to some formerly enslaved people through General Sherman's Special Field Order No. 15 were taken back, and those people were left to live on the streets. Many Black people were rounded up and forced to work as involuntary workers on plantations in the South. The Freedmen's Bureau did help some formerly enslaved people reconnect with family who'd been sold away. The bureau also helped formerly enslaved people with name changes or simply allowed them to pick a last name because so many of them didn't have one.

And of course, this is the time when the Night Riders and Ku Klux Klan came into being. It was a sad, sad time for Black people as they tried to navigate their way through freedom and Jim Crow laws, but the glory in it is that so many Black people survived so that others could thrive.

As for the names you see in the book, many of them are the actual names of people who lived in the Happy Land or people they dealt with in and around the area. People like Reverend Ezel really did travel back and forth to the Happy Land, bringing formerly enslaved people who needed a place of belonging. Rachel and Wiley Bennett lived in the Happy Land, and Wiley Bennett did in fact purchase the land at auction when it was sold due to debts owed by Robert Montgomery.

John Markley and his wife, Sallie Markley, lived in the Happy Land. John was a blacksmith and used his skills to create pots, pans, and silverware out of metal once he and his wife relocated to Hendersonville. Sallie was a storyteller and delighted people in Hendersonville with stories of the Happy Land for many years after they left.

My research also yielded the names of Louella and William Montgomery's children, and I am sad to say that yes, it is true that Louella's first child, Lily, died. In the book, I show the incident occurring at birth, but my research did not yield the exact age of the child at death. The names of Robert Montgomery's children are borne out in the research as well. There is no indication that any of his children other than Elmira lived in the Happy Land.

Research also shows that Louella's brothers, Ambrose and Henry, lived in the Happy Land with her. However, I must confess that I do not know what became of Louella's mother. But my writer's heart wanted a reunion, so I wrote Brenda Bobo—the woman who actually did teach Louella about plants that heal—into the story toward the end. Please note, Brenda Bobo's appearance in the story did not change the outcome. I stayed true to the history that was presented to me as I wrote about the deaths of both kings and the land in jeopardy after King Robert's death. Louella was left to figure a way forward.

Many of the other names I used in the story—such as Reverend Walter Allen, who taught school in Possum Hollow, and Ben F. Posey, who owned the grand home that some of the Happy Landers found work at—can be found in the book *The Kingdom of the Happy Land*, written by Sadie Smathers Patton.

How Did It All End?

Although information from Serepta's and John Davis's grave records indicate that the Kingdom of the Happy Land was in existence for over seventy-five years, my research indicated that it lasted for about forty years. Perhaps even longer than that if you count the fact that Jerry Casey, the last known person from the Happy Land to live on the property, died there in 1918. But based on my research, the property was no longer in the hands of the Happy Landers at that time. Jerry had been allowed to stay on for services rendered, and Elmira came back to the Happy Land to take care of Jerry until he died. Therefore, the property and the structures still remained at that time.

However, the kingdom began to collapse as the railroad tracks were laid down through North Carolina and South Carolina. Customers in other cities and states no longer needed the services provided by the Happy Land Teamsters.

But let me back up, because the court case of 1889, right after the death of Robert Montgomery, is an actual case that occurred. Robert Montgomery died owing $500, and that debt precipitated the serious decline of the Happy Land.

Thankfully, after the land was sold at auction, Louella was able to hold on to some of it due to the twenty-five acres from Elmira and the land Wiley Bennett was able to purchase at auction. The reason I'm able to state that the land was still in the possession of the Happy Landers after Wiley Bennett purchased it at auction is that Wiley was one of the Happy Landers. And as the story goes, the Happy Landers put all of the money earned into one pot and then it was divided among the people. Therefore, it is easy to surmise that the money Wiley used to purchase the land back came from Louella.

However, after 1889, things became increasingly difficult for the Happy Landers as jobs in the area dried up and more and more of their people moved to areas like Hendersonville, Greenville, and Spartanburg, which I mentioned in the book. With so many people leaving the kingdom, there wasn't enough money coming in to pay the taxes on the property. It is believed that the kingdom broke apart sometime around 1910, and Louella and Elmira later moved to Hendersonville to live out their remaining days.

Disparities with Statements in the Book
The Kingdom of the Happy Land

It is important to note that Sadie Smathers Patton received all the information she included in her book about the Happy Landers from the children of the first settlers in the Happy Land. William Montgomery lived only a few more years after they made their home in the Happy Land, so many of the people she interviewed never knew King William. They knew only King Robert and Queen Louella.

This is the point where logic intersects with research. I had to ask myself, *How did Louella become queen if she was Robert Montgomery's sister-in-law?* There must have been a king before Robert, and he must have been William, Louella's husband.

The book *The Kingdom of the Happy Land* does mention that there was a king before Robert, but it fails to make the connection that the first king was Louella's husband. This book further states that once Louella moved to Hendersonville, William came to live with her. At this point he was blind and "useless" (Sadie Smathers Patton's words, not mine).

William couldn't have been both dead and blind and "useless," so based on the research, it would appear that Louella remarried once she moved to Hendersonville.

I truly pray that you enjoyed this retelling of the Kingdom of the Happy Land. Although the completion of the railroad, tax issues, and debts owed by the second king brought down what had once been a place built on the motto of "all for one and one for all," that is not the important part. In my humble opinion, the important part is that they lived—that they didn't let slavery beat them. That they built something their people were proud of for many decades.

Long live the memory of Queen Louella. Getting to know the only queen ever to rule on American soil has been a great honor.

Thank you for reading this important story.

Blessings,
Vanessa

ACKNOWLEDGMENTS

Even though writers sit at a desk and write the words that readers will see in books, the book doesn't become that glorious thing it is meant to be without the help of many, many others. Allow me a moment to give credit where it's due.

As always, I first must thank God for the gift of writing and the ability to get out of bed each morning and do the thing I love so much.

Please know this: the person I am thanking next deserves high praise. I have tears in my eyes as I write this because meeting this woman caused a paradigm shift in my career that I will forever be grateful for. I thought I was just contacting #1 *New York Times* bestselling author Lisa Wingate to ask for an endorsement for my book *Something Good* because I like her books, but it turned out to be a God connection.

Not only did Lisa take time out of her busy schedule to read and endorse *Something Good*, but she also told me about the Kingdom of the Happy Land people. I'm not sure why she trusted me with this story since I was not a historical-fiction writer. At the time, I had been writing only inspirational women's fiction, but I have now caught the historical writing bug. So, Lisa, thank you from the bottom of my heart for trusting that I would be able to bring Queen Louella to life for readers.

I jumped at the chance to write about the Kingdom of the Happy Land people but didn't have the first clue about writing a novel set in the nineteenth century and all that it would entail, so I truly need to thank my writing sisters for the time we spent talking over scenes and plots and language . . . It was a lot. But thanks to Vanessa Riley, Michelle Lindo-Rice, Rhonda Mc-Knight, Michelle Stimpson, Jacquelin Thomas, and Pat Simmons, I was able to complete the task of writing what I consider my greatest accomplishment as a writer thus far.

I have to thank my former agent, Natasha Kern. This was our last project before she retired (tears in my eyes again). I am so thankful for having her guidance in my career all these years and am excited that she finally gets to spend more time with her family, her church, and gardening. She deserves it. But Natasha loved this book from the moment I mentioned it to her and happily sold the idea of my becoming a historical-fiction writer to my publisher, HarperCollins / Thomas Nelson.

My editor, Laura Wheeler, was just as excited as I was about this story. Her developmental edits, along with Becky Monds's, helped to turn *The American Queen* into the masterpiece it has become. Make no mistake about it, their encouragement was everything.

A big thanks to Chandra Sparks Splond for her insight during copyediting. This book has been edited and rewritten and edited some more. I hope y'all enjoy it because I put work in.

Uncovering some of the elements that allowed me to share the story of real people who once lived would not have been possible if not for Mr. Ronnie Pepper. He works at the library in Hendersonville, North Carolina, and is the president of Henderson County's Black History Research Committee. You can find more info on the Happy Land at his website: https://blackhistories.org/2020/07/01/the-kingdom-of-the-happy-land/. I contacted Ronnie Pepper after reading an article about the Happy Land that mentioned his name and his organization. It also indicated that he was a storyteller and often told the story of the Happy Land.

The library Mr. Pepper works at had the only copies of *The Kingdom of the Happy Land* booklet that was written by Sadie

Smathers Patton in the 1950s. Mr. Pepper made copies of that document and emailed them to me. The information I discovered based on the interviews that were conducted with the children of former Happy Landers provided the missing pieces to my research. So thank you so much, Mr. Pepper.

Now that I have spent close to a year wrapped in the realm of the Happy Land, I hand off the finished product to the marketing, publicity, and sales team at HarperCollins / Thomas Nelson. And I want to thank each of you in advance, for your labor will not be in vain. As readers get to know this unsung history of a kingdom on American soil that was built on the motto "all for one and one for all," I believe they will rejoice at this new discovery.

And finally, I would like to thank my family for putting up with me going on and on about Queen Louella. I couldn't help it. She was truly a remarkable woman, and it was my great honor to write her story.

My husband, David Pierce, and my daughter, Erin Miller, fed me as I worked to meet the multiple deadlines for this book, and for that I am truly grateful.

And to each and every person who will spend time reading *The American Queen*, I want you to know that I worked hard to deliver a story that will cause Queen Louella to reign forever in your heart. I hope you enjoy.

References

Online Resources

Ballard, Shannon. "Episode 85: The Kingdom of the Happy Land." April 12, 2021. *Southern Mysteries*. https://southernmysteries .com/2021/04/12/thekingdomofthehappyland/.

Carden, Gary. "The Kingdom of the Happy Land." *Smoky Mountain Living*. September 1, 2009. https://www.smliv.com/stories /the-kingdom-of-the-happy-land/.

"Davis Slave Cemetery, Kingdom of the Happy Land." Henderson Heritage. https://hendersonheritage.com/davis-slave-cemetery -kingdom-of-the-happy-land/.

Elliston, Jon. "The Happy Land: Former Slaves Forged a Communal Kingdom in Henderson County." *WNC Magazine*. Winter 2021. https://wncmagazine.com/feature/happy_land.

Elliston, Jon, and Kent Priestley. "The Kingdom of the Happy Land." *Mountain Xpress*. February 7, 2007. https://mountainx .com/news/community-news/0207happyland-php/.

Green, Gary Franklin. "The Kingdom of the Happy Land." In *A Brief History of the Black Presence in Henderson County*. Asheville, NC: Biltmore Press, 1996. https://blackhistories.org /2020/07/01/the-kingdom-of-the-happy-land/.

Hill, Michael. "Buncombe Turnkpike." *Encyclopedia of North Carolina*. Edited by William S. Powell. Chapel Hill: University of North Carolina Press, 2006. https://www.ncpedia.org /buncombe-turnpike.

Schenck, Missy. "African-American History of Henderson County,

Part Two." Charleston Mercury. https://www.charlestonmercury
.com/single-post/african-american-history-of-henderson
-county-part-two.

Schenck, Missy Izard. "Kingdom of the Happy Land." *Good News*
(blog). Flat Rock Together. February 6, 2021. https://www.flat
rocktogether.com/good-news/kingdom-of-the-happy-land.

"Serepta Merritt Davis." Find a Grave. Added August 29, 2007.
https://www.findagrave.com/memorial/21247932/sereptadavis.

"The Freedmen's Bureau." African American Heritage. National
Archives. Updated October 28, 2021. https://www.archives
.gov/research/african-americans/freedmens-bureau.

Books

Federal Writers' Project. *Mississippi Slave Narratives*. Washington, DC: Allen-Young, 1936.

Jacobs, Harriet. *Incidents in the Life of a Slave Girl*. Boston: L. Maria Child, 1861.

Jones, Katharine M. *The Plantation South*. Indianapolis, IN: Bobbs-Merrill, 1957.

LeClercq, Anne Sinkler Whaley. *An Antebellum Plantation Household: Including the South Carolina Low Country Receipts and Remedies of Emily Wharton Sinkler*. Columbia, SC: University of South Carolina Press, 1996.

Madison, Mary. *Plantation Slave Weavers Remember: An Oral History*. CreateSpace Independent Publishing, September 2015.

Patton, Sadie Smathers. *The Kingdom of the Happy Land*. Asheville, NC: Stephens Press, 1957.

Roberts, Bruce. *Plantation Homes of the James River*. Chapel Hill: University of North Carolina Press, 1990.

Williams, Kidada E. *They Left Great Marks on Me: African American Testimonies of Racial Violence from Emancipation to World War I*. New York: NYU Press, 2012.

Songs

All the songs the Happy Landers sing in *The American Queen* were written either during slavery or right after. All are in the public domain. Here is the list of songs:

- "Balm in Gilead," African American spiritual, 1800s.
- "Don't Be Weary, Traveller," William Francis Allen, 1867.
- "Go Down, Moses," African American spiritual, 1862.
- "Nobody Knows de Trouble I've Seen," African American spiritual, 1800s.
- "Rock of Ages," Augustus Toplady, 1776.
- "Sometimes I Feel Like a Motherless Child," William Barton, early 1800s.
- "Song of the Free," anonymous, circa 1860. The lyrics used in this book were changed to fit the Happy Land.
- "Steal Away to Jesus," Wallace Willis, 1800s.
- "There Is a Happy Land," Andrew Young, 1838.

DISCUSSION QUESTIONS

1. When you first meet Louella, you learn that she has experienced one traumatic event after the next. Could you understand her need to fill her heart with hate rather than love while she was enslaved?

2. In chapter 4 Louella pulls away from William when he touches the scars on her back. Her scars were external, but they did something to her internally. Have you ever had to deal with internal scars that you wouldn't let anyone get close to? Have they been healed? If not, do you think talking to someone might help?

3. After emancipation, many of the formerly enslaved stayed and worked the land of the people who had enslaved them. They signed contracts that guaranteed payment, but many were not paid. This was one of the issues Louella and William dealt with after emancipation. Given what we know about the hardships for African Americans after the Civil War, do you think you would have stayed on the plantation or left the moment freedom came?

4. As the formerly enslaved people got ready to leave the Mississippi plantation, Robert Montgomery's former slaves decided to leave also. Robert was surprised by this. What do you think that says about the way Robert saw slavery?

5. While journeying from Mississippi to North Carolina, the Happy Landers slept outside and were on constant lookout for Night Riders and so-called officials who would throw them in jail and then enlist them in involuntary labor, yet they risked

it all to find a place to call home. While researching these people, I found myself in awe of their grit. What about you— could you have endured everything they went through in order to build something special?

6. After losing her baby, Louella felt like "God was always making mistakes when it came to the things that mattered to her." Have you ever dealt with a situation where you thought God made a mistake with its resolution? If so, I pray that God has healed your heart and that you still believe in His goodness and His love for us.

7. The same night Louella was crowned queen, she woke to a cross burning in her yard. Sometimes it seems as if we go from the highest of highs to the lowest moments of our lives within the space of a few minutes/hours/days. I believe the low moments teach us more than the high moments. Do you agree or disagree, and why?

8. Louella needed William in her life. He taught her to love and to forgive. He also made her a queen. I loved everything about King William and wished his and Louella's love could last forever. But this story is about real people and had to end as it did way back when. How did you feel when Louella discovered her love was no more?

9. Robert was a complicated man to write about. He was a slave owner who passed as white during slavery times. At his death, it was discovered that he had three children who had not lived in the Happy Land. I was challenged to find the other side of him. In reading *The American Queen*, were you able to see any good in the second king of the Happy Land? Did you come to understand him and some of his decisions?

10. In the book Louella felt as if she kept loving and losing. While researching for this book, I found myself thinking, *What a tragic life!* But the more of her story I wrote, the more I began to feel differently about loving and losing. So now I ask you: Is

it better to have never loved at all, or is it better to open your heart to love, even knowing you will eventually lose that love?

11. Louella was very instrumental in the building of the Happy Land, yet there came a day when Robert took her place as second-in-command and was eventually named king, as the men were dismissive toward the queen they already had. When I read about this during my research, I became angry for her and every other woman who has had to strive to be great in this "man's world." A hundred and fifty years later it seems as if women still have the same struggles, although I think things have gotten better. Can you point to examples in this day and age where women rule and/or where we still lag behind?

12. Close to the end of the book, Louella says that God's ways are not her ways but that she finally has peace with that. However, that peace came after years of struggling against some of the things she endured. As we get older and endure our own heartache, do you think it is best to find peace with what is? If not, how would you handle the changes you must endure in life?

13. The scope of this book was so vast and the people within it so amazing that I'm sure you have other questions to add to my list. Let's open the discussion. Was there anything you found interesting about this time period or the people in this historical novel?

14. If you were queen for a day, what kind of queen would you be? Would you be more concerned with dazzling gowns or with the people you served? Name one thing you would do for others as queen of your own Happy Land.

ABOUT THE AUTHOR

Sean Evans Photography

Vanessa Miller is a bestselling author, with several books appearing on *ESSENCE* Magazine's Bestseller List. She has also been a Black Expressions Book Club alternate pick and #1 on the BCNN/BCBC Bestseller List. Most of Vanessa's published novels depict characters who are lost and in need of redemption. The books have received countless favorable reviews: "Heartwarming, drama-packed and tender in just the right places" (*Romantic Times* book review) and "Recommended for readers of redemption stories" (*Library Journal*).

Visit her online at vanessamiller.com
Twitter: @Vanessamiller01
Instagram: @authorvanessamiller
Facebook: @Vanessamiller01